"You're an incredible kisser."

Caine grunted. "Out of practice."

"Well, keep working at it. It's coming back to you." Nora meant herself, too. "I saw you today not only as a man," she said, "but as a real...human being. A lonely human being, not a member of law enforcement."

"I am a member of law enforcement."

Nora leaned back in his embrace, enough to see his face in the moonlight. She felt entirely intent for once on not caring about others but focusing on herself, and she didn't care. The notion was somehow freeing— for these few moments not to feel responsible for every person in her life, for everyone she loved. The day's cooking, cleaning, entertaining, caring had drained her, leaving her vulnerable.

So had Caine's kisses. Nora decided to indulge her notion. And herself. Not even stopping to question her actions, she whispered against his parted lips.

"And I can be a very bad girl."

Leigh Riker

Leigh Riker is an award-winning author of thirteen novels—some, it seems, written from the back of a moving van. An Ohio native with an English degree from Kent State University, she has lived east, west, north and south, from New York to Kansas, and various points in between. In the process she "raised" one husband, two sons, four cats, several dogs, numerous guinea pigs, gerbils, birds and a horse. Always, of course, with a sense of humor.

Oddly enough, she still likes to travel, and firmly believes that change and new experiences, make life interesting.

A member of Romance Writers of America, the Authors Guild and Novelists, Inc., she is a sometime contest judge and former creative writing instructor. Always ready for a new challenge, she is now at home (for good!) in the mountains of Tennessee or in Cabo San Lucas, where she keeps trying, like her heroine in *Change of Life*, to become ever more and more...herself.

Please visit Leigh at her Web site, LeighRiker.com.

Change of Life

Leigh Riker

CHANGE OF LIFE

copyright © 2006 by Leigh Riker

isbn-13: 978-0-373-88122-2

isbn-10: 0-373-88122-3

This edition published by arrangement with Harlequin Books S.A.

TheNextNovel.com

 HARLEQUIN®

PRINTED IN U.S.A.

From the Author

Dear Reader,

Change— good, or sometimes not so good—is a part of life. Big surprise. But lucky for me, I'm a Gemini and we thrive on change.

It's a good thing, too.

After leaving my original home base in Ohio, I spent a few years in New York City, then married and began a series of long-distance relocations that may not have suited someone born under a different astrological sign. The Gemini Twins, however, don't like to be bored!

Like my heroine, Nora Pride, I'm always happiest at home...wherever that may be. The births of children, or grandchildren (by the time you read this, my new little granddaughter will be here), the loss of parents or beloved pets, the triumphs and challenges of career, even the progress of a marriage, are all a part of the fabric—the changes—of our lives.

Above all, these changes are essential, necessary, often exciting. They make life interesting and provide us with ever new opportunities to grow. With Nora Pride, I wanted to explore the changes we face and how we not only learn to survive them but, in the end, thrive.

And now for my next challenge...the start of a new book.

Leigh

For Aidan...

An old Irish blessing

May the wind (of change) be always at your back.

CHAPTER 1

Nora Pride was having a heart attack.

Wearing her best black silk power suit, in the middle of an Interior Design Association luncheon at the Sandestin Hilton, of all places, she broke out in a sweat that seemed totally unrelated to the still-blistering end-of-September day outside the posh Florida hotel. The grand ballroom's frigid air-conditioning wasn't doing her a bit of good.

Her pulse raced. It skipped then thumped, hard, and Nora coughed twice, a knee-jerk physical reaction that tried to stabilize the beat. She prided herself, so to speak, on her appearance. On keeping up appearances, in fact.

My God, I can't die in public. That would be humiliating.

Nora fumbled through her handbag for her cell phone, ever ready not only for a quick business deal but also for any emergency, like her mother's unexpected coronary several years ago, in case Nora was needed again in a hurry. Now, it seemed, her own life was at risk. Still, she hesitated to pull out the phone and make a fuss.

At the podium someone droned on.

"…and with the Gulf area's incredible growth rate in housing—a boom that seems to have no end or even a peak—our design talents in this region will continue to be highly sought…"

Nora didn't hear the rest. Her heartbeat thundered in her ears. She suddenly felt light-headed. Should she call 911, or was that premature? She would hate calling in a false alarm, but as her daughter often pointed out, Nora was much better at caring for others than for herself.

Pulse still pounding, she tried to restore a sense of inner calm. This might be simple anxiety, an everyday, garden-variety panic attack. True, she'd never had one before, but…

Weren't cardiac events more typical in the early morning than at noon? Whew, the room did seem hot. Nora glanced across the table. Her gaze landed on her longtime nemesis, Starr Mulligan, with whom Nora had disagreed again only yesterday about a new client they both wanted—badly.

The memory provided a brief distraction. Nora's business, in particular, had been thriving until the past couple of years. During a pair of especially powerful hurricane seasons, some of her clients had, sadly, lost their homes, and until they rebuilt their devastated properties they obviously had no use for Nora's design services. There were no interiors. Then more recently, another, luckier client had reneged on his payment, and although Nora didn't want to refer the account to a collection agency, she needed the money. Her cash flow was hurting, and the competition with Starr wasn't helping her financial picture. Despite some personal misgivings about the new client they both wanted, Nora still needed the job.

Starr reminded her of Elizabeth Taylor soon after her first marriage to Richard Burton. A few pounds too heavy but still attractive, if not the stunning beauty Liz had been in her youth, with that same dark hair and those arresting lavender eyes.

Nora wasn't mean-spirited by nature. She liked helping people, and she wanted to get along with Starr. But no matter what Nora did, they always seemed to wind up at each other's throats. And it was Nora who tended to back down, to let Starr win.

At the moment, Starr's coal-black hair failed to reflect the overhead light, and her normally piercing gaze stayed as dull as dust—Starr's usual reaction to a boring after-lunch speaker. For a second, Nora forgot her own problems to wonder if Starr had fallen asleep with her eyes open. Maybe she was like a canary in a coal mine, and too much carbon monoxide floating through the cold air had zapped her into wide-eyed yet vague unconsciousness. Now it was causing Nora to…blush.

She reached for her napkin to fan herself.

Women didn't have heart attacks at *her* age. Her birthday might be circled on her calendar next week in red—Nora would turn fifty—but she had hoped for more time before she had to fret about her health like Leonard Hackett, one of her favorite clients, who could be a world-class hypochondriac.

She couldn't die. People needed her. Her mother, Maggie, who had already lived two-thirds of her life playing the helpless widow, was beginning to fail. Sooner or later she would require Nora's help, whether or not Maggie wanted it. Then there were Nora's two grown children. Savannah and Browning might sometimes accuse Nora of intruding in their lives (*meddling* was the word they used), but they, too, needed her. And what about her friends? Her dog?

But then, as if she'd been sacked like a quarterback during the Super Bowl, the truth struck her. Nora dropped her napkin with a soft plop on the linen tablecloth and jerked upright on her ivory damask-upholstered chair. Her eyes again met Starr's across the round table.

And wouldn't you know? Starr couldn't resist arching a penciled eyebrow, which drew the attention of several other people in their circle. Worse for Nora, in the suddenly too-quiet ballroom Starr's voice rang out like a Buddhist temple gong for all to hear.

"Hot flash, darling?"

* * *

"Mark, you have to do something," Nora murmured later that afternoon, flat on her back in her gynecologist's examining room. The peaceful blue and gray decor, which Nora had done, didn't soothe her, but to her immense relief he had squeezed her into his schedule. Nora gazed down her body at her spread legs in the stainless steel stirrups she had hated since before her first pregnancy.

Dr. Mark Fingerhut patted her hand. "Nora, relax."

His touch felt warm, comforting. He must remember her tendency to overreact.

"Why do you always say that? *Relax*? You know I despise white coats." Actually, she adored him—all of his patients did—if not, at the moment, the specialty he had chosen to make his living.

Mark pushed his stool back from the exam table. He flicked dark hair from his eyes. They were brown, like bitter chocolate, but compassionate.

"Listen. I know you're feeling a bit needy…"

"What I need, apparently, is to take ten years off my life."

"Would that be chronological?" he said, sounding amused. "Or biological? There's a difference, you know." But of course he could afford to look smug. To Nora, he appeared too young to be a doctor at all, much less a highly respected gynecologist. And her daughter, Savannah, who was perhaps his newest patient, agreed with Nora. His boyish smile belied the fact that he was pushing forty.

"I have women in their early forties who are perimenopausal," he said.

"What does that mean?" Fresh panic beat inside her like a hummingbird's strong yet delicate wings.

Mark sighed, but his dark eyes twinkled behind his black oversize frames.

"In a way, you're overdue." With a quick glance at her chart, he snapped off his latex gloves. "Fifty—actually,

50.8—is the median age at which women in this country stop ovulating, which means some do when they're slightly younger, others a bit later. Like those women, you're about to undergo what was euphemistically known before the sexual revolution and women's lib as The Change. These days, we tell it like it is."

Her heart sank. "My ovaries are dying."

"Well, not exactly. Slowing down, I'd say." His smile broke through as he smoothed his hair. "You can sit up now. Put on your clothes and I'll see you in my office. Then we'll talk."

"About what?"

He stepped out of the room into the hall. "Your future. There are some choices of treatment for your symptoms we need to consider."

Symptoms? Alone, like the dying woman she'd feared she was at lunch, she saw her life flash before her eyes. Her childhood, alone with Maggie after Nora's father died. Her marriage to Wilson, and the flaming torch she'd carried for years after their divorce. The births of her two children, and the joy they had given her, and still did. Despite her recent attempts to smooth away the lines of experience with a little Botox, and those necessary thrice-weekly trips to the gym to keep in reasonable shape, she was clearly, in Mark's opinion, on her way out.

In the empty room, squishing excess K-Y jelly, Nora wriggled into her panties and skirt, tucked in her silk top and then slipped into her shoes. Blinking, she grabbed her jacket.

"The future," she murmured.

She ducked out of the exam room into the corridor, then bypassed Mark's office and kept going toward the reception area and the door that faced the elevator in the hall. He could be wrong. Naturally, Nora had attended informative lectures (only half listening), read the occasional magazine article on the topic (and instantly dismissed it as irrelevant), and talked to her friends (who all suddenly seemed older than she was).

She'd thought she was prepared. But this was *her*. One silly hot flash didn't mean *she* was entering another stage of her life.

Menopause—she shuddered at the term—happened to other women.

Not to Nora Pride.

On her way home, Nora stopped at Starbucks for a mocha Frappuccino, her preferred grande size, although she wasn't sure it would be a big enough pick-me-up today. Back in the car, she pulled out her cell phone to call her mother. In spite of their usual differences, she needed to hear Maggie's voice, needed perhaps to weep in Maggie's sympathetic ear.

Unfortunately, as was often the case, she didn't get the chance. When Maggie answered, Nora said brightly, "Hi, it's me. I know it's been a while," she added so Maggie wouldn't point out that Nora hadn't phoned last week. "How are you?"

"How else would I be? I'm bored. I watch CNN all day. At six o'clock I switch to Fox News. My balanced diet of current events," she said. "Big whoop." Her tone changed in a heart-beat from dry to sad. "If I watch enough TV, it helps me—a little—to bear up after losing your father."

Nora zipped along in the rush-hour traffic, the AC on high, sipping at her Frappuccino while speaking into her hands-free phone. She envisioned her mother's graying hair, corkscrewed into the unflattering style Maggie still preferred. Nora could almost see her mother's baggy house dress and her white ankle socks scrunched down into the heels of her worn-over, laced-up shoes. Like some Ice Age mummy, in forty years of widow-hood Maggie hadn't changed.

"Daddy died when I was ten." Nora willed herself to find the patience she had lost earlier in the day. She threaded her way between an SUV and a semitrailer rig on the narrow stretch of Route 98 that led through Destin. "We both miss him. But isn't it time you got past that, and went on with your life?"

"Life? I'm seventy-five years old," Maggie informed her as if Nora didn't know.

Nora's pulse hitched. "Are you feeling all right? I told you to make an appointment with your cardiologist. If you want me to, I can take you." It wasn't that far from Destin to the Commonwealth of Virginia, but sometimes just far enough for Nora's peace of mind. Now she felt worried. She could block out the time on her schedule, even cancel a few appointments if she had to, to spend a couple of days with her mother. Take care of business, meaning her mother's health.

With luck, maybe Maggie would welcome Nora's company.

Nora doubted that. She envied Savannah, who had spent most of her girlhood summers in Richmond with Maggie. To this day, she and her grandmother were close, and Nora wished she could duplicate their relationship.

Maggie snorted. "Why bother with the doctor? That man books months ahead. By the time I really need him, I won't need him," she insisted.

Nora bit back a sigh. No wonder they didn't get along. Like Maggie, she didn't relish change in her life (take today, for instance), but she'd had her share. Nora was a survivor, and she remained an optimist. She blew a stray hair from her forehead, then counted to ten before she took a last sip of her Frappuccino. "If you don't want to see your regular doctor…" Nora hesitated before adding, "then come visit me. Better yet—" she took the plunge "—live with me. As soon as you get here we'll get you a complete workup."

This was an old argument, and Maggie didn't accept it now.

"I don't want to move to Destin. I have plenty of friends here. I refuse to become a burden on my children."

Child, Nora corrected in silence. Her only brother lived in Hawaii, and Hank Jr. had made it clear years ago that their mother was Nora's responsibility. His interests seemed to consist of a collection of surfboards, the highest seas he could find, and endless women with the kind of deeply tanned skin that wouldn't age well. He hadn't held a steady job in years, unlike Nora, who had been working since she was fifteen. And seeing to Maggie's future rather than her own.

"When it's my time, I'll go." Maggie didn't mean the move to Destin.

Nora ignored that. She didn't want to think about losing Maggie. She slammed her empty cup into the holder on her console, steering a path with her other hand on the wheel through rush-hour traffic past the posh Silver Sands Mall. Overhead the sky was a clear, brilliant blue, and outside the car she knew the temperature still hovered in the eighties. It was too hot to open the windows, but Nora had the urge to inhale the bracing salt sea air along with the ever-present humidity. "The weather's nicer here," she pointed out. "Don't you know how I worry about you alone in that house?"

"It's my home," Maggie said stiffly. She had rarely left it in fifty years.

"Yes, and it has three flights of narrow stairs and an outdated kitchen with faulty wiring. What if there was a fire?"

"My problem," Maggie insisted. "I should think you have enough to handle. What about Savannah, living with that man before they're even married? In my day, that would be a scandal. And then there's Browning, who may have a fancy-sounding job with the government—he's a spy, if you ask me—yet he hasn't a clue about settling down. How many times has he 'fallen in love' in the past six months?"

Nora sighed. "More times than I can count."

She swung her white Volvo convertible, the top of which was up today to shade her from the sun, off the two-lane road onto a side street that connected to her subdivision. And made one more try. "Please listen to reason. I'm your daughter. Your only daughter."

Maggie's tone hardened. "I hate Florida. What would I do

among that bunch of leather-skinned sunbathers in retirement? They look like alligators. Listen to me, Nora Marianne Scarborough Pride, I am still your mother."

After a few more minutes when neither of them budged from their usual positions, Nora said a wistful goodbye, then hung up, feeling frustrated. Well, that had gone badly, which, considering the rest of her day, shouldn't have come as a surprise. First Starr, then Mark, now Maggie. Nora hadn't even mentioned her troubles, after all.

Thank goodness her day was at an end.

By the time Nora reached home in her quiet, off-the-beaten-path neighborhood, she felt drained. The sight of her tidy, one-story house of rosy brick and the winding stone path to her door didn't help for once. The Frappuccino hadn't restored her spirits, either, or her energy, despite its triple kick of caffeine, and neither had her talk with Maggie. Still, Nora smiled as she opened her door.

Before she stepped inside, she heard familiar doggy footsteps. As always, Daisy greeted her in the foyer. Nora felt an immediate burst of vitality and a love that was both given and received. Several years ago, after Savannah had moved out and then Browning, Nora had adopted the silky golden retriever through a rescue organization. In truth, she felt they had saved each other. Unlike Maggie, Nora no longer entered an empty house. And who needed a man? Even her ex-husband had never been as affectionate or as good a companion.

"Hey, girl. Sorry I'm late. Anybody interesting call today?"

She dropped her keys and bag, then bent to hug the dog; Daisy wriggled with delight. Nora kissed the top of her head, then waited until Daisy bumped her wet nose against the hallway table that stood under a gold-framed mirror. It was part of their daily ritual, and dutifully Nora opened its small drawer to retrieve a bag of beef-flavored treats. Who had trained whom? she wondered with another smile.

The pleasure with which Daisy munched on the canine equivalent of a Dove chocolate bar almost wiped out Nora's memory of her day. With a heartfelt groan of relief, she kicked off her Ferragamo pumps. She padded into the living room, Daisy right behind her, and reminded herself that, their differences aside, Maggie was indeed still her mother. And Nora did love her.

For the few seconds until her jaw had unclenched, she allowed herself to take in the tasteful taupe and gold and cream furnishings of her living room. *Hers*. She'd done a bang-up job with its simple but elegant decor, including the rich, darker shade she'd chosen for the walls, and tonight, especially, she needed its welcome sanctuary. It even smelled like home, part discreet potpourri from the bowls scattered throughout the house, part animal even though Nora bathed Daisy regularly, part furniture polish and the lingering scents of the white chicken chili Nora had fixed for dinner last night.

"Hungry, angel?"

There was only one answer to that question. Daisy launched into another dance, hips wiggling, doggy nails clicking all the way into the kitchen. Nora fed her before she headed straight for the chilled bottle of New Zealand chardonnay that languished in her refrigerator. Frankly, tonight she was a hair away from phoning Heath Moran when she'd promised herself she never would again.

Seeing a younger man, no matter how gorgeous he was, didn't seem…well, seemly, as Maggie might say. The months Nora had spent with her hunky health club trainer had been fun—wildly, madly so—but they were over. Love games were for people her son's age.

Nora had just poured a glass of wine when she heard the front door open. Engrossed in her meal, topped with leftover chili for gravy, Daisy didn't look up from her food bowl. Lazy

Daisy, Nora often called her with affection. Daisy didn't concern herself with protecting her mistress. Obviously she recognized the intruder by scent and wasn't alarmed. For an instant, Nora wondered if Heath had come to return her house key—or to offer her a second chance. On her stocking-clad feet she glided out of the kitchen into the living room and to her surprise heard stifled laughter, twice over. Her heart settled for the first time that day, then warmed at the sight of her daughter and Savannah's fiancé.

"What are you two giggling about?" she asked. They stood by the door whispering like conspirators. Nora supposed it had something to do with their upcoming wedding. If one thing had gone wrong in the planning, everything had, and it had become a joke among the three of them. Nora relished sharing their regular reports of the latest snafu as much as she enjoyed supplying her own version of the often-ridiculous events. "If that printer has changed his delivery date again for those invitations, I'll—"

Savannah grinned. "No, Ma. It's nothing like that."

Nora took a first sip of wine and assessed her future son-in-law's not-quite-suppressed smile. His eyes sparkled, as if he knew some delightful secret, and he waggled his eyebrows at her. Nora lifted hers in response. She was happy to see him and Savannah, too, the one bright spot in this day, except for Daisy. She held up her glass. "Would either of you like a drink?"

"Maybe later," he said.

"Nothing for me, thanks," Savannah said.

Nora smiled with pride at her daughter. With her blond hair and creamy complexion, her slender form, Savannah would make the most beautiful bride. And Johnny—well, what could Nora say? He had been a favorite of hers since he was thirteen years old.

He'd grown up very nicely. Tall, lean, and well put together, with those wicked green eyes, at thirty-three he had the kind of sun-streaked hair that reminded Nora of the surfer boys like her brother who abounded on the Emerald Coast but with a better brain. John Hazard, a screenwriter, managed to hide that sharp intelligence and an awesome talent behind his modest charm as effectively as he often repressed his deeper emotions. Not tonight, she realized. He didn't fool her. A cream puff, she thought, but definitely one with a secret. He was all but dancing across her living room carpet like Daisy, though he hadn't moved an inch.

Daisy had finished her dinner. Nora had no doubt she'd licked the bowl clean. All at once she charged around the kitchen doorway, tail waving like a pennant, bright eyes flashing. She aimed for Johnny, a personal favorite, then Savannah. When she'd absorbed another round of hugs and scratches, she finally settled down at Johnny's feet.

"I saw Mark late today," Savannah said too casually, leaning back against the door, her dark blue eyes—the eyes she had gotten from Nora—avoiding hers. "He said you'd been in before me. I thought he seemed a little…down, somehow. Did you notice?"

"No," Nora said with a flicker of guilt. Mark, depressed about something? He'd seemed his usual cheerful self to her. But then Nora had been preoccupied. Maybe she'd overlooked something.

"I'm sorry we missed each other," Savannah said. "Why were you there?"

Nora's heart jerked. "Just routine. You?"

She wouldn't mention Mark's "diagnosis," didn't want to worry them with the words that Nora had decided to ignore. Besides, those two had something in mind. If anything was wrong with Savannah, she and Johnny wouldn't be toying with her like this, as they so obviously were doing. Would they?

"We have some news," he admitted.

"Good news? Or bad news?" Nora didn't need the latter.

"We think it's good," he said.

"We're not sure about you." Savannah reached for his hand.

They were still hovering by the front door, as if they didn't know whether to come in.

A thousand possibilities flashed through Nora's mind. As she'd suspected, the invitations must have been printed with the wrong names, time, or God forbid, date. Or Savannah's wedding gown could not be finished on time. The reception hall had been double-booked by someone else with a prior claim. Savannah's brother couldn't be Johnny's best man after all because Browning was off to Borneo for the government for six months.

"Angels, I can't stand the suspense. You're afraid to tell me, aren't you?"

"We're not afraid," Savannah said, "but maybe you should sit down."

Nora's pulse took a tumble. "Everything else may have gone wrong today, but my daughter is about to marry the most wonderful man on earth for her, and vice versa. I'm over the moon already. Nothing has given me more pleasure than to help plan your wedding."

"Help?" Johnny echoed. "Is that what you call it? As soon as we got engaged, you ran with the ball. 'Let me take care of everything.' There's been no stopping you." But his tone was teasing, his favorite attitude with Nora.

She reassessed him and Savannah. "Please don't tell me there's some problem with your absolutely perfect match."

"No, of course not." Savannah worried her lower lip. "It's just that I'm—"

"We're—" Johnny said at the same instant.

"—pregnant," they both finished. "Nora—Ma—you're going to be a…"

Savannah's next word failed to register. Nora was speechless, stunned. Her gaze dropped to Savannah's flat stomach. She had laid a hand over it, protectively, covering her still-slim figure in her skinny jeans, and Johnny reached out to enfold her fingers there with his. His chin lifted as he returned Nora's stare, but she saw his left eye begin to twitch, a sure sign that he was feeling stressed.

Still she didn't move. For years she had entertained the happy fantasy of her daughter one day becoming a mother, too. Nora loved her family. She had two children of her own, and on his wedding day Johnny would make three.

Wasn't it only yesterday that Savannah had been a little girl in pigtails, playing jump rope during school recess? Crying over her first boyfriend? Giggling with her girlfriends? Learning to ride a horse? Trying on her prom dress? And always, always after Nora's divorce from Wilson, drawing her primitive stick figures of their family, together again? For a second or two, Nora let the sweet and poignant memories drift through her mind.

"Say something," Savannah murmured.

And at last Nora came out of her trance.

"Ohhh!" she shrieked. Startling Daisy, she sidestepped the dog, crossed the room, hauled Savannah into her wide-open arms, then Johnny, too. "Oh, my God! You two…"

She told them how pleased she was, then turned her first, shocked silence into the kind of Hallmark occasion that sold greeting cards by the millions. Daisy was more than eager to join in the expressions of joy. She shimmied and jumped up on people and gave a short, sharp bark of delight. The bright blue metal tags on her collar jingled like a nursery mobile.

"Can you believe it, Ma? Eeeek!" Savannah shouted.

Nora's eyes misted. How many such moments came along, after all, in anyone's lifetime? She and Savannah surrendered to their tears and clasped each other close, erupting now and then as only women can in support of each other on such a happy occasion.

Soon they would talk, as only mothers and daughters knew how to do, together. They would go shopping. For now Johnny was here, and he was a man, excluded by his sex from their female circle. He gazed helplessly from Nora to Savannah and back again with a baffled expression on his face at their display. He, in particular, wouldn't understand such up-front emotion, and Nora finally took pity on him before she and Savannah went crazy all over again, unable to help themselves.

Yet underneath, Nora felt a strange mix of powerful emotions all her own. One minute she was stepping back to think, *It's too soon.* She had wanted this some day, but years from now when she would be ready. In the next instant, she was laughing and crying and holding on to Savannah for dear life. New life.

Her baby was having a baby.

Nora felt close to being hysterical, actually. Even in the company of the people she loved more than her own life, it had been quite a day.

"I'm going to be...*what?*" she murmured.

CHAPTER 2

"You sure don't look like any grandmother I ever knew," Nora heard Johnny say as soon as the restaurant hostess had shown them to their table, "including my own. Both of them."

She struggled not to blush at the compliment.

"You think so? Really?"

"Character is my business, Nora. I'm thinking—" he assessed her for a long moment "—Sandra Bullock for the part."

"She's only forty."

She felt grateful for his flattery, but Nora had lived on a roller coaster of emotion for the past two days, obsessing over Savannah and Johnny's surprising news. Sometimes she found herself smiling at the prospect, then fighting the urge to run and look in her mirror for any obvious signs that Mark Fingerhut could be right. This morning she had called Johnny to arrange one of their regular brunches, and seized the chance to get away from herself.

Besides, she owed him something. The other night when she and Savannah had done their happy dance all over her living room, Johnny had stood there with a somewhat puzzled expression. *What are they screaming about?* She'd seen that male look on his face but, considering his emotionally deprived background, she hadn't known how to include him then. Almost shyly now, she pushed a small jewelry box toward him.

But Johnny hadn't finished. With barely a glance at the box, he left it where it was.

"Fifty is the new forty," he pointed out.

"How about thirty? Could you see me as, say, Catherine Zeta-Jones?" She was teasing, yet Nora felt cheered. "I'd certainly like to think so, and it's true women do take better care of themselves these days. Preventive maintenance." If only Nora could do a better job of that, but there were always other people who needed her. Maggie, for one. And now there would soon be a little one to cuddle. Still, she couldn't resist saying, "In theory, you realize, I'm too young to be a grandmother."

Johnny had the audacity to laugh.

"Too young? Savannah said last night that she has no idea how we'll get all those candles on your cake next week."

Nora choked on her Bloody Mary.

His grin grew. "It'll be a conflagration, a forest fire raging out of control."

"I'd rather ignore it." She waved a hand, dismissing the topic of her upcoming birthday. Dismissing the unattractive bouts of ambivalence she'd suffered for the past few days. "Johnny, seriously. My birthday aside, I can't wait to dispense hugs and kisses, read stories, and even bake Christmas cookies for your child, not that I intend to put on a frumpy apron while I'm doing it."

"Aren't you getting ahead of yourself? Savannah won't give birth for six more months."

"I like to be prepared." In fact, she'd done just that before she met Johnny for brunch. Thanks to a friend who owned a beautiful shop in the Silver Sands Mall, she'd been able to get the gift ready for him on time. This would be her way of making Johnny feel like an even bigger part of the celebration and their family. Idly, he spun the gift box in the center of the table. He still hadn't opened it.

"Please," she said.

But Johnny had lost his smile. "I can't quite believe it myself, you know. We're having a *baby*." He shook his head.

"Do you realize that less than a year ago I was still living with Savannah's best friend? Trying to get Kit on track in her life while I neglected my own? Keeping her kid from turning into a future juvenile delinquent in that crazy household? Not to mention that mother of hers..." He rolled his eyes over Kit's demanding parent. "Now Kit's back in school to finish her degree, Tyler's still a great kid, I'm with Savannah and she's—we're—pregnant. Just call us The Incredibles."

Nora reminded him of something else. "A year ago Savannah was pining away over you, fretting that you'd never see how right you were for each other. You didn't know that? Well, she did. She was working for that awful temp agency—until I finally persuaded her to take a few clients of mine." Before the second round of hurricanes, Nora thought, before her workload diminished. "But you forgot the rest." She felt a fresh glow of approval for her future son-in-law. "You love Savannah with all your heart. And it's a big heart, angel."

This newly revealed side of his personality thrilled her, because Johnny had been the king of suppressed emotion for most of his life. Savannah had opened him like a can of beans, and in Nora's view the change was all to the good. For his benefit, as well. No, especially for his benefit.

Johnny hadn't had the best upbringing, she knew. His father had abandoned his mother early on, leaving her to raise their son by herself, and even after she'd married then left Wilson (she'd been his second wife), it had been hard going. When Savannah came home the first time, dragging Johnny like an abandoned cat, Nora had immediately taken him in. Their bond remained fierce, like a mother tiger with her cub, like Johnny's with Savannah, and Nora felt lucky to share that.

He didn't even try to wiggle out this time. "Sure, I love her," he said. "What's not to love?"

Nora blinked. "You love me, too. Admit it."

"Yep. I do, *angel.*" He used her favorite endearment, still without smiling, and Nora's inner alarm system went on alert. Despite this enjoyable brunch, Savannah was conspicuously absent today, and Johnny hadn't bothered to explain why. "Savannah would have liked to hear me say that," he added.

"Is she all right?" Nora asked. "Feeling well, no problems now that she's expecting?"

Johnny frowned. "She's a little under the weather. Especially in the morning. Apparently, it's my fault."

Nora smiled but she couldn't bear for Savannah to be ill. "The women in our family don't get morning sickness. She shouldn't, either. I'm joking, of course. I do worry about her. Still, she has plenty to do with the Larson job I gave her to design their family room and sun porch. The contractors haven't exactly been cooperative."

His green eyes brightened. "You wouldn't admit to having morning sickness if you were hung over the bathroom bowl like a Christmas ornament every day. And I bet you'd be wearing your best three-inch heels with a string of pearls."

She couldn't help answering his faint smile. "So true."

Johnny moved the jewelry box closer to his plate. But he left it there, and leaving him room, Nora attacked her eggs Benedict. At the luncheon with Starr, or for the past two days, she hadn't been able to eat a bite. Today she felt ravenous. She knew Johnny didn't easily accept gifts—or love, at one time. She didn't know anyone, however, who needed it more.

"So," he said, addressing his vegetable frittata, "what's new with you? We didn't have time the other night to talk. But Savannah told me you've lost some more clients."

Nora sighed. And thought of Starr Mulligan. "Starr keeps horning in on the rest of my people. I'm sure she's feeling the pinch, too, with so much hurricane destruction everywhere, but this morning my first phone message was from a woman in Royal Palms. I'll see her late this afternoon. Starr and I are battling over the chance to redecorate her ten-thousand-square-foot home. Do you have any idea how much money I'd lose if I don't win this job? Which, yes, I do need."

Johnny named a figure. Very close to accurate, in Nora's estimate.

"How did you know that?"

He shrugged. "I listen to Savannah. She's considering your latest partnership offer in Nine Lives. Royal Palms would be pretty good dough, Nora. Better than the first screenplay I sold to Wade Blessing for his initial Razor Slade film."

"You can't be serious. You earn a ton of money." Wade Blessing, the actor, was Hollywood's newest Arnold Schwarzenegger—before he decided to save the state of California from the governor's office. Wade's continuing action films about a mercenary with a heart of gold could be too graphic for Nora's taste, but that didn't matter to Johnny's bottom line.

"I said the first one. Wait until Wade sees my new script." He grinned. "I'm gonna hold him up like a stagecoach bandit."

A few months ago, after Johnny had walked out on Kit Blanchard and she had turned to Wade on the rebound for a while, the two men had suffered hard feelings, but they had since repaired their friendship.

"I thought you were writing something different."

"That, too," Johnny murmured, looking embarrassed. "It's what Stephen King calls a 'toy truck' project. Just for me right now."

"Johnny, it will be a movie. Tell me. When it gets released, the whole world will see it. How private can that be?"

He looked even more uncomfortable.

"Yeah. I know. But that'll be Christmas a year from now at the earliest. I figure I'll be too busy changing diapers to notice the public reaction. Or the reviews. I don't want to talk about it. Wait until wide release."

When Johnny picked up the jewelry box, obviously as a diversion, Nora held her breath. Embarrassed in turn, she fussed with her napkin, waiting for him to at last remove the wrapping paper from the gift. Would he like it?

"I may have overstepped my bounds with Starr," she admitted, returning to their earlier conversation about her own career to distract herself. "We had a run-in recently, and I may have made an impulsive remark or two about that potential client I mentioned, Geneva Whitehouse."

"Earl Whitehouse's wife?"

Nora felt a twinge of unease. "Yes. Do you know him?"

"Only by reputation. He's a pretty big developer in this area. He built a few of the houses in my compound at Seaview. Didn't you do some work for him a while back?"

"Briefly," Nora said, not wanting to discuss Earl Whitehouse, who, despite his stellar standing in the community, was not one of her favorite people. "We were talking about Starr. She and I seem to bring out the worst in each other. Now I wonder if at our monthly business luncheon this week she decided to retaliate for what I'd said." Had Starr's pointed reaction to Nora's hot flash been exactly that? Payback?

Johnny gauged her expression. "Then why not cut her some slack? You might even come to like her."

Nora doubted that was possible, but she didn't say so. And maybe he was right. She and Starr had struggled with each other long enough, and it was up to Nora—always the ready helper—to take the first step. Then she saw that Johnny had removed the paper, lifted the top of the box and pulled out the gift.

"Uh, Nora." He choked up, and she saw him swallow. "This is for me?"

"It won't suit anyone else, angel."

He slipped the eighteen-karat gold signet ring on his finger. And stared at it. The fine script flowed across its surface, caught the light streaming through the restaurant windows and shone on the one simple word. Five letters that Nora had hoped might mean the world to him.

Johnny's voice was thick. "Sometimes you break me up." Then his gaze met hers, and his smile beamed. "Thank you. You sure know how to get a guy."

The gold ring's inscription read simply: *Daddy*.

Riding on a wave of euphoria long after her brunch with Johnny, Nora decided to take his advice to see Starr that afternoon before Nora met with Geneva Whitehouse. With luck, they, too, might reach some kind of rapprochement.

First, Nora swung by Nine Lives, Inc., where she found a pile of mail waiting on her desk. Her longtime client, Leonard Hackett, one of her most lucrative accounts, was also in her office. Typically, he didn't look well.

Most of the mail was routine, with the exception of an invitation to a charity dinner in Fort Walton Beach for the Heart Association, and ordinarily she didn't mind Leonard's unannounced visits. But why was he here?

Nora tried to listen but, bent upon her meetings with Starr and then Geneva, her mind refused to take in the details. In her experience, it was always better to empathize with Leonard's latest bout of severe hypochondria than to try talking him out of his newest ailment. All she needed to do was make soothing noises.

"I tell you, I'm not long for this world. It will be almost a relief." Leonard slumped in a chair across from her. "I've been ill for years."

"Clearly, it's taken a toll." His neurosis had definitely shredded her nerves and, suppressing a sigh, Nora lifted her gaze from the charity invitation to give him her best look of sympathy.

"I see you're letting your hair grow," she said, hoping to distract him.

Leonard ran a hand over the top of his head where a barely visible fuzz had sprouted. She'd never cared for his—so Leonard had believed—trendy baldness. Now, his gleaming skull struck her as preferable to the gray-brown stubble that took its place.

"I won't need to maintain my looks," he murmured. "I only dropped by—with the utmost effort, I might add—to say goodbye."

Nora's heart lurched. "Leonard, don't be ridiculous."

Needing to discharge her nervous energy, she jumped up from her desk to pour a glass of water from the silver carafe on the sideboard. She held the Waterford tumbler out to Leonard.

"Here. Drink. I have whiskey, if you'd prefer."

"Not good for my liver. My function is marginal, you know."

Nora did sigh then. Leonard frequently tried her patience to the breaking point. Others might laugh at him, but she kept trying in her usual way to—what, save him from himself?

Dutifully, obviously stalling, he took a few sips of water, then set the glass aside. On her cherry end table. Without a coaster. Nora whipped one in the shape of a seashell from the drawer and smacked it down.

"Please, Leonard. No rings."

He stretched his legs out, then crossed them at his bony ankles. If he had ever been the playboy he imagined himself to be, Nora hadn't seen it. To her, he was more like Greta Garbo in drag, playing Camille.

Still, everyone had his illusions, and she maintained a certain fondness for Leonard. He could irritate her to distraction, but he had gobs of inherited money which he didn't mind spending on the houses, condos and co-ops he'd purchased with astonishing regularity over the years.

It was a neurotic cycle, Nora suspected. Leonard became "ill," he managed to survive the deadly disease, then bought himself a new place to live like a fresh lease on life. She had to admit the very notion of his leaving this earth now, after years of threats to do just that, would make her weep.

On second thought, she couldn't continue to agree with him.

She tried to cheer him up. "Your color's good today," she pointed out. "That navy polo shirt makes your eyes look even more, um, blue." Actually, they were almost colorless, but Nora wouldn't be unkind—one reason, she supposed, why Leonard kept showing up without an appointment. He must know he could count on Nora for support. "If I don't miss my guess, whatever illness you contracted during your weekend in the Caymans must be encountering all those little antibodies by now. I'd say that by tomorrow—"

Leonard shifted. "I've talked to Starr Mulligan."

Uh-oh. Here we go. This was the real reason for Leonard's latest impromptu visit. The rest had been a cover-up.

Nora's voice chilled to the temperature of the water in the silver carafe crammed with ice on the sideboard. "I see." He had, as usual, engaged her sympathy for his current illness, taken advantage of her kindness. Now he would tell her the truth. Nora didn't want to hear it.

"Starr?" she said, already rethinking her earlier intention to make amends.

"I wasn't expecting her when she turned up at my condo yesterday afternoon. I was napping, trying to preserve my strength, and not properly dressed to entertain."

"Starr brings her own show with her."

"Yes, well." Leonard cleared his throat. "I think you should know she plans to underbid you on the design for my new house."

"You bought another house? So this medical crisis—" she circled a hand in the air "—was just a ruse."

If he'd purchased yet another home, Leonard intended to live for a while. That was good news. Yet he'd almost put one past her and Nora's focus sharpened. If he hadn't been her most constant client for the past fifteen years, if she didn't need him now, she'd feel tempted to throw him out.

"I didn't bid on your job, Leonard. I didn't know about it."

He adopted a contrite expression like a basset hound. "Can you possibly forgive me?"

"I'm not sure. How did Starr learn about this property in the first place?"

Leonard looked away. "Her cousin is a Realtor. He's, uh, my Realtor."

"I never knew that," Nora said.

"He mainly handles commercial property. I wasn't even in the market when he phoned to tell me he had this marvelous listing at Impressions right near Seaview."

"Charming." Nora didn't mean the gorgeous new development at the shore, a few miles from Destin, and not far from the other planned community where Johnny owned a beach home. "You'll be too far from the pharmacy," she informed Leonard, "and the mall. And probably from the water."

"I can practically walk from my kitchen into the Gulf."

"I see," Nora said again. If her life kept going this way, she wouldn't need to worry about her presumed perimenopause. She'd have a stroke. "So you've gone behind my back, bought a marvelous new home—and Starr has great plans for it." Nora couldn't help the next words that came from her mouth, Maggie's long-ago teachings aside. "Well, congratulations. When she fills the place with hideous pseudo pre-Columbian art and charges you a fortune, please don't call me."

Leonard sounded like a little boy. "Nora."

She pressed her fingers to her forehead, easing the frown that wanted to form. Her latest Botox injections were supposed to be at their peak effect, and her forehead shouldn't show a ripple, like the surface of an unused swimming pool in the sun.

She took a deep, steadying breath. "I'm hurt, Leonard."

How could Starr steal her most lucrative and ever-present client? Just as she wanted to take Geneva Whitehouse? What would Nora do without Leonard? It seemed worse than her usual question: What to do *with* him? He had been the pain in her ribs for years, but she was, well…used to him. He had his gentler side, and until now a certain loyalty, although it wasn't showing today.

"It's a beautiful house," he said in a soft, tempting tone.

And with that Nora realized she'd been played like a fine Stradivarius. Leonard had made the hackles rise on her neck, made her forget Mark Fingerhut.

She rubbed her imaginary frown. "You were trying to tempt me. The problem is, I've never provided estimates on your 'projects' before. If you can't give me carte blanche this time, then by all means realign yourself with Starr Mulligan. I hope you won't be sorry."

Like a hermit crab, Leonard scuttled in his baggy khakis across the office to seize her hand. "Please, Nora. I do value your input."

"I refuse to be manipulated." She withdrew from his cold grasp. "I thought we were friends," she added in a gently scolding tone and, ignoring his hangdog expression, ushered him out the door.

She knew Leonard's taste in home decor. She would simply redo his new quarters in a month or two. For twice the price.

For the time being, she decided to let him squirm.

As for Starr, they would talk, all right. But there would be no truce.

By the time Nora got to Starr's office, having needed an hour to gather herself after Leonard's betrayal, she learned that Starr had left for the day. Disappointed, Nora drove to her last appointment in the very upscale Royal Palms subdivision on the outskirts of Destin. Ready to do some serious arm-twisting, she found the slim, almost petite Geneva Whitehouse waiting—but also, quite unexpectedly, Starr Mulligan.

Nora gritted her teeth, determined to keep her mouth shut until the right opportunity arose to confront Starr in private. Even her latest perfidy wouldn't cause Nora to lose her cool. In grim silence, she trailed Geneva and Starr through the house, expressing the proper *oohs* and *ahhs* here and there over

Geneva's treasures. Geneva, who appeared to be the very epitome of the trophy wife, wanted a new showcase for several of her valuable collections, and Nora and Starr both offered their suggestions.

At a ceiling-high, antique glass-fronted cabinet in the wide hallway, which had a gleaming black walnut floor, Geneva paused.

Peering over her shoulder at the lighted étagère, Nora saw a large number of handblown glass bowls, perfume bottles, and paperweights. A vast amount of gold and silver mixed with crystal sparkled on every shelf. Nora identified Lalique, Orrefors, Waterford—and was that vintage Tiffany?—before her gaze caught on a stunning slender, heart-shaped vase that stood out from the rest.

"That is a gorgeous piece," she murmured. "Very unusual." The light struck and then ricocheted off the cobalt and ruby inside through a swirl of clear glass, creating a rainbow across the dark floor.

"Obviously expensive," Starr said.

"Who's counting?" Geneva smiled, showing a row of very white—and probably fully porcelain-crowned—teeth. Nora guessed she was in her early forties now, but everything about the woman appeared to be perfect, including her youth, or the illusion she had managed to sustain. "It was a present from my husband right before we became engaged," Geneva told them with a loving smile. "His promise, he said then, of our future."

"And you certainly have that," Nora murmured.

Even so, this cabinet was a relatively minor possession. So was the vase, which Nora assumed held a more sentimental price tag. The rest of the house was a monument to expensive taste and extravagance, from the lush sofas with goose down cushions to the brushed nickel-framed paintings on the silk-papered walls. She couldn't wait to get her hands on the redesign job. As soon as she got home, she would draw up her plans. Something a shade less traditional, she envisioned, a tad more lean and contemporary to complement the obvious bling that Geneva appeared to treasure.

Almost twitching, Nora waited until Geneva drifted off into the kitchen. Should she use cherry or alder wood for the new cabinetry? While she pondered the choices, Nora and Starr were alone for a moment, and Nora spoke her mind.

"How dare you?"

Starr arched an obviously waxed eyebrow. There wasn't a stray hair, or even a hair on her head, out of place. Her bland expression didn't alter, not even a blink. "I beg your pardon. Haven't you heard of capitalism, free enterprise?"

Nora clenched her teeth. "In other words, it's every woman for herself."

"If you mean Leonard Hackett, we competed, you lost."

"And you feel entitled to steal my clients from under my nose?"

In response, Starr looked pointedly at Nora's beak. She'd never felt especially proud of her nose. A trifle too long, a bit narrow, it would appear in her mirror to be a classic slash of a blade, but with just a slight bump over the bridge. That might work on a man, on Johnny for example, or Heath Moran.

The thought of Heath gave her a twinge of regret. In spite of her best intentions, after Johnny and Savannah had left the other night Nora had given in and called him, needing some kind of affirmation that she was still a reasonably attractive woman. But Heath hadn't answered his telephone. Maybe he had his reasons, and Heath had decided she was right about the difference in their ages.

Would Nora also inherit her mother's flabby underarm gene, her spreading cellulite? She could already imagine her breasts becoming a sad ski slope under her raw linen blouse, which by now had turned into a mass of wrinkles.

"Starr, *darling*." She repeated Starr's word from the luncheon. "Let me give you some advice."

"Unsolicited, as always?"

Nora smoothed her blouse. "I don't know who scheduled these two meetings at the same time, but I can guess. Wasn't Leonard enough? No," she answered her own question, "you had to call Geneva, and when you learned I would see her today, you 'dropped by' a few minutes earlier. Of all the nerve. If I were you I'd make some polite excuse and leave." She indicated Geneva, who was opening and closing the doors to the immense pantry only a few feet away. "You can put in your bid another day."

"Another day and you'll have contractors all over this place."

"Just tell Geneva—"

"What? That I'm the better designer? Most of the Florida Panhandle already knows that."

Nora felt her blood pressure surge. After her recent near brush with a cardiovascular event, she needed to keep calm. No more of those unanticipated...flushes.

She would maintain control if it killed her. Of her temper. And her body.

"You're not going to rile me, Mulligan. Don't even try."

Nora whirled around, intent upon charming her soon-to-be client and nailing down the deal. Her mind spinning with ideas, she started toward Geneva.

Starr charged after her.

When she jerked Nora around, pulling her arm almost out of its socket, Nora had no choice but to freeze in place. Starr glared at her.

"I want this job. I intend to have it. One way or another."

For a few seconds, Nora stared her down. Then with a cool look of dismissal, she pulled her arm free and continued on into the kitchen. She didn't care whether Geneva heard her or not.

"Someone will die first," Nora muttered.

CHAPTER 3

Detective Calvin Raji Caine had a hangover.

On this hot September morning, it pounded behind his eyes and through his fogged brain. Last night's six-pack roiled in his belly, which he fully deserved, but if anyone spoke too loud in the next few hours, he wouldn't pull his punches.

Caine wasn't proud of what he called his therapeutic drinking, which had started after his wife, Annie's, death, but occasions like that three years ago, and at the moment this one, tended to throw off his good intentions. Right now, his job wasn't helping him to reform.

"Guess I picked the wrong line of work," he said, but it was all he knew.

Caine wound his way up the long, paved drive to the White-house address.

Good Lord.

Did people really live this way? He knew they did. In his job Caine saw all kinds of homes: grand estates, middle-class brick ranch houses, single- and double-wide trailers. The small bungalow he'd shared with Annie popped into his mind as well. Neat and tidy, it had smelled of good food and furniture polish and most of all, love, when she was still alive. He hated going home now.

Solitary confinement, Caine called his place, which echoed with a sense of emptiness now that she was gone. He'd never planned on living there alone, or being a bachelor again. Well, alone except for Annie's cat. Caine was the orange tabby's sole companion now, just as the tomcat was his. He guessed they suited each other, one of them as irascible as the other. Once, he supposed, they'd both been normal guys.

What the hell. He might as well question Geneva Whitehouse about some petty burglary she'd reported earlier that morning or he'd start to feel tempted to go find a little hair of the dog and call a beer or two his lunch—not that Caine had ever done any drinking on the job. He didn't expect the interview to amount to anything. Probably the Whitehouse maid had lifted an item or two, giving herself a nice five-finger bonus.

He rang the bell and heard discreet chimes from within.

The woman who answered would have sucked the breath from an ordinary man, one who still had red blood flowing through his veins. Reed-slim but full-breasted, Geneva Whitehouse wasn't tall, yet she carried herself like a supermodel. An ash blonde with wide blue eyes, she wore a gold wedding ring on her hand next to a flashy diamond set in platinum that must weigh four carats.

"Ms. Whitehouse. Calvin Caine." He flashed his badge. "I'm the investigator assigned to your case. I'd like to ask you a few questions."

With the introduction he handed her his card. As she studied it, the striking blue of her eyes went flat, like an unpolished stone, and the sparkle disappeared except from her ring.

"Please come in."

Caine felt the back of his neck crawl. Right away his head began to throb again and he felt lost. The house was huge, in all ways. Big entry hall, big rooms, big ceilings, big air-conditioning system if the chill was anything to judge by. He thought of his own decrepit bedroom unit, cranking out stale air all night, not helping him to sleep. He kept meaning to replace it. Too bad he didn't have the inclination to change the AC, his clothes, whatever.

In the living room she studied him. "Would you like a drink? Soda, coffee, something stronger?"

He must look as if he needed one. The temptation he'd suppressed rocked him back on his heels. "No, thanks. I'm on duty. I won't take much of your time."

Geneva Whitehouse perched on the arm of a very expensive-looking sofa. She invited him to sit down, but Caine stayed on his feet. He took out his notebook and clicked open his pen.

"The missing vase," he said, prompting her to begin.

"Yes, of course. I noticed it was gone this morning when I got up," she said. "It's quite valuable, although not of museum quality." She named a figure that widened Caine's eyes anyway. "My husband had it custom-made for me from his own design." She blinked. "As you might guess, it has even greater sentimental value." She worried her bottom lip. "Do you think you can get it back?"

"We'll try." He scribbled on his pad. "When did you last see this vase?"

With a longing look toward the hall, she indicated the now-empty space in the curio cabinet, a look that reminded Caine of himself at home in his empty house. "Yesterday afternoon, I think, just before five," she said.

Caine asked the usual questions about anyone who had access to the house or grounds, anyone who might know the layout and her daily routine. In his experience, most people followed the same schedule, in the same order, each day without any significant deviation. She mentioned the gardener, her cleaning service, the pool boy. "But they haven't been here as recently as—" Her gaze popped open even more. "Oh, goodness. I've been so upset, I almost forgot. I've been interviewing interior designers. We're going to have some work done on the house—" needlessly, Caine thought, but it was her money, or her husband's "—and two women were here yesterday. One of them admired that particular vase. It does stand out," she added.

Caine needed specifics.

"Nora Pride," she murmured, sounding reluctant to say the name. "Her firm is Nine Lives, Inc. in Destin."

Sounded more like a pet store to Caine. She gave him the other woman's name, Starr Mulligan of Superior Interiors, and Caine rolled his eyes. Geneva Whitehouse didn't see him because she had glanced away, but when her gaze met his again, his cop instincts began to hum. Caine saw doubt in her eyes. She didn't know whether to tell him something.

"Anything you can give me, Ms. Whitehouse, will be a help. Sometimes the smallest detail can sound a bell."

She fidgeted with her ring. "Something else does bother me, Detective Caine. I'd be less than a good citizen—and not very helpful to you—if I didn't tell you that when they were here, Starr and Nora argued."

Geneva Whitehouse gnawed on her lip again. It was a great lip, full and plump and ripe, but Caine reminded himself that he didn't have much interest in women these days. His work had become his life. And besides, she was married. Caine liked to think he was a principled man.

"I wasn't in perfect earshot," she continued, bringing him back to the reason for his visit. "While I was looking at the shelves and cabinets in the kitchen, Nora took Starr aside. I could hear the buzz of their voices, then they rose before Nora's dropped a little…" She flushed, prettily.

"Go on."

Geneva Whitehouse hesitated. "Maybe I'm jumping to conclusions. The vase was here when they left and later, I think, when I left home myself. I was supposed to meet my husband for dinner, but he was detained at work so I ended up eating alone in the restaurant." She all but wrung her hands, looking more unhappy than her husband's necessary lapse seemed to warrant. "I don't see how anyone could have gotten into the house while I was gone. We have an alarm system and it's always monitored. Earl insisted on it as soon as we were married."

And she had become a blue blood by law, Caine thought. He made a little "hmm" of encouragement. This was Geneva Whitehouse's first marriage, he knew, but it was her spouse's third trip around the matrimonial track, and each time he had downsized in terms of his bride's age. Earl Whitehouse was a prominent local builder and Royal Palms was his project.

Talk about career development. Without ever holding a job, Geneva Whitehouse had become an instant multimillionaire.

In the next breath she knocked him flat again.

"I hate to say anything against Nora, really. But I saw how determined she was to get my business." Geneva Whitehouse reported Starr Mulligan's similar statement, then stopped.

Caine sighed to himself. Getting a witness to talk could be as hard as bathing Annie's cat. For another moment she couldn't go on. Or at least that's how it appeared to Caine, who felt his anticipation rising with every empty second.

She tried again. "Nora said—"

His tone was gentle yet insistent. "Yes, Ms. Whitehouse?"

"The burglary here is one thing and I'm heartbroken over my vase. But, well, I couldn't help but overhear. Detective Caine, Nora threatened someone…with murder."

Nora stared down at the just-received wedding invitation on her desk and thought of violence. And here she'd imagined she had put her past—her marriage—behind her at last. She reread the formal words.

Mr. and Mrs. William Baker
Request the honour of your presence
At the marriage of their daughter
Heather
to
Wilson Pride

The creamy vellum sheet was decidedly stubborn, if an inanimate object had any such quality, or it would have disappeared by now, zapped by Nora's fervent wish that she hadn't been included in the guest list. Attend her ex-husband's wedding? Nora shuddered, but the words on the invitation hadn't altered, either. She wished she could simply ignore them and the troublesome date that she had tried, only a few months ago, to make sure would never happen.

She wasn't proud of herself for attempting to sabotage Wilson's newest "love of my life," and now it seemed she had definitely failed.

Nora leaned around her desk to catch Daisy's eye. The golden retriever was lying in her usual spot between her and the door to her office. Several months ago, taking into account her lost clients, Nora had been forced to lay off her receptionist, and Daisy had kindly offered to work for free. Three times a week she kept Nora company at work, while supposedly discouraging intruders; in return, Nora dispensed extra doggie treats and kept a Chinese porcelain bowl of cold water on hand in lieu of a salary.

"Well, Daisy," she said, "what do you think of Wilson and his bride? It's a good thing he didn't ask you to be in the wedding. I would never have forgiven him for that. But does he really think I want to—"

Nora heard the outer door open.

Apparently her ears were better than Daisy's. The dog hadn't gazed at Nora for more than a second before dropping her head again onto her paws, letting her floppy ears fall over her eyes, and going back to sleep. Now she didn't move—until Nora's visitor appeared in her office doorway. Detective Caine, apparently. The policeman had called to say he was dropping by.

The Walking Wounded, was Nora's first surprised thought. And, for some unknown reason she might never understand, all of the blood drained from her head straight down to her Jimmy Choo pumps. For a second, she swayed in her ergonomic desk chair.

Quickly, even in her distress, she took inventory of the detective. His rumpled black Dockers, his herringbone jacket, his shirt and tie were good quality and well-tailored but looked uncared for, like the man himself, it seemed. His craggy, hard-jawed face, shadowed by a late afternoon stubble, had seen too much living, Nora felt sure, with a sharp, masculine nose and shrewd yet puppy dog-sad dark eyes. His head of thick, dark hair, with just a hint of distinguished gray at the temples, clearly needed a stylist.

Yet he drew her gaze again. He reminded Nora of herself right after she had left Wilson and unwillingly struck out on her own, feeling ironically abandoned. She was feeling that now after getting the invitation to his wedding while she was still single and likely to stay that way.

Nora, the saver of other lost souls ever since her divorce, felt almost sorry for Caine. So did Daisy, apparently.

The retriever's eyes opened, then brightened, and her plumy tail began to flap in greeting against the carpet. So much for Daisy's new career as Nora's quasi-secretary and protector. The detective smiled a little, then bent down to give Daisy a good scratch behind the ears.

"Ms. Pride?" he prompted.

"Yes," she said. "I'm Nora Pride."

"Nice dog."

Daisy rolled over for an expert tummy rub, gazing at Calvin Caine like an adoring strumpet. "She certainly seems to like you."

Nora smoothed her limp skirt, wishing she'd had time to powder the shine from her nose. She reminded herself that he was a cop and not to underestimate him, though it was clear he liked animals, usually a plus in Nora's book. Why did he want to talk to her? He hadn't said, but Nora's heart did a three-sixty roll. She had a stack of unpaid parking tickets stashed in the glove compartment of her car. Had the department finally tracked her down? Why send a detective?

He gave the surroundings a cursory yet professional assessment: Nora's glass-topped desk, the wall of shelves behind it neatly sprinkled with books, a tidy stack of interior design journals and the latest issue of *Architectural Digest*. Then his gaze returned to Nora. He looked her up, then down.

"I have a few questions," he said.

When he stood, Nora inspected his badge, tucked his card away without looking at it and then gave him another careful scrutiny like the one he'd given her. He had a decent build, good shoulders and a straight spine, if not of the same height and breadth as Heath Moran, who still hadn't bothered to answer her numerous telephone calls.

Hugh Jackman, she decided of Caine. A more mature Hugh Jackman.

Then he murmured, "Geneva Whitehouse."

Geneva? Almost before Nora could take in the name, the questions came at her like bullets. This wasn't about parking tickets. When had Nora left Geneva's house yesterday? Who could vouch for her whereabouts last night?

"I was home, alone." Perversely, considering the situation, Nora wished he would smile. She'd like to see what he looked like then, because she suspected he didn't smile often. Or maybe she was trying to divert herself from her obsessive study of the wedding invitation a few minutes ago—that is, until he brought up Starr. And the apparently missing vase.

"Yes," Nora admitted, "I did see Starr yesterday."

He had picked up on her cool tone. "You're not friends."

"I didn't say *that*. We're, well, more than acquaintances. We're competitors in interior design." Oh, you bet. Nora had barely been out the door yesterday before Geneva Whitehouse called to inform her that she'd chosen Starr to do the work on her home. The sudden decision had wounded Nora, but she tried not to show it. "Ours is a small world, Detective Caine. One can't afford to make enemies."

"Would you call Ms. Mulligan an enemy?"

Nora felt her cheeks heat. Before she knew it, they were as hot as a pancake griddle, and she could sense the blood rushing through her veins, centering in her chest and making her feel breathless. Nora fought the strong urge to fan herself with Wilson's invitation. Her skin must look as red as fire. Dear God, she was having another of those flushes, worse than before. Caine's fault. That alone was enough to make her dislike him.

"Starr and I may have had words a time or two, bless her heart. She doesn't have the best…disposition. But we both know where our bread is buttered." She had formed a small lie, hoping to tamp down the fiery blush spreading across her skin, hoping to defuse his keen attention. "If you must know, yes, we sometimes quarrel." A new insight struck her. "I suppose it's almost a hobby for us."

Her heart thundered like a cannon during a twenty-one-gun salute at Arlington Cemetery. Nora looked from him to Daisy, who was now curled at Caine's feet as if she belonged to him rather than Nora. Surely he didn't think…

"Do I look like a common thief to you?" she asked.

Nora drove home in a blue funk, her fingers trembling on the steering wheel of her convertible. She knew she hadn't conducted herself well in the interview with Detective Caine. Still, she wasn't behind bars tonight for something she hadn't done. Look on the bright side.

Daisy certainly did. She hadn't stopped smiling since Caine walked into the office, not even when Nora worked late then dropped her off at the vet's on the way home. Daisy didn't know it, but she was staying overnight at the clinic to get her teeth cleaned.

Alone in the car for the rest of the ride, Nora put down the top and let the warm, sultry Gulf breeze blow through her hair. Overhead the sky had darkened to a velvety blue, and she glimpsed a few stars trying to come out.

She was putting her key into the door of the home she'd worked so hard to pay for as a single woman—an honest woman—when a hard hand covered her softer one. Her pulse jerked in alarm. She hadn't recovered from Caine's interrogation, and Nora half expected another attack right at her door.

Then she smelled him, that recently familiar scent of man and the pricey cologne she had given him for his birthday. Instead of a real assault, to her relief this was some fantasy come to life in her doorway.

A hoarse masculine growl threatened to melt the skin at the nape of her neck. There was no "Your money or your life" forthcoming, but every square inch of Nora's flesh quivered. He didn't bother with talk. He didn't have to.

Heath Moran seemed fully involved in a replay of that scene from the 1969 film *Butch Cassidy and the Sundance Kid*. The young Robert Redford. Katharine Ross. A classic now. Like Nora.

Before she could breathe again, he gently nudged her inside and shut them both into the cool darkness of her entryway. He pushed her up against the closed panel of the door and set his delicious, wicked mouth on hers, and she went limp.

"Why the hell do you keep torturing me like this?" Heath mumbled, his mouth pressed to the cleavage above the top button of her silk blouse. "Three flipping weeks without a word from you. Then I get that desperate-sounding tone on my answering machine. The Steel Magnolia in full meltdown mode. You're enough to drive a man out of his freaking, already-insane mind."

"Heath—"

Nora didn't get the chance to continue. Or explain, as if she could. Clearly, he was a man bent upon a mission of the utmost importance. Critical. *Now*.

Within the next heartbeat, Nora agreed with him.

She felt his hard body against hers, the press of his already-stiff penis against her through the coarse fabric of his cargo shorts. He would be out of them in the next five seconds if she didn't take control.

"You didn't answer my call."

"I'm answering it now." She barely understood his muttering. "I was at work last night. Or did you already forget that Thursdays and Fridays I'm on the schedule?" Before she could push him away, his mouth dipped lower and he had unbuttoned her sufficiently to slip his hand inside her blouse. The heat of his palm on her breast, his fingers snaking inside her bra, felt like heaven. His breath came in pants. "The club's...short-handed right now. One of the trainers...quit and I'm working...more hours."

"Some excuse. And your cell phone battery died? I called both numbers."

"Sounded important." He nuzzled her half-exposed breast. "So is this."

Nora fought not to whimper.

She didn't think she could resist much longer. When she moaned, Heath smiled against her other breast.

"You want it. You know you do. You want me."

"You do have...your skills. And here I thought—" she couldn't help the movement of her own body "—that you were nothing more than a sadistic personal trainer. I'm still hurting," she murmured, trying to be rational. "Those last pull-ups were murder."

"A month ago? And you're still sore? I doubt it." Heath laughed a little, but he sounded winded. "Through tormenting me, then? Because if you are, we can get down to business here."

Heath was forty-two and a stud muffin, as Savannah might say, the likes of which Nora had never known up close and personal until a few months ago. That is, until she'd finally re-discovered her common sense. She'd already made one mistake with Wilson, as today's announcement reminded her. When compared to Wilson's more cerebral, poetic nature, Heath might be embarrassingly physical, more of this earth with his sandy brown hair and eyes the color of topaz, and he was sensible to the core, but he was still a man. And men dumped her, or forced her to dump them, no matter what they promised.

"I can't, Heath." She pulled back, smoothed her skirt and rebuttoned her blouse. Her whole body felt sensitized as she glanced at his still-dazed face. "This is ridiculous. I'm—"

His head jerked up. "If you'd only get over this cockamamy theory that I'm too young for you, Nora, we could have some fun. Again."

"We're really not compatible." Except in bed. She couldn't deny that. What was she waiting for?

Heath's voice stopped her. "I still scare you, don't I?"

Nora couldn't disagree. "Old habits—like Wilson—are hard to break." And then, there was Detective Caine with his questions and his sorrowful eyes, the inspiration for yet another, different blast of heat. This time Nora couldn't pretend it hadn't happened.

Heath ran a hand through his thick sandy hair. He was ob-viously frustrated. "I'm not a habit. You've been divorced for over two decades. Isn't it time to be happy again? With someone else? Me, for instance."

She had to turn away not to jump his bones. He wasn't just a pretty-boy face, a pack of muscles and six-pack abs. It wouldn't be fair to him. Or to her.

He followed her into the living room, where Nora switched on the lamps so as not to leave them in the seductive darkness that had fallen.

"I didn't expect to find you here," she admitted.

Their brief affair, a first for Nora, had taught her a few

things. She wasn't cut out for hot sex without strings. She also wasn't above enjoying it.

That thought, at least, was comforting. Heath's tone was not.

"Look, I've been a good boy. I left you alone for *weeks*. Believe me, that wasn't easy. Then all of a sudden you call me, but I can't figure out why. I stew about that for a couple of days, but when I get here—against my better judgment—you light up like one of these lamps. Then just when things start looking good, and I feel human again, you go into some deep freeze. What the hell happened, Nora?"

"I'm sorry."

"Forget that. *What?* Your future son-in-law disapproves of us? That doesn't sound like Johnny, or Savannah. She introduced us, for God's sake."

Nora took a deep breath. "She's pregnant."

When she turned from lighting the last lamp, Heath was staring at her.

"Pregnant. And that means…"

"I'm going to be a…you know." Nora turned away.

"Well, that's it, then." If Heath slammed the door for good this time, she couldn't blame him, but she wouldn't watch him leave. Instead, he stalked her across the room. "There's no use pretending that it's not all over now," he murmured too close behind her. "A *grandmother*."

Her throat had closed. "That's a good thing, but…" She couldn't go on.

"Jeez, Nora." Heath turned her into his arms. He did have the smoothest moves. She never saw them coming. "Do you think that matters to me?"

A slight thrill ran through her. "It matters to me."

"So why did you call me, then?"

"I wanted…" She didn't know.

"Comfort?"

"Maybe. A little." A lot. A whole cartload of the stuff. "I needed…"

"Reassurance?"

He had gone from bemused bewilderment to curiosity. Now she heard irritation. She might as well finish this off.

"And I had a…hot flash." She didn't quite choke on the word this time.

Neither did Heath. "Well, of course you did. You'll turn fifty next week."

I'm not ready. I'll never be ready. Please don't make me.

She felt petty, immature, but couldn't stop herself. "Then I came home the other night and Johnny was here with Savannah. They told me about the baby. Then yesterday Starr Mulligan—"

"That witch?"

But even that wasn't all. Nora told him about her latest quarrel with Starr, but couldn't bring herself to say she was being accused of a crime. Who on earth could have taken Geneva's vase? And she couldn't tell Heath about Wilson's marriage.

He raised his eyebrows. "Sounds like you've had a weird couple of days."

"Well, yes, and if you include Leonard Hackett—" To her absolute horror, she gulped back a sob. Nora whirled away.

Heath stopped her. His hard, sinewy arms wrapped tighter around her more slender frame. She felt Heath's chin come to rest on the top of her head. He rocked her lightly back and forth, letting her feel that he still wanted her.

"I have a few good ideas to make you feel better." His sexy tone almost undid her. "Want to hear them? It's a free offer," he said in a tempting voice. "Better than a sweaty workout at the club."

Nora gave him a shaky smile.

"My life is changing too fast," she whispered.

But Heath still had her in his arms. He felt strong and good and he wasn't laughing at her. He just held her.

And, despite knowing that no good could come of it, Nora let him.

In that instant she felt vanquished yet determined, like a modern-day Scarlett O'Hara.

Tomorrow, as Scarlett had claimed, would be a better day.

If it wasn't, Nora knew exactly what to do about Caine.

She would just have to hire her own Dream Team.

CHAPTER 4

The next day, Nora was still a free woman.

That pesky Caine wouldn't get the best of her.

And neither would Starr.

On another hot and humid morning with the temperature already climbing, Nora gave the broad front door of Geneva Whitehouse's home another determined blow with the brass knocker. She'd tried the doorbell, which had summoned no one. Now she waited in the blazing sun, then heard the click of heels on wood in the entry hall.

For a second, the back of her neck prickled. She felt she was being observed. Then the tap of stilettos clacked again, going quickly in the opposite direction. Her gaze homed in on the discreet brass peephole in the door.

Not to Nora's surprise, Geneva obviously wasn't glad to see her. A temporary setback.

She leaned on the bell with one finger, lifted the knocker again with her other hand and set off a cacophony inside the house.

"Ms. Whitehouse," she called through the closed door for good measure.

Tap, tap, tap. The returning sound of heels was agitated.

"Geneva, please. Open up. We need to talk."

"There's nothing to say. Our business is finished."

No. It was not. She wouldn't leave until Geneva Whitehouse reconsidered her decision to choose Starr for the redesign of her home. Ten thousand square feet, Nora reminded herself. The very numbers made her salivate.

She could imagine Starr's gloating triumph when Geneva chose her instead of Nora. The insult wouldn't stand.

Apparently this had been her week for outrageous insults.

Nora blocked from her mind the sudden image of Caine's dark, brooding eyes, his accusations. He hadn't gone quite that far, but he'd implied as much, and she knew she was a definite suspect in the burglary here at Geneva's house. Nora desperately needed to repair her reputation.

Damage control. In spite of her aversion to Geneva's husband for reasons of her own, she couldn't afford to lose business. If Geneva would only hire her after all, and she liked Nora's work, she might recommend her to her friends.

Through the still-closed door she heard heavy breathing. Geneva was still there, as if hoping Nora would get discouraged and give up.

"Please," she said again, softening her tone to convey the courtesy that Maggie had ingrained in her long ago. "This won't take long. I just want—"

"Go away." Geneva's voice shook.

Nora took a step back as if she'd been slapped. Geneva really was mad.

Nora reached for the black leather portfolio she'd left leaning against the brick wall beside the door. She chanced a look through the frosted glass panels that flanked it but could detect no movement or the outline of Geneva's body. She must be pressed to the door itself, eyeing Nora through that peephole.

Nora tried another tack. "I have something to show you," she said in a singsong tone. "I think you'll be sorry if you don't take at least a peek."

The door crashed open, rattling the glass.

"Are you threatening me?"

Shocked, Nora clutched the big briefcase to her front. Her

heart had begun to thump ominously, and for a moment she felt breathless.

"No. Of course not. I have some sketches here..."

With a weary sigh, Geneva clattered away from the open door. "Come in, then. But I won't change my mind. After Detective Caine and I spoke, I know that wouldn't be wise."

What did the man say to her?

Nora clenched her teeth. "I am not a criminal." She followed Geneva inside, the cool air washing over her like a damp cloth against her heated skin. "That man has problems of his own. And if you believe Starr—"

Geneva clipped toward the nearby living room, right past the antique, glass-fronted curio cabinet that had held the now-missing heart-shaped vase. Nora glanced at the barren space on the shelf. The cause of her current troubles, or one of them.

Her business might depend on these next few moments— she had no doubt they would be very few—but so did her shaken sense of self-worth.

She perched on the edge of an obviously costly sofa. "I have never been accused of dishonesty before," she said, zipping open the black case to draw out her sketches. "If you need references, I'll provide them. I'm terribly sorry for your loss, but I can assure you I didn't take your vase. What would I do with it?" Nora gave her a weak smile. "Adorn another customer's home with a stolen object? Hardly. Keep it for myself—and wait for the day when Caine barges in to catch me in the act? Sell it on eBay?"

For the first time she noticed that Geneva, who sat on the matching sofa opposite, didn't look quite herself. Maybe Nora shouldn't have tried to make a joke. Geneva's normally perfect blond hairstyle looked in disarray, and her blue eyes lacked their usual sparkle. Her gray sweatpants and T-shirt matched the pallor of her complexion beneath its tan. Even while wearing those three-inch heels, black with fetching crystal beads across the instep, she looked thrown together. Of course, she'd had no reason to expect company.

Geneva's mouth quivered.

"All right, then. Show me."

Nora had expected a bigger fight.

"Really?" She handed Geneva the first of half a dozen drawings, her ideas for the main rooms of the Whitehouse home. Despite Geneva's decision Nora had put them together last night and she felt they'd turned out well. There would be none of Starr Mulligan's typical touches, no garish colors, strange artifacts or overstuffed furniture. The fact that Starr did possess an eye for arrangement, and that her judgment on wall coverings could be pleasing, didn't enter into Nora's assessment. "As you can see, I've gone for a minimalist effect. Neutrals, clean lines, a contemporary look that should serve as a natural background to highlight your treasures."

Her sharp glance made Nora swallow. Perhaps she shouldn't have reminded her would-be client—her temporarily lost client—about the missing vase or any of its scintillating companions.

"This sort of design is all the rage now. I think you'd be very pleased with the outcome—"

"Or else?"

Nora faltered. "Why, of course I'd be happy to work with you on any changes, minor or more extensive."

"Nora. As you know I've already hired Starr Mulligan."

"Yes, I do know." She cleared her throat. "And I realize my comment to her was less than, well, businesslike. I'm sorry you heard it. Starr and I have our differences, but they shouldn't concern you. It's the job that really matters."

"Does it?" Geneva's strained tone alerted Nora. There was something wrong here, even more wrong than Nora being replaced by Starr because of some silly misunderstanding. She'd already apologized, but maybe not enough.

"I am sorry, Geneva. I made a bad impression, but that's why I'm here. Other than to show you my sketches, of course, which I had hoped might speak for themselves. And me," she added.

"The sketches are beautiful."

"You like them?"

Geneva's blue gaze swept over the last drawing in the stack. For an instant her eyes brightened, but then, to Nora's horror, they filled with tears. A few brimmed over, and before she stopped to think, by instinct Nora had fallen to her knees onto the thick carpet in front of Geneva's sofa. She reached out to pull Geneva awkwardly into her arms. "There, there. We can work something out."

"I doubt that," Geneva wailed.

Maybe she felt terrible about her earlier decision. She might feel torn between Nora and Starr but regretted her rejection of Nora based on such tissue-thin evidence of a crime. Maybe now she wanted to make amends, as Nora did, but wasn't sure how.

Nora rocked Geneva in her embrace, as she might one of her children even now. Geneva clung to her, sobbing as if her heart had broken.

"I don't know about you," Nora said after a few moments, "but I can't sit on this rug as if I'm in a Japanese restaurant with one of those little tables that are no higher than a foot."

Geneva Whitehouse didn't smile. She pulled back, embarrassed by her display of emotion, and avoided Nora's searching gaze. Geneva studied the pale cream carpet, the wall covered in an exquisite gold-washed French paper, the violated curio cabinet just visible in the hall, then the deep crown molding that edged the double tray ceiling before at last she met Nora's eyes. Nora had misunderstood.

"Oh, Geneva. Please tell me what's wrong. What have I done that can't be corrected? Certainly you don't believe Detective Caine—"

"No," Geneva murmured. "It's not him."

Unable to speak, she gestured at the elaborate living room before she followed Nora's lead and struggled to her feet. They faced each other with the marble-topped coffee table between them, a gorgeous piece of stone that Geneva hoped would be incorporated in the new design. Right now the house was the furthest thing from her mind. Odd, when it had consumed her for so long.

"My husband...lately, he hasn't been very attentive. He works almost every night—not in his study here, as he used to do, but at his office in town. When I called there last evening, I—I got his voice mail." The last was uttered in a shaken tone. "I thought then he was on his way home, but he didn't show up until three in the morning. I know because I was still awake." She made a futile gesture. "I don't know what's happening..."

Nora sat beside her again on the sofa. She took Geneva's cold hand.

"You're freezing, angel."

Geneva shivered, feeling more bereft than she had since before she met Earl and at last escaped the life her parents had wanted for her. But had she only exchanged one misery for another after all? "I can't seem to get warm."

Nora looked eager to help, but it was clear she didn't know how.

"When my relationship became...difficult, I didn't feel warm for weeks." Nora blanched, as if realizing what she'd said. "Not that I think you have the same problem," she hastened to add. "Marriage is a long-term investment," she tried again. "One that sometimes doesn't work as we'd like. What I'm trying to say is, there are always ups and downs. I wouldn't worry," she said. "Don't even think about my experience."

Geneva withdrew her hand from Nora's clasp. The memory of that other existence, and of one recent night, were still fresh in her mind. "A few nights ago when Earl was home, I went up to his study—it's next to our bedroom—to ask him something and I found him at his computer. That's not unusual, but when he noticed me standing in the doorway, he blanked out the monitor, I think so I couldn't see what was there. He looked…guilty. I don't know that anything was wrong, but it didn't feel right."

Nora looked away. "Your husband is probably embroiled in one of those *male* things that always seem to consume them." She flushed. "That is, men get caught up in rectifying some global injustice or correcting the company balance sheet while we women do so in our smaller way without much fanfare."

Geneva sniffled.

"Is that what your husband does, too?"

"Not any longer. I've been divorced for some time. But I'm sure he does," she added quickly. "Or he will, with his new wife, as he must have with the others. He's getting married again soon. I'm invited to the wedding."

Geneva's eyes widened. She dabbed at them with the handkerchief Nora handed her, using the delicate lawn fabric and Swiss embroidery to blot her smeared mascara. When she saw Nora wince at the stain, she set the cloth aside.

"That," Geneva murmured, "was more information than I need."

Nora wasn't being very tactful, but Geneva knew she was trying, and it wasn't easy to deal with a hysterical woman. Geneva wondered miserably if she was turning into her mother, the stage mama of all time who had been given to outrageous displays of temper and tears.

She couldn't hold back her worst fear. "What if Earl is having an affair? Or visiting Web sites with nubile women on display?" Women younger, prettier, than Geneva now?

"Wilson's first peccadillo nearly killed me," Nora admitted, not helping at all, "and I wouldn't wish that on anyone." She couldn't seem to stop herself. "For a long while I regretted that it didn't kill Wilson instead, even when I still loved him with all my heart." Nora paled again. "Oh, my God. That doesn't mean you should worry about Earl." But something in her expression told Geneva that Nora felt exactly that about Geneva's husband.

Geneva looked at her hands. "I was his trophy wife, you know. We've been married for fifteen years," she said, her voice gathering strength now that she'd stopped crying. "When we said our vows, I was barely twenty-five. Now I'm forty, and no matter how little I eat or how long I spend on the treadmill every day, I'm still ten pounds heavier than when I met Earl—" She broke off, then began again, "I've done a thousand sit-ups, a million leg lifts, or I did until I quit my health club. But my face...oh, God."

"Nonsense." Nora adopted a perky expression. "Forty is the new thirty, even twenty-something. You're a beautiful woman, Geneva. Stunning. Certainly you know that. I'm sure Earl does, too." She gestured at the room, as Geneva had. "He must love you very much. This house, the car you drive, the exquisite pieces you display..." Nora trailed off, as if not wanting to tread too near the subject of Geneva's missing vase again. Another reason she'd spent so much time crying today. "Those are material things, I know, but many men use them to express how much they care. It's easier, you see, than admitting their feelings."

"You think so?"

"Positive." When her stiff-upper-lip approach seemed to work, Nora plowed on. "Maybe you and Earl could talk tonight."

Geneva shook her head. "He called just before you rang the bell. He has a dinner meeting at seven. He won't be home until late again."

"Ah," Nora said.

Geneva felt about to tear up all over again. "What if he doesn't see me as a desirable woman anymore? Then what?" she demanded of Nora, who had no answer. Geneva didn't notice. She swept the half dozen sketches of Nora's designs off the marble table. "If he wants another woman, *she'll* be the one who lives here! Not me."

Nora looked horrified. "This house isn't in your name?"

"We own it jointly," Geneva said.

"Then at least you have a half interest, which is probably worth a great deal in Royal Palms, should the worst happen. It won't, of course. You're just feeling neglected, and insecure. It happens to all of us," Nora assured her. "But there's no sense giving in to a major depression. That's not healthy, and good health is the first defense." She rummaged in her handbag and came up with a card. "This is my doctor's number. Mark Fingerhut. Call him. He can give you a lift in no time."

Geneva examined the card. "An obstetrician?" Her mouth trembled. If only she could have given Earl children. He'd said he wanted only her, without anything else between them except her perfect body, but maybe a family would have provided a stronger bond. Given them something to hang on to other than Geneva's beauty. It had been her lifelong curse. And it was all she had.

"He's also a gynecologist," Nora said. "But he can refer you to the right person if you'd like Botox injections, for example." Nora composed her face into a serene expression. "They were the best thing I've ever done. I'd send you to the man I used, but he just retired."

Geneva stared at her, then down at the card. Nora fished in her bag for another, handing it to Geneva with a flourish. "This might come in handy, too."

Geneva read the name. "'Heath Moran.'"

"I belong to this club where he works. He's absolutely marvelous, and quite easy on the eyes," she added. "Not that I think you need some fine-tuning, but if you're really concerned about a fitness program, join the club and get a personal trainer. Heath is just the man."

"I hadn't thought about a trainer…"

But whatever worked, Geneva decided. She had to do something. Why would Earl remain interested in a woman who didn't look her best, who had moped around all morning wondering how to fix their life together? Only a day or two ago she had been so excited about redoing her home. With a little pick-me-up she soon would be again.

Nora's sketches were lovely, and she had tried to be of help about Earl, but she would have to wait while Geneva reconsidered her decision. She wasn't in the mood to make one now.

"I don't see what else you can do, Ma," Savannah Pride said with a worried frown. Her mother was pacing the kitchen. "You'll have to wait. The rest is up to Geneva Whitehouse."

"I can't believe how I messed things up. You should have heard me, Savannah, babbling on and on, putting my foot deeper in my mouth with every word. I said all the wrong things. Wait? I probably won't ever hear from Geneva Whitehouse again. And I'm not a person who likes to sit on her hands."

"Well, this time you'll have to. You tried to help," Savannah added. "There's nothing more you can do." In the condo she now shared with Johnny—wonder of wonders, he had finally committed to the relationship she had known was destined from the start—she poured Nora a glass of wine and then opened a sparkling water for herself. "I know how hard it can be to find the right words."

She shot another look at the kitchen clock, wishing Johnny would get home. Earlier, Savannah had entertained her best friend, Kit, and her four-year-old son, Tyler, both of whom Savannah adored, but they'd gone home. She needed reinforcements before either she or Nora went into extreme breakdown mode. Better to concentrate on her mother's problems than her own.

"I hope Geneva's fears are groundless," Nora said. "But you know how I feel about that man. I wouldn't trust Earl White-house as far as I can see him. Thank goodness I didn't blurt out my experience with him."

"Thank goodness you didn't," Savannah agreed.

Nora sipped at her wine. "And speaking of marriage," she suddenly said, "what on earth are we going to do about your wedding?"

"Do?" Savannah repeated blankly. She didn't care to have her relationship with Johnny mentioned in the same breath as Earl Whitehouse. She crossed her fingers behind her back as if to ward off trouble.

"I don't see being able to hold the ceremony until the middle of next year." Nora ticked off the months. "It's almost October now, which means a due date in April if my math is correct."

"April Fool's Day," Savannah murmured, which had amused her and Johnny. This baby was the best gift she could give him, and vice versa. But the notion terrified her out of her remaining wits. A mother? A wife? All in the same half year? Sure, this was what Savannah had wanted with all her heart, but her first delight and surprise at the happy turn of events were gone, and she was feeling the slightest bit queasy tonight, not only from morning sickness, which, ironically, seemed to last all day.

There were definitely adjustments to be made, and Savannah admired her mother all over again. Nora charged ahead without the least bit of hesitation, but Savannah was indeed a late bloomer who wasn't sure of her capabilities in the new roles she had admittedly chosen. Whether or not she felt qualified to handle this newest phase of her life, she was in it now.

If one thing was certain, Savannah had learned when her parents had split, it was that life perpetually changed, often in astonishing ways. It was up to her to manage this change. But what if she couldn't?

She couldn't tell Johnny how she felt. She had eased him into the notion that it was all right—and perfectly safe—to love her, that she would never break his heart, and that after his shaky start in the world of relationships, they could live happily for the rest of their lives. If she uttered one word of doubt, she feared he just might bolt. What if he felt trapped?

Savannah realized she hadn't heard whatever her mother said.

"…when the baby arrives, we can replan the wedding."

Panic flashed through Savannah's uneasy middle. She laid a calming hand over her stomach. "Ma, there's no reason to postpone the wedding. Everything's on track at last, and the seamstress you hired can put some kind of inverted pleat in the front of my dress."

Nora looked horrified. "Ruin a dress that cost half the earth? I think not."

"You're worried about how I look?" Savannah waved a dismissive hand. "If Demi Moore could pose with her naked, pregnant belly for some magazine, and every other celebrity on the planet has taken up an attitude of 'let it all hang out,' I don't see why not. At least I'll be fully clothed. It won't be ruined, Ma. I want to get married now."

Nora studied her face. Savannah's words had come out—been blurted, really—much faster than she intended. They sounded desperate. She didn't want to lose Johnny.

"Angel, is there something you haven't told me?"

Savannah didn't meet her eyes. "Could we not talk about this right now? The clam chowder I ate for lunch is threatening to take the reverse route in my digestive system." She turned away from the look on Nora's face. Another second, and her mother would be shoving saltine crackers down her throat. "Enough about me, Ma." She looked at Nora. "Why is your face flushed? The wine? Or are you having a hot flash?"

"One," Nora muttered. "Two at the most."

To Savannah's relief, the front door opened. But it wasn't Johnny.

Savannah's brother, Browning, strolled into the kitchen carrying a big bag from Kentucky Fried Chicken and wearing his usual What, me worry? grin. If he only knew...

"Hey. My two favorite girls. Thought I'd drop by for dinner before the football game tonight and—uh-oh," he said, taking in both their faces. He dropped the bag on the counter, spun around and headed back the way he'd come. "Guess I'm outta here."

Savannah caught him by the collar. "Oh, no you aren't. This is a surprise, but I need fresh troops—and you're it." She poured the last of the wine into a glass, which only made him wrinkle his nose. Browning preferred beer. "You just missed Kit and Tyler." When he groaned at her teasing, Savannah said, "Take Ma into the living room while I find some clean plates for dinner."

It wasn't long before Savannah heard Nora's agitated voice from the other room. Obviously the subject of Detective Caine had come up.

Savannah unpacked their take-out dinner while her brother listened to Nora vent about the missing vase. When Savannah poked her head around the kitchen door to check on them, he was leaning back, arms spread across the back of the sofa with his grin still in place. It took a lot to ruffle Browning. He had nerves of steel.

"Let it go, Ma. You told the cop what you know—that you're innocent. Forget him."

"I should be that lucky. The vase is valuable, but even more so to Geneva, it's an emotional loss. She won't give up until it's found. Neither, I'm sure, will Caine. Why expect less? This hasn't been my week, angel."

Savannah almost pitied her brother, stuck with two women who were trying to deal with their topsy-turvy lives. How could he understand? Browning had too many friends of the single male variety, all of whom tended to act like adolescent, hormone-driven boys half their age. Like Nora, she had nearly given up hope that Browning, at twenty-six, would mature—and find a good woman to marry so they wouldn't have to worry about him.

Not that Browning actually needed care.

He had grown into an amazing man, tall and lean with muscle, yet almost rangy like her Grandfather Pride, but with his own father's perfect bones and Wilson's vibrant coloring. Long-lashed hazel eyes, dark hair. Why on earth didn't some woman grab him?

Many had tried, Savannah knew.

Browning insisted he liked his bachelor state as much as he enjoyed his government job. His friends. His weekends at the beach with any available blonde, brunette or redhead who answered his come-here smile. He practiced a persuasive variation of it on Nora now. Savannah had her own opinion. Her friend Kit might have a few issues, but she could very well be a match for Browning. If only he thought so, too…

"Ma, sit down. You're wearing a hole in Savannah's carpet." He patted the seat beside him. "Finish your wine and tell me the rest of your troubles."

"Don't encourage her, Browning." Savannah ducked back into the kitchen and ran the garbage disposer, as if the noise might shut out their conversation. And her own fears.

When she came out with a tray full of cutlery and plates, Nora was gazing into her chardonnay as if the wine tasted like acid and might kill her at any moment.

"I can't stop thinking about that detective or about Geneva. If you had seen her, Browning, just falling apart this afternoon… Not only did she lose something precious, now she's worried about her marriage, too."

"It wasn't a pretty sight, I'm sure. Ah, here we are." He glanced up, sounding relieved when Savannah set their dinner on the coffee table. Fighting a wave of nausea at the smells wafting from the cartons in front of her, Savannah plunked down on the carpet, cross-legged.

"That may not be a healthful position for the baby," Nora cautioned.

"I'm not even showing, Ma. The baby only weighs an ounce."

"Well, don't say I didn't warn you."

Browning snickered, not seeing Savannah's alarmed expression. "Hey, look. The Colonel's best chicken, extra-crispy, with mashed potatoes. It doesn't get much better than this."

Nora took one bite of coleslaw then set down her fork. "I have the impression Caine would see me behind bars."

Browning snorted.

"If so, Johnny would bail you out," Savannah said. "He'd call Wade Blessing in L.A. and get the name of the best shark attorney here in Florida. A whole dozen of them, if necessary, just like O.J.—"

"My thought exactly," Nora said.

"—and all this will be an unpleasant memory," Browning put in.

Nora smiled. "You're a sweet boy. So is Johnny when he tries. And Savannah, you're always a dear. You'll make a good mother, a fine wife—if that's what's bothering you."

Savannah nearly choked on her potatoes. Her mother knew her too well. "Whatever happens, Ma, we'll all stand by you." *And you'll stand by me.* She'd always known that. "Are you feeling bad, too, about Dad's wedding invitation?"

"Of course not. I told you, I've put that behind me."

"Then he did invite you?" Savannah asked.

"Well, yes. I thought it was a little strange, but then we have made our peace in recent months." Nora blinked. "Thank you, angels. Family and friends are everything."

Savannah reached out a hand to her.

"Ma, you're not going to cry, are you? You've been our Rock of Gibraltar, the one who fixes things and helps us."

"I wonder if I can fix them now." Nora threw down her napkin. "How could he possibly think I'm guilty of stealing a *vase*?"

"Caine has to consider everyone who had contact with Geneva or was in her home," Browning said around a mouthful of chicken. "But you'll see. Tomorrow he'll come crawling. And apologize."

Nora was in her office the next afternoon, still pondering the welcome support she'd received from her children, not only about Caine but Wilson, too, when she realized that Geneva Whitehouse was in the reception area.

Maybe she'd come to return Nora's portfolio, which she'd left behind yesterday.

Daisy left her place, and her nap, on the carpet to pad into the other room, her tail not quite wagging but definitely interested. This was the first sign that Daisy might be willing to acknowledge Nora again after the dog's trip to the vet's for her dental cleaning. When Nora had picked her up the night before, after leaving Savannah and Johnny's condo, Daisy had pointedly ignored her.

Now Nora's eyebrows arched.

"Please send her in," she told Daisy. Nora rose from her chair and went around her glass-topped desk to grasp Geneva's hand. She felt much warmer today. "How nice to see you again so soon. You're looking better."

"I called Mark Fingerhut," Geneva reported. "I'll see him tomorrow. But that's not why I came." She took the chair Nora indicated in front of the desk, and Nora resumed her place behind it, sensing that the unexpected visit was of importance. "I've decided Earl does look as if he's been working too hard and my adding to the pressure he must feel by making waves wouldn't be good for our marriage. I can't thank you enough for listening to me yesterday. I'm sorry I fell apart."

"I'm a woman, too, Geneva. What do we have if we can't help each other?"

Geneva smiled. She wore stunning off-white pants with a cream-colored jacket, topped by a filmy scarf in shades of rust, gold and a muted beige. Her handbag was Louis Vuitton, her shoes Ricardo Ricci. Her hair and makeup looked flawless again. It was like looking at a different person from yesterday, one who had her act together.

Geneva said, "I think we can help each other with the design for my house after all. I may have been hasty about hiring Starr and I have another idea."

Nora's heart began to thump. *Say it. Choose me.*

With a slowness that made Nora's pulse triple in anticipation, Geneva handed over her portfolio and then drew a pair of sketches from her own bag. She laid them on Nora's desk. She glanced at Nora with an expectant expression.

"Well? What do you think?"

Nora studied her own design for the breakfast room, a cheerful study in clubby rattan chairs, a round glass table, and swatches of impressionistic color—deep blue, pink, and yellow—in the cushion fabric. Then she saw the other sketch.

The home office design, which wasn't hers, had a pleasing look, she had to admit, with a light pickled oak for the computer desk and cabinets, a rich hunter green for the carpet, paint for the walls in a soft, neutral taupe that lent a restful air. The chairs were scattered with sunny yellow throw pillows.

"Very nice. But I don't understand," she began with a sense of dread.

"You and Starr." Geneva sounded as if the combination was obvious. "When I studied the sketches you brought yesterday, then looked again at Starr's—" she indicated the pair of drawings "—I knew I wanted you both to do my house."

"You heard us, Geneva. We're hardly friends."

"Nora, I can't decide between you. I like some of your drawings, others of Starr's. I haven't talked to her yet, but when you both see which I've chosen for all of the rooms, you'll see that they complement each other perfectly. I know I'm going to be very happy with the joint result."

"But—but—" Nora stammered. She couldn't imagine anything worse. Except being a suspect in the burglary at Geneva's home.

Geneva beamed. "I can't wait to get started. This has already given me a fresh lease on life." She paused. "I'm sure Earl will love it, too."

Wow, Nora thought. Yesterday Geneva had been a full-blown basket case.

"I really don't think…" Nora tried, already seeing Starr's face in her mind.

"The customer is always right. Is there any reason why this can't work?"

The question sent Nora's stomach into free fall toward her shoes.

Only because we might kill each other.

CHAPTER 5

Was half a loaf really better than none?

In a brief "discussion" with Daisy, Nora had convinced herself that it was. Considering the business she had already lost and the two possible clients who had more recently bailed out to use another design firm—word was definitely getting around town about the burglary—Nora's answer had to be yes.

It didn't take long to realize that Geneva's unorthodox suggestion had another benefit beyond the half share of the design fee Nora would earn, assuming she and Starr could actually work together.

She could quell the local gossips who were beginning to have a field day with her misfortune, and finally demonstrate her innocence in the burglary.

Her life had been spinning out of control long enough. It was up to her to resolve her problems. And as always, that meant seeing to her business and to her family.

After Geneva had left her office, Nora decided on her first course of action. She picked up the phone to call Mark Fingerhut.

"Nora. What can I do for you? Having more of those uncomfortable hot—"

"My will is stronger than a few little hormones," she said. "I feel fine." As long as she didn't come into contact with Detective Caine, Nora added silently. "I wanted to thank you for agreeing to see Geneva Whitehouse."

"No problem. We had an opening and she sounded quite upset."

"I'm sure you can deal with her concerns."

"If I can calm you," he said, a smile in his voice, "she'll be a piece of cake."

He sounded upbeat. Nora had never seen Mark in a sour mood, so maybe Savannah had just caught him in a bad moment. Still, she hesitated, not sure she should mention the other reason for her call. "I was also wondering if you might have room for another patient. My mother," she added. Nora had been ruminating about Maggie since their last call. "I've been trying to persuade her to come to Destin. She's had some problems with her health in the past and I'm worried about her."

"Sure. We'll set up an appointment for her, too. Let me connect you with my receptionist."

"Well, not just yet. We're only in the planning stage." At least, Nora was. Laying the groundwork with Mark, she told him what she knew of Maggie's heart condition and that her mother undoubtedly hadn't taken care of herself in general, especially as a woman. "I hoped that if I approached this from a different direction and talked to you first, I might convince her to make the change. She definitely needs an exam."

"I'll be glad to take a look at her."

"She can be difficult," Nora felt obliged to warn him. At the other end of the line Mark laughed.

"Why am I not surprised?"

Maggie Scarborough was the lucky recipient of Nora's next call. She listened to her daughter, then started to frown. All at once Virginia wasn't nearly far enough away.

"Nora, I know you were trying to be a good daughter," Maggie lectured her in the stern tone she used whenever she felt hemmed in by Nora. "But I'd really rather you didn't discuss my private affairs with a stranger."

"Mark Fingerhut is a practicing physician, not some Peeping Tom."

Maggie tightened her grip on the telephone receiver. "No man has seen me *that way* since your father died."

"Well, then this is your chance," Nora told her.

Maggie bristled. *Cheap thrills?* She held the phone away from her ear, glaring at it. The squat black telephone was a relic, Nora had once said, but it worked for Maggie, who saw no reason to replace it with something more modern. What use did she have for one of those newfangled things with a TV screen that told you who was calling? If she wanted to know, she'd pick up the phone. If she wanted to read, she'd buy a book. And get some reading glasses.

Nora's voice sobered. "Maggie, I really want you to come down. You need a checkup and Mark is very gentle. He'll see you, then recommend a good cardiologist. I think you'd feel a lot better."

"I feel peachy right now." So her heart gave a little flip now and then. She wasn't about to take all kinds of medicine again—she'd tossed out every single bottle after her one heart attack—and that's what doctors were. Pill pushers. She'd probably been misdiagnosed in the first place, and hadn't they told her the attack was minor?

Besides, she hated to fly and Destin was hours away. The thought of having some brute practically strip her naked in the security line didn't hold any appeal. And she knew they did that all the time to vulnerable women like her without a man like Hank to protect them. "I'm staying where I am. You tell Dr. Fingerling that if I ever need him, I'll keep him in mind."

"Fingerhut." Nora made a strangled sound. "I don't believe you. People try to help, and all you do is resist. You're the most stubborn person I know."

"It's a family trait."

Maggie took a deep breath. Her chest did feel tight, but only from the anxiety caused by Nora's call, and she didn't want Nora to worry about her. "It seems to me you have enough troubles of your own. Starr Mulligan, for example." At the start of their conversation Nora had informed her of some woman's suggestion that Starr and Nora work together. Ha. On Maggie's last visit to Florida—the last one, to be sure—she and Nora had run into Starr at a coffee shop. It didn't take long for Maggie to decide that Starr was not her kind. Maggie and Nora had their issues, but Maggie was loyal, and concerned herself about Nora. "I hear from Savannah that you're mixed up with the police," she said.

Nora didn't seem inclined to share any details. "I'm sorry she told you that." She huffed out a breath. "It's nothing. I'm more concerned about finding enough work, taking care of my family— and, as you know, dealing with my exasperating mother."

"Guilt doesn't cut it with me. I won't change my mind."

"Maggie—"

"Anyway, I'm allergic to dogs. I itched for a week after that big goofus of yours spent every night on the guest room bed with me. Not to mention the heat. Every time I stepped outside, I nearly fainted. Even the thought of another trip gives me hives." She took a breath. "Take care, Nora." Irritated by Nora's pressure to leave Richmond, Maggie couldn't resist a last dig. "Let me know when they pull down the Wanted flyer of you at the post office."

When she hung up, she could still hear the sputtered response from the other end of the phone. Feeling guilty, Maggie collapsed into her chair. Her silly pulse was leaping all over the place. She shouldn't upset herself like this.

Every time Nora called, Maggie told herself she wouldn't allow their chat to disintegrate into another quarrel. And every time it did.

But this was her home. She wasn't leaving. Not even for her own good, as Nora might interpret it. She rested her head against the chair back and thought of Hank. She couldn't leave him here.

As long as she felt his presence in the house, kept his clothes hanging in the closet, drank her morning coffee every day from the stout earthenware mug he had preferred, she was still as young inside as the day Hank Scarborough had proposed to her, down on one knee in the proper way, with his own heart showing in his eyes. At seventy-five, she still felt like his bride.

Maggie put a hand over her heart and gently patted herself as if she were comforting Nora or her brother when they were babies, then later Savannah and little Browning.

She wasn't alone here, Maggie told herself. She wasn't afraid.

Nora assured herself that she had done what she could with Maggie, at least for the time being. The thought had become her mantra because her mother was clearly impossible, but that was nothing new. And Nora still loved her. Yet for one moment she had hoped Maggie would finally agree to move, to begin to make some changes in her life, and after forty years to move on at last. To Nora, getting her out of that old house was the first step.

Savannah didn't seem to have such issues with her grandmother, whom she loved unconditionally and didn't try to change. Well, she wasn't Nora. She wasn't the one person responsible for Maggie.

When she got home, to her surprise Nora found her entire family assembled in her living room. Daisy rushed to greet her. For a second, with her hand buried in Daisy's fur, Nora was startled. Her birthday? Already? No, that and the party, which her children had planned themselves, were still three days away. Then she remembered with a jolt that she'd told Savannah about Detective Caine's call late this afternoon while Nora was still fretting about Maggie. He wanted to question her again.

And there he was, another living problem, leaning against

her living room mantel in his under-pressed clothes with those intent dark eyes that saw straight through her, his arms folded across his chest as if he felt irritated that she'd kept him waiting.

Savannah sat on the sofa, looking worried and much too pale. She wasn't eating well, Nora knew, and last night's crispy fried chicken had sent her rushing for the bathroom. Was her pregnancy progressing in a normal fashion? Nora wasn't sure, but she had her doubts.

Johnny had his arm around Savannah, and he wore a non-committal expression, but behind his green eyes his sharp mind was whirring, Nora knew, like the hard drive on her computer.

Across the room, Browning lounged in Nora's favorite, deep-cushioned chair-and-a-half, his gaze studying Caine as if to make sure the man didn't move to snap a pair of handcuffs on his mother. At least Browning hadn't brought one of his un-suitable dates with him tonight.

"Well," she said, "Detective Caine. I'm glad someone was here to let you in. All of them." She glanced at the others, then at her watch. "We did say seven-thirty?"

"It's seven forty-five. You're late."

"Fashionably," Nora murmured. Her watch must be running slow. She dropped her handbag and briefcase on the entry table, then took her time dispensing Daisy's usual treat from the drawer. She straightened her hair in the hall mirror, wishing she'd had time to change into something more casual. But why should she care? She wasn't trying to impress Caine. She wandered into the adjoining living room where, to her irritation, Daisy abandoned her. The retriever waggled over to Caine, who gave her an absent-minded pat before she settled down at his side.

Browning shook his head. "That dog is useless."

"A traitor," Johnny added, biting back a smile.

Nora said, "Lazy Daisy." The dog was slumped against Caine's leg.

Savannah loved her, too, but agreed, "She'd probably let

anyone walk away with this house for a couple of doggy treats, Ma."

Nora was quick to defend her. "Daisy is my lovebug. No, it's all right if she prefers Detective Caine for the moment. She's actually keeping him in check." She smiled a little at him. "Am I supposed to elaborate now on my whereabouts the night of the Whitehouse burglary and the following morning? You already have the names of anyone I talked to that day and the day before," Nora added, but then rattled off her movements for the time in question once more. He was probably hoping she'd make some kind of slip. When she finished, he consulted his notepad, Daisy's shiny nose bumping against the back of his hand as if to take part.

"None of those contacts saw you the previous evening," Caine reported, "when the burglary most likely occurred. After you and Starr Mulligan quarreled in front of Ms. Whitehouse. The only people who talked to you said they were cell phone calls. You could have been anywhere instead of at home. Of course, you may have missed remembering a call or two from here on your land line—and we'll take a thorough look at those records, as well."

Browning leaned forward and then checked himself, as if he'd been about to spring up and throttle Caine for browbeating his mother. Instead, he draped his forearms over his spread thighs and stared down at the floor.

"This is nuts," he said in a taut voice. Obviously he'd changed his mind about Caine's imagined apology. "My mother is a pillar of this community, to use a popular cliché. She's a successful business owner." Well, that may have been stretching the point, Nora thought. "She pays her bills without having to resort to theft. You tell me why she would possibly want to lift a vase that meant nothing to her."

"Some very well-to-do women, successful women, are kleptomaniacs. Like that actress a few years ago." Caine tensed. "But I ask the questions here, Mr. Pride."

"Let me answer," Johnny put in. He drew Savannah closer, but Nora didn't miss her daughter's increasingly distressed expression. "Nora's the most decent woman I know—with the exception of my fiancée," he added quickly. "Nora is like a mother to me, and I'd trust her with my life. Dozens of other people would, too, including everyone in this room except you."

Caine maintained his cop face. "I'm not making judgments."

Browning took a breath. "Go ahead, search the house. Tear it apart if you want. You won't find a thing."

"Let's not get carried away. I don't have a warrant."

Johnny said, "Then you don't have probable cause, which means you have no evidence, only a circumstantial case that wouldn't hold up in court. I doubt the prosecutor would touch this with a very long pole. Nora might have had opportunity—"

"—she had no motive," Browning supplied, his eyes snapping with temper like that in Johnny's voice.

He was about to plow on in Nora's defense, bless his heart, when Caine stopped him cold.

"She had motive." He looked straight at Nora. "The IRS."

Suddenly she couldn't breathe. How on earth had he acquired that information? Nora felt her face heat, and all at once her pulse was racing away with itself again like a Formula One car on the track. What better reason did he need for Nora to steal an expensive vase? If her finances were in jeopardy...

"The Feds are after you?" Browning glanced at Nora.

She forced herself to lock gazes with Caine. "A notice from the government doesn't give a woman motive to burglarize a client's home, Detective."

Nora had been suppressing this other matter for days, overwhelmed by everything else that was happening in her life. The notice was a formality, a meaningless throwaway...like Wilson's wedding invitation, which she had yet to answer. "The IRS notice probably came to the wrong taxpayer."

Caine disagreed. "Your background check says differently.

You may be in a lot of trouble, Ms. Pride. You make it sound like nothing, but are you sure it's just a mistake, a silly mix-up over a few pennies?"

"The problem will be straightened out in no time."

"Ma," Savannah spoke for the first time, "why didn't you tell us?"

Nora sent her a sympathetic smile. "Look at you, poor darling." She let her gaze slide to Johnny, then Browning. "I didn't want to worry you, angels. But Detective Caine has saved me the trouble of admitting that, yes, I did receive a memo that asks—no, requires—me to present myself and my financial records at the IRS office. For a possible audit."

"An audit? We'll go with you," Savannah promptly said. Browning and Johnny agreed, and Nora felt her heart swell with love for them.

"You may meddle in our lives all you want," Johnny murmured. "But we'll by damn meddle in yours, too. Especially now." When Nora started to say something, he said, "Don't bother to object. Have you talked to Paul?"

"My accountant refuses to return my calls, but really, Johnny..."

He frowned. "What if he's in Brazil by this time, with your money? The money he failed to send the IRS last April."

"Several Aprils, apparently," Nora said with a sigh. She'd nearly forgotten Caine, who straightened from the mantel, startling Daisy from her near-doze against his leg. "The man is a CPA," she explained. "I trusted him."

"He's probably a crook." Browning shot to his feet and crossed the room before Nora's racing heart could pound another beat. He pulled her into his arms and held her tight. "Detective Caine should set his sights on the right people. You didn't swindle the government, which is usually pretty good at swindling everyone else, and you sure as hell didn't steal that woman's vase." He scowled at Caine. "Are we done here?"

Caine raised an eyebrow. "For now."

He slipped the notepad into his inside jacket pocket and then strode toward the front door with Daisy following in his wake, her tail swishing. On his way past Nora, they paused. Ignoring Browning's furious look, he said, "Ms. Pride, I'll be in touch."

She half smiled to soften the words. "I hope not."

Not unless he had positive news to report.

Caine had to admire Nora Pride's family support. It said something good about her character and her love for them, an emotion Caine had had little experience with in the past few years and wasn't likely to experience again any time soon.

They all believed her to be innocent, and their love for Nora Pride was written all over them. There was more. He'd already talked to her boyfriend, whose very appearance had irritated Caine for some reason he wasn't ready to examine, and the man had raved about Nora. Caine would also interview her client, Leonard Hackett, who had vouched for her on the phone without reservation, even, he'd said, when he feared Nora might never speak to him again.

Even her gynecologist, never any woman's favorite person, wanted to help clear her name and repair her reputation.

Caine had pretty much seen it all in his twenty-six-year police career, at one time or another, but he'd rarely seen such a display of overwhelming belief in a suspect. Nora Pride took the prize. The other, unwelcome feeling that had taken Caine by surprise when she walked into the living room wouldn't go away, either.

Despite his suspicions, he couldn't deny that she was an appealing woman. She had sleek brown hair with hints of gold, most likely some expensive salon-job highlights. Soft yet determined eyes. And that suit she wore. It had probably cost more than Caine's entire wardrobe, not to mention her shoes. Pointy-toed, three inches high, the kind of lethal stilettos that were in fashion these days, they were an accident waiting to happen. They sure made her legs look good, though.

He didn't know why he had noticed her figure tonight or the other day in her office but he had. Nice chest. A still-slim waist. If he were so inclined, those legs would make him want to run his hands up those top-of-the-line hose that shimmered in the light, straight to the business heart of the woman. And he didn't mean interior design.

No wonder she and Starr Mulligan had quarreled. Nora Pride made Caine want to argue just by standing there.

Was she guilty?

Everyone's a suspect, he reminded himself.

And although she surrounded herself with friends and family and insisted, as they'd said, on meddling in everyone's business, Caine saw that she wasn't very good at accepting help in return.

Hell, at least she had a real life. As a widower, Caine poured his energy into his job. After-hours, he was a recluse.

And their differences didn't end there. Nora Pride was compulsively neat. Caine hadn't shined his shoes since his wife passed away. Nora's home was well kept and, of course, well decorated, while Caine's more sparse bungalow was lucky to see a vacuum cleaner once a month.

He would check out the rest of Nora Pride's contacts and see what turned up. One thing he knew: She wasn't going to get the best of Calvin Caine. The only thing he might have in common with her was a surprising attraction to each other, based on the way she blushed when he looked at her. But they both would be wise to ignore it.

Especially him.

CHAPTER 6

Nora didn't need—or want—Caine's interest. Never mind his sultry dark eyes, his exotic middle name (was he part Indian?) or the way he made her face warm whenever their gazes met. She wasn't a moony adolescent, easy prey for any strange but attractive man. Not after Wilson, and particularly after that wedding invitation. In spite of her brief fling with Heath Moran, she knew better.

She'd endured a long battle to forget Wilson, and Nora had enough on her mind. It would be an even longer time before she forgot Caine's questions in front of her entire family last night. She needed to do something to clear her name—and soon. She wanted to resolve everything else, too: the issue of Maggie, of Savannah's troubling pregnancy, of the IRS. To top matters off, her dreaded birthday loomed straight ahead. Nora didn't want to think about that.

When Leonard Hackett had called to make her day, Nora's mood had plummeted another few notches. So why was she standing now at Leonard's new front door in the exclusive subdivision called Impressions, a mile down the road from Johnny's other place, a beach home in Seaview? On such a humid afternoon when the air seemed almost liquid, Nora couldn't say. Madness, perhaps.

Foolish judgment, probably. They were both possibilities. Or was it that she simply couldn't turn her back on their long and, until recently, firm friendship?

"Nora." Leonard flung the door wide, inviting her in with an eager smile that almost transformed his thin face. His pale eyes didn't quite meet hers as he ushered her through the porcelain-tiled entry and into his living room. Nora didn't waste time on greetings. She came right to the point.

The real reason she was here, she told herself, was because Leonard had mentioned his morning visit from Calvin Caine.

"What did the police officer say to you?"

"He asked questions. I answered them to the best of my ability. Naturally, I assured him that you're a woman of sterling character." Leonard paused. Clearly, Caine's interrogation wasn't first in his mind. "Nora, I've been devastated since our last meeting. Totally. I don't want to leave things this way between us. Please say you forgive me."

Nora wasn't quite ready to forgive. She gave herself a few minutes to take in Leonard's new home, its vaulted ceiling, rough stone fireplace, floor-to-heaven windows, and panoramic view of the ocean mere steps from the house, just as he'd promised. Her breath caught. She was still upset with him, still wounded by his betrayal with Starr, but she had to admit Leonard had great taste. And oh, what she could do for his decor…

Next, she studied his person. He'd acquired a light tan since she'd last seen him, and he appeared to have gained a few pounds. His tan chinos were crisply pressed, and his Ralph Lauren polo shirt, a bottle-green shade that oddly enough made him look more healthy, didn't show a single wrinkle.

Nora reminded him that they were talking about Caine.

"Please don't worry," Leonard begged. "I can see how distraught you are. I did my best, Nora. The rest will come in time." He paused to form a faint smile. "If the worst happens, you'll look splendid in prison orange."

His little joke failed to ease Nora's mind.

"I wonder if the police know what they're doing."

"Let's hope they do. I can only imagine how painful this must be for you." Leonard seated her by the windows in a shaft of sunlight, and Nora put on her dark glasses, in part to hide the shadows under her eyes. She hadn't slept well. When he offered her a drink, she hesitated, tempted, but then refused. She needed her wits about her, and if she chose the excellent wine he'd mentioned, she'd feel tired. If she selected coffee, she'd feel more wired. She knew Leonard made espresso strong enough to kill a mastodon.

He perched on the arm of an obviously new chair. It was upholstered in a luscious pale tan suede that made her designer's heart beat faster.

Other than the chair and matching sofa where Nora sat, there was no furniture in the room. She waited until Leonard returned from the kitchen with a mug of his freshly brewed espresso. "Did you buy these pieces at Nordruff's?"

He shook his head before taking a sip of the coffee. "No, Alexander's."

"They must have charged you a fortune. Full retail. Their markups are ridiculous." Then she noticed the slight flush under his new tan. "Ah, I see. Starr Mulligan. I hope she got you a good price."

"Nora." Leonard sat beside her. He smelled subtly of lime with a hint of…was that rubbing alcohol? One of his home remedies for some undisclosed ailment? At least he wasn't complaining about his health. "You and I have been friends as well as customer and designer for a long time," he said, which had been Nora's thought, too. "Let's not allow this misunderstanding to keep us apart."

Nora raised an eyebrow. "Misunderstanding?"

"Starr can be very persuasive. Before I knew it, I'd agreed to consider her bid even before you presented one. Or would have for the first time, if I'd asked."

"Forget Starr. This is a matter of trust between us, Leonard.

Unfortunately, that trust is broken and I don't know how to get it back."

"It's not as if I've cheated on you like Wilson." He tried to reach for her hand. "Our friendship is important to me, Nora. You know that."

"Then why did you betray me? After so many years of acting as your sole designer on house after condo after downtown loft after seaside cottage, how could you choose Starr because she happens to be 'persuasive'?"

Leonard hung his head. "I was at a weak moment. My health, you know, and then she turned up—right at my door—with this marvelous set of sketches that were unlike anything I've seen before. Oh," he said, catching himself, "I'm sorry. I didn't mean your drawings haven't been equally wonderful, no, perhaps even better, but—"

"Please stop while you're ahead."

For a long moment he sat there. "I don't know what else to say. I made a, well, not a mistake exactly, but a choice that I now regret. If I had ever thought that considering Starr would mean losing your friendship—"

"How could you not know?" The hurt flashed through Nora all over again. "For years Starr and I have been rivals. This was simply another way for her to get back at me again, and I must admit, she did—not that I'm willing to be her victim. Then she provoked me to the point of making some absurd threat—or so it appeared. I take full responsibility for what I said. But now look where I am. I've lost my best client—" she gave Leonard a pointed look "—at least temporarily, lost another in Geneva Whitehouse unless I agree to her terms. What's worse, because of Starr, I'm a suspect in a burglary! What should I do? I could lose Nine Lives."

"Nora," Leonard began in a calming voice, then paused. "Work for me, then." He bent to peer into her eyes. "I hear through the grapevine that you may join with Starr on the Whitehouse home."

Nora had left Geneva to broach the subject of sharing her design work, but she hadn't talked with Geneva since. Either Starr had flatly refused, which was probably the best thing, after all, or she was still pondering the offer.

"Where did you hear that?"

He looked away. "Well, Geneva's husband is the developer on this subdivision. So I run into him from time to time. Starr may have mentioned it, too, and then there's my neighbor..."

In the background the doorbell chimed, and taking the likely excuse to avoid Nora's further reaction to the gossip, he hurried to the front entry.

"Tabby," she heard him say. A minute later, carrying a foil-wrapped paper plate, he guided an attractive young woman into the living room. Her tousled auburn curls glistened in the sunlight, and her bright brown eyes sparkled. "This is my new neighbor, Tabitha Whitlaw, from across the street. She's brought us some brownies, Nora, so you'll definitely need that coffee now. Tabby, this is my fr—"

"We've met." Nora had recognized her instantly. "I designed the model unit for Impressions, and then Tabby hired me to do her home."

"Hi, Nora." Tabby took the chair opposite. "I can't tell you how much I love my house. Everyone who sees it goes insane. What a gorgeous job."

"I should give you a stack of my business cards for your friends."

"This house is going to be great, too. Leonard's very excited."

As if embarrassed to be reminded about Starr, he scurried to the kitchen and then back again in record time with the un-wrapped brownies and two more mugs of steaming coffee, always the good host. "I tease Tabby that she should have bought on the ocean side, but she teases me about hurricane destruction."

"It was actually the difference in cost," Tabby said, grinning at Leonard.

Nora glanced between them. They obviously had become

friends in the short time Leonard had been in this all-but-empty house. Tabby's comment made Nora remember her own concerns when they met.

She had wondered then if such a young woman, who didn't seem to have a full-time job but appeared to have plenty of free time, would be able to pay her bill. The worry had proved to be groundless. Tabby's check had been in the mail to Nora, paid in full, almost before she submitted the invoice.

Interesting. Maybe her family had money, Nora had decided, and Tabby Whitlaw lived on her trust fund. A quick image of the notice from the IRS about back taxes burned through Nora's mind, but she quickly suppressed it.

Were Tabby and Leonard more than friends? He'd been divorced for years, like Nora, which had given them more than one opportunity to bare their damaged souls, but she had never known him to have a girlfriend. He'd been too busy with his numerous ailments, she supposed. Until now. Perhaps they wanted their privacy.

Nora set aside her untouched coffee, then rose. "I need to go, Leonard. It was good to see you. Tabby, you too."

He walked with her to the door, a hand at Nora's elbow.

"Please stay. We need to talk."

She patted his cheek. "We can talk at my birthday party."

"I'm still invited?"

"Of course." As if that had ever been in doubt.

Nora whizzed through the gates, left Impressions behind in a blur of blue sky, white sand and pastel-hued houses, picked up Highway 98 toward Destin, and drove straight to Hi-Health Fitness. She was in and out of the women's locker room at the club, wearing her newest black spandex shorts and sports bra covered by a loose singlet with the Nike swoosh across the chest, and then in the upstairs workout area on a running treadmill before the thought had crossed her mind to go to the gym. Evidently she needed exercise to clear her brain of Caine's investigation, Leonard's betrayal and, of course, Starr Mulligan.

Too bad the first person she saw, to her astonishment, was Starr. From across the chilly gymnasium, they exchanged glares. Starr was on the elliptical trainer, pumping away with all her might, her face gleaming with perspiration.

Nora hopped off the treadmill and strode across the room. "I didn't know you belonged here," she said, disappointed that her much-needed workout would only serve as another reminder.

Nora had expected to calm her thoughts by vigorously pounding the treadmill and lifting a few light weights to preserve her bone mass. Maybe by the time she finished she would know exactly what to do to clear her name. She always did her best thinking while she ran.

Starr kept flying along on the elliptical machine. "I joined last year. Apparently we never do our sweating at the same time."

Nora dispensed with the small talk. "I suppose you've spoken to Geneva."

Starr glanced at the ceiling. "Geneva talked to me, yes. It's an interesting proposition, I have to admit, considering our joint meeting at her home. But why would I want to work for half price and with someone who despises me?"

"I never said that."

Starr half smiled as if she didn't believe Nora for an instant. With her dark hair in a youthful ponytail, she was decked out in a pair of bright red tights and a coordinated striped top that put Nora's basic black to shame. Nora had seldom noticed that Starr's figure wasn't half bad. A few pounds too *zaftig*, perhaps, but only a few, which suited Starr's more solid bone structure. Starr's smile faded.

"Why would I want to work with a woman who threatened to kill me?"

Nora blinked. "You can't be serious. I didn't—"

"Oh, please. I heard what you said."

"I didn't say *you*, Mulligan. I said *someone*." Nora felt at a distinct disadvantage. She had said the words, but not in utter seriousness.

"I was the only other person there," Starr pointed out. "Unless you were talking to Geneva."

"Of course I wasn't. I—"

This time Starr grinned. "But then, I should try to understand. I've heard about those sudden mood swings, uncharacteristic outbursts of emotion at your stage in life…"

"That is not why—"

"And all those irritating hot flashes. It's a lot to contend with," Starr said in a too-sweet, pitying tone. She practically patted Nora on the head. "You're looking a bit overheated right now."

Nora glared at her again. Starr glared back. She wasn't even breathing hard, and she appeared to have been on the elliptical trainer for some time, judging by her damp gym clothes. "I may have misspoken. I did say some unkind things before, but I didn't appreciate your loud comment at the Interior Design Association luncheon."

Starr made a tsking sound. "There you go again. Denying the obvious." A small line formed between Starr's eyebrows. "We could compare birthdays but I'll save you the trouble. I'm told there's a party soon for someone's *fiftieth*…" Her goading tone trailed off. Her gathering frown transformed itself into a sunny, thousand-watt smile, and she beamed at someone behind Nora.

Nora whirled around. And saw Heath Moran coming toward them.

"Heath," Starr purred. "Come here and help me adjust my *equipment*." She tugged at the too-snug top whose red-and-white stripes undulated across her ample bosom.

Heath gave them a sheepish grin. His gaze slid away from Nora.

"You ladies enjoying a good, hard workout?"

"Not nearly hard enough," Starr murmured, eyeing him up and down.

Nora turned away. She started toward the treadmills and then stopped. "You decide whatever you like about Geneva," she said with her back to Starr. "You needn't worry about me."

"That's not what I hear, darling. I don't imagine you're spending time with Detective Caine just because he's cute. I'd gladly answer more of his questions. But that's all right. I have time in my schedule to pick up any clients you may lose."

That insufferable woman. Nora marched on stiff legs right past the treadmills, down the stairs and toward the locker room. No amount of perspiration was going to cure her today.

There wasn't enough money in the world for her to work with Starr, she decided. She'd just have to find another big client—if the entire county hadn't heard about Geneva's missing vase, probably from Starr.

Nora hadn't heard Heath behind her. His state-of-the-art running shoes hadn't made a sound on the stairs. He caught her inner arm just before she reached the women's entrance to the locker room. "What was that all about?"

"Starr. What else?"

"She was trying to get your goat."

Nora glanced up at him. "Yes. And she did."

His worried face made her blink. "Caine talked to me, too." He drew her aside, avoiding a woman in tight jeans and heeled boots who exited the locker room in a cloud of Chanel and brushed past them to the club exit. "I told him the truth, that you're a fine person and I know you wouldn't do anything dishonest. I wish you'd called me when that happened. I might have been able to help."

"Thanks, Heath." Nora attempted a smile that failed. "Unless you found a heart-shaped vase in someone's Dumpster, I don't think so. Until Caine turns up some evidence against someone else, I seem to be the prime suspect in a felony."

Heath traced a light, fluttery line along her cheek and his eyes darkened. "I'd like to help. Just tell me how."

"You did a magnificent job of giving comfort the last time I saw you. I couldn't ask for more."

"I'd like you to," he said. "I thought…I hoped we'd gotten somewhere."

Having made her decision about them, she tried to turn away when part of her wanted to stay in his arms. "If you need female companionship, Starr seemed more than willing."

Heath held on to her and grinned. "You're jealous."

Nora wiggled free. "No, I'm not. She seemed to think you were her type."

"*You're* my type." He pulled her back into his embrace, but only for a minute before Nora drew away again. "Want to know what I got you for your birthday?" he asked.

Her heart gave a little flip. "You bought me a present?" After Nora had tried again to break up with him?

"Nice one," he said. "Better be good to me at least until the party, or I might take it back. Then you'd be deprived not only of a great gift, but of *someone* great." He certainly didn't lack confidence, but then why should he? All that muscle and bronzed skin sent a powerful message. Nora wondered why she didn't respond to it in a stronger way.

She eased out from under his arm and into the entryway to the locker room. "The invitation says eight o'clock. Don't be late or all the good food will be gone." She poked her head back out to kiss his cheek. "And bring the present."

She hadn't been serious, of course. Yet Nora knew Heath would bring his gift, and himself, to her party. Nora wasn't jealous but she knew Starr Mulligan would snap him up in a heartbeat. That image didn't bear thinking about, and Nora had turned her energy for the rest of the day to making plans for tonight. And saving herself.

She'd been thinking about the problem of Geneva's missing vase all day, even before she saw Leonard and then Starr. Heath's understanding had sharpened her resolve to take action, to do something about the matter—which Caine seemed to personify. She wanted to see the look on his face when she cracked the case instead. At the moment, filled with a sense of purpose, her mouth dry with anticipation and more than a little fear, she was in the car, driving through the entrance to Royal Palms.

"Ma, where are we going?" Savannah's query brought her back to the immediate issue. "The Whitehouse driveway is there. You missed the turn."

"We can't park in Geneva's driveway. The neighbors will see us."

Savannah turned to face her from the passenger seat.

"You didn't tell her we were coming?"

Nora shook her head. "This is a clandestine operation. Deep cover. Whatever we find will be ours—and get me off the hook."

"You'll get us arrested. They'll say you planted evidence."

"You're my witness, angel."

Savannah blew a stray wisp of hair from her forehead. "When I promised to back you up, I thought Geneva knew. I don't feel good about this."

Nora swung the car off the residential street onto a strip of tree lawn under a big, arching palm another block past Geneva's house. She switched off the ignition, then the lights.

"And I thought you should stay home."

Her family had been through enough with Caine's interrogation. They were dear to stand by her, but Nora would get out of this herself. Or so she'd thought. "What can we do?" Browning had asked last night after Caine left. "There must be something," Johnny had said. They both looked helpless, frustrated by inaction, but Nora had decided not to include them tonight. They would only talk her out of this. It was

Savannah who had insisted on coming with Nora and was now climbing out of the Volvo with a grim look on her face. Nora prayed no one would spot the white car on the street.

"Are you all right?" she asked, fearing another attack of nausea.

"I'm pregnant, not sick." Savannah paused, her still-pale face illuminated by the nearby streetlight. "Well, I'm pregnant *and* sick, but it's a natural process, Ma, really. I'll get used to it."

"You are a brave woman."

"And you're crazy." Savannah followed her across the road and down to the next intersection where they turned in at Geneva's street. "Why don't we call her on the phone and warn her now that we're coming?"

"Savannah, if you're losing your nerve, stay in the car. I told you not to come, and actually I did call earlier to sound her out. I learned Geneva is out for the evening. She won't be back until at least eleven, and I'm not sure she would have understood anyway. Her husband usually works late," she added.

Savannah groaned. "That man. I wouldn't care if he never came home."

"I agree, but Geneva loves him." Nora marched over to check the number on the next mailbox. "Here we are. Do you have your flashlight?"

"Yes," Savannah said tightly. With a small sigh, she followed Nora into the darkened yard. "What if they have motion sensors outdoors?"

"Have you seen anything come on yet?" It was pitch-black. "Let's start our search here." She aimed for the front right corner of the building. "Then we'll work around the perimeter."

"Trampling all the evidence—if there is any—on our way," Savannah murmured.

"You wanted to help." They spoke in whispers, using the two big black Maglites Nora had bought at Wal-Mart, pointing them close to the ground so the beam would stay concentrated. Her own nerves made her begin to babble. "I saw one of those cold case shows on TV. They said evidence can remain for years, long after a crime has been committed. So we shouldn't give up hope that we'll find something."

"Like what, exactly?"

Nora had paid close attention to the show. She shrugged, wishing she could have brought Daisy, but she didn't want to risk the dog barking to reveal their presence. "Footprints. A cigarette butt—those have great DNA. Maybe the thief dropped a glove like O.J. Or a piece of fiber from a coat or sweater. If we're lucky we might find a stray hair, though it would need to have the follicle with it…"

"Good grief."

But her earlier qualms, so similar to Savannah's, had disappeared. Nora was getting into the hunt now, feeling loose again and almost relaxed. Excitement raced along her veins. "There could be a tire track here, even a bicycle tire if the burglar was a kid…let's not overlook that possibility. Yes, maybe some boy stole Geneva's vase for his girlfriend."

"Ma, please don't do this. I was wrong. We should have let Johnny and Browning know what we were doing. What if we get shot? Let Detective Caine complete his investigation. He's trained to do this sort of thing."

"Then it should have occurred to him to look beyond the interior of the house. I doubt he and his forensics people ever thought of it. One missing item," Nora went on, "and not a major piece, like fine jewelry, at that. I have to do *something*. My business is suffering."

Savannah groaned.

Nora had to admit, the area looked pristine even in the dark. A growing disappointment rolled through her the farther they went. She saw no prints, no tracks, no hair or fiber anywhere. Wouldn't it be nice to spy a scrap of fabric or a scarf caught on a tree limb or bush like a streamer of Spanish moss? Or to find an obviously jimmied window in the rear of the house—right here—or a small pane of broken glass that indicated entry?

Nora still hoped they'd soon find the evidence she needed for the plastic bags she'd stuffed into her jeans pockets. She didn't want Savannah to have suffered an anxiety attack for nothing.

Behind her, she could hear her daughter's shallow breathing.

"A few minutes more, and we'll be done. Gone," Nora assured her.

Still, she didn't want to quit before— Suddenly she tripped over a tree root and nearly went flying. Nora struggled to keep her balance and let out a cry.

"Ma, this is trespassing. On private property."

The words were barely out of Savannah's mouth before the blackened yard seemed to explode with light. Nora blinked. Savannah covered her eyes. The back door opened and a man appeared, tall and broad, at the screen.

Nora groaned. She remembered him all too well, and so would Savannah. Nora heard her gasp. It was obviously Earl Whitehouse.

Unfortunately, he recognized them, too.

"What the hell are you two doing out here?" he said.

CHAPTER 7

Nora squinted up at Earl Whitehouse standing at his back door, his image slightly blurred by the screen. The scowl on his face, however, seemed perfectly clear, even though she couldn't make out the details of his features in the glare of the security lights. His aggressive stance said the rest. They'd been caught and he wasn't amused.

"Earl," Nora said brightly. "I didn't know you were home."

"Obviously."

His deep, gritty tone sent shivers down Nora's spine. Suddenly she wished again that they'd brought Daisy with them, but she'd left the retriever sleeping at home. She'd also left Browning and Johnny at his condo watching tonight's NFL game, saying she and Savannah were going to see a chick flick at the multiplex instead. Now Savannah was definitely having second thoughts.

"Ma," she whispered in her ear as she tugged on Nora's sleeve, "let's run. We can make it to the car before Earl can get down the steps."

Nora resisted her pull. "You don't run from a man like that. You stand your ground. In my opinion he's a bully and once you confront a bully, he usually backs down instead." Nora didn't have to mention her last encounter with Earl in the model unit at Impressions.

"Like it's a good idea to test that theory right now," Savannah murmured.

Earl Whitehouse flipped off the floodlights. He swung the

screen door open with one hand. In the other, to Nora's surprise, he wasn't holding a gun ready to use on some intruder as Savannah had feared. Instead, he held a half-gallon carton of ice cream that appeared to Nora from the distance to be her favorite premium brand. "Come inside," he said, his bulky frame backlit by the overhead kitchen fixtures. "We need to talk."

"I don't think so," Nora answered. Belatedly, she flicked off her Maglite. Savannah did the same, plunging them into darkness again except for the glow of yellow light from inside the house. "It's late. We'll just be going. Sorry to bother you."

Earl didn't agree. "Get in here." He stepped onto the porch, waiting until Nora and Savannah picked their way through the dark yard and up the steps.

She'd known Earl Whitehouse was a large man, but now he appeared to be twice his size. He towered over them, his gray eyes looking almost black, his mouth set in a hard line. Nora brushed past him in the doorway, sensing his heat and the coiled strength in his body. He was big and tall and intimidating to Nora all over again.

Once inside, she blinked against the harsh light of the kitchen—a kitchen she wanted to redesign with all her heart. Savannah had been right about their trespassing. Now Nora had lost the opportunity with Geneva, and it would be Starr who redid the space. She didn't know what to do except to go along with Earl Whitehouse and hope he didn't turn them in to Caine.

Earl gestured at the granite-topped center island and a pair of cushioned stools. "Sit down. Start talking."

Nora didn't know where to begin. She could feel Savannah's tension as they took their places at the counter. It was up to her to protect her daughter and to get them out of here. Safely.

"Well," she began, "as you know, Geneva has lost a treasured vase. The police have questioned me for some reason but they haven't come up with the actual perpetrator." Earl Whitehouse didn't look pleased with her explanation. He stood on the other side of the island, judging Nora with his gaze and eating his ice cream.

"So you took matters into your own hands."

"We tried," Nora murmured.

"Honestly, we meant no harm," Savannah put in. "We didn't find a thing that might point to someone else and clear my mother's name. Why don't we agree to forget the whole thing?"

"I have half a mind to call the police," Earl said, dipping his spoon into the ice cream carton, but he didn't even glance toward the phone. "This doesn't look good for you, Nora."

"No," she had to agree. "It doesn't."

Nora felt a rapid rush of regret. What had she gotten herself and Savannah into? She knew Geneva wasn't home. They were alone with Earl, and pretty soon Caine would be here, too—if Earl didn't decide to deal with them himself. Like Savannah, he had a point. She'd only made herself look worse. She'd unwittingly stepped into Earl's path again, and the reminder of their past at Impressions wasn't pleasant, either.

"You don't like me much. Do you, Nora?" He looked not at her but into the ice cream carton. He couldn't have seen her distasteful expression.

"Isn't that like asking someone when he stopped beating his wife? There's no answer to that, Earl. Considering the fact that you have us both where you want us..."

"Geneva is very upset about her vase."

"Yes, and I'm sorry she lost it—"

"I suppose you don't know anything about that," he said for her. "You're innocent."

"Innocent of everything but invading your backyard tonight, yes. Please don't turn us in. We—I mean, I—was only trying to..."

He looked from her to Savannah. "I should call the cops but I won't." He didn't elaborate. But why wouldn't he call? Maybe she'd misjudged him, and he really wasn't a bad guy. Maybe she'd even misinterpreted her last run-in with him.

Relieved, Nora was already sliding off her stool when Earl's voice stopped her. "Where do you think you're going?"

"Home. Where I belong. It's kind of you to overlook our little 'visit' tonight but we really should be—"

"Going," Savannah said, rising to her feet and starting for the door.

Earl waved the carton in her direction.

"Your daughter interrupted our little 'visit' once before. She didn't see the real situation then, either. Why don't we all share a dish of fudge ripple and let bygones be bygones?"

It was an offer Nora couldn't refuse.

The situation struck her as bizarre. Savannah's expression told Nora that she agreed. Was Earl trying to buy her silence about those moments with him in the model room at Impressions? Would he tell Geneva about tonight? She hoped not. But before she knew it, they were sitting around Earl Whitehouse's granite counter with huge bowls of ice cream, chatting as if they were all best friends, and Nora was wishing she had a piece of cake to go with the ice cream.

Happy Birthday to me…

There was no avoiding it. The balmy, early October night of her fiftieth had arrived. Feeling another rise in the temperature of the room, Nora flapped the hem of her new peach silk tunic in the air. For good measure, she blew down the front of its low U-shaped neckline, although the faint breeze she created didn't help. She wasn't looking in the mirror, but she supposed her exposed skin looked way too pink and blotchy. No wonder.

Two days after Earl Whitehouse had trapped Nora in the humiliating glare of floodlights with Savannah during their "investigation" in his backyard, she was having yet another hot flash—an issue Nora should discuss with Mark if he showed up tonight. Obviously they could be triggered by stress.

"It was your own fault, Ma," Savannah had said, arms crossed over her increasingly shapely chest as they had driven home that night. There were benefits, other than the resulting baby, to her being pregnant. Savannah's shape looked lovelier every day, which Nora imagined pleased Johnny. Her daughter's scowl did not please Nora. "You're lucky he didn't call the cops, Ma, or we'd be in jail right now."

"You warned me, angel. I stand corrected."

"That's it?" Savannah gaped at her in astonishment. "Then I don't suppose it will surprise you when Geneva rescinds her offer to hire you and Starr."

Nora's spirits had fallen then. "You're right. She probably will."

By now Nora realized she'd acted impulsively. Wrongly. Worse, they had discovered no evidence to clear her name in the unsolved burglary. Nora gauged her chances to redo Geneva Whitehouse's home as somewhere between poor and miserable. Not that Starr seemed inclined to cooperate.

The fallout from this latest embarrassing incident threatened never to end. Even Browning was barely speaking to her, and Johnny had sermonized until Nora suffered yet another flush from his tongue-lashing, which she admitted she deserved. He remained furious that she'd put his future wife and child at risk. Nora couldn't blame him, she'd been a bad girl.

Giving her appearance a cursory glance in the mirror, she left her bedroom as if prepared to face the guillotine. What if Earl Whitehouse had been holding a gun, rather than a carton of Fudge Ripple ice cream, when he opened his back door? As Savannah had said, he might have shot first and asked questions later. Johnny had every right to scold her.

Not that she was ready to forgive him for treating her as if she were Lucrezia Borgia, whose devious poisons had wiped out a good number of the Medici family.

Nora frowned. Oddly enough, Earl Whitehouse hadn't seemed half so irritated with her. After his initial demand about their presence on his property in the black of night, he'd backed off. His first threat to phone the cops had eased into a grudging agreement of Nora's plea not to report her nefarious activity. She'd imagined Caine answering the call. Instead, to her vast relief, Earl had behaved like a reasonable person. Nora was still wondering whether to trust him or her previous instincts.

Suddenly a brighter thought occurred to her. Nora might still have a chance. A slim one, but still... Maybe Earl wouldn't tell Geneva, who hadn't been home that night.

The question was, did she feel lucky?

Nora all but slunk into her living room, where the furniture had been pushed back to allow for better movement among her guests. She disliked the effect. Normally, Nora liked to entertain, but she would have preferred a quieter celebration tonight, smaller, with only her children around her. Instead, her one official role in this party had been to offer her home as the setting, and the room was festooned with crepe paper streamers in happy colors: peach like her tunic and flowing pants, hot pink, and a subtler mauve, a display of gaiety in some of her favorite colors that made her heart sink even lower. The stage was set, however. Too late to change it.

In the dining room Nora reassessed the table laden with heavenly-smelling food. Getting in the way of the caterers, she inspected the crabmeat canapés, marinated mushroom caps, tiny quiches with golden-brown crusts, cheese-filled puff pastries in silver chafing dishes. Even the platters of crudités looked inviting.

"Make sure everything stays hot," she cautioned the caterer's assistants, unable to stop herself.

But Nora felt her stomach roll. The bar set up in a corner of her kitchen seemed more the thing for tonight, if she'd been so inclined. Earlier, keeping their minds on the task rather than their recent adventure, she and Savannah had pulled down every suitable glass from Nora's cabinets. She had made sure there was plenty of ice.

Perhaps she should have taken Savannah's suggestion to hold the party at Johnny's beach house, which was bigger. But Nora had insisted on staying home, closer to the circle of friends who were also invited. If she needed to escape into her room for a quick cry, she wouldn't have far to go.

Like the good friend she was, Daisy agreed with her. She looked no happier than Nora. At the opposite end of the kitchen, the dog peered through the mesh childproof gate that had been stretched in the doorway to keep Daisy from mingling with the guests. Ostracized, she lay on the wooden floor of the back hallway just outside the laundry room, her head resting on her front paws, looking like some cartoon character who had been flattened into a ribbon by the villain's truck. She sighed heavily and studied Nora with sad doggie eyes.

"I know, sweetie. It's like prison. Maybe we can plan a jail-break later."

For both of us, she added silently. When the front doorbell chimed, Nora felt another flash of heat blaze through her body. How would she survive the night? Her children's hearts were in the right place, but even though they'd done most of the planning for once, and she'd let them as often as she could, she didn't feel like celebrating.

She felt no more substantial than one of Savannah's stick-figure drawings. When she reached for the knob, her hands were shaking. Why feel nervous? It must be Savannah, who had gone home to change clothes. There might be a lingering tension between them after Earl, but Savannah would never ruin her birthday.

Nora flung open the door and gasped.

If the woman standing there had been wielding a gun like

Earl Whitehouse in Johnny or Savannah's imagination, Nora couldn't have been more shocked. On her front porch, holding a small, brightly wrapped package in her hands, stood Maggie.

Nora blinked. Her mother had repeatedly refused to make the trip to Destin. Yet here she was on Nora's doorstep.

"Surprise," Maggie said, wearing her usual shapeless dress under an equally ancient-looking sweater.

And Nora thought, *Let the games begin…*

"Don't get your hopes up," Maggie said, immediately taking the offensive. If she let Nora start rolling, she would lose control of things, and Maggie was still unsure about being here in the first place. She hadn't been able to resist Savannah's arm-twisting about Nora's birthday, though. Then there was the fact that she hadn't yet met her favorite granddaughter's fiancé and the more unsettling news that Savannah was already pregnant. Maggie had to see for herself.

Before she knew it, she had been on a plane—shaking all the way—from Richmond to Destin, where Savannah met her.

She might never recover from the shock.

Maybe Nora wouldn't, either. She was still standing in the doorway, staring at Maggie as if she had seen the ghost of Hank Scarborough instead.

"I'm here just for a few days," Maggie informed her.

In the background she heard a dog barking. Daffy, she thought was her name. Or was it…? Before she could search her memory banks for the right word, Nora took the gift from her hands and then beckoned her inside. Her carefully made-up face looked funny now. Maggie didn't move. For an instant, she wondered if Nora was about to dissolve in tears. She seemed amazed yet overwhelmed. Was she unhappy with the surprise? Wasn't this what she had wanted?

But then, Maggie wasn't sure she liked it, either. She'd been railroaded into coming. Leaving the home she'd loved for fifty years had been an act of temporary insanity. All at once, she wanted to turn and run.

"Ma, say something." Savannah emerged from the shadows of the porch, where she'd been watching their reunion. "Gram came all this way to celebrate your birthday." She took Maggie's arm, guiding her into the house past a still stunned-looking Nora as if Maggie were some kind of cripple. "Let's get you something to drink, Gram. You must be thirsty after such a long trip. The air in those jet cabins is always too dry."

The dog was still barking, and Maggie could smell fur. She sneezed.

"I'm not even in the house and I'm allergic," she said.

Finally, Nora found her voice. "Maggie, I can't believe you're here."

"Well, I am. Let's not get mushy about it."

"Really," Savannah said with a shake of her head. She looked toward the door. "Johnny, please come help me. You can get Gram's bag from my car. Browning, find her a comfortable chair. And give her a big hug, will you? For heaven's sake, your grandmother deserves a better welcome."

Maggie shuffled into the living room. Savannah's notion that she needed to sit down stung her pride, but her feet were killing her. She usually spent much of her day at home—where she belonged—in carpet slippers and a robe. She didn't have a need to get dressed, never before noon when the soaps began on TV, and she wanted to look her best for those hunky male stars. "Just looking," she always told Hank, her guilty voice ringing in the stillness.

Today she'd crammed herself into these godawful shoes before the sun was up. Never again. She'd gone before Nora recovered from the shock.

"It's not easy to get from there to here," she said, remembering the bumpy flight to Florida and the nightmare of searching the confusing jumble of carousels for her luggage, an old duffel bag that had belonged to Hank. Was the duffel blue or gray? She couldn't remember. "My clothes were all over the place in that airport. I hope those pre-verts enjoyed looking at my underwear."

"Her bag's zipper split," Savannah explained.

"This is my one visit. Don't try to make it more, Nora." She half fell onto an upholstered chair. In the soft cushions Maggie almost sank to the floor. She might never be able to get out again. Then her vision was obscured by two large male bodies, and two pairs of broad shoulders blocked her view of Nora and the rest of the room.

"This can't be Browning." As he bent to her, Maggie reached up to pat his face—and a handsome face it was. His lips pressed to her cheek in a quick kiss. "You were a boy last time I saw you. Now look. All grown up."

"That's a matter of opinion," Savannah said with a cheeky smile. She and her brother had hammered each other for years, even when they were small, and Maggie clucked her tongue as if to say "behave," the way she used to in the summers with them.

"Hi, Gram." But it wasn't Browning who spoke. On her other side stood a tall, strong-looking surfer boy with riveting green eyes. One of them, the left, was twitching.

"You must be Johnny." She glanced at her granddaughter. "Good choice."

Maggie tried to resist, but there they were. Her family. She had missed them. And now, a glance at Savannah's stomach reminded her that she would soon become a great-grandmother! But hadn't Maggie delivered Nora only a year or two ago?

Savannah was rattling on about her chosen husband—a good-looking devil, all right, almost as fine as Hank—when Nora suddenly came to life.

In the background, the doorbell was ringing again.

"Would someone please get that?" she said. "The other guests are here."

"Ma, you should be in hiding." Savannah spun her around, but Nora dug in her heels, an expensive-looking pair of very high little nothings with the twinkle of rhinestones.

"This isn't a surprise party." Nora rolled her eyes. "The last thing I need is another surprise."

CHAPTER 8

Nora's home soon filled with people who loved her and with the happy chaos of a successful party in progress. The rich aromas of good food wafted through the air, her favorite songs swirled through the speakers from the CD player. Before she stopped to think, she was actually having a decent time. For once, she managed to put Caine and the burglary out of her mind. And it was great to have Maggie here at last, right on time for her birthday.

Be careful what you wish for. The few days together could prove daunting, because Nora meant to pressure her about a permanent move. But maybe she shouldn't worry, at least tonight. Once she'd stopped sneezing over Daisy, her mother seemed to be having a good time, too.

Nora worried about her daughter instead. She didn't like Savannah's increasingly washed-out appearance or her obvious lack of energy. After the incident at Earl's house, Savannah had been exhausted, making Nora feel even more guilty for letting her tag along when she was clearly unwell. Which troubled Nora. When she was pregnant, both times, she had relished the process. She'd never felt better in her life, actually. Her skin had glowed, her figure had blossomed—if not as quickly, she realized, as Savannah's had. And at the time, she reminded herself, Wilson had loved her.

There was no question in Nora's mind that Johnny loved Savannah.

"You sure you're okay?" he kept asking.

Johnny ushered her to a chair near Maggie in the crowded living room, then hurried into the kitchen to fetch Savannah a glass of ice water. When he came back, Nora noted that his left eye was still twitching.

She would have tried to help, but Nora got swept up in the good wishes of another friend who had just walked in the door. Leonard was here, dressed to the nines in summer-white slacks, even in October, and a cheerful burnt-orange cashmere sweater with a V-neck that seemed to announce it was autumn and Halloween was on the way.

To her further surprise, Geneva Whitehouse soon showed up—without Earl, thank goodness. Geneva didn't stay long, but she left a gift and repeated her offer to Nora about working with Starr Mulligan.

Another surprise. Interesting, Nora thought. She'd been right about Earl Whitehouse. Obviously, he hadn't told his wife about Nora's late-night visit to their property without permission.

The question was, why not? Perhaps Earl hoped to use Nora again to showcase another of his new subdivisions. She'd done a first-rate job with the model unit at Impressions and then on Tabby's house. Or maybe, after Nora's run-in with Earl a year ago in that same model home, he realized he couldn't afford to antagonize her. He wouldn't want Geneva to hear about that. *Let bygones be bygones.*

The theory didn't quite convince her, but she put it out of mind.

Again, she needed to take action. Savannah's concerted effort to put Maggie at ease wasn't helping to restore Savannah's color or her flagging energy.

Nora sailed across the room, stopping on her way to steer Leonard toward a fresh tray of Gulf shrimp, then to lower the volume on the CD player before she came to a halt in front of

Savannah's chair. Her mother was holding court, and although it was good to see her engaged in social activity, Nora felt her teeth begin to grind.

"You're monopolizing Savannah. And her fiancé. Why don't you mingle for a while?" She reached a hand to draw Maggie from her chair. "I'll introduce you to the rest of the people you haven't met."

Maggie resisted. "I'm fine right here. Let people come to me."

Nora huffed out a breath. Her mother had always relied on others, especially Nora, even when she was miles away in Virginia.

Nora turned, spotting Leonard with his plate of shrimp and a large dollop of cocktail sauce. But before she could introduce him to Maggie, Nora heard a sudden commotion from the kitchen.

A sharp bark rang out, overriding the Shania Twain CD that was playing, and then Daisy exploded into the living room, tail wagging, body wiggling, an escaped jailbird on the loose. The dog headed straight for Maggie, the worst person she could have chosen. Maggie sneezed, but Daisy didn't notice that she wasn't welcome. She leaped up in obvious joy to at last be part of the festivities and landed in Maggie's lap, her front paws braced against her collarbone, her tongue sweeping out to deliver a wet kiss.

Maggie screamed.

Why was it that an animal could pick out the one person in any crowd who didn't want her around, then select that person for special attention?

"She's afraid of the dog," Nora muttered to no one in particular.

"I am not." Maggie grunted at the pressure on her chest. "I can't breathe."

"Daisy, down," Nora ordered but the dog, as usual, didn't obey. Daisy marched to her own drummer.

Maggie sneezed again and couldn't stop. Her eyes turned red, and a big hive sprung up on her skin. It took all of Nora's strength and some of Johnny's to drag the golden retriever away from Nora's mother. Everyone in the room was staring—that is, until Daisy decided to greet them, too.

Nora didn't have the heart to confine her again. Daisy was having too good a time, and why exclude her when she only wanted to share Nora's birthday? Nora asked Browning to get Daisy's leash and sent them outdoors to walk off Daisy's pent-up energy. Maggie sagged back in her chair, vowing to leave the very next morning "before this beast eats me alive."

Nora sighed. So much for her fantasy that she and Maggie would get along this time and put an end to their lifelong inability to be in the same room without arguing. That was all Nora really wanted for her birthday.

After she had given Maggie an antihistamine, Nora turned back to Savannah. Johnny was changing the CD to something lively. Then he circulated through the room, asking people if they wanted another drink or steering them toward the buffet.

"You've knocked yourself out," Nora told Savannah. "Your job is done, angel. I thank you for it." She lowered her voice. "You did your best to make Maggie feel welcome. But now I want you to rest."

"Ma," Savannah said, glancing at the stack of presents in the corner under Nora's indoor palm tree as if it were Christmas, "it's time to open your gifts."

"They can wait." In fact, she didn't want to be the focus of attention. "I was stalling until Mark arrived, but the caterer told me he just phoned to say he has an emergency delivery. Twins. He may be at the hospital for most of the night." Which also meant Nora wouldn't be talking to him about her ongoing symptoms.

"You're treating me like an invalid." Savannah's tone didn't sway Nora.

With determination, she put a hand on Savannah's shoulder

and then turned her toward Nora's bedroom. "We'll call you when the package-opening begins. May I get you a plate of something healthful to eat?"

She never got an answer.

As Nora urged Savannah to take the few steps to the temporary retreat, her worst fears came true. Suddenly she found herself clutching thin air. In horror, Nora watched Savannah lose consciousness and then drop to the floor.

On her way down, she nearly knocked Nora off her feet, too. Nora dropped down beside her daughter's still form. Johnny was there in another instant. They both assessed Savannah's chalk-white face and closed eyes.

"Wake up, babe." He lightly patted Savannah's cheeks.

Frozen, Nora wrung her hands. For once, she didn't know what to do. This was her child, her baby.

The crowd quickly gathered. Even Leonard hurried across the room, his features drawn. He pulled out his cell phone. "My doctor is on speed dial. I can get through to him in a minute."

"Hold on." Browning, who had just returned with Daisy, knelt beside Johnny, across from Nora. To her amazement he held a vial of old-fashioned smelling salts "Maggie's," he said. He waved them under Savannah's nose; after another moment, she began to come around, aided by a few swipes of Daisy's tongue. Her eyes fluttered open.

"Oh, God, I'm so embarrassed." Her unfocused gaze shifted from Browning to Nora, then back to Johnny. She lifted a hand to his worried face. "I'm okay, really. For a few seconds, the room went black. That's all."

"*That's all?*" Johnny's left eye twitched at double speed. "Thanks, Leonard, but we don't need your internist. We need Savannah's doctor. Browning, get Mark Fingerhut. I don't care if he's delivering every other woman in town." He lifted Savannah in his arms. "I never knew having a baby would be such an ordeal. What happened?"

"I'm not *having* the baby. I'm growing the baby," Savannah said weakly.

"Do as he says, angel," Nora murmured. "Let us take care of you."

"You always do." But with that, Savannah subsided, looking disoriented by her brief loss of consciousness and as white as the woodwork on one of Nora's interior design projects.

Maggie was right behind them. "Pregnant women faint," she said.

"Not mine," Johnny answered, his mouth a grim line.

He laid Savannah on Nora's bed, and Nora hurried to unfold a cranberry wool throw to cover her. She plumped up some pillows.

Savannah studied them all again, bringing the world into sharper focus. "I'm fine. Really. I just need a minute…"

Johnny tried to insist that they either phone the doctor or head for the nearest emergency room, but Savannah wouldn't hear of it.

"All right. But you're not moving from this bed." Johnny brushed a hand over her forehead.

"First thing tomorrow," Nora added, "you'll be seeing Mark Fingerhut."

"Ma…"

"You can stay here overnight."

The party continued in the other room, although people peeked into Nora's bedroom now and then to assure themselves that Savannah was, indeed, all right. After that they returned to the Gulf shrimp and the quiche, and, most likely, to the bar in her kitchen. Everyone seemed a bit shaken, like Nora. The buzz of conversation rose again and the music—this time, Joe Cocker's classic song, "You Are So Beautiful"—swelled.

"You really are," Nora said, bending down to Savannah. "You have no idea how much we love you, and we want only the best for you and the baby."

"I know, Ma." Savannah's voice sounded sleepy. The ordeal Johnny mentioned had clearly worn her out. And all those preparations for Nora's birthday party. Not to mention picking up Maggie at the airport. That couldn't have been easy, especially with the damaged duffel bag and Maggie's faulty memory about what she was looking for. Savannah had been running around all day. Now Nora hoped that was all it was.

"Stop twitching," she said to Johnny. "Go take charge of the music, angel. We need something upbeat next but not too loud."

He refused to budge. His hand gripped Savannah's more tightly. "The last time I left her in your care, you nearly got her killed."

Nora raised her eyebrows. "Let me handle this. Woman to woman. I may even redeem myself in your eyes." She looked pointedly at the signet ring on his finger. *Daddy*. "There are things only a mother can do."

His warning look said it all. She'd better be successful this time. When she was alone with Savannah, Nora sat on the edge of the bed. She took Savannah's cold hand in hers and looked for a long moment into her still-not-quite-focused eyes. "Tell me how you're really feeling."

"Tired." The one word was heartfelt. "I never seem to get enough rest. Maybe you're right. Tonight I did too much. But I wanted this party to be perfect for you." She tried a smile. "I have to admit, though, I was on the verge of passing out from the second Maggie and I left the airport terminal. But she came," Savannah murmured. "That's what counts."

A light flashed in Nora's mind. "And you paid for her ticket."

"Well, yes," she admitted. "Call it one of my gifts for your birthday. But you know how she is. I almost had her, then she brought up the money issue. 'I'm not a wealthy woman. I'll be lucky if I make it through retirement without becoming a pauper.' You still send her money, Ma, don't you?"

"Every month. If she's worried about her future, why won't she relocate and let me help even more?"

Savannah's tone softened. "I think she doesn't want to leave Grandpa."

They looked at each other before Nora glanced away, blinking. Was that it, then, and not the fact that Maggie didn't want to be with Nora? She would have to examine that later.

"I'm more worried about you right now, angel. So is Johnny. There's something here that doesn't seem right. You're three months along but you still have morning sickness, which may just be hanging on, but then there's this fatigue. I don't want to alarm you, but it's as if your body is being asked too much, demanded of in some excessive way."

Savannah yawned. "You're making me more tired. I've been to see Mark regularly since I first suspected I might be pregnant. I already have an appointment scheduled with him next week."

"That's not soon enough." Nora paused. "What haven't you told me?"

Savannah hesitated. "Well, I've had some spotting but only a little." At Nora's terrified look, she said, "He's going to do a sonogram plus the exam. If there's anything wrong, he should be able to see it." She paused. "I doubt there is, but if it will make you and Johnny feel better, okay. And maybe we'll find out whether this is a girl or a boy." Her eyelids drooped.

"We'll see," was all Nora said. She wanted her daughter to be well. Why hadn't Savannah told her this before? "Now rest. Mothers need their sleep."

Back in the living room Nora was besieged with expressions of concern about Savannah's welfare. She reassured everyone that Savannah was fine, even Johnny, who looked longingly toward the bedroom's closed door. Nora distracted him and the crowd with the gift-opening for her birthday.

Her mind wasn't on it.

Still, Maggie's present brought tears to her eyes. Sentiment, or more worry about Savannah? She missed her presence, listened for every sound from the bedroom that could mean a trip to the emergency room. Fearing an imminent miscarriage, Nora blinked as she drew out the framed picture Maggie had brought of herself, Nora's brother, Hank Jr., and Nora when she was ten years old. It was in a beautiful antique silver frame, and Nora cherished the photograph at the same time she missed her father in the picture. He'd been gone only a few months then.

She had just opened Geneva's gift of a day at an upscale spa when the front bell rang again. Nora's gaze darted among her guests. She didn't think anyone was missing except—

Heath Moran walked in the door, a bulky gift in his arms.

To Nora's dismay, Starr Mulligan was at his side. Plastered there, actually.

"Well." Nora struggled with her shock, then remembered her manners and stepped back from the door. "Come in. Both of you."

"I ran into Starr at the club," Heath explained, handing Nora the package. He leaned down to give her a kiss, but when he drew back Nora remembered their last meeting at the gym. He looked a bit hurt. "Starr had no plans for tonight, and I wanted to stop by so…" He ran out of steam.

"You invited her."

"Yeah. I did." His voice held a note of challenge. "We wanted to wish you a happy birthday."

Right. Starr Mulligan would probably wish Nora nothing but the worst for "someone who threatened to kill her." As Nora took her light jacket, Starr looked up into Heath's eyes with the forced adoration of a woman on the make. Heath and Starr seemed an unlikely combination. Or a calculated one?

This had been, as she feared, some birthday.

Nora didn't know how many more surprises she could stand.

* * *

Much later, Nora woke with a start, jostling Daisy next to her on the bed from some delicious doggy dream. According to Nora's alarm clock, a beautiful little French carriage piece she had acquired at an estate sale while shopping for one of her clients, it was 3:00 a.m. In the dead of night, she sat bolt upright in bed, her heart slamming, her palms damp.

Daisy came alert in a second, her eyes bright in the darkness, her face a mask of furry concern. "It's all right, girl. Go back to sleep," Nora told her.

She had survived the birthday party, which was already history. Now her entire body felt hot again, but Nora knew instinctively that this wasn't another hot flash.

This was different. Worse.

She threw off the covers and got out of bed. "Stay," she said to Daisy who, to her amazement, flopped back down on the comforter. Nora's cotton Natori nightgown clung to her like a wet shower curtain. Even her hair felt as if it were dripping water where it straggled around her face.

"Whew," she muttered, fanning herself, then headed for the bathroom, hoping she hadn't eaten something tainted during the party. It wasn't as if, in her worry for Savannah, she'd been paying attention to what she ate.

She ran up against the closed bathroom door.

She'd almost forgotten about Maggie. Nora wasn't alone. Although Savannah and Johnny hadn't stayed, Nora's mother was still in the house "for a few days." Did Maggie feel ill?

To her relief, Nora realized she did not. Now that she was in the hall, the cooler air wafted across her skin and through her short nightie. Still, her pulse kept pounding. Fear for herself, or for Maggie? Worried that her mother might be having another heart attack, Nora called through the door. "Maggie? Are you all right?"

The door opened on a beam of blinding light from within.

Maggie stood there, as she had on the front porch earlier, her hair lit wildly from behind like a nimbus, and with that expression Nora knew too well.

"A woman my age," Maggie proclaimed with a hint of disdain, "doesn't get through the night without at least one visit to the powder room."

"I see."

"You, too?" Maggie asked with a gleam in her eyes. *Misery loves company.*

Nora didn't answer. She pulled her damp nightgown away from her chest.

Maggie's gaze followed the motion. "Ah-ha. Night sweats."

"I beg your pardon."

"I had them for years. At your time of life, you wake up drenched, change your gown or pj's and sometimes the sheets, go back to bed, then get up all over again."

Nora rejected the idea. "I've never had one before."

"I suppose you've had the hot flashes, too?"

"Just a few," she admitted, forgetting tonight's series of them. She said weakly, "Night sweats?"

"It's because of…you know. What do they call them? Hormones. Up and down, here then gone. It can drive you crazy. Latest news is, those pills don't help, either."

"Hormone replacement therapy? Of course they do," Nora said, although she hadn't decided whether to ask Mark for a prescription. She'd read some alarming articles over the past week or so; there had been some negative studies. Because he hadn't come to the party, where Nora had thought she might chat with him in a casual way, they still hadn't talked. "The pills are supposed to manage the symptoms," she told Maggie. "Why else would they sell them?"

"They ruin your heart, the TV said. Maybe your bosoms, and I heard they can cause Alzheimer's. Who needs that? I can't remember as it is right now. They might be worse than nothing. Who makes those claims anyway?" she said as if Nora worked for the FDA and her testimony was being challenged by Congress. "The pharmaceutical people, that's who," Maggie answered herself. "What do they care about except their own profits? Money, money, money. That's all I hear on TV. Greed and murder."

"Maybe you should read a book instead. Mother—" Nora rarely used the term unless she was exasperated "—you're alive and reasonably able to function because of the drugs those companies developed."

Maggie's gaze fell. "Not anymore. Besides, they cost a fortune."

Nora knew what that meant. "You quit taking your medications?"

Maggie shrugged her thin shoulders. "Blood thinners…beta blockers…water pills…" She made a dismissive sound. "The side effects are worse than the disease. I threw them away. I feel fine without them."

"Compliance can be a problem with the elderly." Nora turned away in exasperation, then immediately whirled around again. "And you really think you should live alone?"

"I'm still able to make my own decisions without your interference."

"No," Nora said, "I don't think you are." But her throat tightened. Her emotions were on overload, what with the party, her birthday and Savannah's fainting spell. Not to mention Heath turning up with Starr Mulligan. If Nora had reeled at Maggie's surprise appearance earlier, that didn't mean she wasn't happy to see her mother. Their differences aside, Nora didn't want to lose her.

Maggie seemed to agree. "What are we fighting about? What about you? There were enough candles on that cake tonight to burn down the whole block. You're going to be a grandmother and I'll be a great-grandmother. Think about that, cookie."

Nora's mouth twitched. "You're right. It's kind of a good news/bad news thing, isn't it?" She paused. "Maggie, this may be the first time in recent history when you and I have shared a common view. How do we balance the joy with its reminder that we're slowly being replaced by a new generation?"

"It wasn't long ago," Maggie agreed again, "when your father and I were young. Now he's gone. Where does the time go? Please don't remind me that I have fewer years left than I have behind me."

Nora didn't welcome the reminder of her own birthday tonight. "That's true, isn't it? For both of us?" But then she smiled a little, ever the survivor. "We'd better look at the bright side and make the most of what we've got." She hesitated again. "I really would feel better if you agreed to see Dr. Fingerhut while you're here. I'm sure I could get him to work you in."

"After you," Maggie said.

"I already saw him. I left his office, without hearing his explanation of my choices in treatment—including those pills." Too late, she realized that she sounded just like her mother.

Maggie pounced on her. "Nora, we're more alike than you know."

Nora couldn't lecture her mother about her medications when Nora wasn't ready to take them, either. Nor did she know if she ever would be.

Night sweats.

Hot flashes.

Mood swings, as Starr had pointed out.

Nora should take her own advice.

The Big 5-0 had arrived. With a vengeance.

CHAPTER 9

"So, what do you think?" With an anxious expression, Geneva Whitehouse turned her face to one side then the other. "How do I look?"

Nora couldn't see a difference. She hadn't seen a line or wrinkle in the smooth surface of Geneva's complexion before, which had made her wonder why Geneva felt she needed to improve her appearance.

"Beautiful, as always," Nora told her.

To her surprise, Geneva didn't smile. "That's what people have been telling me," she murmured, her gaze downcast, "from the time I was a little girl." She shrugged off the compliment. "After a while, the words lose their meaning."

"You must have been a gorgeous child," Starr Mulligan piped in.

"And I have the cheap trophies to show for it. Funny," Geneva said, "but I've been a trophy myself since I was five years old. That's when I won my first."

"You did the kiddie pageant thing?" Nora asked. Geneva only nodded, looking unhappy. "And you just had the Botox?"

"This morning. It must have worked since it doesn't seem to show."

In the airy living room of her home, Geneva avoided looking at Nora or Starr. The very thing she had wanted didn't seem to have made her happy after all. It was almost as if Geneva felt some other improvement was required of her.

Geneva had asked Nora to this impromptu luncheon—but for what purpose other than to gauge her appearance? She'd claimed she wanted to make up for missing most of Nora's birthday party, but then why invite Starr, too? Nora sensed from Geneva's stiff posture that there was more to come.

"I want to thank you again, Nora. I know I already did, but that was before I saw Doctor Fingerhut. I feel like a…new woman already. After a full checkup, which I'd been neglecting to have, he referred me to someone for the treatment."

"I'm glad you're pleased. Mark and I have been friends for years."

Geneva's too-bright smile was fixed firmly in place, and firm was the word for it. She sat down in front of the marble coffee table to dish up their lunch from the Belleek soup tureen waiting there. The heady scents of shrimp and cream and—was that basil she smelled, or rosemary?—lifted into the cool air.

"Heavenly," Nora said, taking her plate. The casserole contained her favorite penne pasta, carrots, a smattering of tiny mushrooms. Starr waited until Geneva went to the kitchen for the rolls.

"You should control your appetite, Nora. At a certain age, a woman's metabolism slows down." Starr attacked her own dish with gusto. "I'm lucky I don't have to watch my weight." She was no more than three years younger than Nora, assuming she told the truth about her age. "And clearly I'm still attracting younger men."

Nora refused to take the bait about Heath. Inside she was still smarting. Whatever had possessed him to bring Starr to her party? Revenge for Nora's rejection? It was too much.

But Nora kept quiet. If there was any chance she might still get the Whitehouse job, she wanted to preserve it.

Maybe Geneva meant to let Starr down gently today.

When they had finished eating, Geneva reached down beside the sofa for a manila envelope. Nora's pulse began to

pound. "I invited you both here today because I think it would
be a huge mistake for you not to work together. Personal issues
aside," she said, "your ideas for this house are stunning. Here,
let me show you what I like." On a cleared section of the long
table she laid out the rest of Nora's sketches, then Starr's. "I
love this one of my bedroom, Starr. But I absolutely must have
Nora's for the library." One by one she pointed to the drawings
until Nora realized that there were equal designs for her and
Starr. No favorites, Geneva was saying. She was apparently an
equal opportunity employer.

Starr bristled. "I already told you I couldn't—"

"Work with Nora?" Geneva whisked aside the sketches to
pour steaming coffee into three floral-patterned porcelain cups.
"Don't be silly, Starr." She paused. "Would it help if I added a
bonus? Complete the job on time without quarreling, and I'll
give you each an extra fifteen percent."

"Well…" Starr stirred cream into her coffee. She didn't
look at Nora, but it was obvious that her mind was clicking
through the calculations.

"Well," Nora echoed.

She held her breath.

Half a loaf had seemed better than none, but this was by far
a superior offer. With an incentive bonus, the total came closer
to her original bid.

"Let me leave you to talk." Geneva rose gracefully from
the sofa and cleared their plates from the table. "I'll be back
with dessert."

When Geneva had disappeared, Nora leaned forward in her
chair. "We'd be fools not to do it."

"She really wants both our designs, and I have to admit she
has a good eye for color, proportion, style…"

"Money talks?"

"Money is the last thing on my mind," Starr insisted, which
didn't convince Nora.

She heard Geneva's footsteps returning from the kitchen. They had no more time. It was now or never.

"Well?" she said again, inclining her head in that direction.

"I suppose we could call a truce. That would be something new."

It was the practical solution, Nora agreed, one she'd considered before, and she did need the extra money. There was no telling what would happen when she met with the IRS. She held her breath again, hoping Starr wouldn't disagree.

"We'd have to find some way to get along," Starr said grudgingly.

"We're civilized adults. I'm sure we can."

"I'm not so sure," Starr said, "but..."

Nora thought better of belaboring the issue. "Let's do it," she said.

And Starr answered with the beginning of a smile. "Yes, let's."

"Why not? It could be fun." Nora saw Geneva in the doorway, carrying a tray of golden crème brûlées on wafer-thin Irish china, but she couldn't resist one last question. "The money's not the only temptation, is it? Working together is another bonus for you. I think you've finally realized—" she used Starr's words "—that I'm the better designer." Nora wasn't proud of herself for retaliating in kind, but Starr's appearance with Heath last night had brought out a streak of resentment. She had the not-quite satisfaction of seeing Starr's spine stiffen and her smile freeze.

"In your dreams."

Still feeling dazed, Savannah pulled into Nora's driveway, cut the ignition on her new Lexus SUV—planning ahead for their family, Johnny had said when they bought it—then climbed out of the car. Carefully.

After seeing Mark, she felt as fragile as a carton of eggs, which wasn't a bad metaphor. She still hadn't gotten over the shock.

If Johnny had been at their condo, she would have gone there. He had a right to know first. But she had urged him not to miss a scheduled meeting in Miami with Wade Blessing about a script and had assured him she would be fine. The truth was, he made her nervous. If something was wrong, could he take the news? It was Nora who had urged Mark Fingerhut to see her today rather than next week. No surprise there. Her mother was nothing if not persistent. And of course, when he heard about Savannah's spotting, Mark had immediately carved out some time for her.

When she walked in Nora's front door, she wasn't sure what to say. This wasn't the kind of news to blurt out without thinking. She glanced around, wondering why Daisy hadn't rushed to greet her. Her absence provided the opportunity for Savannah to stall.

"Where's the dog, Gram?"

Maggie had been watching TV, cuddled up in Nora's favorite chair, and when she turned and saw Savannah, her face lit up.

"There you are." During their shared summers when Savannah was growing up, Maggie had become highly attuned to Savannah, and vice versa. Maggie frowned. "Daisy's out back in the yard. I can't imagine how an invisible fence—what kind of fence is one you can't see?—can hold her in when she had no trouble jumping over the gate at your mother's party but— Child, what's wrong?"

"Nothing." Her stomach did flip-flops. "Is Ma home?"

"Changing her clothes. She had lunch with Starr and Mrs. Whitehouse."

"How did that go?" Buying more time, Savannah riffled through the mail on a side table, searching for the latest bridal catalog. Such wedding-related items often came to Nora's house. Now the event would have to be canceled.

"It went badly at first," Nora said, rounding the corner from the hall that led to her bedroom. She batted a stray pink balloon left over from last night's party out of her way. "Then to my amazement as much as hers, we actually reached an agreement."

"With Mulligan? You're kidding."

"We're going to do Geneva's home after all," Nora said. "Together. You may want to watch the fireworks when you have time."

"I have my hands full already with the Larson condo." Savannah realized that would be a problem for her now, too. "Maybe I can finish by next week and then…" She stopped.

Maggie and Nora looked at her with curiosity.

"And then," Nora encouraged her.

Savannah couldn't go on. She'd been thrilled, naturally, to learn she was pregnant. A surprise, she'd thought then, but it was nothing like this one. The thought of carrying Johnny's baby, having his baby, loving his baby with him by her side still brought tears to her eyes. The persistent nausea she could deal with, and Mark had given her a script for some medication to calm that down. But there was nothing to ease this latest development, and Savannah wasn't sure she could tell her mother or Maggie now that she was here.

Nora's gaze sharpened. "You did see Mark today?"

"Yes."

Gingerly she sank down on a chair near Maggie. Nora peered hard at her.

Savannah never had been able to hide her feelings. She felt her throat tighten. All at once she wanted to throw herself into her mother's arms and weep.

"What did Mark say?"

Both Nora's and Maggie's faces showed their growing concern. Nora bent down to frame Savannah's face in both hands. But still, Savannah couldn't speak. She merely shook her head and waved a hand in the air, asking for a moment to compose herself.

"You're not ill?" Nora's eyes held sympathy, but also fear. "I knew there was some kind of problem. It's the spotting, isn't it?"

"Not exactly," she managed, feeling even closer to tears. One minute she was elated, as high as the colorful balloons that had festooned her mother's living room last night, the next, she was well on her way to becoming a sloppy mess. Again. "And no, I'm not sick, Ma."

For a moment she gave thanks that Johnny wasn't home. He worried about her endlessly, fussed over every little thing, and when he heard her news his left eye would never stop twitching. He'd been slow to commit to their relationship. Would this new complication send him running after all?

"Tell us what Mark said, Savannah. Now. Did he do the sonogram?"

"Yes." She'd seen all the little fingers and toes, heard the heartbeats.

"You're not having a miscarriage?"

"No." She took another shaky breath, wondering how she would ever do this. Marriage, motherhood, especially now. "Mark wants me to go to bed."

"He what?" Nora blinked, and made the wrong interpretation. "You don't mean to tell me he came on to you today?"

"That doctor is a pre-vert?" Maggie asked, her tone outraged. "I knew it. If he laid one finger on my granddaughter…"

Savannah managed a faint smile. "Gram, he's had his hands on me more than once." Then she realized what she'd said. "I mean, he does his job. That's all." She shook her head. "No, that doesn't sound right, either. Of course he didn't do anything inappropriate. What I'm trying to say is—" her voice trembled "—he wants me on bed rest for the duration of my pregnancy."

Nora paled. "There's something wrong with the baby."

"No, everything's all right. I even know the sex."

"A boy?" Nora guessed, as if to say that she knew most men wanted a son.

"A girl," Maggie said at the same time, because she'd always wanted another granddaughter.

"Yes," Savannah answered.

"A boy and a girl?" Nora's eyes had widened.

"Twins?" Maggie echoed.

"Yes. And, we think, another boy."

They gaped at her. There, that hadn't been so hard after all. Savannah's threatening tears took another direction and she felt her smile spread across her face. The news was mostly wonderful, except for the bed rest part, which was awful. Six more months in the house wouldn't be…child's play. Then, that quickly, she was crying as soon as she uttered the one word that frightened her to death.

"Triplets."

"Two boys? *And* a girl?" Johnny said, his face draining of all color.

"Johnny, sit down." Nora guided her future son-in-law to a nearby chair in her kitchen. He hadn't stopped pacing since he'd arrived several hours after Savannah's announcement. His face looked ashen, and his left eye tic was in full swing.

Nora patted him on the head. "They're quite a surprise."

"Three babies? Even the beach house will be tight, but we sure can't stay in the condo once they're born. And what about Savannah's work?"

He kept his voice low. Her daughter was in the other room, lying on the sofa as Mark Fingerhut had instructed. Nora had insisted that everyone needed dinner before Savannah and Johnny went home to deal with this new situation. She stirred the pot of spaghetti sauce on the stove, then hurried to pour Johnny a hefty glass full of chardonnay.

He made a face. "I hate this stuff. It tastes like flowers."

"Drink it. You need it."

Instead, Johnny lifted his gaze to hers. "Nora, you know I

love Savannah. Just like you, I'll love these kids. That's a given. But I wasn't counting on this. God," he murmured, "three cribs, three strollers—"

"They make them for triplets, angel."

"—all that other gear infants seem to need. Baby swings and diapers by the carload and trips to the pediatrician, three times over… And what about college tuition? I wasn't cut out for this," he muttered. Then immediately, "What am I saying? And here I thought my days of being a no-commitment jerk were over."

Nora bustled to the refrigerator to pull out the makings for a salad. The lettuce looked a bit wilted, but its center would be fine and the tomatoes were still good, just harvested from the small garden she kept in her backyard. They were the last of the season. After Savannah's announcement on top of Nora's agreement to work with Starr, she'd plunged into a furious weeding session while they waited for Johnny that had failed to ease her nerves or her mind. She decided to calm him instead.

"The urge to panic is the curse of first-time parents."

He darted an anxious glance toward the living room. "You think she's really all right? How will those three fit inside her as they grow? How will she possibly breast-feed them all? And with Mark insisting upon bed rest for the next six months, you'll be in a bind at Nine Lives…just when Savannah was enjoying her job with you."

"Savannah is done. For now. Any last details on the Larson condo will give me the chance to get away from Starr now and then," Nora assured him. "The Larsons should be finished well before we start at Geneva's. I'll fit Savannah's other clients in around the Whitehouse redesign."

He grunted before taking a cautious sip of his wine. "You're handling this awfully well."

"I've had time to adjust." In fact, Nora had been planning an all-day shopping expedition with Savannah for maternity and baby clothes and tons of toys and equipment when she heard the news, but in the hours since, she'd come to terms with the fact that Savannah would now be bedridden.

And how would *she* manage that? Nora's smile tried to become a frown. Johnny's concerns were partly hers, too. For his sake, and Savannah's, she had tried to minimize the situation. "It's pretty exciting, you have to admit," she said. "I know Savannah is used to being active, on the go. We'll simply have to keep her entertained. When the babies arrive, we'll form some kind of child-care brigade."

Johnny didn't look convinced. He looked terrified.

The poor man had gone from being a confirmed bachelor to a man in love to an expectant father who probably didn't know one end of a baby from the other.

"You should talk with Savannah," Nora suggested.

"I don't want to worry her. She'll think I'm some kind of lightweight."

"And you imagine that macho attitude will help things?" Nora shook her head. "You need to work together. Admit your fears."

Johnny stared into his now-empty wineglass. His voice hardened.

"No, Nora. Not now."

She had opened her mouth to make a stronger argument when Maggie wandered into the kitchen. She inspected Nora's spaghetti sauce and the whole wheat pasta waiting for the pot of water to boil, then meandered over to the kitchen island to poke her nose into the salad making.

"That lettuce looks done for, Nora. I saw the other day on *The View* that the majority of food poisoning now comes from produce. You wouldn't expect that, would you? Savannah sent me out here to get her some crackers and cheese. Why don't you take them to her?" she asked Johnny, obviously wanting to be alone with Nora, who imagined Maggie had been eavesdropping.

Nora tore the fresh pieces of lettuce and dropped them in a big wooden bowl. "I've been cooking for my family since I was ten years old."

Maggie's lips pursed. She waited for Johnny to fix Savannah's snack, then leave the kitchen before she said, "Your memory is failing. You did not cook for me when you were ten, Nora. Not even at fifteen when you got your first job at the corner market. I always put a meal on the table, every night, even when my heart was breaking."

Nora glanced at the kitchen doorway. Johnny had disappeared into the living room, and she heard the low murmur of his voice, then Savannah's. A moment later, her daughter was weeping. "Oh, dear," Nora murmured. She abandoned the plump tomato she'd been about to slice, laid her best paring knife on the counter, and headed for the other room.

Maggie's tone stopped her. "Leave them alone."

"She's my child," Nora said, her step faltering. "She needs me."

"She needs that beautiful man, the father of her babies." Maggie's tone softened. "We never know when life is going to hand us another difficulty, Nora. When your father left us so suddenly—"

She turned back. "Yes, Mother. I remember. I felt the same way when I left Wilson. Well, almost. But it was as if a part of me had gone, too." She sighed. "I guess it really was for a long while until I managed to stop carrying a torch for a man who had already moved on." And soon would again, she thought. Still, her gut instinct was to go to Savannah now, to offer comfort, to somehow ease Johnny's eye twitch and reassure them that everything—*everything*—would be all right. After all, this complication was a joyous one.

"Those two can handle their own problem," Maggie told her.

"With my help," Nora insisted. She took another step, then halted. "And yours," she added. "I don't mean to sound harsh, but we need all the hands we can get. Instead of sitting in front of the television all day, you might get up, move around and find something useful to do for your granddaughter."

"My tickets to Virginia are already bought."

"We can change them," Nora said.

To her surprise Maggie didn't argue any further. "*Triplets*," she said. "Can you imagine?"

Nora leaned across the table in one of Destin's premier cocktail lounges—or, to be more accurate, a popular local bar and casual restaurant on the beach. From the deck, the view of the Gulf was gorgeous, and a lowering sun cast wispy yet fiery tentacles of red and orange across the horizon. But Nora barely noticed the deepening sunset. Even though the temperature as evening fell was still in the midseventies, she shivered in the slight breeze.

"You're certain Savannah is okay? Healthy?" she said. "And the babies…"

Mark Fingerhut's answer should have been enough. "Perfectly in synch with every obstetrics manual at my disposal."

"You're teasing me," Nora said, not reassured at all.

"I wouldn't dare."

Mark's appraisal of her made her fidget. This wasn't the first time, by any means, that they'd met for drinks after both of their office hours had ended for the day. As she'd told Geneva, she and Mark had become friends over the years. When Nora had called, he had quickly offered to buy her a glass of wine, presumably in thanks for her referral of Geneva Whitehouse, but Nora knew he really meant to set her straight about Savannah.

"I suppose that, like Maggie, you think I'm a meddling mother."

"Nora, relax." It wasn't the first time Mark had told her that, either, but the simple advice never worked for Nora. She took a small sip of her wine and then set it on the table again, still troubled by her failure to help Johnny and Savannah.

"You're not the pregnant one," Mark pointed out. "Savannah is...fine." Nora heard the qualified tone. "That's all I'm going to say. You wouldn't want me to violate the new privacy laws, would you? My doctor-patient contract?"

"I'm her mother. Mark, I need details."

He sighed. "What would we do without your fine hand in everything?" He glanced around to make sure they were alone and no listening ears were at a nearby table. He lowered his voice. "There are risks, of course, with any multiple births—"

"What kinds of risks?"

"Well," he said, as if still reluctant to elaborate when Nora knew better. This was the sole purpose of their meeting here on a day when Mark was on call for the night and drinking seltzer with lemon. He must have felt called upon to give her the business before he actually imparted information. "Naturally there's a greater weight gain with three fetuses, so the mother's abdomen becomes excessively enlarged. It's harder for her to breathe, and there's more pressure on her internal organs. There's a bigger chance that she could develop toxemia or eclampsia, and because of the growing triplets' sizes in comparison to that space available to them, we can expect an early delivery." He hesitated. "The issue will be to keep Savannah comfortable until the babies are big enough to survive." Another heavy pause followed before Mark told her the whole truth. "Then, well, there's a slight problem already."

Nora felt herself turn pale. "She has been spotting, I know."

"Yes. Some. Not much."

"Is she in danger of losing the babies?"

"Not at the moment, but my examination turned up what we call an incompetent cervix. A weakness of the muscle. Thus, I'll put in a suture to support it, and I've taken the precaution of prescribing full bed rest even sooner than I would under completely normal circumstances with multiples."

"Mark, she'll be bored to death."

He removed the slice of lemon from his glass and dropped it on the table. "Boredom won't kill her. Believe me, Nora, having three babies at once—especially for a *primipara*, a first-time mother—is enough to contend with. We don't want to lose one or all of them by failing to practice prudent management of this pregnancy." He paused again. At least he was including Nora now in the process. "And a fascinating time it will be. Triplets occur in approximately 1 out of every 9,300 births, in several possible combinations, and it appears from the sonogram that Savannah's babies are a set of twins and a singleton, that is, the trio derived from two eggs. That means the twins— the boys—are identical, but all of them are a definite miracle on Nature's part."

"Yes, very exciting," Nora agreed, remembering Maggie's reaction. "Do you think Savannah will be able to carry close enough to term for their safety? And hers?"

"That's my job. Let me do it, okay?" Mark frowned. "Not many people seem willing to accept that concept these days. Barely a month goes by without some former patient threatening to sue me for malpractice."

Nora blanched again. "You're not serious."

"In fact, Savannah may have seen one of them ahead of her appointment one day. I was a little cranky. The other woman had just told me I'd hear from her attorney." He cleared his throat. "Not that I've killed anyone lately." His smile was weak. "We live in a litigious society, Nora, and everyone's out for the easy buck. You know, like those people who claim the fast-food coffee's too hot or the one who found a finger in his chili. Like those corporations, I'm a handy target."

"Poor Mark. Savannah did say you seemed low."

He finished his seltzer before adding, "Between managed care, privacy laws and the endless paperwork required by the insurance carriers, plus Medicare and Medicaid forms, there's a lot less time these days to spend with my patients. That part of my business is what I most enjoy." He pushed away his glass, eyeing Nora's still untouched wine. "For medicinal purposes only," he said with another forced smile, "why don't you drink that? My problems are one thing, but they're not for you to worry about too, Nora. I hear from your daughter, not to mention several other people, that you're in trouble yourself. A possible felon…" He let the rest trail off.

Nora's pulse lurched. "That ridiculous rumor is all over town. I lost another design bid yesterday with the clients' vague explanation as to why they chose someone else when my bid was obviously the better one." Her phone had been unusually quiet this week. Then another thought occurred to her. "You've spoken with Detective Caine, haven't you?"

"He was one of the people. I gave him an A-one report card on your character. Which," he added, "I'm not sure he believed. My professional credibility aside, he seems to have formed his own opinion."

"He's a suspicious man." Although he claimed not to be.

Mark acknowledged that with a lift of one eyebrow. "And you seem to have raised his suspicions."

"Geneva spoke to you, too. Didn't she?"

Apparently Nora had no secrets. She needed her own privacy law.

"I didn't say that. But I'm sure this will straighten out in its own time. In the meantime," he said, "it might be wiser to—"

"Keep my nose out of everyone's business?" Nora took a hefty swig of her now-tepid wine. "I suppose you're right, but it's not easy. My daughter's well-being is important to me. So is the rest of the family. Maybe my need to step in stems from being a single mother all these years. For a long time, I was the only person they could count on."

He beckoned their waitress for the check. "All I'm saying is, don't try so hard." He reached across the table to squeeze Nora's hand. "You feel like ice," he said in a chiding tone that reminded her he was her physician as well as her friend. "For the record, I do believe you're innocent. Let this happen as it will."

A nice thought, but time would tell.

People were always telling Nora to sit back, to let life take its course. Instead, she fought the waves like one of the tourist swimmers who often battled the riptides along the Gulf Coast and sometimes lost. She couldn't help it. Nora had grown up in Maggie's home, reliant upon herself rather than her mother, even as a child, increasingly certain that it was up to her to make things work.

She'd done the same with Wilson. That had been her fault for marrying a dreamer with no practical sense about everyday matters, but still…

Was Maggie right that she didn't remember with accuracy? Or maybe everyone she loved did need her to keep them safe and well.

She'd even felt some brief tug at her heartstrings for Caine when they met.

Now her life was changing again, as it did with startling regularity. Whether Mark advised her otherwise, she meant to help Savannah and Johnny.

By the time she arrived for her appointment at the district IRS office the next day, Nora also had her accountant to worry about. Paul showed up at least, much to her relief, but it appeared that his record-keeping and documentation on her behalf was not acceptable to the federal government. Had Browning and Johnny been right about him? At least the man hadn't fled to Brazil.

Nora experienced a moment of all-out panic—envisioning herself in the not-so-attractive orange jumpsuit Leonard had joked about, her unmanicured hands wrapped around the bars of a cell—before the young IRS agent kindly suggested a second meeting at another date. Nora and her accountant would have time to form their defense before the full audit began.

Oh, joy.

But, of course, that wasn't all. When things happened, they happened in clusters. On her first morning at Geneva Whitehouse's home nearly a month later, Nora rang the bell, wondering what the day would bring with Starr Mulligan. When Geneva finally answered, Nora bit back a scream.

Geneva's beautiful face was a mass of black and blue welts. Her eyes, even behind dark glasses, Nora could see, were all but swollen shut.

"Oh, Geneva," she said, one hand to her heart.

Nora had never liked Earl Whitehouse, but was he also a wife beater?

CHAPTER 10

"I swear," Nora told Starr Mulligan another month later, "at first I thought Earl had abused her. I was even ready to call Caine."

"You must have been desperate."

"A last resort." Nora couldn't have agreed more. She'd known her share of problems with men, mainly Wilson, but no one had ever hurt her in the physical sense. She couldn't bear to think that Earl had hurt Geneva. If he had, he belonged behind bars.

"Imagine how embarrassed I would have been if Geneva hadn't explained so quickly about her bruises."

"A face-lift." Starr reviewed her own image in Geneva's front hall mirror. She was dressed today in jeans and a sweatshirt because the day was cool. She wore at least a full pound of makeup on her face.

"I think she'll have a very good result. Once the rest of the swelling goes down, she might look close to twenty again—if that's still important to her." From what Geneva had said about her childhood, her self-image wasn't that healthy.

"Twenty sounds a bit drastic," Starr mused. "But if I ever need one…"

Nora was surprised. "Would you? Get a face-lift, I mean?"

"Sure. I'd think about it."

"Surgery isn't my favorite indoor sport," Nora admitted. "And in spite of the fact that Geneva is perfectly fine, thank

goodness, the thought of those bruises still makes me shudder."
She paused a moment. "And just think what the surgery covers
up. I once heard Lauren Hutton— Remember her?"

"The first supermodel."

"No, that was Suzy Parker, the redhead, wasn't it? Lauren's
the one who spent a lot of time in Africa taking pictures of wild
animals after her career had peaked. She sells cosmetics for
mature women now on the Home Shopping Network. Or is it
QVC?" Nora paused, realizing that she and Starr were having
an actual conversation, if not a serious one. They had a similar
frame of life experience. "Anyway, Lauren said she'd never
have 'work' done. If she did, she would never know how she
would have looked otherwise."

"Interesting," Starr said. "But she's probably lying."

"Well, that was years ago when she was still in her prime—
not that she doesn't look good now." Nora bustled into the living
room where she had been supervising the removal of Geneva's
old wall-to-wall carpeting before Starr had arrived for the day.

The two Mexican workmen were making good progress. On
a tour of the rest of the project, she led Starr to the kitchen
where the local cabinetmaker was tearing down the cupboards
amid a great deal of screeching as nails gave way and, on his
part, swearing.

"Not bad," Starr said over the noise. "One month and we
have most of this down to the bare bones. If the furniture
comes in on schedule, we should finish the whole thing well
before our deadline."

"And get our bonus—or rather, bonuses."

Starr scowled. "What's a little extra here and there to you,
Nora? You already have it all. Nine Lives. A home of your
own—"

"So do you, Mulligan." The switch of mood stunned Nora.
She knew Starr had a condominium near the beach.

"A family," Starr went on, as if she hadn't heard Nora. "I

must admit, I envy you. And now three grandbabies, no less. How is Savannah holding up?" she asked before Nora could respond to her attack.

"As well as can be expected, not to make a pun," Nora said. "She hates being confined to home and bed, but I dropped my mother off this morning to spend the day with her at least. Who would have thought?"

"Your mother, too," Starr continued her list of Nora's pluses in life. "She's still here?"

"Amazing," Nora agreed.

"Well, my mother's gone, my ex and I split years ago, and I haven't seen my only son in what seems like forever."

The admission came as another surprise. Nora had never thought of Starr as a perpetual victim like Maggie. Starr seemed much tougher, more resilient. Certainly she could be aggressive with Nora. But actually, she'd never thought of Starr having a personal life, much less a family of her own. "Where does your son live?"

"Houston. He has a wife and little girl. She's four."

Nora blinked. "I didn't know you were a grandmother."

"The only time I've seen her was when she was born. You don't know how lucky you are. Occasionally they send me a picture. Unless they need something, I don't hear from them.

If that were her granddaughter Nora would have been on the first plane to Texas, but she only said, "Starr, I'm sorry. Sorry you don't hear from or see him."

Starr gave her a curt glance as if to say, "Sure you are," then walked from the noisy kitchen into the breakfast room. So much for camaraderie. Starr slumped down onto one of the new, floral-cushioned rattan chairs and picked up the water bottle she'd left on the round, glass-topped table beside her usual tote bag stuffed full of supplies for the day. Starr would finish another two bottles, Nora had learned, before quitting time. In the past four weeks, she and Starr had discovered a lot about each other, yet this latest bit of information about Starr's after-hours existence, which seemed a lonely one, unraveled some of Nora's previous impressions—most of them less than positive—and some of her initial judgments—equally negative—about Starr.

That is, until Starr looked up at Nora with a too-sweet smile. Starr peered closely at her. "Are those gray hairs I see, Nora?"

Nora's lips tightened. "And here I was, trying to like you," she finally said.

All of a sudden, she missed Geneva, who often kept their interactions as civil as could be expected. But today, Geneva wasn't home; she hadn't been able to tolerate the sounds of destruction throughout her dismantled house and had finally left to do some shopping, wearing the huge dark glasses that had hidden her swollen features for weeks.

The working environment could have been worse, but Earl Whitehouse was out of town. A business trip, Geneva had told them, and she was glad. He didn't like the noise or the mess, either, she said, to which Nora had uttered a soothing, "I know it's upsetting to have your personal space torn apart. It must feel like a violation. That's very common among clients. But try to have patience, Geneva. The long-term benefits will soon outweigh this short-term chaos."

Behind her, Nora had heard a definite choking sound.

"Pollyanna," Starr had murmured.

Nora considered herself to be an eternal optimist, but now they both seemed less than glad to be alone with each other. Yet as Nora had supposed before they started the job, Starr rarely let her out of her sight.

Had Geneva asked her to keep an eye on Nora while she was gone, just in case Nora felt the urge to help herself to another piece of crystal, or was Starr afraid that Nora would get all the glory if she didn't participate one-on-one *ad nauseum* in the redesign of the Whitehouse home?

Nora didn't get time to speculate.

She wasn't out the door from the breakfast room to the hall, intent upon inspecting Earl's new library while she calmed herself, when Starr trod on her heels. Nora bit back a scathing remark but kept going.

They hadn't killed each other yet, but the day was young. Still, Nora found it hard to resent a woman whose only son never came to visit.

Was it possible Starr had a heart—a broken one, like Maggie's—after all?

And Nora did have much to be thankful for. Savannah, Browning and now Johnny, who would become officially family once the wedding took place—the new date for which was one more thing she needed to address. And her home was comfortable. She couldn't imagine that, as a designer's home, Starr's house would be any less suited to her, but Nora did admit to having one advantage: the coming triplets.

What if, like Starr with her granddaughter, she rarely saw them once they arrived? What if Nora lived far away, like Maggie in Virginia, or as Starr did now from Houston, and couldn't visit often enough to become a real part of their lives? To help shape them?

That would never do.

Mark might chide her, Johnny might accuse her of meddling as Maggie had, but Nora's family, and her friends, needed her.

Heath, for instance.

She wasn't quite ready to forgive him for bringing Starr to her birthday party, but Heath had been very contrite.

"I'm sorry, Nora. I ran into her at the club and we started talking. I told her I couldn't have a drink with her, that I was on my way to your place."

"She actually invited herself," Nora guessed. Starr had been speculating for years about the inside of Nora's home. And of course she couldn't resist the urge to gloat over that fiftieth celebration, if that was the correct word. Nora hoped she was satisfied.

But couldn't Heath have said no?

"She was too persuasive," he'd clarified, just like Leonard, and Nora let it go at that. The way Starr had looked at him during the party, as if Heath were a delicious candy bar by the same name, just oozing rich chocolate, convinced her to stay quiet. Nora was determined not to see Heath, anyway.

Certainly, she couldn't accept his gift. The bulky package had turned out to be one box inside another within another, each smaller than the last until, finally, Nora drew out a birthday card that contained a voucher. Heath, who had just started a side business as a computer consultant when he wasn't working at Hi-Health Fitness, was a wizard at the keyboard, and he had created a beautiful invitation for Nora to spend a long weekend with him at an inn in the Florida Keys. Of course she couldn't go.

She still felt guilty and wondered if she had somehow led him on.

She went into the library where another carpenter was hammering the new shelves into place. Oh, they were gorgeous, rich cherry with brass trim.

Starr said right behind her, "I hate to say it, but you were right."

She couldn't believe Starr had actually complimented her taste.

"I'm glad I—we—altered the design for this room. The pickled oak would have been too pale against the neutral walls Geneva wants. We needed more drama in here."

They talked for a few minutes in Southern fashion with the carpenter, who knew Starr's cousin the Realtor who had sold Leonard his house at Impressions, before Starr's attention was distracted by a car pulling up the drive alongside the library windows.

"You have company," she said with a gleam in her eye.

Nora glanced outside—and willed a sudden flood of too-familiar heat not to flash across her skin.

"Caine," she murmured. "Nothing lucky about that."

With a disgruntled glance at the house, Caine slammed the door to his unmarked police car and then strode around the yard to the Whitehouse front entrance. Damned if he'd knock at the kitchen door where all that racket was coming from. He already had another headache, and he wasn't about to slink in the back like some servant. Which was exactly how he'd been made to feel an hour ago.

He was mad enough at Earl Whitehouse to eat snakes.

To his further dismay, the first person he met was Nora Pride.

"Well, well," he said. She had her nerve, revisiting the scene of the burglary. Unable to stop himself, Caine looked her over from today's loose white shirt with flowing sleeves to her well-fitting dark slacks. "I had no idea you and Geneva Whitehouse were pals these days."

"How did you know where to find me?" Her expression remained bland. Caine hadn't come looking for her, but Nora Pride didn't know that. "First, my office, then my home," she said, "now here. If I didn't know better, I might assume the Destin PD is stalking me." She paused. "Or that you're sweet on me."

"Huh," he muttered, feeling a faint warmth in his neck, then stepped inside. The din there was even greater than before, and when he took another few steps he ran into Starr Mulligan of Superior Interiors, Inc. Again, it surprised him to see her and Nora in the same room. From what Ms. Mulligan had told him when he'd questioned her right after the Whitehouse burglary, she had a low regard for Nora Pride. His prime suspect had expressed the same opinion of Starr Mulligan.

Two months later, to his utter disgust, Caine was no further in his investigation than he'd been during that first round of interviews. Which was his problem right now.

He surveyed the area. "Is Ms. Whitehouse home?"

"No, she's not," Nora said. "May we take a message?"

Oh, yeah, he was the errand boy, all right. He had just opened his mouth when a workman appeared in the kitchen doorway. "Ladies, I got a problem here with the end wall cabinets."

Starr Mulligan shot Nora, then Caine, an arch look. "I'll take care of it," she offered, then disappeared with the burly guy who had a claw hammer in his hand. That left Caine alone with Nora Pride, never a comfortable position for him to be in. She always got under his skin and Caine always felt she'd taken the best shot, not that he understood why they were sparring in the first place. He'd decided it was a woman thing, beyond his male comprehension.

He looked after Starr Mulligan, the safer choice. "Quite a woman," he said. "She reminds me of someone…that actress who did the horse movie…"

"Elizabeth Taylor. In her youth," Nora added. "Are you a movie buff?"

"Now and then. Mostly then," he said and smiled a little. "I like a good thriller. My wife, Annie, loved movies. I don't go by myself." He cleared his throat. Caine resisted the urge to reach inside his jacket for his notepad, which he sometimes used as a prop to hide his discomfort in an awkward situation. He knew the message he needed to deliver by heart. It was still making his gut sour and his headache grind in his skull.

The police chief had called him in to the office that morning before Caine even loosened his tie. His butt wasn't on the mashed-in seat of his desk chair when the summons came. "Get in here, Caine." And then, the hammer on his job had dropped. Maybe he should have become a carpenter, not a cop. The chief eyed him with displeasure.

"Earl Whitehouse was just on the phone. He wants to know what's happening with their burglary."

"Not much," Caine had confessed. "I've questioned everyone who might have a connection to the theft. I've requestioned most of them. The lab turned up zip, *nada*, on the small bit of possible evidence they found. No viable prints, no hair or fiber at the scene, not a single tire impression in the yard."

"Whitehouse is hopping mad. His wife's vase is still missing." The chief shot a look at the ceiling as if to say, "Help me." He obviously didn't think a piece of heavy crystal could be worth all the fuss. Caine had to agree with him, but the chief hadn't been through. "Find something. Fast. He's a hotshot in this town, Detective, and it's your job to close this case. When can I expect to see that file on my desk?"

Caine sighed. The pulsing in his temples grew worse. Now, he gazed at Nora Pride, who was a damn sight better to look at than the chief, never mind how she unsettled him. But he still had no answers. His investigation was at a dead end.

"I doubt you're here to admire Starr Mulligan," Nora finally said when he didn't continue their movie discussion. "As for Geneva Whitehouse, I'll be glad to tell her you came by." She had reached around him to open the front door—dismissed again, Caine thought—when his hand covered hers. Just as abruptly he snatched it back, his skin tingling from their brief contact.

"I'm here to update her on the case. I'll try later."

"While you're here, is there anything you can tell me?" Her voice quavered with need. Not the kind of need he'd been thinking of when their hands met, or when he walked into the house and saw her standing there like a delicately packaged surprise just for him. "I work for Geneva. So does Starr."

Caine felt certain he'd missed something. "You and Ms. Mulligan? And Geneva Whitehouse? The same Whitehouse who reported her missing vase and wondered what you knew about it? Who told me you'd made a threat? The combination seems unlikely. She actually gave you a job?"

Her slender back stiffened. "Some people can be convinced of a person's innocence with a few simple words about trust. Geneva believes in me. She likes my design and she liked Starr's, so for a change we agreed to join forces for her benefit."

"And yours," he pointed out.

"It's a business, Detective Caine. But we're also human beings—and as such, as women, we can be flexible."

Caine didn't pretend to understand the connection. He was rapidly getting in over his head. When Annie was alive, she'd sometimes done the same thing, spun him around with feminine logic until he couldn't tell up from down. Caine decided he'd rather attend an autopsy.

"Human beings," he repeated. "Some people have an appetite for greed. Or revenge," he added, but the sudden fire in her eyes warned him not to pursue the topic. "All I can tell you is that my investigation continues. We're following a few leads."

"Ah, so you have nothing."

She'd seen right through his standard cover-up and Caine rubbed the back of his neck. "Earl Whitehouse is—shall we say—concerned that the burglary remains unsolved."

Nora blinked. "The chief is putting on the heat?"

"Yeah. You could say that." Caine's eyebrows still felt singed by the chief's blistering tirade.

"How strange," Nora murmured.

His cop instincts went on full alert. "Strange? How so?"

"Well, I... Never mind." She tried to turn away, but Caine turned her back again with a hand on her upper arm. He stared into her velvety eyes.

"If you have anything I need to know, spill it."

"I'll have to take the Fifth on that, Detective. It was just a thought—which might incriminate me. Your views about me are already enough. If I haven't said so until now, your visit to my family was an invasion of my privacy—and a humiliation."

"Nor—Ms. Pride, this is a police matter. Nothing personal."

She waved a dismissive hand, as if his authority didn't matter. "I've been deeply hurt by your obvious suspicions. All I can tell you is, I, um, ran into Mr. Whitehouse one evening and—"

"Define 'ran into.'"

She hesitated. He watched her face turn bright pink and her hands clench into small fists. He remembered the satiny feel of her skin and gritted his teeth.

"My daughter and I, well, we decided to look for something that could, uh, be of use in clearing my name."

Caine fought back a groan. "Don't tell me. You came here."

"Yes, we did," she admitted. "But no one was supposedly home at the time." She didn't go on, as if her explanation made perfect sense.

"Help me out here," Caine said. "Help yourself. Keep talking."

She thought for a moment. "I know this sounds bad now, but I honestly didn't think then that there was any harm in—"

"Trespassing on private property?"

"That's what my daughter said. But—"

He rolled his eyes. "Tampering with a crime scene?"

"Disturbing evidence, yes, she said that, too," Nora confessed. "But really, Caine, I was only trying to help. To help myself." She repeated his words as if he had given her permission to troop through the Whitehouse yard. "I know it wasn't the wisest decision, and my entire family is still unhappy with me because of it, but I'm not sorry I tried. You practically admitted that the case has gone nowhere."

"Did I say that?"

"If it hadn't been for Earl Whitehouse we might have found—"

"You mean Whitehouse caught you?"

Her blush deepened. "It was…embarrassing. As I said, I didn't expect him to be here. But when he opened the door, after his first surprise he didn't seem that upset."

"He didn't report the incident," Caine said for her.

She brightened, as if she'd just discovered he was smarter than he looked. "No. In fact, he seemed eager to forget it. His wife was distraught enough, he said, over the loss of her vase. I'm positive he didn't tell her that we were here because soon after that Geneva hired me—and Starr—to redo her home."

"Huh," Caine said again. Her story was interesting.

"Geneva seems satisfied that I had no part in the burglary." She paused. "Which, of course, I didn't."

"You don't have to convince me."

He withdrew his notebook after all and jotted down a few notes on Earl Whitehouse and his odd shift of attitude about the case. First, he hadn't cared that much. Now, it seemed, he did. And then, Caine scribbled a line about Nora Pride and his new doubt that she had filched a vase that didn't belong to her.

Very interesting…

Savannah had never been so bored in her life. Spending every day in bed or, if there was wild excitement, on the sofa, wasn't her idea of a good time. Thank heaven Kit Blanchard, her best bud, had stopped by today with Tyler, her second-best buddy.

Savannah had read him a few books and greatly enjoyed his company. At four years old, Tyler seemed to have a rich under- standing of the world, which he often expressed in fascinating ways. Kit, her red curls jiggling, her eyes flashing with the drama she thrived on, had despaired today that he would ever stop talking like Elmer Fudd, but to the bedridden Savannah that was hardly a major problem. Typical of Kit, though. It as- tonished Savannah that her soon-to-be-husband had once lived with the volatile woman who was his complete opposite.

"Too bad you'll miss Johnny," she told Kit. "He won't be home until later."

"I doubt he'd be eager to see me. He still tiptoes around our breakup—which, I must say, has worked out nicely for you."

Kit leaned over to hug her. "I'm happy for you, Savannah. You're far more right for him than I was."

Savannah's smile faded. "I'm worried, though. The triplets will be a huge adjustment for him. For me, too," she added, then hesitated before she went on. "I'm not sure I'll be able to handle them."

"Johnny was always great with Tyler. Right, kiddo?" Kit playfully ruffled his dark hair.

The slender little boy who nestled against Savannah's side on the bed quickly grinned. "Me and Johnny are fwiends."

Kit rolled her eyes. "See what I mean? It's 'friends,' Tyler."

"I know. I wike to say it wike that."

Savannah grinned back at him. He was tweaking Kit, but she suspected that he hung on to the childish speech pattern for himself, too. Like her brother Browning, who'd been shattered by their parents' divorce, Tyler's early experiences with his mother and difficult grandmother had stunted his development.

"I 'wike' the way you say it, too," she said, cuddling him close. "Do we have time for another book?" She didn't relish being alone again, and bored.

"I have to go, Savannah." Kit gathered up Tyler's toys, a collection of small cars and more books, stuffing them into her already overloaded tote bag. "I have a class at six. Criminal psychology," she said, rolling her eyes. "You wouldn't believe the things people are capable of." She helped Tyler into his light jacket.

He resisted. Tyler sniffed the air. From the kitchen wafted an enticing aroma that smelled very much to Savannah like cookies. Maggie was baking.

"What about tweats?" he asked. "Gramma Maggie said I could have some."

"Tyler," Kit began, already starting to self-destruct. She wouldn't want to be late for class. Kit had just returned to school to finish her college degree—and, Savannah hoped, to continue taking charge of her life at last.

"Ask Maggie for a take-out bag," Savannah suggested, re-arranging herself in the lumpy bedding. She laid a hand over her abdomen, stopping Kit before she left. "Go ask her now, Tyler, while I say goodbye to your mom." When he skipped out of the room, she turned to Kit. "What if I can't do this?" she said. "How did you manage with Tyler when he was a baby?"

"My mother helped—if you can call it that," Kit said. "Later Johnny was there. You can see how he loves Tyler. He'll be a terrific father, Savannah. You'll be a wonderful mother." She hurried to the door, leaving Savannah to deal with her forced confinement again without them. "Take it one day at a time. That's all you can do. That's what I'm doing."

"Isn't that the cutest pair?" The door had just closed behind Tyler and Kit when Maggie carried a plate of fresh-baked cookies into the bedroom of the condominium her granddaughter shared with Johnny. That little boy was enough to broaden the smile on her face. Her whole being felt brighter today.

"Tyler's a gem. Kit's a work in progress," Savannah said, "but she's trying."

Maggie snorted. "If she stays away from Johnny, we'll get along fine."

In the weeks since Maggie had arrived in Florida she had fallen in love with Savannah's soon-to-be husband, the father of her three babies. Maggie felt increasingly torn. She didn't know whether she wanted to stay longer or fly back to Virginia. Hank must be missing her by now.

"Don't worry. Kit and Johnny are definitely done. The best thing about their relationship was Tyler." Savannah shifted in bed to a sitting position in the rumpled sheets. Her nose twitched. "Are those peanut butter?"

With a satisfied nod, Maggie set the plate beside her.

Savannah took a first bite of the cookie she'd chosen. "Mmm," she said with a sigh of pleasure. "Thanks, Gram. Your special cookies."

"I haven't made them since the last summer you visited me."

"Really? Why not?"

"The recipe turns out three dozen. If I ate them all myself, I'd weigh a ton."

Savannah assessed Maggie's still-slender frame. "You could never eat too much. I, on the other hand—" she waved the cookie at her growing abdomen "—am turning into a manatee." Her eyes glazed with tears, which were common these days. Hormones, Maggie supposed. A woman was captive to them all her life, their excess or their lack, even in her case their total absence. She hated to see her granddaughter in distress.

"Is there anything I can do to make you feel better?"

"Yes. Shoot Mark Fingerhut." Savannah pressed her lips tight. "No, Gram. What am I saying? Listen to me. I'm in danger of becoming a bona fide monster."

"Who said that?"

"Browning. Of course, I did nearly take off his head when he brought me roses the other night. And pizza, with everything. Because I love them both, I could have acted more grateful. What a guy. But I'm so jealous of anyone who can walk out of here on two legs." She paused. "The rest of you come and go, spreading cheer, baking cookies—seeing the world beyond these four walls."

"It's a beautiful day but not that warm." Maggie had never realized the weather actually changed in Florida. "You're better off indoors."

She sighed. "I just lie here, getting bigger every day. Waiting."

Hoping. But Savannah didn't say that.

Maggie chose a cookie for herself then sat in the rocker by the bed. "You know what Mark Fingerling said. You're not to worry. It isn't good for the babies, either." She gazed fondly at

Savannah's five-month belly. She looked easily another two months beyond that. "The triplets are moving now, aren't they? That's when it seems real—and worth every moment in this bed. Including those moments when the little ones were only a glimmer in their father's eyes."

Savannah blushed. "Gram, you leave my fiancé alone. He's mine," she said with a grin that gladdened Maggie's heart.

Maggie flushed. "I like that boy. I didn't realize until Nora's birthday how much I missed this family. If you were never going to come to Richmond again, I guess I had to come here."

The thought surprised her. Somehow, her few days' visit had turned into months. She'd changed her flight home several times. Thanksgiving had come and gone. And now the Christmas holiday was near. Up north, Maggie spent most of her days alone in the house she'd owned for half a century. Many of her neighbors had moved away, as Nora wanted her to do, but at least for now she had company. Oh, how she had missed her granddaughter's summer visits. Missed Savannah.

Maggie and Nora's relationship was another matter. She put that out of her mind as Savannah sent her a smile. Her spirits lifted.

"I'm glad you're here, Gram."

Flattered, she offered Savannah another cookie. "Keep eating. You may gain a few pounds, but the twins and my great-granddaughter need nourishment. When they're born, I'll rethink my position on Virginia."

"You'd consider moving to Destin? That would be—"

"More than sensible," a familiar voice said from the doorway. Maggie glanced up to find Nora there, but she refused to discuss the issue any further. How could Nora understand the magnitude of such a move for Maggie? Savannah, either? Maggie wanted to keep her options open.

"Peanut butter," Nora said with an interested glance at the half-empty plate. "I shouldn't, but…" She selected a cookie.

"You always did make these best. Not that either of you should be eating them. Maggie, your arteries must be filled with sludge."

Maggie smiled. "They're my arteries. I'll dump whatever I like in them."

Nora chose to ignore that. She bent over to kiss Savannah's brow. "How are you today, angel? Comfortable?"

"Not."

"Then I have just the thing. I stopped on my way home to do some Christmas shopping, and I brought you something." Nora hustled out into the living room and came back with a large package. "This is a pregnancy pillow. It will cradle your abdomen in the coming months, but it should mold itself to you, as you like, even now."

"Thanks, Ma." There were a few moments of opening the package, then shuffling the thing around until Savannah and Nora seemed satisfied. "You, too, Gram. You take good care of me."

"What else would I do?" Maggie had begun spending her days at Savannah's condo, going back to Nora's after she served dinner to her granddaughter and Johnny, and then only to sleep, in part to stay away from Nora, who kept telling her what to do.

For a short time in Nora's hallway on the night of her birthday, Maggie had hoped they might connect again. But the moment had passed, and then Nora had advised her to make herself useful. Maggie had decided to make herself scarce.

This new activity, after years of watching TV all day, should have exhausted her. Instead, Maggie felt energized. Her chest pains hadn't troubled her since she got here, come to think, and even her mind felt sharper.

Of course, she knew she was only kidding herself. She kept too busy to ponder the fact that sooner or later some ailment would kick up, and Nora would pressure her to sell her house, to give up the life she knew in a place where real winter happened every year, to put herself in Nora's hands through the long, humid summers here until Maggie was too sick, too forgetful to care.

But was her fear really about time running out?

Or having to make a change in her life?

"Humph," she murmured then snatched up the now-empty plate. "Better get the kitchen cleaned up before the men get home."

Then Maggie heard Nora say something to Savannah, and Maggie stopped in the doorway, sensing another battle about to begin.

"Feeling cozy now, angel? I wanted to talk to you about the wedding."

"Ma," Savannah began, already sounding stressed.

"Well, of course it had to be postponed once we knew about the triplets. When the babies come, and your figure is back to normal, we'll have the wedding—even if it would have been best beforehand."

"Johnny and I could get married right here. We don't need all those people you insisted upon having. Simple is better. I could still wear my dress. We can let out the seams."

"That is not going to happen."

The front door opened and Johnny walked in. He joined Maggie in the bedroom doorway, where she was shamelessly listening. For once Savannah was taking the brunt of it. Of course Nora saw this as caring for the people she loved.

Johnny addressed Maggie. "What's this? Another skirmish in World War III?" He eyed Nora with a jaundiced expression. "*Whose Wedding is it Anyway?* That's not just a TV show, Nora. This is our life. Savannah's and mine. It's our decision."

"Oh, dear," Savannah murmured.

"No, I need to say this." Giving Maggie a quick hug, he ambled across the bedroom to kiss Savannah. He laid a real lip-lock on her, taking his time, and both Nora and Maggie looked away to give them a moment of privacy. Then he straightened, nailing Nora with another look. "When we marry, how we marry, is up to us. Whether Savannah wears that damn dress altered to the hilt or without a stitch taken, is up to her. Whether my sons and my little girl are born within wedlock is definitely up to me."

"Johnny, be reasonable," Nora said, but she didn't quite meet his eyes.

"I am reasonable. From now on, our marriage plans will be ours alone to decide. Without a middleman, er, woman. I won't spend the rest of our lives humming a tune to the lyrics of 'Mother-In-Law.' Do I make myself clear?"

Nora's mouth tightened. "I was only trying to help."

Having said his piece, he took a few steps to pull her close and Maggie watched, transfixed, surprised. No one had ever handled Nora so well, forcefully but with an underlying affection that couldn't help but take the wind out of her sails. "We love you. But we also love each other and it's our show." He kissed her soundly on each cheek. "Now, what's for dinner?"

Savannah gaped at him from her nest of pillows.

Nora stared after him as Johnny strode from the room, asking over his shoulder if anyone else wanted a drink—except Savannah, who could have water or juice. Men, Maggie thought. You had to love them. They handled things and then were done. Women could obsess over them for weeks. Or, in her case, remain paralyzed by indecision, maybe for forty years.

Maggie laughed at the still-shocked expression on Nora's face. She'd never had this much fun. Certainly not alone.

"He's a keeper," she told Savannah with a triumphant glance at Nora. "I wouldn't dream of going anywhere."

CHAPTER 11

"You'd move here?" Nora had echoed, unable to believe Maggie.

"I didn't say that. But I can hardly fly back to Virginia now while Savannah is carrying triplets. You can see how much she needs me. But her condo is too small. She and Johnny need their privacy. You have plenty of room. We'll just have to work it out."

Nora was still pondering that—and Johnny's unexpected scolding of her—the next morning when she arrived for work.

By the time she opened Geneva's front door and stepped inside to the usual noise, which assaulted her eardrums louder than any rock concert she'd ever attended in her youth, she still hadn't come to terms with the fact that the people she loved might soon shift away from her. What if they stopped needing her altogether? As Starr's son had with her?

One thing seemed clear. There would be no more intervention on her part about the wedding. Her nose was still out of joint. Naturally, Maggie's new cooperation wouldn't last, but for now she ought to enjoy it. But did her mother mean to take over with the babies, too?

Was Nora in danger of ending up alone, just like Maggie? Or Starr?

Wouldn't that be ironic?

Had her mother at last found a way out of her solitude, her role as a helpless widow for the past forty years? And where did that leave Nora? It was she who'd begged Maggie to come to Florida, then suggested—strongly—that Maggie pitch in to help.

It wasn't bad enough that they were the worst two roommates on earth. Forget those few moments in the hallway when Nora had confessed to her first night sweat and Maggie had talked briefly about her own future.

To top things off, Caine hadn't seemed to Nora quite so prickly the last time they met, but as far as she knew he hadn't let her off the hook about the theft of Geneva's vase, either. Her report on Earl Whitehouse had interested him, though. What to make of that?

When Nora strolled into the Whitehouse living room, to her surprise she found Geneva sitting on the sofa beside Heath Moran, both of them looking oblivious to the noise around them. Starr was apparently late. Nora hadn't seen her car in the drive, and if Starr had been here, she would have been pressed against Heath's other side. Geneva looked up.

"Nora, I asked Heath to stop by this morning. It occurred to me last night, after I got back from the gym, that the bonus room on my second floor might make a wonderful home exercise area. It's not that I don't like the club," she said hastily with a reassuring smile for Heath, "but Earl gets so busy, it's not convenient for him to make the trip to Hi-Health after work. He's hardly home as it is. Maybe this will give him a new motivation to spend more time here."

Nora tried to gauge Geneva's statement and her expression, but she was still wearing big dark glasses to cover the last of her bruises. Her face appeared serene and her tone sounded confident, so Nora decided she was more concerned about the home gym for the moment than about Earl's continuing neglect.

"An exercise room is a great idea," Nora said, avoiding Heath's gaze. "Have you looked at the space yet?" She started toward the stairs.

"Done," Geneva said, halting Nora's progress. "Next, Heath

will bring me—us, I mean—some catalogs about equipment. We're thinking Cybex."

Heath nodded. "You can't go wrong. It's high quality and adjustable, suited for women as well as men. It'll last you for the rest of your life. Looks good, too." He rose to his feet. "I've got a couple of fitness magazines in the car. They may give you some ideas." On his way past, he paused. "Nora, can you lend a hand?"

How heavy could they be?

Heath tilted his head toward the front door. "Please," he added.

Outside, Nora let out a sigh as he rummaged through his car trunk for the men's health magazines. He came up with a crumpled pair of them, dog-eared at the corners, their covers showing men with rippling six-pack abs—like Heath's—and muscular arms. Their skin gleamed, as if they were sweating.

"Oil," he said, following her gaze. "They use it for competitions to highlight their muscle definition."

"I see."

"No, Nora. You don't." Heath ran a hand through his hair. "Look, I've almost called you a dozen times since your party. The one time I did, I apologized about Starr Mulligan, which didn't seem to do any good. I don't know what else to say— except you were right."

Nora gazed at the overlapped magazines in his hand. At the men on the front. None of them measured up to Heath. "Right about what?"

"I could have said no. She was trying to flirt with me, I knew that. In fact," he went on, his eyes troubled, his expression ashamed, "I'm not proud of this, but I wanted to make you jealous. It was mean-spirited of me. I'm not normally like that, but I couldn't seem to help myself." He gave her the hint of a smile, one corner of his mouth crooked up in a boyishly appealing way. "Did it work?"

"Oh, Heath. You are the most charming man." He ran rings

around Caine in that department. He was better looking, too. If only she felt that necessary spark. "You know how I feel. And your gift was a lovely idea, but I can't go with you to the Keys. This—" she circled a hand in the air "—wouldn't be the best thing for either of us."

His expression fell. "You think Starr would be? For me?"

"*No.*" The single word came out sharply. "That is, a relationship on the rebound is never wise." Nora should know. Heath was her rebound from Wilson, though it had taken her twenty years to make the plunge. And a fine swim in Gulf-warm waters it had been. Still, she and Heath were over. She couldn't let him continue to hope otherwise. "I—I've never been a heartbreaker before. I don't know how."

He turned slightly away, slapping the rolled magazines against his muscular thigh. "Nora, you broke my heart the instant I laid eyes on you."

Nora still felt shaken by her conversation with Heath. But by five o'clock she was also worried about Starr, who had not shown up for work. After the last tradesman had left for the day, Nora and Geneva decided to check on her. Starr's excuse earlier had seemed vague, and Geneva informed Nora that Starr's voice on the phone had sounded weak. A woman living alone, as Nora well knew from Maggie, if not herself, could be a tragedy waiting to happen.

If Starr had fallen, she might be lying there on the floor, helpless. Nora and Geneva picked up Chinese takeout and a bottle of decent wine and then drove to Starr's condominium, not far from Johnny and Savannah's high-rise building along the shore.

Nora had never been there before. She didn't know what to expect.

On her way with Geneva to the condo, Nora had stopped at home to let Daisy out after her day alone then to feed her.

The dog had looked so forlorn at being left alone again, Nora didn't have the heart not to take her with them. If Starr disliked animals, Nora could leave the dog outside for a little while—just until she assured herself that Starr was fine.

When Starr opened the door, Nora took a sharp breath.

Starr's obvious surprise at seeing the two women and a dog on her doorstep didn't make her look any less ghastly. Her skin had the unhealthy hue of a green tomato, and her brilliant amethyst eyes looked sunken in their sockets. Wearing only a lavender silk wrapper that should have enhanced their color, and in bare feet, she held a hand to her lower abdomen.

Nora had never seen her in less than full battle makeup. For a moment, she couldn't move.

Starr looked as if she'd taken a punch herself, and for one instant Nora remembered Geneva opening the door to reveal her bruises. She didn't wait for an invitation.

Geneva pushed inside right behind Nora. "Oh, you poor thing. We were right to feel worried. We've brought dinner— some egg drop soup as well."

Starr didn't say a word about Daisy, whose tail was waving hard enough to create a breeze. She led the way into her living room, a tasteful yet eclectic array of furniture with subtle pastel cushions and some truly beautiful framed, impressionistic artwork that shouldn't have surprised Nora but did. The lush Aubusson rug on the floor was divine, she had to admit.

"I'm not really hungry," Starr told them.

"Stomach flu?" Geneva edged back toward the door. "We'll leave you alone, then. Just eat when you can. Drink lots of fluids. My immune system is a bit compromised after my surgery. I wouldn't want to catch—"

"I'm not contagious, Geneva." Starr sank onto a wide chair upholstered in a dramatic leopard-skin print, the one eye-popping touch in the elegant room. "I'm having my...well, you know. It's a curse, as they say."

Nora moved into action. So that was it. "Here, Geneva. Take this bag into the kitchen. Dish up the food. And bring us some glasses. Do you have a corkscrew?" she asked Starr who, in a weak voice, said it was in the drawer of her center island. "You need drugs. I have Tylenol and Aleve, name your poison. Daisy, sweetheart, lie down. You don't mind the dog?" she asked Starr. "Daisy is the absolute best at giving comfort when a woman feels low. She'll give you a nice doggy hug."

"I'm too far gone to care. Do as you like," Starr murmured, but she seemed touched by their concern. Her employer and her archrival, but obviously she needed someone to care for her and Nora was good at that.

She adopted the no-nonsense tone she used with Savannah. "We've spent weeks together on Geneva's house. I'll make sure you survive until we finish." Nora sat on the footstool near her chair, stroking Starr's clammy hands. "Do you always feel this bad?"

Starr shook her head. "No, but lately I'm not myself."

Daisy washed her other hand with her floppy pink tongue while Nora waited for Starr's explanation. In the kitchen she heard Geneva banging about, pulling down plates, searching through the drawers for the corkscrew and some silverware. In the cool air, a drift of White Shoulders perfume filled Nora's nostrils. Starr lay back in the chair, eyes closed.

"One month I'm normal, the next I'm like this." She gestured toward her stomach. "I don't know what's wrong with me. I skipped several cycles completely."

Nora studied her. "Has it occurred to you we may be in the same state?"

"No." Starr put a hand to her forehead. "I'm younger."

"Mark Fingerhut told me that perimenopause can begin at any time, even as early as the late thirties."

Starr groaned. "You're kidding. Really, Nora…"

"I think you should see him."

Geneva returned from the kitchen carrying a tray and wearing a big smile. She'd obviously overheard. "I'm sorry. This isn't fun for you, Starr. I know. But Nora refers everyone to Mark Fingerhut, including me. He should pay her commission, but he's really a great guy. I think Nora is right. You should make an appointment."

"You can't lie around looking like Violetta in *La Traviata* or Mimi in *La Bohème* on her deathbed," Nora agreed. "If nothing else, think of our bonuses."

"I'm not an opera lover."

Nora popped out two pills from a plastic bottle, poured Starr a hefty glass of wine, and said, "Drink. You'll feel better. If you like, I can call Mark in the morning for you."

Geneva backed her up. "He'll take equally good care of you."

"I am not going through The Change," Starr insisted.

Which cracked Nora up. "Oh, *darling*. It's not a choice, believe me." But, wait. She couldn't help smiling like Geneva. No wonder Starr had recognized Nora's first hot flash so quickly.

"I haven't had more than one…maybe two," Starr said.

Nora grinned. The denial echoed her own at first.

Starr wasn't thrilled with Nora's advice, but she did agree to call Mark herself, as if she didn't want Nora involved. There would be no harm in making sure that her body was in working order, Starr said. After that, it didn't take long for the analgesics to take effect, aided by the wine, and soon she was able to enjoy her meal with Geneva and Nora. Oh, and Daisy, too.

Nora fed the dog sweet and sour chicken, then a helping of her favorite crab Rangoon, and pretty soon Daisy was smiling, too.

It was the best time Nora had had in months.

Her whole family seemed to be mad at her half the time. She'd wounded Heath but didn't know how to mend the damage. She worried endlessly about Savannah, worse than Johnny did. She didn't often try to help Browning, who had always insisted on making his own way, and of course there was Maggie. Her suddenly independent mother. And then, there was Caine.

Tonight she forgot all that. She shared dinner, wine and laughter with…well, she couldn't call Starr a friend and Geneva paid her salary, but they were all women. Together.

"Here's to us." Nora made a toast. Their glasses clinked.

She had helped Starr, at least.

She was having fun.

"Here's to me," she murmured.

After dinner, they all got a little silly, Nora had to admit. Nora went out to her car and came back with one of her gifts for Savannah: a set of rubber duckies for the bathtub, along with a yellow towel and washcloth, that made everyone smile. When Daisy needed to go out, she suggested a walk along the beach after they had walked the dog. The night was cool but balmy, and a million stars twinkled in the black velvet sky.

At the edge of the sand, Nora stopped to remove her shoes. So did Starr and Geneva. Barefoot, they stepped onto the still-warm footing underneath. There was nowhere on earth that had a better beach. The Gulf Coast sand was very fine, very white, and had the consistency of powdered sugar. It was the result, Nora had once heard, of granite rock that tumbled downriver from somewhere she couldn't remember being pulverized on its way to the sea, into the world-renowned color and texture that she had never seen equaled. Nora always wanted to come back to the Emerald Coast.

In the dark she watched Daisy streak along the beach parallel to the froth of dainty whitecaps close to shore. The dog seemed happy to chase the waves when they washed onto the hard-packed sand in front of her, and before Nora could stop her, Daisy was soaking wet. In front of the three women, Daisy shook herself until they shrieked then the dog shimmied back into the shallow water.

Feeling utterly peaceful, Nora walked between Starr and Geneva. Starr was feeling much better, she could tell, but Nora wasn't as sure about Geneva. Neither the woman's startling beauty, nor the wealth her husband had heaped upon her seemed to make her happy.

"Geneva, tell us about your pageant days," Nora coaxed.

The darkness seemed to lend Geneva an unexpected air of confidence. She smiled, showing perfect white teeth, before she said, "You really want to know?"

"Of course we do," Starr chimed in. "Did you have a talent?"

Geneva grimaced. "In my teen years, I played the piano. In the earlier days I danced and sang."

"What did you sing?" Nora asked.

Geneva's smile widened. "'Tomorrow,' or whatever it's called. You know, that song from the Broadway show *Annie*. I did a soft-shoe number, too."

"Show us."

"Oh, no, really, I..." But Starr joined in the request.

Looking embarrassed at first, Geneva did a little dance on the damp sand, her shapely legs flashing in the moonlight, her movements becoming more spirited as Nora and Starr offered their encouragement and Daisy raced back from examining some seashell that had washed in to yip and bark around Geneva as if she were singing, too. Geneva didn't have a bad voice.

"Did you like the pageant thing?" Nora asked when their applause had finished. The air smelled of seaweed, and the lingering scent of diesel fuel from a passing boat offshore. "It sounds like kind of a sad life—like JonBenet Ramsey."

"I didn't mind it," Geneva said, "until I was older. Then I wanted to be with my friends on weekends, not at some junior miss event in Atlantic City." She paused. "The parents liked it, though. Some of them."

"Yours?" Starr asked.

Geneva shrugged. "My mother, mostly. She was an attractive woman, and I think she felt she'd given up her own future to marry my dad."

Nora wondered if that applied to Geneva, as well, with Earl, but she didn't pursue the issue. As if inspired, Geneva launched into another, more upbeat song complete with a dance routine that would have made Al Jolson envious many years ago, and soon they were all laughing, clapping for her again.

This time when she finished, she made a little bow and said, breathless, "Gee, I thought I'd forgotten that. Or wanted to. I had a pretty strict upbringing, really." Her tone grew wistful. "While my friends were having fun, I was forbidden to drink soda or eat candy. Mom was preparing me for a film career in Hollywood, and I needed these perfect teeth for close-ups. What about you, Nora?" Geneva asked.

"I needed braces."

Grinning, Nora watched Daisy streak off down the beach, leaping and jumping and generally enjoying herself, before she finally answered, knowing the flip words weren't what Geneva needed.

"I didn't have an early career. I grew up seeing to Maggie's welfare after my father died. I married Wilson when I was barely twenty. We had ten mostly good years together before we divorced and I became a single mother with two kids to raise. I still miss what we had at first. But I didn't make something of my life," she said, "other than the traditional roles until I was thirtysomething. After we separated, I went back to school, completed my interior design training, and worked with a local hotshot. About fifteen years ago, I started Nine Lives."

Starr rolled her eyes. "And now he's getting married for the fourth time."

"Fifth, counting me," Nora said. "I just RSVP'd and said no to his wedding invitation."

"As you should," Geneva said.

Then Starr offered her own background. "I never wanted to be anything except a designer. I had no plans to marry or have children. Then I met my ex, and everything clicked—for a while—before I found myself on the street again with no support check and a five-year-old boy to raise." She glanced at Nora in the dark. "I guess I'm not the most maternal person."

"Maybe you haven't given it your best try," Nora murmured.

Then, before she could say more, they were comparing men.

"It's a good thing we don't have kids. Earl leaves his dirty socks on our bedroom carpet," Geneva confessed. "He may be a dynamo in real estate development, but he really needs a maid."

"Don't they all?" Starr added her own two cents. "Mine never put a plate in the dishwasher. I don't imagine his son does, either. I've heard my daughter-in-law complain."

"You should have taught him," Nora said. "Wilson is clueless around the house to this day, and Browning isn't the most adult person in the world, but he learned to do his laundry before he was twelve. I'm still hoping that will clinch the deal for him with some delightful young woman. But I'm not holding my breath. Browning is still the Gulf Coast's most eligible—and active—bachelor."

"Hmm," Starr said, her eyes on Daisy, who was barreling back down the beach toward them, her doggy tongue lolling from her mouth, her ears flying in the soft night breeze. "I guess you're still the better mother, then," she said, as if Nora had been trying to compete with her again.

"Girls, please." Geneva lifted her face to the stars. "I can't say I've had a better time since I married Earl. Why is that, do you think?"

"Women understand each other," Nora said. "Other than that, I don't think we should examine the issue too deeply."

Because the conversation suddenly seemed too serious, they searched for something else to do. Before Nora knew it,

Geneva had started to hum another tune, something she and Starr recognized. And with the moon high overhead, the glint of silvery light on the water and a million stars in the sky, they began to dance. Heads thrown back, shoulders squared, hair flying, they took turns singing tunes from the past, the newer songs each had found meaning in, a selection of timeless classics. "Tomorrow," and then "Yesterday" and Helen Reddy's "I Am Woman." Distracted from her tide pool wanderings, Daisy yowled her version of the half-forgotten lyrics, too. It was like a ritualistic, primitive happening, and with the dog wriggling between them, they finished with their arms around each other, feeling a connection they never had before.

They returned to Starr's condo, still laughing and talking, sharing the small tidbits of their lives—and the bigger, more important things—until at last Geneva and Nora decided they should leave.

With warm hugs all around, they left Starr grinning after them from her doorway, and with a quick pat on Daisy's head, Nora loaded her into the Volvo.

"If only dogs could talk," she said.

With a backward wave for Nora, Geneva went up her front walk, feeling a little tipsy. Ordinarily she didn't drink much, and neither did Nora or Starr, she assumed. But Starr had really tied one on tonight. When they returned to her condo, she had offered another round of the wine left over from dinner. As their designated driver, Nora had cut herself off earlier, after one glass, for which Geneva felt grateful. Sometimes Earl drank too much when they were out, and she always feared they wouldn't reach home alive.

Geneva passed the spot on the driveway where Heath Moran had stood behind his car that afternoon with Nora. Their silent conversation from Geneva's vantage point behind the front window had appeared to be less than romantic. Heath even looked a little sad, though he'd seemed all right later.

Geneva and Heath had spent most of the day together poring over the magazines he'd found, measuring the bonus room again for the best arrangement, then using Earl's computer in his den to study some of the online manufacturers' sites. At first she'd had trouble accessing Earl's programs, but Heath had figured out Earl's password. Pleased with the progress she and Heath had made, Geneva turned to watch Nora drive away.

It had been the right decision to hire her and Starr to redo the house. She'd had her doubts at first, but now the project seemed as much for Geneva herself as for the benefit of her marriage to Earl.

She opened her front door and let herself into the darkened house. God, tonight had been fun, the most she'd enjoyed herself in a long time. She'd never imagined the three of them could laugh so much, and as with any group of women, some of that laughter had been at the expense of the men in their lives, past or present. Including Earl.

Geneva stopped to inspect her face in the hall mirror.

Her bruises had mostly faded. Nora and Starr had said she looked wonderful tonight, but the magic words made her wonder what they'd thought of her before. Except for a few smears of lingering yellow bruise across her cheekbones, she felt pleased with the effect. And those she could hide with a cover stick or what, during a lengthy discussion of makeup, Nora had termed "Spackle."

The question remained: would the changes please Earl?

Oddly, Geneva discovered that the answer didn't seem as important as it might have only a short time ago. Even the curt message from Earl that she discovered on their answering machine—"I won't be home overnight. Taking the company plane to Boston for an early meeting tomorrow"—didn't alter her mood now.

After tonight, she was feeling good. Her thrice weekly workouts at Heath's club were toning her body, firming her legs and lifting her breasts. She looked sleeker, more svelte, almost as good as she had when she met Earl. Soon she'd be ready to shop in earnest. A new wardrobe, new makeup, new jewelry and, of course, new shoes. Lots of shoes.

What made a girl feel better about herself than that?

Yes, she'd definitely done the right thing.

With a little smile she turned away from the mirror. And let out a startled cry that echoed in the stillness of the dark foyer.

To her horror Geneva ran smack into someone standing in the hall. "You scared me!" Shocked, Geneva raised a hand to her chest. "What are you doing here?"

In the darkness she couldn't see the face, but the taller figure, the taut line of the mouth, the glitter of purpose in those eyes took her breath away. Geneva had been adored for most of her life, if only for her beauty. Her looks had always paved her way, even covered the path with gold. She'd become Earl's beloved trophy wife, although she wasn't as sure of him these days. She wasn't used to such open hostility.

Everything happened too fast. Within minutes, her worst fears were realized.

The tone of voice, the truth, soon dulled her mind. She couldn't take in the words, yet she understood their message. That led to a brief scuffle before Geneva's quick, panicked step away from the danger she sensed. She heard outrage and then screams, some of them her own as she tried to defend herself. Then, just as she turned her back to run, she caught the peripheral image of a raised object and, before she could move, felt the heavy weight crash into her skull.

The hallway, the house, the world went instantly black.

The blow didn't hurt.

Geneva felt nothing.

* * *

Nora's first call the next morning on her way to work was to Mark Fingerhut. If she left the appointment to Starr, Nora had decided, she might never make one. As soon as Starr felt human again, she'd conveniently forget the exam, or so Nora assumed.

When she flipped her cell closed, she was smiling. Of course Mark would see Starr. Nora didn't feel any satisfaction that Starr was apparently facing the same fate—that is, natural life event—that Nora was, but it amused her all the same. It almost seemed like poetic justice.

That is, until Nora remembered seeing Starr's coal-dark hair against her pasty-white face, the obvious pain on her features. If she and Geneva hadn't arrived like the Mounties to her rescue, Starr would probably have suffered in solitude until dawn. Besides, the night had proved to be delightful, and their dancing with abandon on the beach in the moonlight remained in her mind. They should do it more often.

The thought surprised her, but Nora couldn't wait to begin work today. Their unlikely trio had given her a real boost, the first that was entirely for Nora in some time. She'd always been a single mother, a breadwinner, the one who fixed everything. Maybe she needed more time, more fun, for herself. She marched up to the double front doors and twisted one brass handle, but it didn't give.

Locked?

Geneva was an early riser. Sometimes she went to the gym before Nora arrived, although she was usually back by now. Sometimes she jogged around the pricey subdivision of Royal Palms, joining a neighbor here, an old friend there, on her run. In either case, she left the door open for Nora.

She rang the bell. For no apparent reason, a slight prickle of alarm ran up her spine and raised the fine hairs on her neck. She looked around. Geneva's Mercedes sat in its usual spot, but none of the workmen's trucks were parked in the driveway or along the edges of the yard. She didn't expect Starr this soon—they'd told her to sleep late this morning—but the tile workers were supposed to begin by eight o'clock. It was almost nine now.

The unusual silence in place of the usual noise brought an attempt at a frown. With the schedule, and Geneva's promised bonus, in mind, Nora dialed a number.

"We showed up," the contractor protested. "Nobody answered. Me and the guys are at another job. We'll see you tomorrow."

"I'm here now, Eddie. You can't come back today?"

"Nope. We're already set up here. My clock's tickin' too, Nora." To the clap of a tile cutter in the background and his men's voices, he disconnected the call.

Nora slapped her phone shut. She couldn't afford a lost day. And how had she thought they'd get into the house before Geneva returned? Or was she really gone? Nora walked around to the rear door but found it locked, too. There was no note on the door. At the front again, she pressed her face to the side panels, but their frosted glass revealed nothing inside.

Nora stepped back.

They'd all been out late last night. Maybe Geneva had simply overslept and didn't hear the workmen, or Nora, at the door.

Picking up a handful of pebbles, she flung them at the upper-story window that she knew to be part of Geneva's bedroom suite. She waited a moment, but no face appeared at the glass. What if, like Starr, Geneva was sick? The rich crab Rangoon hadn't sat too well with Daisy.

Finally, in desperation Nora called Starr.

"'Lo?" Starr sounded groggy.

"I'm sorry I woke you. It's Nora."

"For heaven's sake, don't you ever stop pestering people? I said I'll be there at noon." She was about to hang up, Nora could tell, their previous night's camaraderie forgotten, when Nora said, "Wait! I'm here at the house. I can't rouse Geneva.

No one else is here. Eddie said they tried to get in earlier but got no answer, either. And the door is locked."

Starr thought for a moment. "Got a credit card?"

"Yes, but—"

"Then you have two choices. Use it. Or call the cops."

Nora remembered her recent talk with Caine, then her unauthorized visit to the Whitehouse home and the glare of floodlights when Earl had opened the back door. She didn't care to revisit the situation, but this was different.

"Maybe I should call her husband."

Nora dialed his office, but his secretary informed her that Mr. Whitehouse was out of town. Nora's heart thumped. If anything was wrong, just as she'd found last night with Starr, Geneva would be alone.

Nora decided to use the credit card.

Feeling like the felon Caine must think she was, Nora slipped into the house. Sunlight flooded the entryway but didn't cheer her. There were always half a dozen people here, but now the place felt abandoned, even creepy. Taking a deep breath, she walked toward the main hall, her Ferragamos clicking on the dark walnut floor. The sound echoed, magnified by the stillness.

"Geneva?" she called softly.

To Nora's dismay, she heard a low moan.

She clattered a few more steps—and saw Geneva lying on the floor. In a pool of red.

"Oh, my god! Geneva! What happened?"

Geneva didn't move. Nora could barely see the rise and fall of her chest, and her blond hair splayed out across the red all around her, making Nora's breath catch. Her stomach rolled. Her mind went blank.

She, who couldn't resist the urge to help anyone, felt suddenly frozen, just as she had when Savannah fainted. Apparently Nora wasn't always the one who could help others.

Then Geneva groaned again. And Nora came out of her trance. She knelt to feel for Geneva's pulse, finding it weak but steady. Thank God. Geneva didn't open her eyes.

"Earl..." was all she said.

CHAPTER 12

"It wasn't Earl who did this," Geneva kept saying.

Nora and Starr couldn't believe her.

"Typical," Nora muttered, becoming more frustrated by the minute. "Women who are abused often, ironically, defend the very men who abused them. I read that once in Oprah's magazine." She lowered her voice so Geneva wouldn't hear the rest. "I *knew* Earl Whitehouse was up to no good."

"Maybe she's afraid he'll come after her again."

Starr and Nora whispered between themselves, casting anxious looks at Geneva. Nora hadn't moved her from her fallen position on the marble floor of the hall until Starr arrived. Nora knew she should have called an ambulance, but Geneva had begged her not to. Nora's then-frantic call to Starr had seemed the automatic next step after their previous evening together. Nora needed assistance. Like her, Starr had been concerned that Geneva might have a neck problem and they shouldn't move her at all. It was Geneva who finally struggled into a sitting position, then repeated her plea not to call an ambulance or the police. Her eyes were still filled with unshed tears.

"Earl would never hurt me."

Nora made an exasperated sound. "Then who would, Geneva? Who else could have entered your house last night?"

"Earl said he was flying to Boston," she insisted. "He was already gone."

"*If* he was telling the truth. Maybe that trip was his way of setting up a convenient alibi." Nora, who didn't have one for the night of the burglary here, would highly recommend it. The notion made her consider another possibility. Could this attack be part of another burglary attempt?

"I'm telling you," Geneva said weakly, "it wasn't Earl. We may have our problems, but I know my husband." She hesitated, her gaze fuzzy and unfocused. "I don't know who hit me, though. I can't seem to remember…anything."

Nora laid a freshly dampened cloth over Geneva's forehead. She felt as if she were fussing over Savannah or Browning with some childhood fever, but Geneva's situation was far worse. If she couldn't remember, she couldn't be sure about Earl. And Geneva was in no shape to determine what might be missing, like the crystal vase, from the house. "Well, whoever did this will be punished. We'll see to that."

"I really think we should call 911," Starr said again. "Geneva can't remember who hit her, whether it was Earl or someone else. She needs a doctor. Maybe she has amnesia."

Nora agreed, but Geneva stiffened. She was resting now after the two women had wrestled her into a living room chair, her feet up on its matching hassock, the cool cloth on her head—a thick, folded Egyptian cotton terry cloth towel, no less. The bleeding had almost stopped, but Nora worried that her worst injuries couldn't be seen. Geneva's scalp was becoming more contused by the second. What if her brain swelled, too? Starr was right. The need for medical help came first. They could argue about Earl later.

Nora started for the phone beside Geneva on the end table. Before she picked it up, Geneva's weak hand covered her wrist.

"Please, Nora. Don't. I'll be fine."

Nora gaped at her. She could sense Starr's matching expression. "Fine? Someone—" she didn't mention Earl this time "—tried to bash your head in. How could you be fine?"

Geneva made another attempt. "Scalp wounds always bleed like mad. It must look worse than it is. It doesn't even hurt…that much."

"Don't be ridiculous." Nora had seen her wince. "You're probably in shock." But when she tried to withdraw her hand from Geneva's tenuous grasp, Geneva tried to tighten her grip. The attempt failed and her hand fluttered back to her lap. Her eyes kept opening, then closing, each effort more difficult than the last.

"I don't want my own doctor," she said, a half-hearted surrender. "He'd only tell Earl."

Good point, Nora thought. "Then I'll phone Mark." His name flashed into her mind as quickly as Starr's had. He would be discreet, if that was what Geneva wanted most. At least he could tell them whether she needed to get to a hospital.

Geneva groaned at the suggestion but didn't protest again. By now, Nora imagined, the first shock was wearing off, as it was for Nora and Starr. While they waited for Mark, she chattered to Geneva, trying to maintain her conscious state. She wasn't sure if Geneva heard her.

"What happened here?" was the first thing Mark said. In the hall, he gazed in shock at the pool of red on the floor. Then he hurried into the living room to seek out his patient.

Nora babbled an edited version of the scene she'd found.

"An unknown assailant knocked her cold? With what?" Mark asked, sounding shaken. Nora assumed he had little experience with blunt force trauma in his practice. A screaming woman in labor was more his territory. "This was quite a blow, Geneva." He flashed his little penlight in each of her eyes, gauging their response. "A baseball bat?"

"I didn't see what it was," she murmured, flinching as he gently probed her skull and the growing contusion. "I guess I was struck from behind."

While he completed his examination Nora and Starr faded into the background and looked for an obvious weapon, but they found nothing. The occasional groan or moan from Geneva turned Nora's stomach. She supposed it didn't do much for Starr, either. Her voice sounded subdued even when she said under her breath, "Cute. Very cute."

In the living room doorway, Nora turned to her.

"Dr. Fingerhut," Starr said. "Is he married?"

Nora glanced at Mark. She'd never thought of him as marriage material from a personal standpoint, but he was a reasonably attractive man. Compact, square, and nicely built if not overly muscular. And at close to forty, he still had his hair. "I made you an appointment," she finally said. "You can ask him yourself." Nora sent her a more pointed look meant to tease. "Really, Mulligan. I wonder about you. Is it possible you invented a female problem last night just so you could meet men?" Her birthday party was still fresh in her mind, yet now Nora almost welcomed the distraction. "I had no idea I was to become your personal little black book."

Starr only smiled. "You're still peeved about Heath."

"I was never peeved, I—" She didn't finish. The latest object of Starr's affection walked toward them, leaving Geneva alone in the living room.

Mark frowned. "Nora, Ms. . . . ?"

"Mulligan. Starr Mulligan."

His gaze slid over her. "Ah, yes. So we meet. . .sooner, rather than later."

Nora stepped between them. "How is she, Mark?"

"I don't know. We haven't— Oh, you mean Geneva." His lips twitched. He must know exactly what they'd been talking about. Him. Then he sobered. "I don't like the look of that scalp wound. She may need some stitches to stop the bleeding entirely. Her pupils are equal and reactive, but she may have a slight concussion. Amazing if it's not worse than minor."

"She should have an ambulance."

"That would be my recommendation, but I met a lot of resistance when I suggested it. Any idea why she's so reluctant to get checked out in a more suitable environment? That's for her own safety."

"We think she's afraid," Nora said.

His frown deepened. "Domestic abuse? She didn't indicate—"

"No," Starr said, "she won't. She doesn't 'remember.'"

Mark rubbed his neck. "I told her the hospital was her best bet. Frankly, I'm not eager to be held responsible if something goes sour. I have enough trouble in my practice, never mind poaching on some neurologist's gig." He paused. "Especially since I'll be in court next week." He'd mentioned a lawsuit before. "That trusted patient I told you about decided to stab me in the back."

"Mark, how awful. I'm sorry it came to that." Nora laid a hand on his arm as they walked to the door. "I'm being audited by the IRS myself," she added as if their differing troubles provided common ground.

Starr moved closer. She'd been ignored long enough. She gazed up at Mark. "If Geneva won't go to a hospital, then what can we do?"

"She can't stay here alone," Nora said, elbowing Starr back a few inches. "I'd take her home with me, but Maggie's staying in my spare room."

Starr didn't have a guest room, but she was still studying Mark. He fidgeted by the front door, obviously ready to leave.

"I'd put Geneva up for the night on my den sofa," Starr finally offered. "But you know, Nora, it would be simple for a certain someone to find her at my place, or yours. We both work for Geneva, after all."

She had a point. If Earl Whitehouse had been Geneva's attacker, and she had suppressed the memory of the horrible assault in order to keep her sanity, they needed a different choice. Nora grabbed her cell phone.

"Let me see what I can do."

* * *

"We didn't clean up the blood."

Starr's comment brought Nora's head up from her dazed contemplation of her lap. Hours later, the sight of Geneva's front hall, then the gash on her head, still had her hands shaking and her thoughts scattered. It wasn't every day, thank goodness, that she saw such a grisly scene.

Geneva was fast asleep in the master bedroom of Johnny's second place, a beach house outside of Destin, not far from Leonard Hackett's home in Earl Whitehouse's newest subdivision at Impressions. But they could have been on the moon for all anyone except Johnny and Savannah knew. Well, and Maggie, who had also been there when Nora called to ask if she could borrow the house key for a friend. No one would trace them here. For tonight, Geneva was safe. Nora kept telling herself that.

"We don't want to clean up," she said at last, although the memory of Geneva's front hall was not a pleasant one. "Earl couldn't know we'd find her."

"You mean *you* found her." Starr gazed at her blankly. Maybe she felt as upset as Nora.

"If it was Earl Whitehouse, then let him squirm. Let him walk back into *that house* tomorrow where he supposedly loved Geneva—where he just tried to *kill* her—and find everything as he left it. Let him wonder where Geneva went."

"And if it wasn't Earl?" Starr asked.

"If not, then he'll be shocked. In either case, we'll be there to gauge his reaction. If Earl didn't do it," Nora added, "the person who did might come back hoping to finish the job. Any burglar that vicious wouldn't want to leave a witness."

"Still…" Starr hesitated. "If it wasn't him," she went on, her bare feet curled beneath her on Johnny's white leather sofa, "the first thing Earl will do is call Caine."

"Then we'll know Earl was innocent." At least that would seem more likely.

But Starr wasn't the only one who had objected to Nora's theory. Savannah hadn't been thrilled either to hide a fugitive.

"Ma, let the police handle it. A crime was committed."

"Nora," Johnny had said, "you're playing with fire, intervening again in Geneva Whitehouse's relationship instead of ours this time. Mark was right. She belongs in the hospital."

"Or you could wind up in prison," Maggie put in.

Nora's temper had snapped. "For what?"

"Kidnapping," they all said at once.

She'd bitten back another reply. "May I have the key or not?"

Nora did have a well-developed conscience. She wouldn't jeopardize Geneva's safety or her health. On their way to the beach, at Nora's urging Geneva had agreed to stop at a twenty-four-hour emergency clinic where another doctor had found no damage to her brain other than the slight concussion Mark had suspected. So here they were, with Geneva asleep except for the regular times when Starr or Nora woke her to make sure she hadn't slipped into a coma.

"We'll have to cancel the tile men again for tomorrow," Nora said. "We can't have them showing up before Earl Whitehouse."

Earlier, after they'd settled Geneva in Johnny's wide bed on clean sheets and urged her to drink some clear broth, Nora had phoned a dozen hotels in Boston until finally she located the one where Earl had stayed last night. Still, he could have bashed Geneva beforehand, flown in later, and managed to make his early appointment in Boston. Private jets could zip you here and there without the inconvenience of security or flight delays. It didn't take that long to get from Florida to Massachusetts.

Had he and Geneva quarreled last night after Nora dropped her off? And did Geneva now want to forget the unhappy event that had led to his losing control and then hitting her hard with some heavy object? All Nora and Starr could do was speculate, but it was, in Nora's view, an educated guess.

"Tomorrow we'll take the next step."

* * *

To Nora's relief, Geneva had stayed safe at the beach house all night. This morning, Geneva had awakened looking somewhat better, although she still didn't remember what had happened. Until she did, and Earl Whitehouse was either arrested or cleared of what appeared to be attempted murder, she wasn't going home if Nora had any say in the matter.

The tile workers weren't happy about a second day without any progress on the Whitehouse master bathroom, but Nora explained, "It can't be helped, Eddie. Mrs. Whitehouse is indisposed. She couldn't bear the noise today." She scrambled for a plausible explanation. "Migraine, you know."

Eddie grumbled. "I can't afford lost pay. You'll find the hours on my bill."

"We can talk about that later."

With an aggrieved sigh she hung up, in danger of getting a headache herself. It was late-afternoon before she and Starr drove to the Whitehouse home, leaving Geneva in Maggie's care—and Daisy's. She wasn't an effective protector but Earl, or whoever, didn't know that. After last night's initial protest, to Nora's surprise Savannah had insisted she'd be fine on her own for a few hours. Even Maggie's voice had held a certain excitement when she agreed to help, as if she vicariously enjoyed being part of the project to save Geneva.

The first thing Nora saw when she opened the door was the now-dried pool on the hall floor. Her stomach lurched.

"Poor Geneva," Starr said. "She really could have been killed."

"Let's go upstairs." Nora skirted the scene to head for the second story and Geneva's bedroom suite. She would need fresh clothing, some of her favorite toiletries, and makeup, of course. What woman could be without her cosmetics? Even a still-beautiful woman like Geneva needed a certain amount of artifice to feel on top of her game. "Find a suitcase, a tote bag, shopping bag, something to carry this," she said to Starr. "I'll pick out a few tops and pants."

"Maybe her workout stuff, too. Once she feels better, it might be therapeutic for her to go with us to the club."

Nora had never seen so many gorgeous clothes. She ran her hand over sumptuous silks and soft-as-down cashmeres. Then a wave of unexpected sorrow washed through her. Such expensive things were just that, she knew: things. As Nora had seen after Geneva's Botox injections, they didn't guarantee happiness.

Wilson had also lavished Nora with the very best during their marriage, even when he couldn't afford it. In a way, Earl Whitehouse reminded her of Wilson, married three times to ever-younger women and now working on his fourth since Nora. Had Earl caused Geneva the ultimate *un*happiness as well? Was she right, after all, that he'd been cheating on her? And maybe that was why they'd quarreled?

Nora turned away from the immense wall of closets, a bundle of clothes in her arms. And heard the downstairs door open.

Stark fear shot across Starr's face. Someone was in the house. Nora imagined her expression must look the same. They were trapped on the second floor, and only last night someone—someone with a terrible rage—had come after Geneva in this same house.

"What do we do?"

"Who do you think it could be?"

They both spoke at once. Earl Whitehouse was the logical person, and they'd planned to wait for him. But it was only four o'clock, hours before Nora expected him to return. Still, he had a key to the house. They heard heavy male footsteps in the foyer, then in the hall. The footsteps stopped, and Nora imagined she heard a sharply indrawn breath, though she must have been too far away to actually hear the sound.

"It's him. I know it," Starr whispered.

Suddenly Nora had second thoughts. She looked wildly

around for some means of escape. But there was no outside door to a balcony or deck in Geneva's master suite, and the windows in the garden-style bathroom were sealed shut.

Footsteps sounded again, coming up the stairs.

Clump, clump, clump. Closer, closer.

Nora's memory kicked in, and all at once she was cornered in the bedroom of the model unit at Impressions with Earl Whitehouse crowding her, reaching for her. She was still holding Geneva's clothes when Earl appeared in the doorway. Busted.

"Change of career?" he asked, barely glancing at Starr. "Or more of the same? You make a very bad cat burglar, Nora. *Where's my wife?*"

Earl Whitehouse was not in a good mood.

In fact, to Nora's surprise, his scowl at Nora, then at Starr, couldn't hide the ashen pallor of his face. His hands were trembling. This wasn't quite the reaction Nora had expected but...

"Geneva is safe. No thanks to you," she said.

He blinked. "What are you talking about? I've been in Boston. What's all that...*stuff* downstairs? And why are you holding Geneva's clothes?"

Nora dropped them on the floor, but she wasn't about to tell him where Geneva was, even if he did appear about to lose his lunch from anxiety. She'd been accused of theft before. Now things looked even worse for her. Kidnapping, Maggie had said. But this was about Earl, she reminded herself, not about Nora.

"Someone attacked Geneva last night. It wasn't either of us, I assure you."

His tone hardened in disbelief. "And you suppose it was me?"

Nora didn't answer. Neither did Starr. They both stared at him.

"What possible reason would I have to hurt my wife?" He paused, but Nora saw his gaze shift away to focus on the nearby bed, king-size with a full canopy and rich brocade hangings that hadn't been replaced by something lighter. "Is she hurt?" he asked. "Downstairs, is that her bl—" He couldn't go on.

Either he was a very good actor or Earl Whitehouse was genuinely shocked. Nora began to doubt her first suspicions. Her little trap wasn't going well at all for any of them.

"Geneva suffered a laceration to her scalp," Starr supplied. She had seemed to recover quicker than Nora. "She's going to be fine." In her tone Nora heard her own, *no thanks to you.* "So." Starr edged toward the door, dragging Nora along with her. "We'll just leave now. Leave you to…" *Clean up the mess.*

Earl stepped between them and escape. "Not so fast."

Fifteen minutes passed while Nora and Starr tried to explain themselves. Then downstairs Nora heard the front door open again. She darted a glance at the fallen clothes on the carpet, the waiting roll-on case Starr had found in the closet, then the cell phone at Earl's waist.

She had no doubt this time. She knew who was climbing the stairs. She almost knew what he would say.

In the next heartbeat, Calvin Caine filled the bedroom doorway.

"Nora Pride," he said, his eyes taking her in first. "We have to stop meeting like this."

"I hope none of you touched anything downstairs." Caine prowled the bedroom, his little notebook already in hand, clicking his pen on and off until Nora thought she might scream. "The forensics team will be here soon." He looked at her. "Any idea what weapon was used to hit Geneva Whitehouse?"

"No." They'd already discussed the possibility of a second burglary. Did he think she'd done it? "Why don't you ask Mr. Whitehouse?"

Caine turned to him. Earl Whitehouse only shrugged.

"How would I know?"

"It's routine." Caine sent Nora and Starr out of the room so he could question Earl alone. In the hall they pressed their ears to the door. "Where were you last night?" Caine asked.

"Boston." Earl Whitehouse sounded irritated. "I took the company plane yesterday rather than get up this morning before 4:00 a.m. to make an early meeting there today. You can talk to my secretary, the pilot and co-pilot. After we landed I checked into my hotel. I had a slight altercation with the desk clerk, who should remember me because of the incident. The waiter at the hotel restaurant, too, where I had dinner." He rattled off the information in a brusque, businesslike manner that made him sound more than accurate and, Nora thought, superior. "I ate grilled scrod with vegetables and had a bottle of muscadet." He smiled faintly. "Would you like me to spell that for you?"

Nora couldn't tell, but Caine appeared to be less than amused by Earl's attitude. She put one eye to the crack in the door and could see Caine's fingers tighten on his pen. "I'm a beer man myself, but go on."

"Later I stopped at the lobby bar for a nightcap. Talked with the bartender on duty. We discussed the Red Sox's chances for the pennant next season and watched part of a hockey game that the Bruins finally lost. I went to my room a little after eleven." He paused. "That should cover it, don't you think?"

"And today?" Caine said.

Earl Whitehouse heaved a put-upon sigh. He watched Caine scribble on his pad. "I slept from eleven-thirty or so last night until six. Got up, showered, dressed and was at a breakfast meeting by eight, maybe a little before. I then met with the board of directors at Bay State Home Builders—there's been some discussion about my purchase of the company—and finished by eleven. My plane was in the air by noon. As soon as I landed in Destin, I drove straight home." He hesitated. "I've been a little concerned about Geneva lately."

Nora bristled. That sounded properly husbandlike, and doting, which Nora knew was at odds with what Geneva had

said about her marriage. Still, in Nora's experience Earl wasn't
an honorable man. She didn't buy his alibi. She dragged Starr
back into the room, certain he was lying.

"If you were so concerned, why did you strike her?" Nora said.

"Ms. Pride, please." Caine rubbed the frown line between
his brows.

Earl Whitehouse exploded. "I've told you what I know, Detective. This is just one more example of police incompetence.
Despite my demands to the chief, the investigation of the
burglary in this house is still open and my wife's vase is still
missing. Now this vicious attack on Geneva. Why don't you
question Nora Pride?" He shot a hard look at Starr, too. "Why
Geneva hired her after the trouble before, I couldn't tell you.
Her kind nature, probably." His voice shook with emotion.
"And what did that lead to? Geneva might have died!"

"I didn't touch her! And I did not steal that vase!" Nora
couldn't help her own eruption. "You didn't seem particularly
concerned about its loss when we met in your backyard!"

Earl Whitehouse turned red. He didn't know that Nora had
told Caine.

To Nora's surprise, Starr leaped to her defense. "Nora and I
may have had our quarrels in the past but we've worked
together since then. I've never seen Nora take so much as an
extra spoon of sugar for her tea, much less try to steal *anything*
from Geneva."

"All right, ladies." Caine flipped to a fresh page in his
notebook. "Your turn. Mr. Whitehouse, we'll check out your
story. No interruptions, please. You may wait in the hall."

Earl didn't budge. "They were the last people to see my wife
last night," he said. "Geneva phoned my office around five
o'clock. She left a message with my secretary that she would
be with Nora Pride and Starr Mulligan for the evening. I got
the message when I landed in Boston. I left Geneva a message
in return on our answering machine so she would know when

she got home that I'd made the snap decision to fly out sooner than I'd planned. Then today I come home to find these women rifling the closets."

"I see." Caine wrote another sentence or two. Then he turned to Nora.

"Starr wasn't feeling well yesterday," she explained and caught Starr's warning look that begged Nora not to elaborate about her illness. "We took dinner to her. Then we sat around and talked, as women do. We took a walk on the beach. Geneva and I left around eleven. We were surprised that the time had gotten away from us. We'd had a good three-way conversation," she added, with a glance at Earl. "Very revealing. Then I drove Geneva home. I left her at her front door. I didn't go in," she said.

"Huh." Caine scribbled some more.

Earl Whitehouse fidgeted as if he could barely contain himself. "Detective, it's more than likely that these women either quarreled with my wife at Starr Mulligan's home or continued some argument here. Who knows whether Starr stayed home? Maybe one—or both—of them wasn't happy with 'working together' and wanted to dissolve this awkward partnership. The fight escalated—and Geneva got whacked with the nearest object one of them could pick up. They're covering for each other," he said. "Geneva had promised these women a hefty bonus to finish this job on time. Maybe they decided to 'negotiate' for more? Or one wanted the whole bonus for herself and hoped to cut out the other one? But Geneva wouldn't cooperate."

"It's a theory," Caine murmured.

Nora's heart sank. She sent Starr a look of sympathy, then lifted a shoulder in a half shrug. Caine saw the motion.

"You claim you—and you alone—left Geneva Whitehouse at her door. When you drove away," he went on, "did you notice anything unusual? Someone lurking near the house, maybe?"

"No."

"What about another car parked deeper in the drive, in the shadows under a tree, or along the road nearby? Waiting? At night this would be an even less busy area than it normally is."

"No."

Nora declined to embellish her statement. The more she said, the worse it became. Hadn't Caine ever heard that the spouse was the first, and most likely, suspect?

He closed his notebook. He snapped his pen shut and slipped both items into his inside jacket pocket. He nodded at Earl Whitehouse, then at Starr.

As he passed Nora, he glanced at her with an expression she couldn't read.

But Earl hadn't finished. He took a spread-legged stance in the middle of the room, his arms crossed over his chest, which was puffed out in an obvious attempt to make himself look bigger, more powerful. "Find the person who attacked my wife, Detective Caine."

Caine didn't look at him. "We'll do our best, Mr. Whitehouse. I'll tell the chief you said hello."

He studied Nora for another brief second until her face began to glow, then he shook his head.

"Don't go too far. You're a person of interest in this case. Again."

CHAPTER 13

"One minute." At Nora's car, Caine covered the door handle with one capable-looking hand before she could open it. "Where is Ms. Whitehouse?"

"We're *not* kidnappers." Nora thought she saw Caine's mouth twitch but he only looked at the ground between their feet. So did Nora. "Geneva's at an undisclosed location where she can be safe."

His gaze lifted, a warmer light in his dark eyes. "You're a *CSI* fan, right? *America's Most Wanted?* I recognize the lingo. You can either give me the address," he said in a low, controlled tone, "or get her on the phone and let me speak to her. Now."

Nora chose the latter. A few minutes later, Caine seemed satisfied that Geneva was indeed safe, had gone willingly, and didn't want to leave wherever she was just yet. He handed Nora her cell phone, then headed back into the Whitehouse home. By then, the forensics team was there to process the scene of the attack, including a thorough search for the missing weapon. How soon would they finish? Earl Whitehouse, Nora heard him say at the door, was eager to restore order to his home. Of course he would be. The sooner the police left, the sooner he could cover the rest of his tracks.

Now Nora and Starr were at her condominium where the mood was much different from their female camaraderie over Chinese takeout last night. Some miles away, Geneva was nursing her bad headache and Nora had promised to bring her more painkillers. Pacing Starr's living room, Nora thought she could use a few tablets herself.

But first, she and Starr were having another heated discussion.

"How can Earl Whitehouse simply fire us?" Starr asked from her perch on the sofa. She'd had the luxury of changing from her work clothes into a pair of comfortably tattered jeans and walking around in bare feet.

"He's paying the bills. That's a direct quote," Nora murmured, pacing the room some more. Even her light wool slacks, a concession to the cooler weather in December, and her Dupioni silk blouse felt tainted from the encounter with Earl Whitehouse and Caine. Nora would swear the unwholesome scents from that house were now embedded in her clothes.

"So what do we do?"

"Earl Whitehouse didn't hire us. He can't fire us. Only Geneva can."

"But she said he controls the money. He'll probably change the locks tonight. He was pretty mad that we'd taken her away from home and won't tell him where she is."

Nora took a brave stance. "I'm not worried about Earl Whitehouse. I still think he assaulted Geneva. I don't care what she says, nothing else makes sense." Unsettled by Caine's most recent interrogation, Nora whirled around in the center of the room. For a moment she allowed herself to be distracted while she regained her equilibrium. "Did I tell you last night, Mulligan? I, um, like your home. It isn't what I expected."

"What did you expect? Lava lamps, velour sofas, a Christmas tree with multicolored strobe lights?" Starr sounded amused. In the corner of the room stood a traditional blue spruce tabletop tree decked with tiny white lights and tastefully scaled-down decorations.

Nora hesitated. "Let's just say I admire what you've done here."

"And at Geneva's?" Starr pressed.

"For the most part, yes."

Starr's expression softened, but her lavender eyes turned somber. "Last year, I didn't even put up a tree. No one was coming for the holidays, as usual."

Nora felt an unexpected pang of sympathy. "What about Thanksgiving?"

Starr shook her head. "I went out for dinner. Alone."

"You should call your son."

Nora and Starr had discussed her lack of family before. Now they had a different issue to address. Nora said, "We're both suspects this time in Geneva's attack, you know."

"You more than me." Starr blinked at the sudden change of topic.

"No, as Earl said, we were the last two people to see Geneva before she was attacked. For all Caine knows, we did it. Together, it would have been easy for us to overwhelm her. One of us could have held her while the other took a shot. Odd," Nora murmured. "There wasn't anything at the house or in that hallway that I could see that might have been used to hit Geneva."

"Whoever it was brought the weapon with him and took it away."

"Earl Whitehouse," Nora said again. "He probably got rid of it." His comment about paying the bills revealed his attitude toward Geneva; he didn't respect her as anything *but* a trophy wife. And it made Nora like him even less than before. "Geneva told me she feared he had lost interest in their marriage."

"Hmm," Starr said. "But she also claims that her workouts at the club and her new look after the face-lift will improve not just her self-esteem but, she hopes, their relationship."

"And Earl hasn't left her," Nora agreed.

"Darling, they never do until someone's waiting in the wings. Men like their creature comforts too much—and regular sex, of course. Earl Whitehouse won't take the chance of losing Geneva unless he's sure that he's found true love with another woman."

"That's harsh, Mulligan."

"In my experience, it happened to be true."

Nora blinked. "Your husband cheated on you?"

"Like the old song says, 'And don't it make my dark eyes blue.'"

"Brown eyes," Nora murmured. "And I can't imagine that such a betrayal kept you down for long." She assessed Starr's expression and her still-beautiful lavender gaze. "As a matter of fact, you probably handled that much better than I did."

"Wilson fooled around?"

Nora looked away. "I caught him one night by the pool below our bedroom window in the hot tub with a twenty-something. She didn't last long, but she was the end of our marriage. I left the same night. With Savannah and Browning."

"Nora, I never knew that."

She shrugged. "It took me twenty years to get over him. How pathetic."

Starr grinned. "I made it in less than two." Then her smile faded. "On the other hand, I'm still single and my son seems to prefer his father. It won't be long before my granddaughter learns to like her Grampy better, too."

Nora returned to the subject at hand. "The question is, how do we prove Earl's guilty?"

"Of cheating on Geneva?"

Nora thought a moment. "If he was cheating, and Geneva found out, a quarrel between them makes perfect sense. Possibly because she wouldn't give him a quickie divorce. You know how important her marriage is to her."

"She even changed her face to please him."

Nora disagreed slightly. "But the change has done her a world of good, too. I don't think she sees herself in quite the same way any longer, like some golden Oscar statue Earl can put on the curio shelf instead of a strong woman in her own right. One who makes her own decisions. Who knows what she can accomplish once she really sees that? And remembers what happened to her last night."

"If she does. Which still leaves you as Caine's favorite suspect."

Nora spread her hands. "Don't forget to include yourself. But you're right. We don't know when—or if—Geneva will remember the attack. So where does that leave us? I say we look for the real culprit ourselves. Now."

Starr pondered that for another long moment. "Find evidence against Earl Whitehouse on our own? I don't know, Nora."

"Once word gets out about Geneva's attack, we'll lose business. I'll lose even more business than I did before," Nora added, "but so will you. Our reputations are on the line. We can either hang separately, as we usually did until we hired on with Geneva, or we can work together—just as we have on her house—to clear our names." Nora thought of the still-missing vase, then the attack on Geneva. "Once and for all," she added.

Savannah leaned back against her stack of pillows and, for once, didn't resent the fact that she was fated to spend the next few months in bed. She might still feel bored, but she'd never been so pampered in her life.

Her entire family, including Maggie, had hovered over her since Savannah got the news that she was having triplets. Nora came to see her every night after her first stop at the beach house where Geneva Whitehouse remained. Browning and Johnny had brought her so many bouquets that their bedroom looked more like a funeral home. Even Kit had surprised her this afternoon with a gift.

Tyler Blanchard lay curled in the crook of Savannah's arm. He had one leg crossed over the other, his knees up, with one foot swinging through the air. Savannah had just finished reading him his favorite book, *Where the Wild Things Are*.

"The story doesn't scare you anymore, Tyler?"

"Nope. I'm not fwee years old, Sabannah. I'm four."

"I see." She suppressed a smile. "Definitely more grown-up. I can understand that monsters under the bed or in the closet wouldn't be a problem for you now."

In answer, he cuddled closer. She and Tyler were good friends, and Savannah especially cherished the hours he'd spent with her lately. Nothing lifted her spirits more or made the clock move faster than a visit with Tyler.

With Kit back in school, working hard to complete her degree, she used Savannah more often to babysit. Savannah didn't mind. Just as good, she would be married before the babies were born. She and Johnny had decided to go ahead with a wedding without Nora's help, though they had yet to choose a date. Still, one thing nagged at her. One day at a time, Kit had advised. But Kit had only one child, not three.

With a little tug at her heart, Savannah gazed down into Tyler's eyes.

"Could you ask Grandma Maggie for a glass of water? I'm parched."

"What does 'parched' mean?"

"Very dry," Savannah said.

"You mean wike a 'tini?"

"A what?"

"That dwink in a mouth that gwins."

"Grins?"

Johnny strolled into the bedroom.

"I think he means gin. In a classic wide-mouthed glass."

Savannah's gaze widened. "A gin martini?"

"Kit's happy hour choice on Friday nights." He shrugged. "What can I say? They're all the rage."

"She wikes 'em with stwawberries," Tyler agreed. "She only has one. Wike me," he added. "I get a Shirley Temple—even if she is a girl."

Savannah shook her head. "I hope Kit doesn't take this child to bars."

"She and Tyler are okay," Johnny assured her, bending over the bed to kiss Savannah hello, then ruffle Tyler's dark hair. "Aren't you?"

Tyler frowned. "I'm not weal fine. Not without you."

Johnny's expression melted. He'd become Tyler's surrogate father several years before, when he and Kit were together, and his deep relationship with the boy was all that survived. "I miss you, too, buddy. I'm glad you're here today."

Tyler beamed. "Me, too. Mommy said Sabannah needed to get cheered up." Then he squirmed down in her bed, bumping arms and legs against her, until he laid his head against her tummy. Savannah rested a hand on his shiny hair. "I can hear the hearts!" he announced, glancing up at her with wonder in his eyes. "Did you hear 'em, Johnny?"

Johnny smiled. "Yep. Plenty of times. Pretty neat, huh?"

"Wow. There's a whole bunch. Is there weally fwee babies in there?"

The question made Savannah's pulse quicken. She was a bundle of rampant hormones these days, with an ever-changing array of moods, but that didn't answer the question: how was she going to cope?

"Two boys and a girl," Johnny told Tyler. "What do you think of that?"

"Neat." He switched ears, listening to Savannah's abdomen and smiling to himself. Johnny exchanged a look with her as if to say, "We'll be all right. It's just like three of Tyler, that's all." But Savannah wasn't soothed. Sometimes at night she lay awake, wondering what kind of mother she would be. As good as Nora, but not as intrusive at times? Like Maggie during their summers together? Would there be anything left of her to give to Johnny?

As if to push away the alarming thoughts, she laid a protective hand against her growing belly. And silently apologized. Feeling unsure of herself was bad enough. But she wouldn't do anything to harm her triplets.

"They could be my bwothers," Tyler said. "Oh, one sister, too. But a girl's okay. As long as she doesn't cwy."

"Would you wike—like—a brother?" Savannah asked.

He nodded vigorously against her stomach. "Yep. But Mommy says she needs a husband first."

"Good idea," Johnny murmured.

Kit was a single mother, always had been. Savannah had been her labor coach when Tyler was born. She had some knowledge of childbirth, at least, which might prove different in itself, but other than her occasional weekends with Tyler, Savannah remained ignorant about kids.

"Johnny," she said in reprimand.

"Kit's come a long way, but she's not there yet."

"Is that why you weft her?" Tyler eased away from Savannah to sit up, leveling Johnny with a hard look. "Mommy cwied when you did."

"Yeah. I know. I'm sorry, Tyler." Johnny sent her a help-me look, which Savannah chose to ignore. "We talked about that, remember? We decided we were okay with it. Pals again."

Tyler studied Johnny for a long moment until Johnny's left eye twitched. Then Tyler slipped from Savannah's bed and flowed into Johnny's arms, all sturdy little boy and staunch little man.

It hadn't been easy for him with Kit. At least she was showing signs of a new maturity, and when she finished college, Savannah hoped Kit and Tyler would really be all right. After all, Kit was training to become a psychologist, like her very difficult mother.

Johnny was still holding Tyler when Browning walked into the room.

"Hey," he said. "What a crowd scene. How's it going, Ty?"

"'Kay." Tyler flashed Browning his usual look of suspicion, as if he never knew quite what to make of Savannah's brother. Which, she admitted, was true of many people much older than Tyler.

"When's he going home?" Browning asked them, probably wondering if Kit was due to arrive any time soon.

"I go home when Johnny takes me."

Browning arched an eyebrow at Johnny.

Savannah piped up, "Actually, I thought it might be your turn, Browning. Tyler's going to eat dinner with us, but then you could run him home—and say hi to Kit."

"We'll feed you, too," Johnny said, trying not to smile. He knew what she was up to. Savannah had been playing matchmaker with Browning for a long time.

"You're out of your mind." Browning took Johnny aside. "Walk into that barracuda's den? No way."

Johnny didn't give him any rope, either.

"You're a chick magnet," he said, meeting Savannah's eyes over his head. "You can charm her to death."

"No, thanks—"

Browning got no further. Johnny steered him out of the room while Savannah read Tyler another of his favorite books.

By the time dinner was over Tyler's eyelids were drooping. Savannah looked pointedly at Browning, and without further protest, which he no doubt knew would be futile, her brother herded Tyler from the apartment toward his car. He knew when he was beaten. Savannah only hoped he wouldn't drop Tyler off at the curb in front of the house to avoid seeing Kit. He knew better than to try.

"'Bye, Sabannah," Tyler called back. "'Bye, Johnny. I wuv you guys."

"We love you, too," they said in unison.

The door closed. Silence fell. Johnny eased into Tyler's former position on the bed beside Savannah. "What a great kid. Ours will be, too," he said. "I want to make sure we include Tyler, though. Sometimes he feels I abandoned him when I haven't. Kit and I were just a bad combo."

"But what about us? What about our babies, Johnny?" She hesitated. "I don't know if I'll be good enough."

He rolled over to gaze into her eyes. "You're the best thing that ever happened to me."

She gave him a mock pout. "You just say that because you wuv me."

He nuzzled her throat. "Does Doctor Fingerhut have any idea how cruel he is? First he confines my bride to her bed— my bed—for the next four months. Then he tells me, 'No sex.'"

Savannah's smile was mysterious. She drew Johnny closer, pulled his head down to hers, and kissed him until their ears rang. It was the best way she knew to soothe him, to soothe herself. And, for the moment, to forget her worst fears.

"Trust me. There are all kinds of ways," she said.

Gingerly, Geneva rolled over in bed. The motion made her head ache and her vision blur. As she opened her eyes, the room spun around her. With a small groan, she fell back against the tangled sheets. A cold, wet nose bumped against the hand that hung over the side of the bed.

Daisy whimpered a little, as if worried that Geneva had taken a turn for the worse.

"Feel better?" Maggie hurried into the room carrying a huge helping of yet another of her casseroles on a festive-looking blue Fiestaware plate.

"Much better," Geneva hastened to tell Maggie. "I'm sure I could eat in the kitchen tonight." She struggled to a sitting position. The movement caused her brain to whirl even faster; she dropped back down again, hugging her pillow for stability.

"Nonsense. You stay right where you are."

Next to the bed, Daisy danced an anxious jig, her liquid

brown eyes riveted on Geneva. "Maggie, you shouldn't be doing all this. Put a couple of sodas in the fridge, a yogurt or two, and I'd be fine alone. I don't need Nora tonight, either."

"Being alone is overrated."

The hitch in her voice caught Geneva's fuzzy attention. She couldn't seem to concentrate, yet she couldn't miss Maggie's tone.

"You were alone until you came to Florida."

"No, I had Hank. My husband was still with me every morning, noon and night for forty years. Frankly, I feel guilty leaving him up there in Virginia while I'm down here in the tropics."

"Subtropics," Geneva said, trying to make her smile.

"Alone and being lonely aren't the same thing."

Maggie set out the dinner on the hospital-type wheeled table beside the bed. Nora had rented it from a local medical supply house, and Geneva had to admit the idea had been sound. She really couldn't make the short trip to the kitchen even when she wanted to.

She couldn't forget the attack, either—if not its details.

The lack of memory continued to disturb her. She'd never lost track of time in her life, and it bothered Geneva to have such a gap. If only she could remember…

Yet all of Nora's determined efforts to jog her memory had failed.

She picked up her fork, but didn't eat. Daisy's eyes fixed on Geneva's hand, obviously hoping she'd drop a morsel of tender beef. Outside a car door slammed, and a woman's footsteps clattered up the walk. "Nora?" she said.

"She's late. She promised to pick up dessert. Guess she didn't feel like having dinner first."

Geneva bit back a smile. She knew Nora hated her mother's cooking. The aroma of beef stew rising from Geneva's plate didn't exactly thrill her, either. Maggie's casseroles left much to be desired.

Like Geneva's faulty memory.

And the phone call she'd shared with Earl.

"Come home," he'd said in that abrupt tone that always made her feel uneasy, and even those two words had struck a wrong chord within her. If she couldn't recall what had happened in the hallway of their home, how could she be absolutely sure that her attacker *wasn't* Earl? Until she learned from someone else that he was innocent, Geneva wasn't going anywhere. She would be wise to heed Nora's opinion about Earl. Just in case.

She had, however, told him that Nora and Starr were to continue with the design work on the house. "I don't want those two snooping around," he'd said, but half the job remained undone, and there was lumber, tile, carpet and drapery fabric everywhere. The kitchen cabinets weren't finished and the new home exercise area hadn't even been started.

Geneva frowned at her dinner plate. Why could she remember all that but not who had struck her from behind? Geneva was still staring at her food, feeling frustrated that she couldn't remember, when Nora walked in.

Maggie's glance was cursory before she went out to the kitchen without a word for Nora. Geneva picked at her food.

"She looks tired," Nora said, staring after her mother.

"She knows you don't like her stew." Geneva bent to place her dish on the floor where Daisy could reach it. The dog lapped up the remaining gravy and bits of meat with a definite sense of appreciation.

Geneva and Nora laughed, but Nora's smile quickly faded when Geneva said, "Maggie's been working too hard. But she's enjoying herself—and life—again for now, Nora, taking care of me. And Savannah. She always comes in or leaves with a smile on her face and a twinkle in her eye."

"That must be for Johnny," Nora murmured. She took a seat on the chair by Geneva's bed. "How are you today? Get any sleep?"

"I didn't wake up until noon when Maggie got here and I've been napping all day. My head still hurts, but unless I move too fast my eyes and my stomach are more cooperative."

"Good." Nora paused. "Earl came to the house while Starr and I were there. He didn't seem happy to see us, and he doesn't want us back."

"I know. I spoke to him. It's all right, Nora. I want you to finish the house. But I told him I wouldn't be home for a while. At first I felt guilty, then I decided how much I like it here. I've never been on my own, ever since Earl and I married."

Nora glanced at another of Savannah's framed stick-figure drawings on the bedside table. This one was of Savannah, Johnny, and Tyler. "It's a very relaxing space. Savannah did a good job. It was her first. You're welcome to stay, Geneva, as long as you need."

"I hate to intrude." Daisy had her face pressed to Geneva's leg and, lightly patting the covers, Geneva invited her aboard. She took comfort in stroking Daisy's silky coat and letting the dog lick her hand—just as Nora must have intended when she brought Daisy today to keep her company.

"You're not intruding. Besides," Nora said, "Johnny and Savannah won't be coming to the beach until the triplets are born."

"That's kind of you...of them." Geneva picked at an imaginary piece of lint on the bedspread. "Nora, do you really think the two episodes are connected? The theft of my vase—Earl's engagement gift—and the attack on me in the hall?"

Nora elaborated on her theory. "If it was Earl, maybe he was trying to frighten you with the first burglary. He might have taken the vase to scare you. Such an emotionally linked piece was difficult to lose, and the fact that it was the only thing the burglar took then makes me suspicious. Goodness," she said with a little laugh, "I sound like Caine."

"But if that's true..."

Still, the notion didn't seem right. Earl was direct, often controlling, but she doubted he would use some kind of psyops method just to drive her away. More likely he would have asked for, even demanded, a divorce—and what could Geneva do? Earl controlled the bank accounts, all the finances. He made the decisions. "Don't worry your pretty head," he always told her.

Now Nora was obviously worried.

Geneva lifted her hand from Daisy's head. "If he meant to scare me off, it didn't work."

"So he escalated with another attempt. You quarreled and he struck you. He took off for Boston and checked into that hotel to give himself a plausible alibi. With the private jet, he could fly any time. Who would know?"

"The federal aviation people." Geneva studied Nora for a long moment, noting the sleek lines of her black suit, the polished gleam of her expensive black pumps, the black handbag on her lap. Her head began to spin again, and for an instant her vision dimmed. Geneva lightly shook her head to clear it—and so did her brain.

All at once she remembered!

She was back at the house in Royal Palms. Nora had dropped her at the front door, then driven away. Geneva had used her key, walked inside, shut off the security system. She'd listened to Earl's message on the answering machine about his trip to Boston, but before she could reset the alarm for the night, alone in the house without him, someone had crept up behind her…or had been there all along, watching.

"It wasn't Earl," she said again. "It was someone dressed all in black." She paused, a puzzled frown forming as she remembered the struggle, her attempt to flee from danger, then the crash of a heavy weight against the back of her skull.

She pictured the figure…taller than Geneva, not as slight yet smaller than Earl and not as broad.

"Nora," she said, "it was a woman."

CHAPTER 14

"Maybe you think too much," Starr said. "If Geneva says it was a woman who struck her, we should probably forget playing Sherlock Holmes. She must have worn gloves because the cops didn't find any prints here."

Nora paced the hallway of the Whitehouse home. It was Christmas Eve, and she hadn't finished her shopping. Her tree was half-decorated and she still needed to pick up her fresh turkey at the market by five o'clock. Before that, she had promised to drive Savannah to her appointment with Mark Fingerhut; wonder of wonders, Savannah had convinced Maggie to go with them "just to meet Mark and see if you like him." To cap off the festivities, Nora had a late-afternoon appointment of her own with the IRS. The day was too full for her comfort, but everything had to be fitted in somehow before the holiday tomorrow.

Today's schedule was almost enough to make her forget Earl Whitehouse.

Nora's heels echoed in the high-ceilinged space of his entry hall, and she could feel Starr's gaze on her as Nora strode across the dark walnut floor. Surely there must be evidence here. Somewhere. But even Nora's report of last night's talk with Geneva hadn't made Starr more enthusiastic about their quest.

Nora missed Savannah, who had provided support during the mission to find evidence in Earl Whitehouse's yard. She turned to stride back the other way.

"Geneva still loves her husband. She's recovering from a concussion that rattled her brain, so maybe her thought processes aren't what they should be right now. That's where we come in."

"In the first place, we thought the attack might be too painful emotionally for Geneva to remember."

"But don't you see? Now that she does remember," Nora said, "it may be even more painful to know that her own husband tried to kill her. That makes the theft of her precious vase pale by comparison."

"What are you saying?"

"Geneva may want to throw us off track, take the suspicion from Earl and lay it on some unknown woman—if there really is one. My money's still on him."

Earl Whitehouse was nowhere to be seen. Hoping to avoid him, Nora and Starr had arrived later than usual, expecting to be locked out this time—in fact, to find that he'd changed the locks. But the door had opened easily to Geneva's key. The dead bolt hadn't even been turned and the security system had been left unarmed, as if Earl expected—even welcomed—them.

Nora's first move had been to walk through the entire house, inspecting each room, making sure that Earl had truly left for the day. When she'd finally checked the garage, she'd found his car gone. But like a silent reminder that Geneva was still recuperating at the beach house from her injury, her Mercedes sat looking forlorn and lonely in the second space. Nora had last seen it in the drive so Earl must have moved it.

Now that Eddie the tile guy had also arrived, in a surly mood, and the carpenters were banging away more happily in the nearby kitchen, she and Starr could get to work themselves.

"If we must do this, where do we start?" Starr's tone was aggrieved. "Frankly, I'd rather concentrate on completing this job. Just being in this house gives me the willies. I keep imagining Geneva lying in that pool on the floor. I can feel the attacker about to sneak up behind me, too."

"Mulligan, we're not looking for some faceless man with a hook."

"Hook?"

Nora half smiled. "Didn't you ever sit around a Girl Scout campfire or a senior class retreat and tell horrible stories about murder on Lover's Lane?"

Starr shivered. "Oh, you mean that guy without a hand. Reaching into the car where two kids are making out—always the popular kids wearing their Tommy Hilfiger or Abercrombie outfits—and killing them with his vicious steel hook?"

"That's the one. Urban legend."

"I was never part of the 'in' crowd, so I didn't pay attention to the stories."

"Don't tell me." Nora gazed at her. "You were one of the Brains."

"If you must know, I spent my high school career on the honor roll." Starr barely avoided rolling her eyes. "Let me guess. You were prime bait for the man with the hook—except that your hair was brown, not his usual preferred blond."

Nora didn't answer. She'd never been at risk. She hadn't dated until she was in her last semester before college, partly because Maggie wouldn't allow her to, partly because Nora had been taking care of her mother most nights, but also partly because she'd been in the middle of her geek phase then. But what a surprise now. She and Starr had both been far removed from the gorgeous cheerleaders who attracted the football team captain or the star of the state championship basketball team.

Nora had gone from her mother's home to Wilson's without ever being on her own. Like Geneva, she'd turned from a dutiful daughter into a devoted wife, one whose loyalty had proved to be misplaced, and then she'd become a hands-on mother for Savannah and Browning, the sole breadwinner for her family. No time off for good behavior. Now she was caring for Maggie again, whether or not Maggie realized that. Nora's commitments were strong and very important to her. But were they enough? The night with Geneva and Starr and the moon had made her wonder.

She tried to dismiss her own doubts.

"We turned out just fine, Mulligan. Let's get going."

After another quick survey of the entry hall where Geneva's accident had happened, she headed for the stairs, trying not to mind that the living room, without Geneva in residence, didn't display a nine-foot Christmas tree decorated to the hilt. There wasn't a twinkling light in sight. The lack of holiday spirit unsettled her. The racket coming from the kitchen, where the carpenters were finishing the new cabinets today, and the guest room bath, where Eddie and his coworker were setting tile, had given her a headache. No wonder Earl Whitehouse had disappeared.

Which, of course, worked to Nora's advantage.

Except for Eddie and his crew, the upstairs rooms were neat and tidy. Beds made. Draperies pulled back to let in the morning sun. Each room had an adjoining en suite bathroom where the new sinks sparkled and the towels hung in regimental order. Because Geneva had said that Earl left his socks on the floor, Nora's bet was on Geneva as the person who maintained such a tidy day-to-day environment.

When Nora had first met Geneva, her radar had flashed on alert for a different reason. Her beautiful home, her sleek car, her collections of silver and crystal and jewelry seemed just a facade. Nora had known right away that Geneva Whitehouse, despite her natural beauty, was an unhappy woman. Even Earl's gift of the beautiful, missing vase was just another part of his control.

But the Trophy Wife was changing, and Nora felt sure there would be more to come once she and Starr solved Caine's two-part case for him.

She entered the master bedroom and looked around. Starr hovered in the doorway. "Come here," Nora said. "You look through the dresser drawers. I'll take the nightstand and shelves."

"What are we looking for?"

"Oh, good grief. Anything," Nora said. "We'll know when we see it. What's the matter, Mulligan? For once in your life, you feel intimidated?" She made a shooing motion toward the dresser.

Ten minutes later, they had found nothing.

Starr was clearly discouraged. "I doubt Earl Whitehouse would leave evidence about himself or his plans for Geneva in his own bedroom."

Nora mumbled, "Hide in plain sight." She rose from her kneeling position on the carpet. The bottom shelf of Geneva's bookcase had revealed nothing more than had the upper shelves. Zero. Maybe Starr was right.

But Earl's study was next door, a casual room where he could retreat to work at the computer rather than in the formal library downstairs. Undaunted, Nora marched into the other room.

"Ah-ha," she said, eyeing Earl's computer. "Where does a man leave his personal information? Suppose he even hired someone to hurt Geneva."

"A hit man?"

"It's possible. And his e-mail might prove it." The state-of-the-art system already whirred and glowed. A quick scan of its electronic desktop showed her the usual collection of icons. Nora ignored the video games but clicked on a financial program. *Could be a gold mine here.* Maybe they'd find a large payment for services rendered.

The program denied them access.

"Try this one." Starr leaned over her shoulder, sounding more engaged in the process now. "He belongs to AOL. There are all kinds of possibilities there. Chat rooms, message boards. We can look at his e-mail then the log of the Web sites he's visited—just like the FBI under the Patriot Act."

Again, the double click refused to open the program.

Nora keyed through the rest of the software offerings with the same result. "None of these applications will open. Geneva had trouble, too, at first when she was looking at fitness equipment for the house. Earl might have changed his password again."

"Now what do we do?"

Stumped for a moment, Nora suddenly smiled. "Heath."

Starr blinked. "Nora, that's a lovely idea. I'd do Heath in a second but—"

"Potty mouth. I don't mean Heath as in stud extraordinaire. I mean Heath as in high-tech wizard with his own consulting firm." She pulled out her cell phone. "He wants business. Today we're it."

"Ma, really. You'll get Heath in trouble, too," Savannah said. "I'm glad he didn't pick up your call. Detective Caine should handle this."

Nora had left another message on Heath's machine, wondering if he was avoiding her again just when she needed his help. Then she'd tried to put aside her concern about the Whitehouse case and her own damaged reputation. Christmas was looming, with most of her errands still to be run, and on the way to the doctor's office that afternoon she felt Savannah's accusing gaze from her place in the passenger seat of Nora's car.

"Caine has had plenty of time. He hasn't handled anything." Ignoring a quick flash of his dark, attractive image that could cause heat to rise in her face, Nora glanced in her rearview mirror at Maggie in the backseat, but to her surprise her mother didn't chime in to offer her opinion. Meeting Mark Fingerhut in a social setting might be acceptable to Maggie, but Nora wondered if her mother felt apprehensive about seeing him at his office in a white coat, even if Savannah's appointment was the main event.

"Geneva's case is only one incident on a crowded police blotter. Like the press, they'll go on to the next story within a few days as they did after the burglary. Geneva's attack isn't on the same order as the murder they're probably investigating."

"But Geneva is alive, thank heaven. The forensics people will analyze whatever they may have found this time, and eventually they'll make an arrest." Savannah studied her. "Ma, this isn't your responsibility. You came close enough to disaster when we invaded the Whitehouse yard and then when you 'kidnapped' Geneva."

Nora tried to ignore the barb. "Starr and I may well have saved her life, you know. What if Earl—or whoever—had come back?"

Savannah closed her eyes. "There's no getting through to you."

Maggie finally spoke from the backseat. "Does your mother ever listen to anyone? Talk about being kidnapped. Here I am," she said, "on my way to see that doctor I just may change my mind, Nora, and wait in the car. Let Doctor What's-his-name get his kicks with someone else."

"That would be me," Savannah murmured, but she was smiling. She ran a comforting hand over her belly, the motion snugging her stretchy top even tighter against her ever-growing abdomen. In Nora's day—which she refused to think of as the Dark Ages—women had disguised their pregnancies; now they let it all hang out, even in television commercials. Savannah caught Nora's eye and winked. "Mark's a good guy, Gram. You'll like him."

"You'd better," Nora said. "I invited him to Christmas dinner."

Savannah laughed. "Ma, you've invited the entire Gulf Coast."

"Not yet," Nora said, returning her daughter's grin.

She turned in at the medical complex where Mark practiced, adjacent to the hospital where Savannah's triplets would be born. Nora found a parking spot near the door so Savannah and Maggie wouldn't have far to walk. Or, for Maggie, room to escape? With Johnny in New York on business—Wade Blessing was in town for a series of interviews on their upcoming Razor Slade film—Nora was the go-to girl. She'd gotten them here without jostling the babies even once or losing her mother.

As she got out of the car, all at once Nora felt hot all over. The day's tensions must be getting to her. Just when she'd become somewhat accustomed to these sudden power surges and felt she could control them, an especially big one hit her all over again.

"Ma, your face is red."

Nora couldn't blame it on the weather. In December, the air felt as cool as it was likely to get today on the Emerald Coast, and she was even wearing a light sweater on this mild afternoon with the temperature in the sixties.

"You should see her with a night sweat," Maggie put in.

Helping her from the car, Nora sent her a dark look.

"Really, Ma, you should do something about those," Savannah said.

Mark happened to agree. During Savannah's exam, Nora and Maggie watched him poke, then prod Savannah's blossoming stomach; he showed them the last sonogram of the three babies in her womb. The twins appeared to be elbowing each other as siblings often do and Savannah's daughter clearly was sucking her thumb. Mark informed them that fetuses sometimes hiccupped as well. But after Savannah was done, and Maggie had reluctantly been hauled into another examination room, Mark cornered Nora in the hall, presumably to give her his report.

"Savannah is doing fine. I still don't want her out of bed, but I'll let her spend Christmas Day on the living room sofa. And Maggie and I had a nice talk. I'll see her next week for a complete examination."

Nora's pulse jumped. "What's wrong with her?"

"I'll most likely refer her to a cardiologist for treatment—which you asked me about before—but I'd like to make sure everything else at my end is in place and good shape." He looked at Nora. "She didn't much care for my initial diagnosis. I did detect a slight irregularity now and then in her heartbeat."

"She won't take her medicines."

"Do your best to drag her back here, will you?"

Nora promised she would. "Thanks, Mark." She turned away, hoping he didn't have more on his mind, and started for the waiting room to collect Maggie and Savannah. But Mark placed a light hand on her arm.

"And follow the same advice yourself. What about you?" he asked. "I thought we were going to discuss treatment for your hot flashes." He paused. "Your mother wasn't supposed to bring it up, considering the privacy thing, but she tells me you're also having night sweats and mood swings."

"I don't have moods," Nora said. "I just live with Maggie."

He paused. "I didn't miss the fact that you ran out of here before, leaving me to talk to myself in my office." He released her arm. "Nora, don't you think you should manage your own health as well as you do for everyone else?"

"When I have a spare moment," Nora promised.

"Trust me. We can work this out." He steered her toward the receptionist. "Why don't we fit you in next week when Maggie comes?"

Nora was still fretting long after she dropped Savannah at her condo and made sure she was settled into bed with a light snack and some bottled water. Because Mark had been pleased with Savannah's progress, Nora left Maggie at the beach house with Geneva, who was planning to take a short walk on the sand at sunset. Then she drove into town for her meeting with the IRS.

Much to her surprise, Nora's accountant had come up with most of the required documentation, but Paul's casual attitude set her teeth on edge. The short meeting adjourned with another planned for soon after Christmas and a stern reminder from the federal agent that this was serious business. Indeed it was. Nora didn't need any more bad news about Nine Lives to jump-start the rumor mill. Worse, she was in danger of going to prison, and that orange jumpsuit was still not her idea of a great fashion look.

Tight-lipped, she parted ways with the accountant in the parking area outside the IRS office. Her own caution that he not think about taking a long vacation in some South American country would have the right effect, she hoped.

Nora stopped at the market just before closing to collect her Christmas turkey. At a store next door in the small strip mall, she bought a few stocking stuffers, including three crib mobiles, and at a nearby Moms To Go she bought Savannah several new maternity outfits that weren't quite as revealing as the one she'd worn today.

But even that wasn't all. Nora had several more stops to make.

With her energy flagging, she picked up a Starbucks Mocha Frappuccino then carried it with her into the Hallmark store. She needed Christmas cards—special ones for Maggie, Savannah, Browning, Johnny and the babies. She already had yellow and blue and pink blankets for each one wrapped in cheerful paper under her tree.

Nora was perusing the selection when someone suddenly wrapped familiar arms around her from behind. Nora didn't have to look. It wasn't Heath this time, but her ex-husband, who always smelled like sandalwood and ink. With a glance over her shoulder, Nora saw Wilson. To her utter dismay, he stood beside his latest bride-to-be who looked to be about twenty years old, although Nora knew she was actually almost thirty, like Savannah.

Wilson kissed her cheek. "Nora, Merry Christmas."

She gazed into his hazel eyes, the same as Browning's. She tried not to stare at his still-trim form or the apparently new, and trendier, clothes he wore. It hadn't occurred to him that her heart might stop at being grabbed without warning. Heather, a slim honey blonde with serious eyes, sent her a look of womanly empathy. "Wilson is getting carried away with the spirit," she said.

Nora found her voice. "My goodness. What a surprise."

"It's good to see you," he said. "But we were disappointed to get your response to our invitation for the wedding."

"We hope you'll reconsider." Heather stayed in the background, but it was clear to Nora that she was already stepping in to keep Wilson on track. Without guidance, he could be vague and dreamy and not quite aware of other people. Or their feelings.

"I'm sorry, but I felt my presence on your special day would be…inappropriate."

"Don't be silly." Wilson released Nora and then reached for Heather's hand, which bore a brilliant rock the size of Pensacola. He looked genuinely crestfallen. "We're expecting you."

"Counting on you," Heather added with a bright smile.

"To add to our bliss," he said. "I've written a poem for the occasion. Savannah and Browning have both agreed to come."

Nora fought down the urge to haul out her cell phone and remind her children of their loyalty to her. Still, she wouldn't. Their father was important to them, too, as Nora had reminded herself so often over the years. Now she reminded herself that she and Wilson had recently made peace.

"Please think about it," he said.

"I will," Nora lied.

"Wilson would really like you to complete our day," Heather told her.

Nora could only think that she should have driven straight home. She felt tempted to let them know that she would have to attend the ceremony alone if she came, which she wouldn't, but she'd bite her tongue through before she admitted that she didn't have a date. Which made two. She was still pondering

the Heart Association dinner, but that decision would have to
wait until after the holiday.

Nora endured more Christmas wishes and a kiss from
Wilson then Heather before they drifted off to buy candy canes
for Wilson's other children from two of his other marriages; he
hadn't had kids with Johnny's mother. Being careful to avoid
any further encounter with Wilson and Heather, Nora quickly
selected her cards, and then left the store, wondering why she
still seemed to care that Wilson was getting married and was
obviously happy without her.

How much progress had she made after all? Not that she
loved him anymore in that way, Nora told herself.

On her way home, she made a last stop at Impressions where
Leonard answered the door wearing a frown and looking pale.
The change startled Nora, who had gotten used to his new,
healthier look. Behind him she saw a scraggly artificial tree that
looked far less ready for prime time than her own half-finished
decorations.

"Nora, come in. That is, if you're not afraid of bacteria."

Nora stepped back in the doorway. "What's the matter?"
Leonard's immune system often failed him, or so he insisted, but
still, she'd thought he was improving, perhaps with Tabby's help.

"Yesterday I woke up with this dreadful sore throat and
stuffy nose."

Nora picked up her usual cue. "You have my sympathies."

She supposed a slight head cold wouldn't kill him, or her,
although that would mean staying away from Savannah not to
risk her babies. Leonard didn't give her a chance to leave. He led
her into the airy living room of his new home where Nora took
a seat on a suede sofa, and moved a half-filled tissue box out of
the way. The room smelled stale and felt much too warm. Or was
she having another power surge? After her morning hunt for
evidence at Earl's house, then seeing Mark, the IRS agent, Wilson
and Heather, and now Leonard, she wouldn't be surprised.

"Wouldn't you know?" he said. "Just when I felt almost normal…"

"Well, a small setback is to be expected."

Leonard slumped in his chair, his flannel pajamas rumpled, a few buttons undone. "My immune system must be in chaos. From stress, I suppose."

"Then I'll let you rest and gather your defenses." Nora stood, then cleared her throat. "Leonard, I stopped by to remind you about Christmas. I hope you'll feel better by then. You're expected at my house around noon."

"I'm not sure, Nora. My illness," he said with a frown, "and then there's Tabby. She's my real concern."

Nora wondered if her first impression of them had been right.

"Are you lovers?" Nora couldn't resist asking.

"Of course not. She's far too young," Leonard said. "But even in the throes of this latest mishap with my health, I'm more worried about her." He darted a glance at the house across the street. The place looked abandoned. Several days' worth of newspapers littered the front lawn, the lush zoysia tropical grass had yellowed now that winter was here. "Tabby has suffered an emotional disaster. It seems she's gotten herself into a mess with another man. Maybe I should have taken her under my wing sooner, but I didn't know about him until recently." Leonard ambled to the window, leaned a shaky arm against the frame and peered out as if he might magically make Tabby appear. "At any rate, they had a terrible fight. I heard them from clear across the street. He finally slammed out of her house, climbed into his car and peeled off."

"People in their twenties often have extravagant emotions."

"I didn't see his face. Tabby told me very little about him, but she's been distraught for days—her nights are even worse—and I've been sitting up with her, which has finally broken my strength. I've been trying to do my best to comfort her."

"That's all you can do, Leonard. You're a good friend."

With that, Nora realized she had forgiven him for his betrayal with Starr.

He turned toward her with a shattered expression. "She's all alone, you know. Her family lives in California. I'm really all she has now, but I don't know what will become of her. Tomorrow she—"

Nora hastened to proffer the invitation. "Bring Tabby with you to dinner. I wouldn't hear of leaving her to fend for herself on Christmas."

Leonard subsided onto his chair again. He pressed a pale hand to his flannel-clad chest, then reached with the other for a tissue. "Nora, what can I say? And after I treated you badly about Starr? You are the dearest, dearest person…"

Leonard was about to weep, and Nora streaked for the front door. "You know better, angel. Get well. I'll see you both tomorrow."

CHAPTER 15

For Christmas, Nora pulled out all the stops. She always did. She loved the entire holiday season from Halloween until New Year's, but Christmas was her eternal favorite. She loved the twinkling lights all over town and on her living room tree, where she draped strings of tiny clear bulbs until the wiring in her house was overloaded. She loved the presents piled underneath the tree, the fragrant pine-scented wreaths hung at doors and windows, the traditional carols that spilled from every shop in the mall. Last night, as always, she had loved to the point of tears the midnight service at her church and from the boys' choir that final cascade of soprano voices in the descant to "Adeste Fideles" that echoed through the nave. Nothing would ruin her day.

On Christmas she could forget her troubles—the Whitehouse burglary, the attack on Geneva, the ensuing loss of clients, the IRS and even Caine.

Nora was up before seven, dressed by eight and in the kitchen at nine.

Not even the rumble of thunder close by could dampen her spirits. A quick glance out the kitchen window told Nora that a storm was moving in quickly, but what did it matter? Except that Daisy hated thunder and lightning, and had already taken up her position under the dining room table. Every time Nora looked at her, the dog's expression seemed to be the equivalent of putting her paws over her ears and rolling her eyes in terror.

"Sorry, girl, but there's no soft white snow for Christmas in Destin."

With the huge turkey almost ready for the oven, she washed her hands then went to answer the doorbell. Grinning, Johnny stood on the porch, his arms full of Savannah, a backpack that threatened to overflow with brightly wrapped gifts perched on his broad shoulders. "Ho, ho, ho. Merry—"

"Christmas, Ma." Savannah bussed her other cheek.

"I couldn't open the door," Johnny explained.

"Welcome, angels."

Maggie appeared in the hallway that led from the living room to the guest bedroom. "Let me take that bag," she said, and removed the backpack from Johnny as he set Savannah gently down on the sofa. Dressed in red sweatpants and shirt for the occasion, Maggie wore too much rouge today. But she seemed to take great delight, as Nora would have, in spreading and then rearranging the gifts under the tree until she seemed satisfied.

The tree was laden not only with lights galore but with every ornament Nora had collected over the years. Special emphasis was given to those she, Browning and Savannah had used each season when her children still lived at home. Without these mementos, it wouldn't have been Christmas. Without her children, too, Nora thought, and felt strangely glad that she'd invited Starr to join them for dinner.

The more, the merrier, was Nora's motto. With her family, Starr, Leonard, Mark, Geneva and possibly Tabby and Heath, there wouldn't be a single inch of spare space in the dining room. Exactly as Nora liked it. She hurried to bring Savannah and Johnny creamy eggnog, which she served in her special Christmas mugs trimmed in gold.

She and Maggie toasted the expectant couple. Then Maggie bustled back to her room and returned with a Christmas-green throw that she tucked around Savannah's growing belly. "You're not to do a thing today," she told her, sounding just like Nora.

"As soon as Browning gets here, we'll open the family presents," Nora said, although she needn't tell them. Every year she followed the same traditions in the same order. It occurred to her that this season Maggie was also here, and Nora lifted a small prayer of thanks to the darkening heavens. This year her mother wouldn't be alone in Virginia, and Nora wouldn't worry about her.

"Before that spy boy arrives," Maggie said, heading for the kitchen, "I'll just get my stuffing mixed up for the turkey."

She wasn't out of sight before Savannah rolled her eyes as if she were Daisy, afraid of the gathering storm. "Ma, she's not making her 'famous' oyster dressing, is she?"

"I'm afraid so."

"Sounds good to me," Johnny said, having never experienced Maggie's holiday cooking. "I like oysters."

Savannah groaned. "Ma, please. Stop her. Or set aside some plain stuffing for me. I love seafood but not oysters while I'm pregnant." She shuddered.

"I understand."

As the thunder built and lightning split the dark sky, Nora hurried into the kitchen where it appeared that Maggie had hauled out every mixing bowl from the cabinets. Maggie had her own memories of Christmas in Virginia. She sprinkled sage and oregano all over Nora's clean counter. Nora gave her Savannah's stuffing request, then said, "You're making a mess of my kitchen. Please clean up as you go."

"You're telling me how to prepare a meal? I was running a household before you were born."

"Of course you were. That doesn't mean I want my kitchen to look like some war has been fought here, too." She slapped a damp cloth into Maggie's hand. So much for their tentative peace during the past few weeks. But then, Maggie had spent most of her time at Johnny's beach house taking care of Geneva, or at the condo caring for Savannah. Nora turned around to leave. She couldn't watch. "By the time dinner is served, I want this place to look as if nothing happened. Christmas is the one day when I need my home to appear like some glossy spread in *Architectural Digest*." A brilliant display of cloud-to-ground lightning illuminated the entire house, and she heard Daisy whimper from the dining room. After a last reminder to Maggie, she would comfort the dog. "Remember my birthday? Humor me. Make it look as if some caterer was in charge."

Maggie sniffed. "When your father was alive, we had fun in the kitchen on holidays. The bigger the mess, the better we liked it."

"I remember oyster juice—or is it called liquor?—all over the floor."

Maggie's tone was smug. "That was only one year. Your father and I got...distracted. Oysters are an aphrodisiac, you know."

"Say what?" Johnny appeared right behind Nora. When she turned, he handed her two empty eggnog mugs. "Maggie, you vixen." Grinning, he peered at the mixing bowl on the counter. "Can I help?"

Nora shuddered. Johnny wasn't a neat cook, either.

She heard the doorbell ring; it was a welcome reprieve. There was Browning, similarly laden with packages and wearing his best smile. "Hey, Ma. Happy holidays." He paused. "I'm being politically correct."

"Come in, you naughty boy." Nora hugged him tight, presents and all. "Merry Christmas to you, too."

The gifts were, as usual, grand. Within the hour, the turkey was in the oven, oyster stuffing bulging, and the presents were strewn about the living room in clouds of hastily undone wrappings and bows. This was Nora's one indulgence for the holiday. She didn't hurry to scoop the beautiful papers and ribbons from her carpet. To her, they looked like bright confetti that contributed to the party atmosphere.

Her family, her friends around her—although by noon Geneva hadn't yet called to say she was ready to join them—good food in the making, enough glowing light from the tree and candles on the tables to make every woman there look ten years younger...Nora wished Christmas would last until March.

Daisy obviously didn't. In spite of the new chewy bone Nora had given her, which now lay between Daisy's paws under the table, she disliked the celebration and the rising storm. The wind began to howl around the house, and Daisy howled with it. She was still voicing her opinion when the lights went out.

Nora was serving chilled white wine, merlot and shiraz, a martini for Maggie, and a sparkling water with a twist of lemon for Savannah when it happened. At the same instant, someone reported that one of the toilets had overflowed. As she shouted for Browning to find a plunger, the phone finally rang. Nora didn't have time to worry about the electric oven and the turkey stalled in its cooking. It was Geneva who had called to cancel.

Nora felt a surge of disappointment. "Not even for an hour or two?"

"I'm at the house, Nora. Not the beach house. Our house." She lowered her voice. "I couldn't refuse Earl's invitation. When I phoned to wish him Merry Christmas, he was so cute and he seemed...adrift without me. He came to pick me up and now with the storm—"

"You told him where you were?" Nora asked.

"He's had our meal catered and afterward maybe we can talk." Earl obviously planned ahead. "Are you sure this is wise?"

Geneva hesitated. "I think it's time."

What could Nora say? She had other disasters to manage. She left Geneva's plate at the table, just in case she changed her mind. But Starr was here now, walking up the path under the first slant of rain and carrying an enormous gift basket, commercially prepared and wrapped in red cellophane. Nora couldn't see her face around it, but she'd know Starr's legs anywhere. Starr had great legs.

By the time Browning had dealt with the plumbing, there were still no lights. Then Leonard arrived with Tabby, who looked wan but lovely in green velvet. Leonard just looked wan.

"I see you're on your feet again," Nora said, kissing him under the live mistletoe she'd tacked up in the doorway, as she did each Christmas season.

Leonard smiled. "I thought a bit of food might speed my recovery."

He had brought several bottles of wine with expensive labels for dinner, and Nora sent him to the dining room to uncork them and let them breathe, cautioning him first not to step on poor Daisy. With a look of confusion at all the chaos around her, Tabby endured the necessary introductions and even Browning's teasing about her choice of an escort for the holiday before he fetched her and Leonard drinks. Nora hurried back to the kitchen to check on the turkey, which was relying on the already-falling temperature to continue cooking. That wouldn't last long, and she hoped the power would snap on soon.

Everyone was making quite merry nonetheless, much to Nora's satisfaction, when the doorbell rang again. Heath, she hoped. But when she opened the door, to her utter astonishment Caine was there. He glanced behind Nora. There must have appeared to be dozens of people in her living room amid the signs of a party in progress that, in the low light, was rapidly becoming even more merry. Caine didn't seem to be celebrating.

"Didn't know you had company."

Nora stared at him, wondering why he hadn't seen the extra cars out front, or if he was here to look for underage drinkers. Caine looked his usual unpressed self, but today his clothes were more casual. His normal sports jacket with the little notebook tucked inside, his regulation dark trousers and not-quite-shined shoes were absent. He wore tight jeans, a Henley shirt in blue and green stripes that managed to make his broad shoulders look even wider, and well-broken-in running shoes. "It's Christmas," Nora informed him, because Caine obviously had no clue. Or he was putting her on?

"Christmas? You mean Christmas Day?"

"Turkey and all the trimmings." If she could somehow finish roasting it. "You have no plans?"

He merely shrugged, as if he couldn't admit the truth.

Nora flinched at the next clap of thunder. The rain was beginning to sweep across the porch then lash against the door. Why was he here?

"I wanted to tell you…" Caine shifted from one foot to the other. "The forensics report is in. They went over the White-house home with the usual fine-tooth comb. There's no sign of burglary. Earl himself took a thorough inventory but found nothing gone this time—"

"As if he's an impartial observer," Nora murmured.

"—plus the weapon used on Geneva, whatever it was, is still missing."

"Which only helps my theory. It was Earl."

Caine shook his head. "Earl Whitehouse's alibis checked out. He was in Boston as he said when his wife was attacked. Even that bartender remembered him. Whitehouse is no longer on my list."

Nora tensed.

"And you buy into that?"

Caine sighed. "Six people have vouched for his where-abouts that night."

"But what if Earl paid them off? His secretary, his pilot and co-pilot depend on him for their income—and for his good will."

"Which doesn't explain the bartender at his Boston hotel, the front desk clerk or the waiter in the restaurant there."

Nora's mouth tightened. "The waiter and bartender work for tips. With a little persuasion the clerk may have fudged the records and changed the time of Earl's check-in. They could probably all use a little extra cash. And money would be no object. Earl Whitehouse is loaded. He's also an arrogant bully. A few bribes here and there were probably just business as usual for him."

"You really don't like the guy, do you?" Caine gazed at her as if Nora were slightly paranoid.

"You don't believe me?" She held his gaze. "I'm telling you, Earl could have struck Geneva, hightailed it to the private air terminal, taken his plane to Boston after midnight. He could cover his trail with the bribes, check in late, and still make his early meetings there—with men he didn't have to pay off."

"You've really given this a lot of thought," Caine said.

Which didn't mean he would give credence to her ideas. If he still believed Earl Whitehouse was innocent, then Nora could guess what he thought about her. Was this untimely appearance on her doorstep meant to apply more pressure?

And she'd thought nothing could dampen her spirits. "So let me guess what this is really about. You decided to come by and ruin my holiday. Can't we agree to view me as a suspect again tomorrow?"

"Maybe it's not about you."

What did that mean? Nora wasn't sure.

"Is that your way of apologizing? Well, thank you very much. Have a nice day." She turned back, ready to slip inside and shut the door. But then something stopped her. Nora spun around again, as if some alien force were pushing at her spine, urging her to confront the strange look she'd glimpsed in his eyes. It was…wistful, Nora realized. Caine was still staring at the people she loved, gathered in her living room around the Christmas tree, drinking and sharing the easy laughter that families often did when they weren't warring with each other.

"Hey, come in and shut the door," Browning called.

"Look, I'd better go—" Caine started to say.

Then in a rush, Daisy emerged from her makeshift storm shelter. She pushed between Nora and the door, then shoved her nose into Caine's palm for a hearty pat. "Hey, girl." She was still carrying the chewy bone in her mouth and drooling.

"Amazing. She's been under the table all day." Nora took hold of Caine's shirt sleeve and hauled him inside, Daisy herding him toward the living room. Maybe she could use honey instead of vinegar to change his mind. "You'll join us for dinner. We have an extra place," she said.

For some reason Caine stuck to Nora like a strip of Velcro. Was he shy in social situations? Still, he made himself useful. "Your power's out?" he asked.

"Half an hour ago. The turkey's not done," she admitted, but before she could say more he was in her kitchen, inspecting the oven, testing the bird. Nora gauged the pan of potatoes boiling on the stove. The cooktop was gas so the side dishes would be fine. The turkey, however…

"Needs another two hours," Caine decided.

"I don't have two hours. We eat at three."

"Not this Christmas, you won't."

Nora gazed at him, feeling panic roll through her in a wave like the thunder that crashed outside. As soon as Caine had stepped inside, Daisy had led him straight to the hall table and begged him for a doggy treat. Now she was buried again under the dining room table, probably praying for the rain to stop. So did Nora. If the power didn't come on…

"Got a Wal-Mart nearby?" Caine asked.

"A mile or so. What can we do? The whole neighborhood is dark."

While Nora replenished everyone's drinks, he rounded up Johnny and Browning for a quick trip to the store. They soon returned with a turkey cooker and a big can of peanut oil, with which to deep-fry the holiday bird on her back deck. Nora thanked him and let him handle the rest.

Dinner wouldn't be that late, everyone told her. They didn't care. When Nora finally began to whip her potatoes, which were justifiably as "famous" as Maggie's oyster dressing, Caine leaned against her kitchen counter, his arms folded, and watched her. Too intently.

"You know your way around a kitchen," he remarked.

She waved the old-fashioned potato masher. "Living, dining, bath rooms, too," she added. "It's what I do."

He half smiled. "Maybe you should get your own cooking show. I used to watch Rachel Ray and Nigella every now and then on the Food Network. But Nigella always made me feel interested in something other than food."

Nora fought the urge to feel flustered. He wasn't talking about her, as he'd said. If she allowed the feeling, she would definitely suffer another hot flash and this wasn't the day for one. Instead, she felt control of her world—and the holiday celebration—slipping away from her.

"Did you really not know it was Christmas?" she asked, fluffing air through the potatoes until they looked like soft white clouds in the sky.

He grunted. "Holidays don't mean much to me. Last Christmas, Nigella and I whipped up some kind of plum pudding. Then called it a day."

Nora dropped the potato masher to her side, as if Caine might decide it was a weapon. "You can't be serious. Who doesn't love Christmas? Or Thanksgiving?"

"A man with no family to enjoy them," he muttered. "Does it matter?"

"Of course it matters." She eyed him over her shoulder. "And everyone has a family. You may not like yours—" *Or they might not like you.* She had to admit, though, Calvin Raji Caine was a very attractive man. In his way.

"My parents are gone. My one brother was killed in Desert Storm, a jeep accident, not combat." He paused. "I lost my wife three years ago."

Nora's hand paused. Oh, dear. She must have sounded callous. How had the conversation changed so quickly into something far more serious? Too late, she remembered his earlier reference to Annie in the past tense.

"I'm sorry."

"Me, too. She was a good woman. We loved each other."

So that explained it…or rather, him. Now she wondered what he must have been like when his wife was still alive, when he was happy and had a family and a home to go to every night, perhaps even children.

"We never had kids," he went on as if she'd spoken aloud. "We wanted them. It just didn't happen." Another faint smile crossed his face. "Maybe I should really blow you away and add that I like a few beers after work. They help me to unwind…to sleep."

"Help yourself," Nora said, gesturing with the potato masher at the refrigerator. "I should have offered you a drink before. But I thought you were…on duty." He had a freshly opened, slightly warm Corona in hand before she could blink.

"Even I get a day off."

"And it didn't occur to you that Christmas was the reason?"

"I forgot. We had a kind of late party after my shift ended last night."

"You drank too much and you live alone," Nora guessed. No one would remind him. He wasn't the type to get a roommate; oddly enough, she suspected he hadn't looked for another woman, either.

"Just me and the cat. Annie's cat," he added, as if the very thought of Caine petting a soft coat of fur, smiling, caring for a helpless animal as easily as he appeared to like Daisy would make him even more…human. He wiped that image from her mind with his next words. "Name's Killer. We got him when I was working Homicide."

"Cute," Nora said, returning her attention to the potatoes. She added another drizzle of cream and a dollop of butter, reminding herself that she always felt uneasy in his company. What had possessed her to invite him for dinner? She tested the potatoes with one finger, then sprinkled on more salt and pepper.

"Cute? So's the apron," Caine murmured.

He startled Nora. She'd never heard that tone of voice from him before, and when she turned around his gaze slid over her figure—down, then up, then down again. She had seen that look. Nora tightened the Christmas-print apron strings tied in a bow behind her waist.

"You like aprons? You'll find another one hanging inside that cabinet door. It's navy blue gingham, not as feminine as mine, but as long as you're here and have no other place to be…" The notion sounded more appealing than she expected. "Browning is a dreadful carver. Johnny has his hands full making sure Savannah stays where she's supposed to be this afternoon." The golden brown bird was already resting in the space between Nora and Caine, its juices settling. The turkey fryer had worked wonders, and Caine had assured Nora that, although the skin was crispy, the meat would melt in her mouth. "The knives are in the first drawer beside you. You do know how to slice a turkey?" she teased.

"Sure." Caine suddenly grinned, as if he'd been having fun all along at her expense. "I've watched an autopsy or two."

Nora paled. "Oh, that is awful." Then with a prim nod of her head, embarrassed, she turned back to dish the potatoes into the big Spode Christmas bowl she always used. Her hands felt clumsy. "Your mother must have aged very quickly," she said.

"I was the bane of her existence. She always expected me to end up on the other side of those iron bars."

"Ha," Nora said, and then, "Why are you named Raji? Was your family—"

"Hindu? No, my mother was addicted to Indian films, especially the Merchant Ivory sort or whatever, those sweeping epics about love and loss. She liked the sound of the name, I guess. Sorry," he said, "not to be more exotic."

Despite his demurral, he was good in the kitchen, probably because he had to be. If he wanted to eat at home, there was no one to cook except him. She couldn't imagine Killer the cat would be much help. Nora tried not to watch Caine but couldn't help herself. With quick, sure movements he found the knife, arranged the beautifully done turkey to his satisfaction on the counter, drew the serving platter close and went to work. He didn't create a mess like Maggie, and Nora couldn't resist a gibe in return.

"This obviously isn't your first time."

Caine laughed, low and a little sultry. "Good one."

The storm rumbled away into the distance, the rain tapered off, and the electricity winked on again, as quickly as it had cut out, startling them both. Before she could react, or pull back, he leaned toward her to slip a sliver of succulent turkey breast into her waiting mouth.

"It's not mine, either," she heard herself say. "Call me Nora."

Had he lost his mind? By the time he finished his second slice of pumpkin pie topped with whipped cream and an extra sprinkle of pecans, Caine was sure he had. Not that the knowledge stopped him.

He wondered if Nora Pride had been right. Had he come by her house on the major holiday of the year just to tell her that Earl Whitehouse's alibi rang true? Hell, no. Caine had enough experience in law enforcement to know when he heard a bald-faced lie, especially from himself. She hadn't even believed him.

He was also certain that Nora saw right through him to the bone-deep loneliness that lived inside. Annie's death had never left him, not on a single night or as he did his job in the middle of every day. The realization that Nora—still a suspect, twice over, as far as the department was concerned—could glimpse the very inner reaches of his soul should have been enough to make him run.

Go home, he told himself. Break open another cold one, nestle into the contours of the leather recliner, flip channels until 2:00 or 3:00 a.m. Stay out of sight. Those all-seeing deep blue eyes of hers made him beyond uncomfortable.

For once he didn't need another beer. Instead, he stayed.

In her living room he sat around Nora's brand-new Christmas present from her kids, a state-of-the-art, high-definition, fifty-two-inch plasma screen TV and watched, rooted, booed, hooted and armchair-quarterbacked the rebroadcast of yesterday's Hawaii Bowl football game. He'd never had so damn much fun.

Every time Caine glanced up, Nora seemed to be watching him, a small, satisfied smile on her tempting mouth. As if she had personally saved him from himself. *Don't go there.*

Then Mark Fingerhut arrived, late, which prompted another round of eating. Starr served Mark his plate, taking a seat beside him.

The evening passed too quickly. Before he knew it, Caine had a turkey-with-cranberries sandwich on whole wheat bread happily settled in the pit of his stomach, and he'd accepted one last glass of an excellent merlot. Never mind the beer; tonight he was living high and, to his further sense of unease, enjoying it.

When he tried to summon his usual image of Annie's face, he came up blank. Which brought Caine right out of his too-comfortable chair between Browning and Johnny, right in the middle of the final two minutes of the football game. It hadn't proved to be a very good one, but again, he'd liked the company.

"Foregone conclusion," he murmured when the two men looked up to find Caine shrugging into his jacket. The score was 42-17. "Guess I'll be on my way."

Nora suddenly appeared behind him. She was holding a foil-wrapped package that smelled, fragrantly, of more turkey and that strange, fishy dressing. "If you must rush off, remember to put this in your fridge when you get home."

He tried to object. He had plenty of food in his freezer, mostly packaged dinners. Nora might want her leftovers tomorrow.

"Nonsense," she said. "I know a hardship case when I see one."

Lord!

Caine said his good-nights, even let Nora's mother, Maggie, plant one on his cheek and beg him to "come back soon." Then he was in the open doorway, wanting in one breath to be in his car heading back to solitary confinement across town and in the next feeling tempted to linger. To keep hearing the easy laughter among Nora's family, to keep catching her gaze on him in that speculative way. To realize that, for these few hours in a near-stranger's house, he'd even felt as if he belonged there.

A half hour later, he was still hanging around.

And the rest of Nora's guests had left.

"I'll walk you out," she finally said, gathering a soft knit wrap around her shoulders and all but pushing him out onto the porch. She shut the door behind them. The rain had gone completely, leaving the usually humid Gulf air feeling sweeter, cleaner and cooler. The chill sent a shiver down his spine, and Caine glowered at her in the dark.

"You'll catch pneumonia." She didn't move to go in, so he said, "I told you, Whitehouse is clean." Was that what she wanted to hear again? "Where that leaves us, I can't say." He wasn't sure he meant just the Whitehouse burglary or the recent attack on Geneva. The day had changed things between them, everything but the buzz of attraction that had always been there. "You can rest assured, however, that I'll keep digging until I can close the case."

Still, she said nothing. She didn't move.

Caine squared his jaw. "You still don't believe me?"

"I believe you. You should believe me, too. Starr Mulligan and I will also keep working, searching…"

"Leave Whitehouse alone. He's innocent."

"More speculation, Detective Caine?" She smiled a little, disarming him but at the same time sending his system into high alert. "I thought you only dealt in 'just the facts, ma'am.' As far as I'm concerned, Earl still could have hurt Geneva *before* his flight." Her tone, he could swear, was teasing, which confused him.

Everything about Nora Pride confused him. Especially today.

"That was Jack Webb, right? From *Dragnet*. This is real life."

"Yes," she nearly whispered. "It is. Think about it. I know I will."

She looked happy but tired. Caine decided to take another tack, perhaps in self-defense. "I was watching you today," he said. "You knocked yourself out for everybody else. But what about you?"

"I like making Christmas for the people I love."

"You should spend more time on yourself," Caine said. But Nora didn't appear to agree. Of course not.

"And you?" she echoed his earlier question. "How long has your wife been gone? It seems to me you don't have a life at all. That's a shame."

She had a point. Caine followed her glance upward to the center of the door frame. Just over her head he spied a suspicious-looking plant tacked to the wood. In the chill night air, it didn't look so good, kind of limp and semitransparent. Still, he recognized its little white berries. And felt his heart kick up.

"I thought we'd put our differences aside. It is Christmas," she reminded him. "You liked being here today, I could tell. For once, I saw you differently, as a man. That's interesting, don't you think?"

"On both sides." But after the admission, which came too easily, Caine didn't know what he thought. In fact, in the next instant he wasn't thinking at all. His brain, too, had taken a holiday.

A second later, his normal analytical powers danced right off the porch, disappearing into the night, leaving him helpless to figure out what was going on here, while Caine took another look at the door frame.

Then, acting on sheer blind instinct, his pulse beating to a primitive drum, he pulled Nora under that wilted sprig of mistletoe—and kissed her.

Fifteen minutes later, Nora came up for air.

They were no longer standing on the porch under the mistletoe or the yellow glare of the light beside her door. She was no longer wondering whether he was right, that she needed more time for herself, a thought she had also entertained. As if to prove his point, and hers, they were wound together in a tangle of arms and legs, in Caine's unmarked police car, deep in the nighttime shadows of her driveway, out of sight from any prying eyes. Maggie was the only possibility left, except Daisy, who seemed to adore Caine. But her mother had gone to bed before Savannah, Browning and Johnny left, right after Leonard, Tabby and Mark. Starr had been the first to go. Heath, she realized in a fuzzy attempt to get her bearings, had never shown.

Alone in the car with Caine, she seemed able to focus only on the feel of his mouth on hers, firm yet pliant and warm, and, above all, skilled.

"Caine," she murmured, drawing back from the kiss, stunned by her own sense of abandon in his arms. This wasn't like her at all. Neither was flirting in the kitchen while he carved the bird.

"Nora," he said, mimicking her soft groan, then went back for more.

She melted. "You're an incredible kisser."

He grunted. "Out of practice."

"Well, keep working at it. It's coming back to you." Nora
meant herself, too. She had enjoyed her brief fling with Heath
Moran. The sex had been good. But, always, there had been
some other element missing. With Caine, and the utter help-
lessness of her response, she never wanted him to leave. "I saw
you today not only as a man," she said at last, "but as a real
human being. A lonely human being, not a member of law
enforcement."

"I am a member of law enforcement."

Nora leaned back in his embrace, enough to see his face in
the moonlight and the scant glow from the streetlight at the
curb behind them. She felt entirely intent for once not on
caring about others but focusing on herself, and she didn't feel
guilty. The notion was somehow freeing, not to feel responsible
for these few moments for every person in her life, for everyone
she loved. The day's cooking, cleaning, entertaining, caring
had drained her, leaving her vulnerable.

So had Caine's kisses. Nora decided to indulge them. And
herself. She gazed at him for a long moment before she moved
into his arms again, then lifted her face, her mouth, to his. Not
even stopping to question her actions, she whispered against
his parted lips.

"And I can be a very bad girl."

Caine lost track of time. He lost track of his own body.
It seemed to have a will of its own.

There had been a brief moment or two in which he'd questioned his sanity again. Then he'd told himself to shut up and pro-
ceeded to take another tour of Nora Pride's lush mouth. At some
point she'd ended up across his lap, wedged between Caine's trai-
torous body and the steering wheel, his hand up under her skirt
and his mouth nudging aside her blouse to seek the soft skin at
the top curve of her breast. Things were getting serious fast. They

were both panting hard when Nora shifted a little to find a more comfortable fit—and hit the horn with her elbow.

A split second later, the porch light flashed on.

Nora shrieked. Daisy barked. Caine groaned in frustration—and guilt.

"Ah, shit."

Like some shocked gargoyle, Maggie's face appeared in the living room window right beside the cruiser, her bed hair wild, her eyes more so, and Daisy didn't look much better. There was a mad scramble to straighten clothes, Caine's, Nora's, about a dozen other people's, or so it seemed. Caught. Caine had busted his share of would-be lovers on dark side roads. Now he was one of them. With Nora Pride.

Obviously she'd decided she didn't want to be there.

She had tumbled off his lap, stuffed herself back into her bra and yanked down her skirt before he fully gauged what was happening. While Caine's head was still spinning, without a word she popped open the passenger door of his police car and all but fell out into the driveway.

"Oh, no," he heard her say just as a Jeep Cherokee pulled up in front of Nora's house. The driver didn't get out. Caine saw a quick flash of a man's angry face in the moonlight, his big-shouldered body and a sweatshirt that read Hi-Health Fitness across his broad chest. The guy shook his head, jammed the Jeep back into gear and sped off.

Nora was across the short strip of Bermuda grass to the sidewalk, up the steps and in the house before Caine could peel away from the curb.

CHAPTER 16

Geneva peeled her long, silky tunic over her head. She shook her hair free, in that way she'd always had since her teen years in beauty pageants, and gazed at Earl across their bedroom. His eyes darkened with obvious desire. He stared at her almost-bare breasts, the leaner length of her torso, her newly nipped-in waist and the long length of her legs.

Only a minute before, Geneva had felt perfectly feline, graceful and appealing as a woman, very much interested in making love with her husband, but for some reason she now fought back a sudden wave of revulsion. Earl didn't seem to notice. He tracked her like a stalking tiger.

"You look great, baby. Been working out?"

Odd, but the endearment didn't strike Geneva as it normally might. When Earl swiftly closed the last distance between them and took her in his arms, her whole body stiffened. It had been weeks since he'd touched her, months since he'd approached her with the old tenderness and really listened to her. She couldn't help getting the impression that he wasn't listening now, that he was comparing her to someone else.

"I belong to a new health club. And I've been walking on the beach."

He nuzzled her throat. Geneva's heart began to pound, not in arousal.

What was wrong with her?

Sure, at first she'd been uncertain about having Christmas

dinner with him. Nora's cautions had stayed in her mind. Yet Geneva knew it wasn't Earl who had hurt her, and she had decided she owed him a hearing of some kind, a few hours together so he wouldn't be alone over his holiday meal. They had never been apart on Christmas since they'd met.

Earl had ordered pheasant in red wine sauce, whipped sweet potatoes, truffles and stuffed mushroom caps, her favorite asparagus with lemon butter, and a pumpkin cheesecake for dessert because Geneva didn't care for pie. They'd even shared some exquisite petits fours as a treat later. There'd been a delicious dry cabernet with their meal, and a rich tawny port with an assortment of cheeses afterward while they opened gifts in front of the living room fire. Or rather, Geneva did. She hadn't brought anything for Earl and suppressed another wave of guilt.

Especially because the thought hadn't occurred to her.

Why not? Why didn't the presents she'd received seem special? And why didn't his touch thrill her now?

With a streak of his thumb, Earl erased the frown that wanted to form between her eyes. He bent to kiss the corner of her mouth, but Geneva turned her head at the last instant and his lips only grazed her cheek.

Without the benefit of Botox, Earl was able to frown. "What's wrong?"

"Nothing. This just doesn't feel right."

He drew back, scowling. "You don't believe Nora Pride, do you? The cops cleared me, Gen. I swear to you, we'll find out who hurt you, but in the meantime you have nothing to fear, especially from me." He tried to draw her toward the bed, his eyes still dark with need. But Geneva held back.

Undaunted, he reached for the zipper of the slacks that draped just right over her hips and now-firmer thighs. Geneva had dressed carefully for the holiday, changing once she'd arrived into the clingy gold pants with that creamy silk tunic that held allure yet didn't promise too much. She'd deliberately worn lighter makeup, no heavy eyeliner or mascara as usual. Maybe she should have twisted her hair into a knot rather than leaving it loose—the way she'd worn it for days at the beach.

Now she edged back until her legs hit the bed.

"Earl, I don't think we should."

His frown deepened. "Why not? We're married."

But were they, really? Geneva suddenly doubted that. Neither did she care for Earl's quick loss of patience with her now. It reminded her of her parents' reaction when Geneva's stomach had knotted before yet another pageant or at some screening session for hopeful teenage models. If she were that young now, they'd be pushing her to go to Hollywood, or to appear on *American Idol*.

She wasn't that young.

She wasn't that needy.

The realization hit Geneva like another, softer blow.

She looked up into Earl's angry eyes—and saw a stranger.

Geneva put out a hand, gently pushing him back so she could ease away from the foot of the bed. She took a few steps toward the hall before Earl swung her around to face him.

"Where do you think you're going?"

She started to say *home*, then stopped herself. She was home, supposedly. And that came as a surprise, too. Funny, but the beach house she'd borrowed from Johnny Hazard seemed more like home to her than this house she'd planned from its multipeaked roof to its four-car garage. There, Maggie had taken care of her and Geneva had walked on the sand, either with Starr and Nora or alone, and she'd really listened to the gulls, enjoyed the blue sky and the stars at night.

She wasn't about to give up her retreat. For too long, she'd been her parents' beautiful little girl, their beautiful teenage daughter, and then Earl's beautiful trophy wife. Now, with her face practically bare and her hair swinging free, she felt stronger than before her accident. She held his gaze. She wasn't about to make love with Earl, either.

"I'm not ready to come back," she said. "I need more time."

Because at some point during her long, solitary walks on the beach, something had happened. Slowly, gradually, one bare footstep at a time, Geneva had discovered something precious, something she'd never realized was missing.

Herself.

"Nothing really happened," Nora said again. If she repeated the phrase often enough, she might come to believe it herself.

Facing her in Geneva Whitehouse's bedroom the day after Christmas, Starr snorted. "You wind up with Caine in the backseat of his car—"

"It was the front seat."

"—and you tell me nothing happened?"

"Well, not much." Nora regretted the confidence. But she'd felt so unsettled this morning when she reached the house, her mouth still tingling from the touch of Caine's lips. She couldn't say anything to the tile guys, who were scoring and cutting handcrafted porcelain squares downstairs in the kitchen. But Nora had needed to tell someone, and of course Starr noticed her mood. "He kissed me," Nora said. "That's all."

"Then why do you feel guilty?"

"It was wrong. I knew better. The case…" She waved a hand.

"Must have been some kiss."

A lot more than one. But Nora didn't say that. She rearranged a newly reupholstered slipper chair in front of Geneva's Mission-style dressing table. She couldn't shake the feeling that something had happened in here, too. Recently. The air had that same heavy quality as in Caine's darkened car. Had Geneva spent the night with Earl? Well, she wasn't here now. Neither Nora nor Starr had heard from Geneva today, and as always Nora worried about her.

At least that felt normal.

Now she needed to focus on her own reality.

Nora remembered Heath pulling up just as she and Caine leaped apart.

Still, the memory of Caine refused to fade. The masculine scent that rose from his skin, a blend of soap and musk and the sharply pungent aroma of some piney aftershave. The feel of his hands, large and capable and warm, against her cooler bare skin. The touch of his mouth, his tongue. The small groans he had uttered against her throat…

"What's next?" Starr asked, jarring Nora at last from her reverie.

"Nothing. I plead temporary insanity. I'm sure Caine doesn't plan to repeat the episode, either."

Starr made a scoffing noise again. "Sure. Right. Is he a man? They never give up wanting some. Look at that yummy Heath, for instance."

"Yeah," said a familiar drawl from the doorway. "What about me?"

Heath strolled into the room, his gaze hooded, his body tense.

"Heath! Oh, there you are," Nora began.

"Oops." Starr headed for the hallway. "I'll just go downstairs. Leave you two to work things out. The tile men are putting in the accent tiles today. I'll just, um, make sure they put them in the right place."

No one heard her. Until Starr's footsteps had faded and they were alone, Heath merely stared at Nora.

"I gather you weren't really talking about me."

How long had he been standing there able to hear them?

He took a few steps closer. "You know, I thought the easy thing would be to skip Christmas at your place. Just stay home, get takeout for dinner, watch TV. Hang out by myself and be safe." He shrugged. "Then I decided, hell, why not? I'll drive over to Nora's after everyone else has gone. We'll have a piece of pie together, nice and easy. But it wasn't easy. Was it?"

"Heath, I'm sorry."

"Hey, I'm the one who should be sorry. I should have got the message the first time." He ran a hand around his sturdy neck, the motion rippling muscles in his shoulder and forearm. "What am I, wearing a Kick Me sign?" he said. "I didn't mean to ruin your little backseat tryst with Caine. My God, *Caine?*"

"It was the front," Nora said again, as if that made it better. "And it wasn't you who ruined things. I made a mistake, moved the wrong way—and just as you drew up out front, Caine's horn blew. Then Maggie switched on the security lights, afraid there was a prowler nearby. And Daisy started barking."

Heath eyed her with skepticism. "You're kidding. Right?"

"I wish I were."

To her surprise, he laughed. "Nora, that's like a couple of teenagers, necking in a place where they shouldn't be. I haven't done that since I was seventeen."

"I never did that," Nora murmured. Not until last night.

He walked closer, a half smile still on his face. "The sky didn't fall, did it?"

"No," she admitted.

"How about the earth? That move for you?"

She had to smile, too. "We didn't get that far."

For a moment he looked relieved. Then he sobered. Heath was all clean, well-put-together man, a male animal in his prime, and Nora had a splendid appreciation of his face and body. Yet that one thing had always been missing for her—the spark, the zing, the sheer chemistry she'd experienced last night. With the wrong man.

It told her something, though.

Heath wasn't right for her, and no amount of time could change that.

When she slipped her arms around his waist and held on tight, Nora heard him sigh. "Is this the part where you ask me if we can still be friends?"

"Forever," she said in a hopeful tone. "You'll find someone wonderful, Heath. I know you will."

He swallowed, hard. "Yeah. I guess. Someone almost as wonderful as you. But I know when I'm beat." He stepped back and headed for the adjoining study. "Better get to work. Shouldn't take me long to hack into Earl's computer."

Nora watched him go. There was one moment when she wanted to run after him, to make him feel better somehow, to assure him that she loved him in her own way. She wanted him to be happy.

Nora rested her forehead against Geneva's four-poster bed and blinked.

"Find someone younger," she whispered to a now-gone Heath. "And far more wonderful."

Last night she'd felt more aroused than she had in years. More than with Heath, bless his heart, or even with Wilson long ago. If she never felt that spark again for the rest of her life, if she ended up alone like Maggie for the next forty years, Nora knew she could never settle for less.

Caine had slept late. When the front doorbell rang, he had that pull-the-covers-over-your-head-and-go-back-to-sleep, escape-from-the-world feeling. If he stayed in bed, he might forget last night with Nora. Forget his own miscalculation.

Not likely.

When the doorbell became more insistent, Caine threw off the covers and padded into his living room, Killer the orange tabby scurrying over his feet to head for safety. The cat's name—Annie's choice—was a misnomer. He had never known a bigger sissy, but Killer wasn't a bad companion. In the high window of his door, Caine saw two heads, one dark, one light. Rubbing his chest, he flipped the dead bolt and opened the door to find Browning Pride and John Hazard on his porch in the late morning sunlight. So much for catching up on his rest on his second day off. Or burying his guilt over last night in his dreams.

Neither one of the men was smiling.

Caine took the offensive. "Well, isn't this a switch? It's usually me pounding on someone's door."

Ignoring him, Browning and Johnny pushed inside, shouldering Caine out of their way. They went straight for his sofa but didn't sit down. Turning around, they planted their feet and eyed him up and down with mutually sour looks. And here he'd thought he'd won them over yesterday. Setting up a turkey fryer qualified as a male bonding event.

"My mother invited you to Christmas dinner," Browning said, as if Caine had committed some crime. His mouth was set in a tight line that showed white around the edges, and in spite of his training, his experience, Caine had the sudden impulse to run. Instead, he stayed his ground. He hadn't done anything wrong...not really. "It was *Christmas*," Browning repeated, as if his crime were one of capital proportions. Death penalty, for sure.

"Good turkey. Nice and juicy. I liked the pie, too."

"Nora wasn't supposed to be your extra dessert." Johnny took a step, bumping his shin on the coffee table. "She invites the whole world on holidays. Don't take it personally."

Caine was in danger of doing just that. He'd spent half his night trying to talk himself out of that kiss—those kisses—in his car. He could still feel Nora Pride in his arms, her soft body and the look in her even softer eyes, the press of her breast against his harder chest. He'd been out of his mind, all right. If the chief found out...

"How did you know?" Caine asked. His guilt must have been written all over him, and he struggled to suppress the haunting memory.

Browning jabbed a finger in the air. "Maggie called us first thing this morning. If you think you can fool around with my mother and get away with it, think again."

"We care about Nora," Johnny said, his expression grim. "Most of the time she doesn't want us to. She thinks it should be her who takes care of us, but Maggie was right. So is Savannah. Nora needs us, too."

"It's about time she realized that," Browning said.

Caine simply stared at them. He couldn't disagree. In fact, he couldn't agree with them more. He'd seen the devotion that Nora's family so readily displayed when he'd questioned her and then again yesterday. It had taken them no time at all to decide she was innocent in the burglary at the Whitehouse home, and then later of the attack on Geneva. Without question, Nora's children and her friends had formed a solid support system, no less effective than a line of SWAT team members in full riot regalia. Caine had to admire that.

"So I tried to tell Nora myself," he finally said. He'd even told her to focus more on herself and let others take their turn caring for her. He didn't think Johnny and Browning would believe him.

It had been a long time since anyone had cared as much about him.

Except for yesterday and last night, when Nora had taken care of Caine. He felt his groin tighten in remembrance, but it wasn't only sex. Nora had really cared. She'd seen the overwhelming loneliness in him as soon as he walked in her door. Seen it better than he did.

It had taken him three beers when he got home to blunt the memory.

"I can understand your concern," Caine told them.

But Browning didn't seem to buy his sincerity. "Don't hurt my mother," he muttered.

Caine bit back a groan. He had no intention of hurting Nora Pride. He had no intention of getting within six feet of her again. Certainly he didn't intend to kiss her. The momentary aberration from his usual state of celibacy was simply that.

For both of them. And yet… Caine had a sudden image of Nora's cozy living room, the scents of home cooking in the air, the rare pleasure he'd taken in deep-frying the turkey for her, the sound of the TV football game and raucous cheers from Browning and Johnny, the sweet taste of pumpkin pie that lingered in his mouth like the touch of Nora's tongue.…

Caine brought himself up short. He'd loved his wife. He'd told Nora that, too. He always would love Annie. But then a new thought struck him. Maybe, last night aside, it was time he got over losing her. Nora Pride was a pretty amazing woman herself, not that they could have anything permanent.

"I imagine she can hold her own," he said to Browning and Johnny. Caine reminded himself that he still had an open case to solve, that he needed to do his job, and that Nora was part of it. "More likely, she'd kill me. That woman is a man-eater."

Johnny almost smiled, but Caine saw Browning's jaw tighten again.

"That's my mom," he told Caine.

Late that afternoon, Nora, Starr and Heath clustered around Earl Whitehouse's computer in his upstairs study. After her morning talk with Heath, Nora kept her distance so he wouldn't feel worse. Suppressing another flicker of guilt because they were about to invade someone else's private system, she peered around him—and Starr, who had nestled against his shoulder—at the computer screen.

After an intense clicking of keys and a few curse words under his breath, a program popped open for Heath, and he was in the heart of Earl Whitehouse's data. It had taken Heath no more than a minute.

"How did you do that?"

He shrugged. "Talent. Nimble fingers," he said, holding up both hands before he dropped them to the keyboard again. "Presto change-o, abracadabra, plus about a gazillion hours of practice. Programming, networking, figuring out software glitches. Damn, I'm good."

"You're being modest," Starr murmured.

In spite of her earlier decision about Heath, Nora nudged Starr aside.

"Let him keep his mind on business." She leaned closer. "Find anything?"

Heath clicked a few more keys. A document appeared. The Quicken software showed them a spreadsheet of Earl Whitehouse's finances. Scanning the page Nora saw the words American Express. Ah-ha. Her pulse accelerated.

"That's his account."

Starr stepped closer to Heath again. "Good place to start. Follow the link."

"Scroll down, Heath," Nora suggested as soon as he pulled up the details on the AmEx Web site. Like many people, Earl used the same few passwords for his accounts.

To her disappointment the entries were mostly predictable. Dinners charged at local restaurants, presumably with Geneva. A bouquet of Thanksgiving flowers sent to New Jersey for Earl's mother or aunt—Nora couldn't tell from the same last name. Earl's tickets on Delta to Jamaica. Nora would have to check with Geneva on that, but she saw nothing that would obviously incriminate him.

"Nothing out of the ordinary," Heath said, sounding disappointed, too.

"There are a lot of entries." Starr pointed at the screen.

"Keep going." Nora wasn't about to give up. She pushed down another wave of uneasiness but glanced at the study doorway to make sure they were still alone. As Nora always did, she half expected Earl to walk in at any second. Then she would be facing a possible breaking-and-entering charge after all. Earl wouldn't be so understanding this time if he discovered them going through his personal electronic files.

"I wish Geneva was here," she said.

Starr, who had objected at first to the search, whirled around. "Oh, stop being such a worrywart, Nora."

"One of us has to have a conscience, Mulligan." Nora didn't mean only over this unauthorized foray into Earl's financial life. She sent a pointed look at the back of Heath's head. His sandy hair glistened in the sun that flooded down from the overhead skylight and illuminated the fine hairs on his forearms, the backs of his hands.

Starr simply leaned closer, letting her chest brush against his upper back. She planted her feet firmly, elbows jutting out so that Nora couldn't come any nearer to them.

Nora did her best to ignore the territorial challenge that should no longer matter. She'd finally made Heath see that their relationship could never go beyond the friendship that she hoped he would eventually accept.

Still, Nora felt terrible.

She switched her position, determined to see the monitor screen. After last night with Caine, her determination to clear her name had become even sharper. She'd lost enough clients to all the nasty rumors going around town. It hadn't been bad enough to be accused of burglary, but then she'd become a suspect in the attack on Geneva, as well. At that point, Nora's office phone had stopped ringing. She'd been forced to return more than a few retainers for her services. There wouldn't be another until the case was closed.

Surely, in the jumble of figures about Earl Whitehouse's dealings, they would find something.

Nora almost didn't see it. The credit charges flashed by, one line at a time, until she realized what she'd glimpsed a few seconds before. She reached out to cover Heath's hand, forgetting the fact that she had no right to touch him now.

"Wait. Go back."

Heath hit the Page Up key, and the figures rolled in reverse.

"There," Nora said. "Look."

Heath and Starr both glanced over their shoulders at her. Heath raised his eyebrows. "What?" His tone was cool, which Nora deserved, yet he sounded interested.

"The notation for the order of some Hunter Douglas blinds. The shipping address," Nora said, but neither Starr nor Heath appeared to be enlightened. "It's one of the homes in Earl Whitehouse's new subdivision."

"So?" Starr said. "He needed blinds for his office."

"I recognize the address. I designed the interior—and suggested those blinds. But not to Earl. It wasn't his office." Reaching around Heath, Nora paged up again, then hit gold, or was that tarnished silver? "They were the last things we needed to complete the job. And there, see?" She pointed at several prior purchases on the screen. "These are more orders. Earl must have paid for the entire home." Nora had had her suspicions at the time.

"It's his subdivision," Heath pointed out. "I remember you doing the model unit for him. What's the surprise?"

"It's not for the model." Nora felt her pulse begin to pound. "This house is across the street and down another block." Geneva's suspicion weeks ago had proved to be true, but it didn't thrill Nora to be right after all. The skunk. "Earl's girlfriend," she said. "He *was* having an affair."

Nora's heart sank. Never mind the challenges that had come with her obvious entry into menopause, which didn't seem so bad now, the complication with Savannah's pregnancy and her postponed wedding, Nora's parting from Heath or her lost clients. Even Maggie and Caine were forgotten. All she could think of now was Geneva.

Starr nearly whispered, "Are you sure?"

"This will really hurt her." Nora didn't hesitate. "But yes, I'm sure."

"How can we tell her?"

Nora didn't know. But the more proof they found, the harder it would become for Earl to deny the truth. "Heath, can we take a look at Earl's e-mail?"

Starr clutched her arm. "Nora, maybe we shouldn't."

A sudden movement in the doorway of the study made them all turn. But it wasn't Earl Whitehouse standing there, as Nora expected. It was a shocked-looking Geneva, whose face had gone as blue-white as skimmed milk.

"Maybe we should," was all she said.

CHAPTER 17

"I think we should kill him," Starr said, not for the first time.

Nora kept driving toward Earl Whitehouse's subdivision at Impressions. In the backseat of her Volvo, Geneva rested her head against the seat, eyes closed, her face still the shocking shade of white that told Nora she was on the verge of a collapse.

"Men can be such weasels," Starr insisted, her lips a grim line and her lavender eyes shooting angry blue sparks on Geneva's behalf.

At the wheel, Nora made a soft clucking sound. Sometimes Starr went too far. No, Starr often went too far. She wasn't being fair about the whole male sex. Her lingering bitterness over her divorce and her estranged son shouldn't include someone like Heath, for instance.

"All men aren't weasels," Nora murmured with a warning glance at Starr.

Geneva blinked, looking as unfocused as she had after being attacked in her home. She was in denial. "I was with Earl last night. I was the one who said I needed distance from our marriage—at least for a while longer. I know I had some suspicions but to learn they're real…I can't believe Earl would do this to me. This isn't like him."

"Maybe it's exactly like him." Starr rolled her eyes. "Get real, Geneva. The man's been married three times. Each of his wives has been younger than the last. It's typical," she said. "Men get that midlife panic but rather than face their own changes, as we have to do, they feed their sagging egos with some new sweetie. It helps them buy into the illusion that they're still twenty-five."

"Starr," Nora murmured. "Please."

"You know it's true, Nora."

"That's a sweeping generalization."

And Geneva had been one of those sweet young things herself not that long ago. Nora remembered their more recent conversation over Chinese takeout, the confidences all three women had shared that night, and she sensed how vulnerable Geneva must feel to know she'd been right after all.

"Earl loves me," Geneva said, as if to convince herself. She pressed a steadying hand to her head, but no wonder she felt rocked by the day's events.

Earlier, she had gazed at Earl's computer, disbelieving of the numbers on the screen. For another hour, they had pored over the incriminating data, the picture of his apparent infidelity getting worse. To her shock, a year ago Nora had received e-mail messages from the same online address—Earl's—she now saw receiving a series of intimate posts from a woman. She recognized that address, too. By the time Heath shut down the computer, Nora had felt sick to her stomach. Earl was cheating, all right. Or he had been. And the person's identity made her feel even worse. But how to make Geneva face the truth now without destroying her in the process?

As always, it helped to know you weren't alone, and Nora cleared her throat. "Geneva, do you trust me?"

"Yes. Why?"

"The AmEx figures—all those gifts and that trip to Jamaica you never took with Earl…I know this hurts, angel, but…" She paused. "Then there are his bank statements, those mysterious withdrawals and deposits to a separate account at regular intervals that tell the story." She hesitated again. "I don't want to say this, believe me, but it's true, just like the computer data and Earl's e-mail, some of it recent, only a few days before Christmas."

Nora took a breath. She *really* didn't want to do this, but clearly Geneva needed the wake-up call. "I'm glad we've gotten to know each other. I consider us to be friends as well as client and designer. But Earl and I have a history you should know about. A year or so ago, as I mentioned, I did the interior for the model home at Impressions. From the start, I liked Earl and he seemed to like me—I mean, in the professional sense. I thought we respected each other."

"Nora, I'd really rather you didn't," Geneva interrupted.

Nora knew she had to, but softened her tone. "One late afternoon when I was finishing up in the guest bedroom there, Earl...cornered me." In the rearview mirror Nora watched the fresh pain flash in Geneva's eyes, saw her first refusal to trust what she was hearing. "I have to admit, he came on pretty strong. I told him, of course, that I wasn't interested. This was well before you and I met, Geneva, but I wasn't looking for a man even then, and if I were I certainly wouldn't have picked a married man—one who clearly prefers younger women." In the end, Nora had been forced to knee him where it hurt. "Frankly, I don't know what would have happened if Savannah hadn't walked in to pick me up for dinner that night. It was an awkward incident, which I took pains never to risk repeating, but it scared me. I completed the job for Earl within the next few days, then left." She paused again. "I'm sorry to tell you this, but it did happen."

Starr muttered, "I don't want to say this, either, but since Nora brought it up...Earl does have something of a reputation in this area, Geneva, certainly among the design community. It's why I didn't accept the offer to do that model home myself."

Nora's gaze shot to Starr. Just when she decided they shared common ground, Starr reverted to type. "That is so not true. I won the bid; you lost."

Starr shrugged. "We can argue later. This is about Geneva. What are we going to do?"

Geneva stayed silent. Nora negotiated the final turn into the gates at Impressions. She drove straight to the house across the street from Leonard Hackett's. His shades were drawn against the midday light, she saw, but today his neighbor's were wide-open. So would her eyes be when Nora and Starr got through with her.

Nora had wanted to leave Geneva at home, to test the waters first. But Geneva had insisted on coming along. This was her life, she'd said. And Starr, always ready to go where the wind blew, had taken her side. Geneva could bury her head in the proverbial sand, go back to Earl as his trophy wife, and pretend she'd never visited the inner sanctum of his computer, thanks to Heath. Or she could confront the issue head-on and at least try to salvage her pride.

Nora feared Geneva still believed in Earl's innocence. It was one thing to get that queasy gut instinct about your relationship with a man, but quite another to find your worst fears had come true. Even after Nora's confession, Geneva might hope they were wrong about him, and this other woman would set them straight.

Nora doubted that. Her inner radar was working overtime. Optimism was a wonderful quality, one she shared with Geneva, but this would also be Nora's chance to clear her name at last. Afterward, she and Starr could help Geneva deal with the emotional fallout. Then Nora could reclaim her position in the local design community and woo back her lost clients without losing any of them.to Starr.

Some corner of her mind told her she should have clued Caine in to the situation rather than try to handle this herself, even with Starr's help. But Nora still felt mortified by those moments she'd spent in Caine's arms like one of Earl White-house's bimbos. She didn't need that kind of reputation, either.

Besides, no crime was about to be committed, she hoped.

Earl had reminded her of Wilson, and undoubtedly re-minded Starr of her ex-husband. Birds of a feather. Nora was still smarting about Wilson's upcoming wedding and still staunch in her refusal to accept his invitation, despite Heather's urging.

She and Geneva and even Starr had all been betrayed by the men they loved.

This might be a once-removed kind of payback for Nora, years too late, but from a personal standpoint, as well as a pro-fessional one, the idea definitely held appeal. Nora was only human. And above all, she didn't want Geneva to suffer.

Of course she'd considered a confrontation first with Earl, but, as was often the case, he'd taken off in the company jet early that morning, this time for south Florida where he was trying to buy land for yet another upscale development. Earl could wait.

Meanwhile the main thing was to help Geneva.

"You really think we should do this?" Geneva hung back on the top step.

"Tabitha Whitlaw is just as guilty as he is," Starr told her and reached around Nora to give the door another knock for emphasis.

"Maybe we should wait until Earl gets home."

"Oh, him, too," Starr said. "Right now, it's not his turn."

"Mess around with a bunch of women over forty," Nora murmured after pounding on Tabitha Whitlaw's front door for the third time, "and regret it."

"Who's there?" said a muted female voice from inside.

"Nora Pride."

"And friends," Starr added.

Nora didn't have time to reflect on the strange feeling that ran through her at hearing the term. She and Starr had never been friends, yet they were bonded not only as unlikely co-workers but by their determination to help Geneva deal with Earl's tacky affair.

"It's Geneva Whitehouse," she called out. "Please open the door."

A strip of light appeared between the door and its frame, then another, wider slice until the security chain caught. Tabby's swollen red eyes peered out at them through the crack.

"What do you want?"

"A few minutes of your time," Nora said. "I think you know why."

The chain slid off. The door opened to admit them, and Nora, Starr and Geneva walked in. Tabby motioned them into the living room where, not quite to Nora's surprise, she found Leonard already lounging on the sofa, a cup of tea on the end table by his elbow, the TV remote control in his hand. He turned off the set. "Good morning, Nora."

He sounded hale and hearty again, an incredible turn-around. Maybe her Christmas dinner had helped. Nora was amazed by Leonard's continuing transformation. He seemed to be having fewer episodes of some dire disease that always went unnamed and was never cured to his satisfaction before another took its place.

"Leonard. You seem to be feeling better."

"Tabby and I take care of each other. Today it's my turn." He glanced at Nora's empty hands. "I was hoping you'd brought us more leftovers from the Christmas turkey." He rose to his feet and then moved to stand, protectively, next to Tabby.

She'd never known Leonard to care for anyone else more than for himself, and for a long moment Nora just stared.

Starr stepped in. "Maybe you'd better speak to us alone," she said to Tabby. "This concerns a very private matter."

"Tabby's relationship to Earl Whitehouse?" Leonard asked. "I know all about that. We've discussed it in detail, one reason

I'm here now." He looked at Nora, reminding her of Tabby's quarrel with Earl.

"I'm so ashamed,'" Tabby murmured, then burst into tears.

Nora readjusted her earlier view of the slim young woman who had fallen for Earl Whitehouse's "charms." And some of her outrage on Geneva's behalf dissolved in a quick wash of unexpected maternal feeling. Tabby was still under thirty, probably unsophisticated from what Nora had seen, and Earl had used her just as he had Geneva.

All at once, she wanted to assure Tabby, who looked very young and vulnerable in a too-large T-shirt and bare feet, that they were unarmed, but the quip seemed out of place. Tabby didn't look at all like a home wrecker.

Leonard guided her to the sofa and sat beside her. "Please say what you came to say. I'm staying right here in case I'm needed."

Nora put an arm around Geneva's shoulders. They and Starr were at a loss. Nora had expected a more defiant attitude, a considerable degree of righteous self-justification from Tabby. This obviously shattered girl made things different.

"You were my husband's lover?" Geneva finally asked in a soft voice that held the hint of fresh tears. She needed to hear her say it.

"Yes."

"Did you love him?"

"He said he wanted to marry me. We had all these plans…"

"Marry you?" Nora echoed. "Earl begged his wife to come home. Does that sound like a man contemplating divorce?"

"I think you'd better start at the beginning," Starr suggested in her best no-nonsense tone.

Still weeping, Tabby looked to Leonard for support. He tightened his grip on her hand, and Nora saw him give her a light squeeze of encouragement. Leonard, thinking of others before himself? She couldn't quite wrap her mind around the change.

Tabby's tone was halting. "I met Earl at his office when I

came to look at the subdivision model. I didn't intend to buy. I couldn't. I was working as a secretary nearby. I was curious because the units at Impressions looked so neat from the outside. I liked their Spanish tile roofs. I was only daydreaming on my lunch hour. I never meant to—" She paused. "I'd just broken up with my boyfriend, and Earl was so nice to me. We talked and talked, and then he asked me to dinner. I didn't know then that he was married, I swear."

Geneva's expression froze. She went from stunned to resigned. "You went to the Villa Capri," she guessed, her tone deflated.

"How did you know?"

"That was where he took me on our first date. I met him when he judged the Miss Panama City pageant. I came in second, and Earl offered to console me over filet mignon."

"Me, too," Tabby said, sounding astonished at the similarity.

"I'm beginning to see a pattern here," Starr murmured.

Tabby blushed. "We ended the evening at the Starlite Motel."

"Across the street from the restaurant," Geneva added.

"You went there, too?" Tabby looked at her lap. "We saw each other for a few weeks after that, here and there. Then Earl said I should live in style, and he, well, he made it easy for me to move into this house."

"In whose name?" Nora asked.

"The deed is in his name. Earl said it would be simpler that way. He is the developer here, and everything belongs to him until it's actually sold, and I didn't have the money for the down payment, much less the monthly mortgage."

"Or the interior design work," Nora said.

"Earl suggested we hire you, or I should. He said he owed you a favor."

"You could say that." Nora remembered Earl's clumsy but aggressive come-on in the bedroom of the model unit at Impressions. She'd been reluctant to work for Tabby in the same development where she might run into Earl Whitehouse at any moment again, but as always Nora had needed the business. And Tabby, she had been assured, would pay top dollar.

"We were happy," Tabby murmured, as if she couldn't believe what had happened. Her unwise decision to get involved with Earl had already cost her dearly, if not in the financial sense. "I'm really sorry, Mrs. Whitehouse."

Geneva sank onto a chair across from her. "I'm sorry, too." She glanced at Nora and Starr. "I should have believed you."

Nora touched her shoulder. "It's not something any woman wants to believe. I know how painful this is for you, Geneva."

Starr turned toward Tabby. "So you and Earl were tucked up here in your little love nest—"

"It was perfect. For a while," Tabby admitted. "Earl listened to me. He gave me gifts all the time. The furniture, and then after I moved in, some jewelry. We took a wonderful trip to Jamaica."

Starr raised her eyebrows at Nora. They'd seen the charges on Earl's American Express account.

"Soon after I moved in, he bought me some smaller items. A Cuisinart because he liked us to cook together, some extra linens in the colors he likes—"

"Blue," Geneva supplied. "Sea-green like the Gulf, and that rich, royal purple."

"He liked red though, too, and how the color swirled with the dark blue in the crystal vase he gave me—until I learned it wasn't his to give." Tabby looked guilty.

Nora snapped to attention. "A vase?"

"Shaped like a heart," Tabby confirmed.

"Oh, no," Geneva nearly whispered.

"Oh, Tabby," Leonard said.

"Oh, brother," Starr muttered.

Tabby frowned. "I'm sorry for that, too. I know it was yours, Mrs. Whitehouse. Earl took it for me, but it wasn't mine to keep. One night, he had too much to drink and talked a lot.

He said the vase wasn't new, and I thought it was an antique at first, but then he slipped. He insisted you wouldn't miss it, that you had so many treasures you wouldn't notice it was gone. That was when he admitted he was married. It was the first time I knew I couldn't trust him."

Nora's eyes widened. "Earl stole the vase from his own home?"

And Nora had been accused of a false burglary.

"He took it," Geneva said, "while I was waiting for him in a restaurant."

Tabby nodded. "I knew you'd really want it, Mrs. White-house, so I said he should take it back. He got angry. If I didn't trust him completely, then maybe we weren't right for each other after all and we shouldn't marry." She gave a little hiccup that sounded more like a sob. "He said maybe I didn't love him the way he thought I did."

"What a manipulator," Starr said. "The creep."

Tabby Whitlaw had walked into his trap like a baby rabbit in Mr. McGregor's garden looking for the first tender lettuce of spring. Nora couldn't sustain her initial anger. In fact, she almost felt sorry for Tabby.

Geneva's years of competing in beauty pageants from the time she was a child had given her an obvious composure under stress that Nora envied. "So you broke up?"

"Not right away," Tabby continued. "Earl had a business meeting in Boston. I was supposed to go with him, but after the argument—our first—we agreed it would be better for me to stay behind and think about our relationship." She sighed. "After he left, I guess I panicked. I still loved him and I couldn't believe things were falling apart. I didn't want to lose him just because he'd lied to me once."

Starr groaned softly. "You mean, twice."

"Yeah, I guess I was naive," Tabby agreed.

Nora almost wanted to cross the room and give her a hug, but she held back, not wanting to appear disloyal to Geneva at the same time she sympathized with Tabby. "You made a mistake, that's all."

"Then I made another mistake," Tabby confessed. "I went to see Mrs. Whitehouse."

Geneva's smooth brow tightened.

"I had to wait a long time," Tabby said. "You weren't home that night so I stood outside the house, imagining that Earl and I lived there together. It's even more beautiful than this one, Mrs. Whitehouse."

"Please. Call me Geneva." Her tone was dry yet hurt. "We have someone in common."

"The longer I stood there, the more convinced I became that Earl and I did belong together, that he'd been telling me the truth when he said his wife didn't understand him."

"Oh, please," Starr murmured. "That's a classic."

Tabby hesitated. "Then you came home, Mrs.—I mean, Geneva—and before you could turn on the lights or set the security system, I slipped in behind you." Tabby shuddered. "I only meant to talk to you, to make you see how Earl and I felt about each other. But you looked so like you belonged there instead of me, comfortable in your home. I wondered what your relationship with Earl was really like and why he didn't just leave you—unless he was lying to me again. Before I knew it—" Tabby swallowed hard "—you and I were quarreling. It was like you were the one in our way, in the way of our happiness together. I lost control and lunged—"

"It was *you* who hit me," Geneva said, and Nora could see the full memory of the attack resurface in her still-bruised mind. She'd said it was a woman.

Nora had, in part, been wrong.

Tabby studied her hands, laced together with Leonard's. "I had brought the vase with me as proof that Earl loved me, not you. But you didn't want to believe what I was trying to tell you."

"We struggled," Geneva remembered. "I turned away,

telling you to leave my house. You shouted, 'Listen to me!' Then you struck me with the vase."

Tabby nodded miserably. "It was supposed to be my engagement gift."

"And *mine*," Geneva told her.

Tabby looked crestfallen. "I shouldn't have done it. But I was so angry, I couldn't think then. As soon as you started talking, I knew you weren't the guilty one, he was. And that meant so was I. I've been hiding the vase ever since," Tabby admitted. "I watched TV for days, afraid that I'd killed you and the police would track me down. They'd come and search my house. I mean, Earl's house."

"Hot potato," Starr murmured.

"So I 'lent' the vase to Leonard. It's in his bedroom on a shelf."

With that, Nora stepped forward. Leonard looked pale. The vase had been in his possession, only a few feet away, when Nora had visited his home.

But wait. Another connection clicked in her mind. "But if Earl gave Geneva that vase, then took it from her when he fell for Tabby…was that the only time he transferred its 'ownership' to another woman?"

"My God," Starr said. "I think you're right."

"You mean, what if—?" Tabby began but Nora cut her off. "It's the gift that keeps on giving."

An hour later, Nora, Starr, Geneva and Tabby were sitting in the living room of Earl Whitehouse's first wife. An elegant, refined woman who was impeccably dressed, she had done well for herself in the divorce in spite of Earl's reluctance, she said, to share his assets. Her home, in a high-rise building that overlooked the beach, was tastefully furnished and well maintained. Every surface gleamed.

"Who was your designer?" Nora couldn't help asking.

The woman smiled at Starr. "Ms. Mulligan. It's nice to see

you again, Starr. I get compliments on your work all the time. She was just starting out then and eager for business," Earl's ex told Nora. "I paid her twice her going rate—and let Earl pick up the tab."

"Divine justice," Starr agreed.

Earl's former wife shifted on her bargello-patterned upholstered chair. "You said something on the phone about a vase?"

Geneva produced it from her large leather tote bag. Leonard had been only too happy to return it to her. He hadn't known he was guilty of receiving apparently stolen property.

Afternoon sunlight streamed through the long windows, softened by sheer linen curtains. But still, color ricocheted through the glass vase in a display of sparkling scintillation like that of a fine diamond, casting a vivid rainbow across the floor.

As soon as she saw it, Earl's first wife inhaled sharply. She put a hand to her perfectly coiffed hair. "I'd almost forgotten how beautiful it is."

An impressive gift, all right, unusual, and presumably unique. At least Earl Whitehouse had good taste, Nora thought.

"You recognize this vase?"

She pursed her lips. "Earl gave it to me when we became engaged. He said it was a symbol of our love. Then he had the nerve to ask for it in the divorce settlement, and I was just mad enough to let him have it. I should have used it to fracture his skull for running around on me."

Geneva made a strangled sound. So did Tabby.

"He filled it with red roses," Tabby said.

"Yes." The woman nodded but frowned. "Are you telling me that he—?"

"You were the first," Geneva said. "At least, I think you were." She gestured toward Tabby who was seated on a Sheraton-style bench near the doorway. "She was the last…to date."

"Incredible. The rat."

"But true, apparently. Like Bill Clinton," Nora said. "He

gave copies of Walt Whitman's *Leaves of Grass* to Monica, and lots of other women he romanced. Can you believe that, he had a whole supply of books, or so I read in some magazine. Or was it his autobiography?" She dug in her purse for her cell phone. "Shall we call Earl's second wife and see what she has to say?"

With a tight smile, Geneva rose.

"No. Let's pay her a visit, too. We'll surprise her."

"Maybe not. But I'd like to see her face," Starr agreed.

By five o'clock, Nora and Geneva had recovered from the repeated shock of learning that Earl had given the same engagement present to four women. He'd even used the very same words.

"At least he could have changed the flowers," Starr remarked.

She, Nora and Geneva rode with Tabby toward the private hangar where Earl Whitehouse kept his company jet. Daisy, after being picked up at home, sat scrunched between Geneva and Tabby in the rear seat of Nora's car. Nora doubted the dog would provide much in the way of protection, but her presence might give Earl something to think about. She smiled at Daisy's soulful gaze, her ears alert as if she understood their conversation.

Earl was on his way home from south Florida and expected soon. The four women were more than willing to wait for him. Even Tabby had said, "I wouldn't miss this for the world."

Geneva gave them a weak smile that Nora could see in her rearview mirror. "I can't wait for his reaction when he sees us."

Nora's heart twisted at Geneva's tone, one reason Nora was leading this raiding party. Geneva had suffered a number of stunning revelations already today, including the one from Earl's second wife. Earl had forced her to sign a prenuptial agreement. In their divorce, almost everything, including the vase, had gone to Earl. After that, Nora couldn't send Geneva into the lion's den alone.

She pulled the Volvo into the lot outside the chain-link

fence where both passengers and the public were allowed to park. Together they all waited until the sleek Learjet had landed, and Earl Whitehouse clambered down the steps onto the tarmac. His bulging briefcase in hand, he started across the restricted area—and saw them waiting, four angry women lined up at the gate. Four determined expressions. Even Geneva looked formidable.

Daisy growled, deep in her throat. Unlike her response to Caine, she appeared not to like Earl on sight.

"What's this? A welcoming committee?" Earl's startled gaze shot past Geneva, then stopped at Tabby. "No, I guess not."

No one had to tell Earl that the jig was up. He'd been caught red-handed. His wife, his girlfriend (Nora disliked the term mistress) and the woman he had once trapped in a bedroom. Starr didn't have quite the same investment in the situation, as far as Nora knew, but she'd been wronged in her life, as well. Starr had a definite presence that lent some necessary support, and perhaps backup. Nora wouldn't have done this without her.

If she had ever wanted to help anyone in her life, it was Geneva, who had never been able to help herself. Always, she had depended on others to define her as a woman, as a person. In the past weeks she'd begun to change, but Nora stayed right beside her now, ready for anything.

So did Daisy, who for once seemed to know her place.

"So," Earl said, opening the gate, "you've met." He meant Tabby and Geneva, of course.

Tabby's still red-rimmed eyes told her part of the story. Even Earl couldn't miss that. To Nora's surprise, as soon as he stepped into the parking area, Tabby flew toward him. She shoved past Nora, knocked Starr aside when she would have put out a hand to stop her, and flung herself at Earl. Surprised, he staggered back.

Daisy tensed, her warning growls deepening. Her eyes flashed.

"You bastard!" Tabby cried.

"Settle down, baby." Earl held her off, Tabby's arms flailing in every direction as she tried to connect with his midsection, then his jaw. "Cut it out, Tabby. People might be watching from the terminal."

"I hope they are!"

Nora hoped Earl didn't intend to hurt her, but in apparent self-defense he pushed Tabby away. With the sudden movement, she would have gone sprawling if Starr hadn't caught her. They battled for balance, with Daisy dancing anxiously around them, barking.

"I trusted you!" Tabby yelled, oblivious to the curious faces that had indeed appeared in the terminal windows. "You lied to me! You lied to me about Geneva's vase. You lied when you said you loved me."

Earl didn't bother to look sheepish. With a twisted smile, he took advantage of Starr's hold on Tabby to pull out his cell phone and punch in a quick few numbers before anyone could prevent him.

"Get back in the car," he told them. "I've called the police. If you want to avoid trouble, leave now."

"He's bluffing," Starr murmured.

"I don't think so," Nora said. She stepped forward, determined to have her say, if in a gentler fashion than Tabby. "Before the cops get here, Earl, let me tell you something. This is just for me, not from Tabby." This was her chance to stand up to Earl as Tabby had done. "I don't need to remind you of what you did. But I swear, you won't trap some other unsuspecting woman like me in an empty house again and frighten her with your lousy come-on. You're history, Earl. You treated me badly then. You treated Tabby like dirt, too. Worst of all, you betrayed Geneva, who loved you, just as Tabby did, with all her heart."

"And we weren't the only ones," Tabby said, her voice trembling. "We know what you did."

When she pulled free of Starr's grip and went for him again, Earl batted her away. Tabby fell against Nora. As Nora set her on her feet again, Earl grabbed Nora's arm, gripping her hard. And Daisy, close at Nora's side, turned into a snarling beast.

To Nora's amazement, the peaceful golden retriever leaped up, barking maniacally. She knocked Earl backward. His arms pinwheeled for a second before he regained his balance, but Daisy didn't back off. She growled and snapped at him, her pearly white canines flashing like razors.

"Down, girl," Nora said, but Daisy's hackles stood on end, and though she backed off Earl she refused to sit. Rumbling in her throat, she leaned against Nora's leg, ready if she was needed again. For the first time in her life, she'd protected Nora.

Geneva cleared her throat and then stepped forward, as if she'd been waiting her turn. "We know about the vase, Earl. Your first two wives weren't any happier to realize what you'd done than we were."

"You decided to stick together," he said. "That's...admirable. But what I did wasn't a crime, Geneva." His chin went up. "I bought the vase, I owned it."

"That's all it meant to you?" Tabby thrashed, again in Starr's hold. She shook her head in disbelief, but then subsided as if resigned. "You know what? You're not worthy of my love, Earl. Or anyone else's."

Nora could have said the same, once, about Wilson, as she supposed Starr could have of her ex-husband. She sent Tabby a sympathetic look. It would take a long time for Tabby to regain her trust, to look for a better relationship than the one she'd thought she had with Earl. The same held true for Geneva.

Earl shifted his weight, glancing toward the road as if hoping to see a police car with siren blaring, lights flashing. He didn't deserve to be rescued, but Nora wasn't eager to encounter the cops again. She hadn't had time to appreciate the fact that her name would now be cleared in the burglary and the attack on Geneva. She wondered what would happen to Tabby.

Starr had turned away with Tabby and was leading her back to the car. Tabby was weeping again, but Nora felt sure her tears came from anger now, not loss. Keeping Daisy near, she moved closer to Geneva.

Earl glared at Nora. "Haven't you butted in enough? My wife and I can talk things out on our own." He gestured with his head toward Nora's Volvo. "Go help your friends."

"I am helping my friend." Nora reached for Geneva's hand and held her ground. She wasn't about to abandon her. Earl had taken in one too many women, and Nora was no more inclined to leave him with Geneva than she would leave Savannah or Maggie to fend for themselves. Earl would only manipulate the vulnerable Geneva into seeing things his way.

But to Nora's surprise Geneva's quiet voice cut into her determined thought. "I'm okay. I'll be all right."

Nora shook her head. "Geneva, he'll only find some way to convince you that you're wrong, that the others are wrong, too, and before you know it—"

"This is my marriage, Nora. Please. Leave us alone."

For a moment Nora stared at her. Wisely, Earl kept quiet. Then Nora realized that, in the depths of Geneva's blue gaze, she glimpsed a new strength that had nothing to do with how other people defined her. Including Nora, who had underestimated Geneva.

Perhaps Earl was even right about Nora. She had interfered too much. Johnny had said so. Savannah, too. Browning had thought the same for a long time. Even Mark and Maggie, and finally Caine, had told her so. And still, Nora had refused to let the people she loved work out their own problems.

Who did she think she was, meddling where she really

wasn't wanted? It was only because she cared so much…or was that the whole truth? She'd think about that later.

Geneva's pleading look, the new quiet confidence in her expression, finally made Nora back away. Slowly.

"If you need me…" she couldn't resist saying before she took another step.

"Thank you, Nora, but no." Geneva had already turned to face Earl again before Nora could blink.

"Well, if you're absolutely sure…"

"I am." Geneva took a deep breath, her total concentration now on Earl. "All my life," Nora heard her begin, "I've let everyone including you, Earl, love me—if that's the word—for the wrong reasons."

Oddly, in that instant as she backed away with Daisy close by her side, Nora felt a new sense of serenity wash through her. Hoping she'd done the right thing but pretty certain she had, Nora walked Daisy toward her Volvo.

She saw Caine's unmarked car wheel into the parking lot. Behind him, she spied two other cars, but they weren't cops, and Nora smiled. One luxury sedan, followed by a subcompact with a rusted shell, careened off the street and screeched to a halt near Nora. Earl's two ex-wives had arrived. There would be more hell to pay for Earl Whitehouse.

Nora had her fingers wrapped around the handle of the Volvo's driver door when Caine climbed out of his car. He assessed the situation with one professional glance. Geneva and Earl were talking softly, much to his and Nora's satisfaction. Geneva would be okay. Starr and Tabby sat side by side on Nora's rear seat. But it wasn't any of the others to whom he addressed his comment.

Caine's dark eyes met hers. He towered over her, big and male and not at all intimidating. He gave Nora the same look he'd given her in his car on Christmas night. His slow smile took her by surprise.

Nora felt her pulse flutter, felt the first telltale warming of her skin. This time it wasn't a hot flash. Nora had changed.

"More trouble?" he asked.

"No," she told him. "Everything's fine."

CHAPTER 18

Nora was still smiling when she reached Savannah and Johnny's condominium. The day after the incident at the air terminal, she wasn't ready to go to work yet. In spite of everything, especially the fact that she'd finally taken a backseat in Geneva's troubles with Earl, she felt quite hopeful about the outcome, whichever way it might go.

The realization was strangely freeing. Like those moments in Caine's car on Christmas, she actually felt more…herself. Like Geneva, it had been years since Nora had focused solely on what *she* needed.

"What are you grinning about?" Savannah wanted to know from her place on the living room sofa. As usual, she was surrounded by snacks, a cold glass of what appeared to be fruit juice, a pile of current magazines, a couple of paperback novels, one of them a grisly-looking thriller if Nora could judge by the cover, and the TV remove control. Her stack of pillows kept her comfortable, and she looked happier than she had in weeks. No, she looked as if she had a secret of her own.

"The world is a very bright place," Nora answered, dropping her purse on a nearby chair and then crossing the room to give Savannah a kiss. "How are my babies today? How are you feeling, my first baby?"

"Terrific. And fine. It's a sunny day. How could I be otherwise?"

"That's a change," Nora murmured, but she gave thanks for it. She'd been worried about Savannah ever since the announcement that one baby had magically become three. Nora sank down on the sofa beside Savannah and patted her ever-growing stomach. "Hi, angels. I'm glad you're treating Mommy well."

"What happened with Geneva?" Savannah reached for Nora's hand. "When you called last night after you got home from the airport, your report sounded tense, and I've never trusted Earl Whitehouse, either." Nora gave her a quick recap, and Savannah frowned. "Finding you with him in the bedroom at his subdivision that day really shook me up. If I'd arrived a few minutes later…"

"He would have had a fat lip to go with the swift kick I delivered. I can take care of myself," she assured Savannah. "I did just fine yesterday—with a little help from Daisy. My heroine." My, she was having a lot of revelations today. Or perhaps they were epiphanies. "Earl is a chastened man at the moment," she went on. "Geneva took care of him perfectly." Then Nora reconsidered. "Of course, there were a few unsettling moments after I left them alone. But Geneva more than held her own. I'm very proud of her. When we first met, she was a hollow woman. Now she seems to be bursting with new confidence, insights."

"I hope one of them was a decision to divorce Earl. I can't believe the way he treated her, not to mention Tabby and the others. Especially you."

"Earl has a problem," Nora admitted. "Geneva has insisted that he get counseling for what appears to be a sexual—or rather, romantic—addiction."

"You mean a Don Juan complex?"

"That's for the psychiatrist to determine." Another revelation. Nora didn't feel the slightest urge to help Earl. She would support Geneva in whatever she chose to do, but that was that. Nora's only other duty was to finish the redesign work on her home. Without Starr, Nora had learned. "Unfortunately, Geneva thinks she may go back to Earl and try to work things out."

"You're not serious."

"Geneva told me he simply fell apart once she confronted him about his behavior. She says she begged her again to come back. Geneva says it made her realize that he's always needed her more than she needed him."

Savannah frowned. "Doesn't sound like a match made in heaven to me. Johnny and I may have issues, but I couldn't be happy with a man who wanted to lean on me like Earl with Geneva. How can she trust him? Is she sure she's doing the right thing?"

Nora's thoughtful expression suddenly became a smile. "Geneva has a generous heart. And who knows? Maybe that's exactly what Earl and even Geneva need. Perhaps she'll gain even more strength by being the one in charge for once. Heaven knows she never was before, considering her parents and her upbringing. But now the power balance in her marriage will shift, that's for sure." Nora paused. "Actually, when you think about it, Earl's addiction gives women absolute power over him, not the reverse. Maybe he's begun to realize that now."

"A change, all right. But I'm not optimistic about their chances as a couple." Savannah reached up to test Nora's forehead with one hand. "Are you sure you don't have a fever? It's not like you to simply back off. For instance, after Geneva got hit with the vase, you insisted on caring for her, even when you were a suspect yourself."

"It's precisely like me," Nora said, and meant it. "The new me." My goodness, she thought as the reality struck home. "It will be interesting to see what develops—from a distance this time."

"What's this?" Johnny had entered the apartment without either of them being aware of it. Nora and Savannah glanced up with twin smiles for him. Johnny leaned over Nora to plant a sound kiss on Savannah's mouth. Then he brushed Nora's cheek before he straightened. "Nora, sitting on the sidelines?"

Savannah laughed, sounding more like herself than in the past difficult weeks. "Ma's had quite an adventure. With Earl White-house—and her gang of lady friends. Don't cross them, buddy."

Nora gazed at him fondly. She felt very lucky to be getting him in her family. "Johnny hasn't given me a moment's worry since you announced your engagement. And speaking of that…"

"Did you tell her?" Johnny asked.

"Tell me what?"

Savannah hesitated. "I was waiting until you got home."

"So you could make me the bad guy?" Johnny sat at the foot of the sofa, and Nora saw his green eyes sparkle. He loved to tweak her. "Well, here goes, then." He took an exaggerated breath. "We've set a date."

He named a day less than a month away, while Savannah was still pregnant. "You mean a small civil ceremony?"

"No, the whole shooting match. Fifty guests," he said. "Maybe seventy-five. Savannah and I are still putting the list together so you won't need to—"

"Where?" Nora asked, feeling left out again and a little hurt.

He shrugged. "The beach house, if Geneva's agreeable."

"She's planning to go home to Earl," Savannah added.

"We didn't think beyond that," Johnny said, "but we want to be married before the kids get here."

Nora realized they expected her resistance, or worse, her suggestions, at every turn. Of course they did. She'd always taken control of events, tried to smooth the way for her loved ones. It was a habit she needed to break.

"Stop right there," she said. "You may hold your wedding wherever you please." She waved a hand in the air. "I'm sure you're equal to the task."

"You mean you don't want to—"

Interfere? Meddle? Nora said with a smile, "No. I don't."

Saying the words seemed to give her a newfound strength, like Geneva. Actually, it occurred to Nora that she and Geneva were very much alike in one way—they had each sacrificed themselves for the other people in their lives. Along the way, Nora had lost a big chunk of herself. Let her daughter and future son-in-law worry about their wedding. Nora had only one idea in mind, and that was hers to address.

"You're certain?" Johnny asked. Clearly, he hadn't believed she would buy his ultimatum about their wedding plans. "We wouldn't want to deprive you—"

"Of course you should. Plan away. I have every confidence that you'll create an absolutely perfect wedding just as you've made a trio of adorable babies without my help. I'll tell you what I'm going to do on your special day."

"What?" they both said at once, a renewed wariness in their voices. Nora's capitulation had come too easily, they would think.

"Enjoy myself," she answered, which she was doing right now. "First, I need to buy a new dress."

"Take Maggie with you," Savannah suggested. "She needs a whole wardrobe."

Nora thought of her mother's usual baggy house dresses and oxford-style shoes. "Well, yes, of course." That idea didn't necessarily hold appeal, but Savannah was right. Her mother could use a bit of updating, and Savannah couldn't handle the job just now. "It will give me something to do."

"Hmm."

"I mean it, angels. I'm out of the wedding planner business. It's all up to you from now on. I'm glad you'll be married before Maggie goes back to Virginia."

"I'm putting my house on the market."

Maggie's announcement came as she walked in the door from Johnny's beach house after spending the morning with Geneva, who didn't seem to need her as much now. In fact, she'd sent Maggie home in a cab. When Maggie said the words, Nora only looked at her.

"Didn't she tell you?" Savannah asked Nora. "She's staying in Destin."

Maggie beamed. "I'm so excited about the triplets. When they're born Johnny has asked me to move in with them at the beach house, that is, after Geneva moves out. There's more room there than here in the condo, and I'll have my own room and bath. Right near the nursery. With three of us to pitch in, we should be able to handle everything."

For a moment, she could tell, Nora felt overlooked. But the move should be good news. Nora had been nagging her for years to relocate. In the weeks of caring for Savannah during her pregnancy, Maggie had realized that she no longer felt like a victim—most of the time, because people never changed completely—and these days, when she looked in the mirror, her eyes did appear brighter. Her step was lively. She had discovered a new sense of purpose.

Being with family had stripped years off her appearance, and she had gradually shifted from dwelling on herself to others, rather like Leonard Hackett with Tabby. Nora might like to think that her first talking-to with Maggie had helped do the trick, but Nora couldn't take all the credit. In fact, Maggie could even tolerate that dog, and in recent days she hadn't sneezed even once. Daisy wasn't a bad sort. Whenever Maggie felt a bit low and was missing Hank, Nora's pet always stayed close to give her a wet kiss and a sympathetic look.

Maybe, Maggie decided, she would pack up the house in Virginia even before it sold and bring some of Hank's things to Florida, just so he could still be with her.

"I'm so glad," Nora finally said, sounding relieved. "With Savannah, Johnny, and you, the triplets will be covered. One person for each baby."

"You can be our pinch hitter. At least in the first weeks, that will be a blessing."

Savannah assessed Nora's face. "You're not disappointed, are you? You know there will always be room for you, Ma, any time. We'll be thrilled to have you spell us for a while here and there. Besides," Savannah said, "you're already the triplets' favorite—"

"Grandmother." The word seemed to trip easily over Nora's tongue. She had even framed a copy of the latest sonogram for her bedside table, and Maggie wanted one for herself. They grinned at each other. They would be the most hip, up-to-the-minute, hands-on grandmas in the whole world.

And a grand new age it would be, as far as Maggie was concerned. A time of exciting possibilities that she had only begun to explore. Who knew what she and Nora might accomplish in the next fifty years? Maggie had even agreed to see Mark Fingerhut again, then a cardiologist. If she needed medication, so be it. Maggie intended to live for a long time. The babies needed her.

"When the triplets are holding their own, I just might buy a house here," Maggie said. And to her satisfaction Nora's mouth dropped open.

Unlike her mother and grandmother, Savannah hadn't moved a muscle for the rest of the day. She didn't have to. Almost as soon as Maggie and Nora disappeared, bound for the Silver Sands Mall a-twitter with plans for their wedding outfits, Kit had arrived with Tyler.

To Savannah's surprise, Kit insisted upon fixing lunch before she left Tyler to "pway with Sabannah" while Kit attended her English class. Tyler seemed only too happy to wait on Savannah hand and foot; he did almost as good a job as Maggie. Back in bed, Savannah was glad her grandmother was getting an afternoon off. The fact that she and Nora had left in high spirits was a bonus.

Tyler was hooting in triumph over his latest win at Chutes and Ladders when Johnny walked in, looking pleased with himself. While Tyler was there he'd gone out to work on a project at Starbucks. Johnny leaned against the bedroom door frame with a secretive smile.

"Big news," he said. "I called Wade from the cell on my way home. We had a good talk. Looks like he'll produce my new script and maybe even play a part in it."

"Razor Slade rides again," Savannah murmured.

"It's early days yet," Johnny went on but then he stopped, having heard what she said. "Not Slade." A faint flush bloomed on his cheekbones. He fiddled with his signet ring. "The other thing. You know."

"What thing?"

"The movie Johnny's been witing," Tyler said, setting up their game for another round. He didn't look at either of them, but he clearly took in every word.

Savannah stared at Johnny. "A four-year-old boy knows what my fiancé is doing at his computer—and I don't?"

"It's a surprise," Johnny said.

"Tell me."

"He calls it *Wubbing Sabannah*," Tyler supplied. He kicked one leg rhythmically against the side of the bed to show her he was waiting to play their game.

"Love?" Savannah echoed. "There's no violence? No car bombs? No hostage situations or shoot-outs in some godforsaken jungle twelve thousand miles from anywhere?"

"Not even a car chase," he admitted.

Savannah blew a strand of hair from her eyes. "Johnny, I've never seen you do anything except Razor Slade. He's your alter ego, the guy who expresses your inner angst—"

"My lack of commitment," he corrected her. "My hang-ups from the past. I'm over them," Johnny assured her. "See? I'm about to be married. I'm a bona fide family man." He scooped Tyler off her bed and swung him around high overhead while Tyler shrieked with laughter.

When Johnny set him down, Tyler said, "Do it again. Make me go higher."

"Johnny…"

Savannah waited until he and Tyler settled once more beside her. Tyler's face was red. Johnny's looked sheepish. She had no doubt he was using the wrestling interlude to cover his deeper emotions. Just like a guy. Just like him.

"What?" he said.

"You're stalling."

He tried another diversion next. "So are you, using this triple baby-making thing to avoid a decision about your mother's partnership offer at Nine Lives." He was teasing, but he had a point. Savannah shifted restlessly.

"I've decided," she said, making a decision on the spot. "I'm going to stay home with the babies until they reach kindergarten. I may fill in now and then if Ma needs me, but my commitment is to the triplets...and you."

"Are the babies almost born, Sabannah?" Tyler asked. "Because I wanna pway with my bwothers. Maybe the girl can pway, too, but not all the time. Only when we let her."

"You and I will need to have a talk," Savannah told him, ruffling his hair. It had taken Kit years to develop a sense of herself as a woman, like Geneva. Tyler would learn the rules long before Johnny, who glanced at her now.

"The script I was stalling about..." He cleared his throat. He spun the *Daddy* ring on his finger again. "It's kind of a reunion story about these two people who met a long time ago and this guy who got all screwed up—his left eye twitches—and couldn't make the commitment to the woman he loved."

Savannah blinked. "You wrote about us?"

"Yep. It's pretty mushy, but I hope you'll like it."

"Oh, Johnny." She reached for him and drew him into her arms. Tyler came, too. "This is a whole new direction for your work." For a long moment, she held them both. And then...and then, she knew. When she looked into Johnny's eyes, she knew he did, too.

"Break it up," Browning said, coming into the room with a tray of soft drinks.

"Where did you come from?" Savannah asked.

"Johnny and I ran into each other at the elevators." Browning lived just down the hall. He passed out the drinks while Tyler, who was never quite sure about Browning, eyed him with his usual suspicion.

"Are you gonna take me home today, Bwowning?"

"Yeah, dude. I think I am."

"So you can see my mom again?"

"What's up, Browning?" Savannah and Johnny said at the same time.

"Hey, she's not as bad as I used to think. What's wrong if I say hello?"

"Last time you stayed when I went to bed," Tyler said. "Do you wike us?"

"Maybe I do." Browning set aside his unfinished soda. "Don't drink and drive, kid. Come on, let's go. I already had one weird conversation today with Maggie. She seems to think I'm some kind of spy."

"Are you?" Tyler asked, looking impressed.

"Just because I work for the CIA? Nah, no way."

He was already ushering Tyler out the door with an excuse that he wanted to get the boy home before Kit got back from class. Savannah stared after them.

At the last second, Tyler turned around, raced back into the bedroom and threw his arms first around Savannah's thick waist, then around Johnny's knees.

"Wet me see when the babies come."

Johnny grinned. "You'll be the next to know."

When they were gone, Savannah looked at him. "Do you really think Browning…"

"CIA? It wouldn't surprise me. Your brother has a lot of hidden depths."

"It takes one to know one," she said.

Johnny settled beside her, his arm around her shoulders, one hand draped across her once-upon-a-time lap. He felt the babies kick at the same instant she did. Savannah turned into his arms. "Johnny, we're going to be okay. Because when Tyler was here, all at once I understood. It won't be easy raising three at once, but we're not entirely ignorant. We've both helped Kit raise Tyler."

"We have some experience." Johnny kissed the top of her head. "You're right. I'm scared to death," he finally admitted, "but I imagine you are, too."

"Terrified," Savannah said, which no longer seemed quite so daunting. She wasn't in this alone.

"It's a huge responsibility but we can do it…"

"One day at a time," Savannah repeated Kit's words, then added one of her own. "Together."

"We didn't have the most stable families, either of us—even though Nora's great—but this one's all ours. Let's do it right." He followed Savannah's gaze to the end table where her newest stick-figure drawing sat, a primitive study of her, Johnny and three tiny babies. He traced her soft, knowing smile with a finger. "I've always loved you, you know."

"Of course I did." Savannah relaxed into his embrace. Johnny's left eye was no longer twitching. "It was just a matter of getting you to admit it."

Nora's arches were throbbing in high heels, although she didn't want to admit it. She stowed her packages in her room, then kicked off her shoes. After an exhausting day, she'd left Maggie at the beach house to share dinner with Geneva and maybe a walk on the sand. It had been a lovely day, warmer than usual at the end of December, and Nora imagined the sunset would be spectacular. She and Maggie had managed their shopping expedition without stumbling into a quarrel for a change, and Maggie was now sporting a new layered hairstyle in a becoming champagne color. Nora realized she hadn't enjoyed her mother's company so much in years. Maybe never. Perhaps there was hope for them.

In the end, she hadn't even been forced to strong-arm Maggie into a move from Virginia to Florida. Amazing.

She had just started to massage her aching arches when a knock sounded at the door. Caine had just raised his hand to rap again when Nora opened it. For a moment she simply stared at him. He stared at her. Caine spoke first.

"You okay?"

"My feet hurt," she finally acknowledged. "Other than that I'm dandy." After a brief hesitation, she said, "Come in."

Caine got no farther than the entryway. He shifted his weight from one foot to the other and studied his shoes. He was a man with something on his mind. "I was worried. That was a pretty intense scene at the airport." He paused again. "Actually, I wanted to apologize. I should have gotten there sooner."

"And why is that?"

"My job is to serve and protect. Earl Whitehouse could have hurt someone...you," he added, which seemed to be his point.

Nora was almost afraid to ask. "What about Tabitha Whitlaw?"

"Geneva Whitehouse refused to file charges in the attack. As for the vase, of course, it was never stolen in the first place. Geneva claimed there was no real harm done." He hesitated before adding, "Tabby has gone home to California."

"That's probably best," Nora said. "Geneva's stronger than she knows."

Caine's expression morphed into full cop mode. "The real reason I'm here is...there seems to be a sizable collection of parking tickets in your name."

Nora blanched. Oh, no. Just when she thought she was above suspicion.

"Only teasing," Caine murmured, breaking into that slow

smile again. "But you might consider paying them off to clear your conscience."

Having heard his voice, Daisy came trotting from Nora's room where she'd been lost in some doggy dream on the bed. Perhaps exhausted from yesterday's airport wrangle, she hadn't noticed Nora even when she dropped her shopping bags there. Now Daisy's liquid eyes blinked. Tail wagging, mouth grinning, she wiggled over to Caine for a sound pat on the head. She gazed up at him with genuine adoration.

"That dog loves you," Nora said.

"You find that hard to believe?"

"No."

Caine bent over the dog, hiding his expression. "She should meet Killer the cat—my cat—sometime."

"Dogs don't like cats." Killer was no longer Annie's pet?

"If there's food involved, they can be pretty flexible. The same holds true for us guys." He glanced around, as if hoping dinner would magically appear.

Her heart beat faster. "Is this a social call?"

"As soon as I tell you that I closed the case, handed my report to the chief at five o'clock, and your name has been totally cleared…yes, I guess it is."

Nora smiled. "How nice of you to drop by. If you'd like to stay, I think I can find us something to eat. Maybe even a beer."

"I'll pass on the beer."

Nora took another look at him, closer this time. Caine looked freshly shaven, and, good grief, his hair was neatly combed. His khakis were pressed with a razor-sharp crease and his black T-shirt appeared to be new. It hugged his broad chest and impressive shoulders, and Nora felt a tingle race through her.

"I had my first call about work in a week," she said. "It came through on my cell while I was shopping with my mother for wedding clothes."

"Whose wedding?"

"Savannah and Johnny." Nora said no more about their plans. She didn't need to. "I already RSVP'd to my ex-husband and his bride."

"What did you answer?"

"No," she said. "And I'm sticking to it."

He repeated her words. "Why is that?"

"You don't think it's odd for a man to invite his ex-wife to his latest wedding?"

"Maybe a little odd." Caine paused. "But why not go?"

"Why would I?" Nora asked.

"To prove to yourself that you're really over him." He hesitated again. "If you want, I'll take you."

"You would?"

"Sure. Why not?" As if they had to start somewhere.

Nora considered for a moment. Was his question also Caine's decision to move on with his life? To put his love for Annie behind him?

Which made Nora think some more. Sure, Geneva would have to make her own decision about her marriage, but Nora's was finally over and, unlike Earl, in Nora's mind, Wilson Pride wasn't a bad guy. He was a poet and a dreamer. Wilson didn't possess much of a practical side, but he truly did love women. Once, he'd loved her. It was one thing that had made it so difficult to get over him. But he would always be the father of her beloved children, and thus an important part of her life, just as Annie would be for Caine. Maybe it was time for both of them to make some changes—and Nora didn't mean only regarding her hot flashes.

She could see herself in Geneva, not focused on who she really was but on pleasing and caring for others. Defining herself through them. No more, she thought. Maybe she'd even let someone take care of her now and then.

Nora smiled at Caine. "How could I refuse that offer—the chance to see you in a suit?"

He grinned. "It's a pretty impressive sight."

"You do own one?" she couldn't help asking.

"A couple of 'em," he said. "For when I have to appear in court to testify—not to make the chief sweat."

Nora took a breath. "Well, since you have such an extensive wardrobe, there's also a charity dinner I should attend for the Heart Association. I need an escort."

"It's a date. Two dates, actually," he said.

A few days later, as Nora finished telling Starr about Caine, they were both perspiring. The weather had turned even warmer, and it appeared that the Gulf Coast might have a very early spring. Perhaps there would never be a winter at all this year—or maybe it would snow on the Gulf Coast tomorrow. In either case, Nora would handle it. Discarding her jacket as soon as she parked the car at the airport, she turned to Starr.

"Well, are you ready?"

"If I could survive that craziness with Earl Whitehouse, I guess I can survive anything—even a visit to see my kid. His wife, too."

"And your granddaughter," Nora added for her. "Take lots of pictures."

Starr got out of the car. "I can't believe I'm doing this. I can't believe I just called them up and invited myself to Houston."

"You should have done it long ago, Mulligan."

"Why? Because you would have? Yeah, like you haven't had your share of foul-ups in this life." Starr waited for her to unlock the trunk and haul out the first suitcase. Starr had packed enough for a year—or was most of the luggage for the gifts she was taking with her? Nora saw the arm of a Barbie doll hanging from an outside compartment. She smiled.

"Who are you trying to kid?"

"Not the IRS, that's for sure." Starr marched across the concrete parking garage toward the terminal. "Any word on your audit?"

Nora ignored the attempt to goad her.

"Paul and I met with the agent yesterday. Everything's cool."

"They let you off the hook?"

"I was very convincing." She paused. "But then, so was my accountant. And this morning the phone was ringing every two minutes, not because of that but because of Earl. Word gets around fast. I guess my reputation here in Destin will soon be restored."

"Well, don't think you're going to hog all the business. I'll be back before that big, beautiful house near Geneva is finished being built. And then we'll see."

"Give it a rest, Mulligan. We just might decide to work together again. We didn't do badly this time. Geneva's very pleased. She told me that if she decides to leave Earl after all, she'll keep the house. It's just what she wanted." Nora waited a beat before saying, "I know how grateful you are that I'll complete the job while you're on vacation."

Starr shook her head, but she was smiling, too. They walked into the terminal, each carrying a bag. But as soon as she set down her share of the load, Nora felt even lighter than the change of weight might warrant.

She waited while Starr checked the bags and got her boarding card. Then Nora walked her toward Security, realizing that the lightness was inside her.

Maybe Starr would find her place with her family, but Caine had been right. Nora had spent far too much of her life dwelling on her lost commitment to Wilson. Even making peace with him some months ago hadn't completely cured her. But since their divorce, what had she done? Turned to her children, her friends, and made her commitment to them instead. Seeing Wilson married would be a positive step for her this time. Now she could make a new commitment. Not to anyone else, but to Nora.

At Security, she held Starr back, suddenly reluctant to let her leave.

"You inspired me," she said. "I called my brother in Hawaii last night. Hank Jr. seemed glad to hear from me. He even offered to help with Maggie—if by long distance." She paused. "You won't stay away too long?"

"So you can swipe half my clients? No way. I'll be back before you know I'm gone." Despite her gruff tone, Starr lingered, too. "Besides," she said, "I wouldn't want to get on your bad side. Mark Fingerhut is bringing me to Savannah's wedding."

"Mark?"

Starr sent her a gloating look. "Don't feel smug about Caine. Mark and I have started seeing each other," she confessed. "And as a result, he's convinced me to let him write me a prescription. As soon as I get my exam, I'll fill it."

"Then maybe I will, too," Nora said. She'd been thinking, like Starr, about a short-term course of hormone replacement therapy, just until her hot flashes were under control. Like her life. "For a year or so..." she said.

"Did you know he's giving up his practice? After Savannah's triplets are born. He's decided to sell and go into academics."

This news didn't quite surprise Nora. "He hasn't been happy with the hassle of malpractice insurance and the rest, I know." But Starr, dating Mark? Well, why not, Nora decided.

As always, Starr herself was full of surprises.

And there was one more to come.

Starr had turned away, her gaze on the X-ray scanner in the distance, but then she circled back to face Nora.

"God," she said, "I feel like I'm in that old movie. You know, the one with Ingrid Bergman and Humphrey Bogart and that French guy in the fog."

Nora blinked. "*Casablanca.*"

"Yeah, that's the one." She took another hesitant step, then stopped again.

Nora saw the doubt in her lavender eyes. And the new awareness of another change that had nothing to do with their business rivalry, or even this exciting new phase of both their lives. Never mind The Change. It went deeper than that, and Starr seemed to sense it, too.

As we get older— not that old, Nora thought —*we don't become wiser (that's for sure), we don't get better (well, maybe a little bit). Like Maggie and Savannah and Geneva, too, we simply become more...ourselves. I am who I am.* And who knew what she would still become?

Nora had always been a survivor. Now she could roll with the punches again, just for herself. New Year's would come soon, the start of another year. The start of the rest of her life.

"You remember what Bogie said to that French policeman," Nora murmured. She reached out to give Starr a light hug. "This just might be the beginning for us...of an amazing friendship."

"You never know."

* * * * *

Experience entertaining women's fiction for
every woman who has wondered
"what's next?" in her life.
Turn the page for a sneak preview of
a new book from Harlequin NEXT,
WHY IS MURDER ON THE MENU, ANYWAY?
by Stevi Mittman

On sale December 26, wherever books are sold.

keep. One night, he had me mind to drink and talked a lot.

Design Tip of the Day

> Ambience is everything. Imagine eating a foie gras at a
> luncheonette counter or a side of coleslaw at Le Cirque.
> It's not a matter of food but one of atmosphere. Remem-
> ber that when planning your dining room design.
> —Tips from *Teddi.com*

"Now that's the kind of man you should be looking for," my
mother, the self-appointed keeper of my shelf-life stamp, says.
She points with her fork at a man in the corner of the Steak-
Out Restaurant, a dive I've just been hired to redecorate.
Making this restaurant look four-star will be hard, but not half
as hard as getting through lunch without strangling the woman
across the table from me. "*He* would make a good husband."

"Oh, you can tell that from across the room?" I ask, wondering how it is she can forget that when we had trouble getting
rid of my last husband, she shot him. "Besides being ten
minutes away from death if he actually eats all that steak, he's
twenty years too old for me and—shallow woman that I am—
twenty pounds too heavy. Besides, I am *so* not looking for
another husband here. I'm looking to design a new image for
this place, looking for some sense of ambience, some feeling,
something I can build a proposal on for them."

My mother studies the man in the corner, tilting her head,

the better to gauge his age, I suppose. I think she's grimacing, but with all the Botox and Restylane injected into that face, it's hard to tell. She takes another bite of her steak, chews slowly so that I don't miss the fact that the steak is a poor cut and tougher than it should be. "You're concentrating on the wrong kind of proposal," she says finally. "Just look at this place, Teddi. It's a dive. There are hardly any other diners. What does *that* tell you about the food?"

"That they cater to a dinner crowd and it's lunchtime," I tell her.

I don't know what I was thinking bringing her here with me. I suppose I thought it would be better than eating alone. There really are days when my common sense goes on vacation. Clearly, this is one of them. I mean, really, did I not resolve less than three weeks ago that I would not let my mother get to me anymore?

What good are New Year's resolutions, anyway?

Mario approaches the man's table and my mother studies him while they converse. Eventually Mario leaves the table with a huff, after which the diner glances up and meets my mother's gaze. I think she's smiling at him. That or she's got indigestion. They size each other up.

I concentrate on making sketches in my notebook and try to ignore the fact that my mother is flirting. At nearly seventy, she's developed an unhealthy interest in members of the opposite sex to whom she isn't married.

According to my father, who has broken the TMI rule and given me Too Much Information, she has no interest in sex with him. Better, I suppose, to be clued in on what they aren't doing in the bedroom than have to hear what they might be doing.

"He's not so old," my mother says, noticing that I have barely touched the Chinese chicken salad she warned me not to get. "He's got about as many years on you as you have on your little cop friend."

She does this to make me crazy. I know it, but it works all

the same. "Drew Scoones is not my little 'friend.' He's a detective with whom I—"

"Screwed around," my mother says. I must look shocked, because my mother laughs at me and asks if I think she doesn't know the "lingo."

What I thought she didn't know was that Drew and I actually tangled in the sheets. And, since it's possible she's just fishing, I sidestep the issue and tell her that Drew is just a couple of years younger than me and that I don't need reminding. I dig into my salad with renewed vigor, determined to show my mother that Chinese chicken salad in a steak place was not the stupid choice it's proving to be.

After a few more minutes of my picking at the wilted leaves on my plate, the man my mother has me nearly engaged to pays his bill and heads past us toward the back of the restaurant. I watch my mother take in his shoes, his suit and the diamond pinkie ring that seems to be cutting off the circulation in his little finger.

"Such nice hands," she says after the man is out of sight. "Manicured." She and I both stare at my hands. I have two popped acrylics that are being held on at weird angles by bandages. My cuticles are ragged and there's marker decorating my right hand from measuring carelessly when I did a drawing for a customer.

Twenty minutes later she's disappointed that he managed to leave the restaurant without our noticing. He will join the list of the ones I let get away. I will hear about him twenty years from now when—according to my mother—my children will be grown and I will still be single, living pathetically alone with several dogs and cats.

After my ex, that sounds good to me.

The waitress tells us that our meal has been taken care of by the management and, after thanking Mario, the owner, complimenting him on the wonderful meal and assuring him that once I have redecorated his place people will be flocking here in droves (I actually use those words and ignore my mother when she rolls her eyes), my mother and I head for the restroom.

My father—unfortunately not with us today—has the patience of a saint. He got it over the years of living with my mother. She, perhaps as a result, figures he has the patience for both of them, and feels justified having none. For her, no rules apply, and a little thing like a picture of a man on the door to a public restroom is certainly no barrier to using the john. In all fairness, it does seem silly to stand and wait for the ladies' room if no one is using the men's room.

Still, it's the idea that rules don't apply to her, signs don't apply to her, conventions don't apply to her. She knocks on the door to the men's room. When no one answers she gestures to me to go in ahead. I tell her that I can certainly wait for the ladies' room to be free and she shrugs and goes in herself.

Not a minute later there is a bloodcurdling scream from behind the men's room door.

"Mom!" I yell. "Are you all right?"

Mario comes running over, the waitress on his heels. Two customers head our way while my mother continues to scream.

I try the door, but it is locked. I yell for her to open it and she fumbles with the knob. When she finally manages to unlock and open it, she is white behind her two streaks of blush, but she is on her feet and appears shaken but not stirred.

"What happened?" I ask her. So do Mario and the waitress and the few customers who have migrated to the back of the place.

She points toward the bathroom and I go in, thinking it serves her right for using the men's room. But I see nothing amiss.

She gestures toward the stall, and, like any self-respecting and suspicious woman, I poke the door open with one finger, expecting the worst.

What I find is worse than the worst.

The husband my mother picked out for me is sitting on the toilet. His pants are puddled around his ankles, his hands are hanging at his sides. Pinned to his chest is some sort of Health Department certificate.

Oh, and there is a large, round, bloodless bullet hole between his eyes.

Four Nassau County police officers are securing the area, waiting for the detectives and crime scene personnel to show up. They are trying, though not very hard, to comfort my mother, who in another era would be considered to be suffering from the vapors. Less tactful in the twenty-first century, I'd say she was losing it. That is, if I didn't know her better, know she was milking it for everything it was worth.

My mother loves attention. As it begins to flag, she swoons and claims to feel faint. Despite four No Smoking signs, my mother insists it's all right for her to light up because, after all, she's in shock. Not to mention that signs, as we know, don't apply to her.

When asked not to smoke, she collapses mournfully in a chair and lets her head loll to the side, all without mussing her hair.

Eventually, the detectives show up to find the four patrolmen all circled around her, debating whether to administer CPR, smelling salts or simply call the paramedics. I, however, know just what will snap her to attention.

"Detective Scoones," I say loudly. My mother parts the sea of cops.

"We have to stop meeting like this," he says lightly to me, but I can feel him checking me over with his eyes, making sure I'm all right while pretending not to care.

"What have you got in those pants?" my mother asks him, coming to her feet and staring at his crotch accusingly. "*Baydar?* Everywhere we Bayers are, you turn up. You don't expect me to buy that this is a coincidence, I hope."

Drew tells my mother that it's nice to see her, too, and asks if it's his fault that her daughter seems to attract disasters.

Charming to be made to feel like the bearer of a plague.

He asks how I am.

"Just peachy," I tell him. "I seem to be making a habit of finding dead bodies, my mother is driving me crazy and the catering hall I booked two freakin' years ago for Dana's bat mitzvah has just been shut down by the Board of Health!"

"Glad to see your luck's finally changing," he says, giving me a quick squeeze around the shoulders before turning his attention to the patrolmen, asking what they've got, whether they've taken any statements, moved anything, all the sort of stuff you see on TV, without any of the drama. That is, if you don't count my mother's threats to faint every few minutes when she senses no one's paying attention to her.

Mario tells his waitstaff to bring everyone espresso, which I decline because I'm wired enough. Drew pulls him aside and a minute later I'm handed a cup of coffee that smells divinely of Kahlúa.

The man knows me well. Too well.

His partner, whom I've met once or twice, says he'll interview the kitchen staff. Drew asks Mario if he minds if he takes statements from the patrons first and gets to him and the waitstaff afterward.

"No, no," Mario tells him. "Do the patrons first." Drew raises his eyebrow at me like he wants to know if I get the double entendre. I try to look bored.

"What is it with you and murder victims?" he asks me when we sit down at a table in the corner.

I search them out so that I can see you again, I almost say, but I'm afraid it will sound desperate instead of sarcastic.

My mother, lighting up and daring him with a look to tell her not to, reminds him that *she* was the one to find the body.

Drew asks what happened *this time.* My mother tells him how the man in the john was "taken" with me, couldn't take his eyes off me and blatantly flirted with both of us. To his credit, Drew doesn't laugh, but his smirk is undeniable to the trained eye. And I've had my eye trained on him for nearly a year now.

"While he was noticing you," he asks me, "did *you* notice anything about him? Was he waiting for anyone? Watching for anything?"

I tell him that he didn't appear to be waiting or watching. That he made no phone calls, was fairly intent on eating and did, indeed, flirt with my mother. This last bit Drew takes with a grain of salt, which was the way it was intended.

"And he had a short conversation with Mario," I tell him. "I think he might have been unhappy with the food, though he didn't send it back."

Drew asks what makes me think he was dissatisfied, and I tell him that the discussion seemed acrimonious and that Mario looked distressed when he left the table. Drew makes a note and says he'll look into it and asks about anyone else in the restaurant. Did I see anyone who didn't seem to belong, anyone who was watching the victim, anyone looking suspicious?

"Besides my mother?" I ask him, and Mom huffs and blows her cigarette smoke in my direction.

I tell him that there were several deliveries, the kitchen staff going in and out the back door to grab a smoke. He stops me and asks what I was doing checking out the back door of the restaurant.

Proudly—because, while he was off forgetting me, dropping by only once in a while to say hi to Jesse, my son, or drop something by for one of my daughters that he thought they might like, I was getting on with my life—I tell him that I'm decorating the place.

He looks genuinely impressed. "Commercial customers? That's great," he says. Okay, that's what he *ought* to say. What he actually says is "Whatever pays the bills."

"Howard Rosen, the famous restaurant critic, got her the job," my mother says. "You met him—the good-looking, distinguished gentleman with the *real* job, something to be proud of. I guess you've never read his reviews in *Newsday*."

Drew, without missing a beat, tells her that Howard's reviews are on the top of his list, as soon as he learns how to read.

"I only meant—" my mother starts, but both of us assure her that we know just what she meant.

"So," Drew says. "Deliveries?"

I tell him that Mario would know better than I, but that I saw vegetables come in, maybe fish and linens.

"This is the second restaurant job Howard's got her," my mother tells Drew.

"At least she's getting *something* out of the relationship," he says.

"If he were here," my mother says, ignoring the insinuation, "he'd be comforting her instead of interrogating her. He'd be making sure we're both all right after such an ordeal."

"I'm sure he would," Drew agrees, then looks me in the eyes as if he's measuring my tolerance for shock. Quietly he adds, "But then maybe he doesn't know just what strong stuff your daughter's made of."

It's the closest thing to a tender moment I can expect from Drew Scoones. My mother breaks the spell. "She gets that from me," she says.

Both Drew and I take a minute, probably to pray that's all I inherited from her.

"I'm just trying to save you some time and effort," my mother tells him. "My money's on Howard."

Drew withers her with a look and mutters something that sounds suspiciously like "fool's gold." Then he excuses himself to go back to work.

I catch his sleeve and ask if it's all right for us to leave. He says sure, he knows where we live. I say goodbye to Mario. I assure him that I will have some sketches for him in a few days, all the while hoping that this murder doesn't cancel his redecorating plans. I need the money desperately, the alternative being borrowing from my parents and being strangled by the strings.

My mother is strangely quiet all the way to her house. She doesn't tell me what a loser Drew Scoones is—despite his good looks—and how I was obviously drooling over him. She doesn't ask me where Howard is taking me tonight or warn me not to tell my father about what happened because he will worry about us both and no doubt insist we see our respective psychiatrists.

She fidgets nervously, opening and closing her purse over and over again.

"You okay?" I ask her. After all, she's just found a dead man on the toilet, and tough as she is that's got to be upsetting.

When she doesn't answer me I pull over to the side of the road.

"Mom?" She refuses to meet my eyes. "You want me to take you to see Dr. Cohen?"

She looks out the window as if she's just realized we're on Broadway in Woodmere. "Aren't we near Marvin's Jewelers?" she asks, pulling something out of her purse.

"What have you got, Mother?" I ask, prying open her fingers to find the murdered man's ring.

"It was on the sink," she says in answer to my dropped jaw. "I was going to get his name and address and have you return it to him so that he could ask you out. I thought it was a sign that the two of you were meant to be together."

"He's dead, Mom. You understand that, right?" I ask. You never can tell when my mother is fine and when she's in la-la land.

"Well, I didn't know that," she shouts at me. "Not at the time."

I ask why she didn't give it to Drew, realize that she wouldn't give Drew the time in a clock shop and add, "…or one of the other policemen?"

"For heaven's sake," she tells me. "The man is dead, Teddi, and I took his ring. How would that look?"

Before I can tell her it looks just the way it is, she pulls out a cigarette and threatens to light it.

"I mean, really," she says, shaking her head like it's my brains that are loose. "What does he need with it now?"

Her daughter was
going through a Goth phase.

Her mother-in-law
was driving her crazy.

And something's up
with her husband.

Maybe she should dye her hair, lose those extra
pounds—anything to get the attention of the man
she loves. But what was he hiding? For the first
time in their marriage, they must be truly open
with each other to rediscover what brought them
together in the first place.

Sex, Lies and Cellulite:
A Love Story

by Renee Roszel

Available January 2007
TheNextNovel.com

HN76

Holiday Wishes

by
Kate Austin,
Stevi Mittman,
Mary Schramski

Three Special Women...
One Unforgettable Holiday

Don't miss this special collection of three
unforgettable stories about the magic of
holiday wishes coming true!

HARLEQUIN®
Next™

HN70

Available December 2006
TheNextNovel.com

REQUEST YOUR FREE BOOKS!

2 FREE NOVELS PLUS 2 FREE GIFTS!

There's the life you planned. And there's what comes next.

By the Way, Did You Know You're Pregnant?

After twenty-five years of wedlock and three grown children, starting over with the diaper-and-formula scene was inconceivable for Laurel Mitchell. But between her tears and her husband's terror, they're waiting for a bundle of joy that's proving life's most unexpected gifts are the best.

The Second Time Around

by Marie Ferrarella

HARLEQUIN®
NeXt™

Available January 2007
TheNextNovel.com

HN73

All women become slightly psychic…eventually!

Lila's psychic ability disappeared
the moment her visions led her to
a missing heiress tied to the bed of
Lila's fiancé. Leaving town to start over,
Lila's journey finds her changing in
ways she could never have predicted.

Slightly Psychic

by Sandra Steffen

HARLEQUIN®
Next™

Available January 2007
TheNextNovel.com

HN75